I0788610

ARILINN

ARILINN

A NOVEL OF DARKOVER®

MARION ZIMMER BRADLEY
AND
DEBORAH J. ROSS

Also by Marion Zimmer Bradley and Deborah J. Ross

The Clingfire Trilogy
The Fall of Neskaya
Zandru's Forge
A Flame in Hali

The Alton Gift
Hastur Lord
The Children of Kings
Thunderlord
The Laran Gambit
Arilinn

Edited by Deborah J. Ross
Stars of Darkover
Gifts of Darkover
Realms of Darkover
Masques of Darkover
Crossroads of Darkover
Citadels of Darkover

A Note to the Reader

Writing *Arilinn*, the third novel in a multi-book project (the first two being *Thunderlord!* and *The Laran Gambit*), turned out to be an adventure in itself. I began it during the confluence of the 2020 COVID-19 pandemic and the California wildfires that year. My family and I were forced to evacuate as the fires raced down the mountains to within half a block of our home. We loaded up our cars in record time and skedaddled out of town. Eventually, we found our way to a long-stay hotel, "we" meaning three humans and four cats. The first weeks were intense. I went to sleep each night convinced that our house, with our library and my mother's piano, things we could not possibly transport at an hour's notice, would be gone … and waking up to images posted by local fire volunteers, showing our street through swirls of smoke but our fence and buildings intact.

Needless to say, these conditions did not promote creative focus. I somehow managed to produce a rough draft. My "rough" drafts are extremely rough at the best of times, and this one set a new record. True, it had a beginning, a middle, and an end, also characters, dramatic tension, words, and punctuation. Otherwise, it resembled the state of my mind: a *flaming mess*. Fortunately, I had the joy of working with a superb editor, Judith Tarr. Off to her went the aforementioned *flaming mess*. What came back was a thorough, sensitive, and insightful edit. As I worked through her comments, a deeper story emerged, demanding to be brought to light. This is why I love revising, by the way! A brilliant editor has the ability to suggest ways to make a story more true to the author's vision, and Judy gave me just what I needed. I'm immensely proud of the result. I hope you enjoy it, as well.

Adelandeyo, my friends. Go in peace and joy.

Deborah J. Ross

Acknowledgments

How do I thank everyone who cheered me on over twenty-five years of writing Darkover novels (and decades of short fiction before that)? The list would surely be as long as this book. My family put up with my disappearing into my office every morning, afternoon, and evening. Juliette Wade, writing partner *extraordinaire*, held me accountable as we each worked on our separate projects on different continents. She and the other "Word Dragons," Janice Hardy and Kimberly Unger, kept me sane when it seemed this project would never end. Claire L. Fishback of *You Can Toucan!* shared invaluable time-management strategies (more accountability). The Marion Zimmer Bradley Literary Works Trust supported me every step of the way.

Exceptional gratitude goes to everyone who's written to me over the years with moving, poignant tales of how my work brought light and hope in dark times and understanding to troubled families. I treasure your trust in sharing your personal stories with me. Hearing how my words have made a difference is the best gift an author can receive.

This is for YOU, the readers who fell in love with Darkover seventy years ago and have remained ever loyal, questioning, enchanted, and dedicated to this marvelous world.

"Arilinn was not the oldest of the Towers, but it was the proudest … claiming that the first Keeper had been a daughter of Hastur's self. Damon didn't believe it, for there was too little history which had survived the Ages of Chaos."

—The Forbidden Tower

PART I

The long Darkovan winter slowly loosened its grasp. Spring burst upon the Hastur estate with the heady aromas of damp earth and the first rush of green growth. The blossoming fruit trees in the castle orchard layered the ground in petals. Those who had neglected their outdoor work now bent to it with cheerfulness, and those who had no excuse invented reasons. More than one otherwise staid servant could be seen, arms flung wide, face lifted to the sun, tucking a flower into a braid, or singing as they went about their tasks. The lord's children were no exception.

Lord Aidan Hastur looked down from the outdoor balcony, watching his two youngest daughters play in the garden. Skirts swirled as they darted here and there, as swift and agile as kestrels. Their adolescent voices brought a smile to his lips.

He turned away from the enchanting sight below, leaned against the cool, close-set stone, and closed his eyes. They were so young, so innocent. How much longer he would be able to shelter them from the sorrows of the world, he did not know. His only certainty was that he would give anything to keep them safe.

Aldones grant my daughters may raise their children in a land at peace, and that my son, my Iain, need never lead men to their deaths.

◆ ◆ ◆

Tossing back the copper-bright curls that had come loose from her braid, Leora Hastur let out a whoop and darted out from behind the garden wall to tag her younger sister, Sharina. Sharina raced down the graveled path. Leora followed on her heels, both of them yelling. The gardener gave a mock scowl as they barreled past.

"Stay out of me beds!" he called after them.

Breathless and glowing with exertion, the sisters slowed to a more decorous pace. From the end of the path, they could be easily spotted from above, and neither would put it beyond their next-eldest sister, Jessamy, to tattle on them. Before they could head back into the garden, however, they heard a galloping horse on the road leading to the castle.

Something is going on. Leora could taste it in the air.

They were just in time to see an unfamiliar rider halt in the courtyard. A stableboy trotted forward to take the reins. By the time the rider had dismounted, the castle steward, the *coridom*, had emerged from the front doors.

"Blue, gray, and white," Leora murmured, her gaze following the rider as he followed the *coridom* inside. The colors belonged to their neighbor and sometime adversary, Carcosse.

"What does *Dom* Merryl want with us?" she wondered aloud.

Sharina giggled. "Maybe it's an offer of marriage."

"If that's true, it would be for Jessamy. We'll just have to wait our turn and trust that when the time comes, Father will make us a good match." She did not include their oldest half-sister, Neave. Mother would never agree to a suitable dowry for a step-daughter from the first Lady Hastur.

"*I* don't want to be wed to some old pimple-faced Carcosse," Sharina said. "Nor to anybody!"

Leora took her sister's arm. "Whatever it's about, we won't find out by standing here."

The entrance hall was empty except for Lorcan, the *coridom*, a dignified man the two sisters delighted in calling *Uncle* although he was old enough to be their grandfather. When they went to him, his somber expression lightened.

"*Damiselas.*" He bowed to each of them.

"We saw the rider from Carcosse," Leora said. "Do you know what it's about? Is he with Father now?"

"What a mystery!" Sharina stood on tiptoe to kiss the old man on the cheek.

"They've gone up to the presence chamber," Lorcan replied. "But you're not to interrupt them with your chatter. Should it be appropriate, *Dom* Aidan will summon you. Until then, I advise you to remember the adage about the rabbit-horn and the scorpion-ants' nest."

Leora had always hated that story's moral that terrible things happened to children who poked their noses where they didn't belong. She suspected it was made up expressly to discourage curiosity.

"And no sneaking around the back passages, hoping for a look!" Lorcan shook one forefinger at them, but his eyes twinkled. "I know you, young scamps!"

"We would never behave in such a disreputable manner," Leora said, gathering her dignity. "What must you think of us?"

"I think," he said more gently, "that your lady mother has need of you this hour, and that you would do well to attend her rather than meddle in men's business. And to remember that rules are not made to torment you but to keep you safe. Go along, then."

Further argument would be futile. She'd only end up sounding childish, and Sharina would follow her lead.

I'm nearly fifteen. I ought to be patient. She knew what her mother would have her do: sit quietly and do needlework or supervise the kitchen or any of a hundred boring things while the men make the important decisions. But how could she help Father if she didn't know what was going on?

The answer was that she couldn't. That wasn't what girls were allowed to do.

"Aren't we going to snoop around and get some answers?" Sharina said, grabbing Leora's arm.

It was *not honorable*, as Father had said a year ago, the last time they'd gone "exploring." Leora's cheeks still burned from the scolding. Father had assumed, rightly, that she had led Sharina into mischief. He'd upbraided Leora not only for poking around where she had no business but for endangering her younger sister.

"What if you'd fallen or gotten trapped? Those passageways aren't safe. What kind of example were you setting for Sharina, who looks up to you? You are a daughter of Hastur and should have known better. I am deeply disappointed in you."

Blinking back tears of mortification, Leora had vowed to never give her father cause to be ashamed of her again.

"No," she said to Sharina with a trace of regret, "not this time. I'm sure we'll find out what it's all about."

◆ ◆ ◆

Aidan went through the household accounts with his long-time friend and paxman, Connor Darriell. The two men met in the comfortable, slightly shabby chamber Aidan referred to as his office. The furnishings were old enough to have acquired a collection of scratches, water rings, and candle burns from generations of careless boys. Aidan was responsible for a goodly number from sneaking into his grandfather's private chamber.

Aidan steadfastly refused to allow Graciela, his present wife, into his office. Connor had once remarked that the lady would not depart without having rearranged everything in such a way to be unfindable, but there had been no malice in his words. Connor and Graciela got along reasonably well, and as for Aidan, he had married her for her family's power and her housekeeping, not for affection. He and Fiona-Maria Aillard, his first wife, had shared a great love and an even greater passion, but it had brought him nothing beyond her death and one surviving and most perplexing daughter.

Connor opened the oversized ledger books, set out a fresh pot of ink, and took his seat beside the desk. They were only a few years apart in age, and Connor had been fostered at the castle since both were boys. It was a common practice among the Comyn aristocracy. Connor gained an education and place in life. Aidan had a companion and aide whom he could trust.

"Young Iain's coming along with his weapons drills," Connor said once they had reviewed the progress of spring planting and a handful of villager disputes.

"I'll get out on the yard tomorrow," Aidan said, "and go a few rounds with him."

"He'll be thrilled."

"Not if he forgets everything you've taught him."

Both men looked up at a knock at the door. Connor made as if to rise, but Aidan restrained him with a gesture, *As you were.*

"Come."

The *coridom's* assistant entered and bowed formally. As he waited for permission to speak, he radiated anxiety.

"What is it?" Aidan shaded his words with kindness. The assistant was one of the younger men training under Lorcan who would assume his duties as he aged. This lad was newly come to the castle from a small forest village under Hastur rule and was still visibly in awe of Aidan, Lord Hastur.

"*Vai dom,* there's a messenger come from Lord Carcosse."

Carcosse? What devilry is he stirring up now?

Aidan kept his features carefully neutral, although he sensed Connor's alertness. He maintained a calm, confident demeanor, aware that rumors were already flying about the castle.

"Shall I have the messenger escorted here?" the assistant asked.

"I'll hear him in my presence chamber shortly."

The assistant's eyes widened. "*Vai dom,* we may require a—a short time to prepare the chamber."

"Then take the time," Aidan said. "As for the messenger, he can wait. Offer him water or watered ale, but keep him in the guardroom." *And under watchful eyes.*

"Yes, *vai dom.*" With another bow, the assistant departed.

Connor turned to Aidan. "The *presence chamber,* my lord?" In the past, the chamber had been reserved for formal, diplomatic use.

Aidan did not bother to answer. He and Connor had been out of step with one another lately. The reason couldn't be helped, nor the resulting ragged edges. With time, those should heal.

He strode over to the window overlooking an interior courtyard. On the far side, one of the household staff opened the window and shook out a duster. How normal, how *domestic* that seemed. He did not want to assume that this message from Carcosse presaged some dire event, perhaps a return to the violence that had overshadowed his grandfather's and his father's times. The thought persisted. He tried to shake it off, lest his fears cause him to bring about that very fate.

"Something was bound to happen sooner or later," he said, trying not to sound as bleak as he felt. "This message could be perfectly benign, an overture to better relations—an invitation to a ball, for all I know. Or an inquiry about a marriage alliance."

"Or something far worse."

"Either way," Aidan said, forcing a lighter tone, "this messenger will take back not only my response but the formal setting in which I gave it."

"In other words, you take Carcosse seriously."

"In other words," Aidan replied with a lift of one eyebrow, "I mean to make him take *me* seriously."

◆ ◆ ◆

The presence chamber was narrow and shadowed, a relic of the past. The benches, secretary's table, and heavy, ornately carved chair in which Aidan now sat, were dark with polish. Aidan hated the place, even though he knew its uses. For the past two generations, the chamber had been the scene of tense diplomatic conferences between Hastur and Carcosse, as well as a place to receive petitions and settle disputes. At times, Aidan imagined he could hear echoes of those times, voices shouting, the tramp of boots, the anger—that implacable, deadly anger—on both sides.

No one now living knew exactly how the feud began. Aidan had grown up with the story of a betrothal feast in which the groom—the young Carcosse heir—and the Hastur bride's mother died. Of poison, of a secretive thrust of a dagger, of tragically circumstantial but natural causes, it did not matter. Each family blamed the other, and Aidan had heard only the Hastur side. The resulting cycle of retaliation had ended with the Carcosse manor in ashes and each side nursing bitterness that, like half-buried embers, could flare up at any time.

Go carefully, Aidan cautioned himself. *Do not make trouble where there is none. If there is a way to keep the peace between us, I must find it. And yet … I cannot trust these people. I dare not.*

Connor opened the door and bade the messenger to enter. Aidan listened while the message was delivered. The rider stumbled over a phrase here and there. He wasn't a trained Voice. Those were very few and greatly sought after, making their services expensive.

"My lord, hear the words of Merryl Zamboro of Carcosse, who salutes his neighbor, Aidan Valdir of Hastur, and sends wishes for the continued good—no, excellent—health of his family. He regrets to inform Lord Hastur that a party of thieves has crossed over from Hastur lands into the domain of Carcosse and there—" he described the area's precise landmarks, "—there unlawfully seized cattle rightfully belonging to Lord Carcosse's subjects. He further—um, testifies—no, asserts—that these law-breakers owe fealty to Lord Hastur and therefore their trespasses are Lord Hastur's responsibility. Therefore, my lord demands one hundred coins of gold in recompense."

If Aidan had been a decade younger, he would have laughed in the messenger's face. The flimsiness of the charges compounded the outrageousness of the sum. It was enough to buy every single cow, bull, and calf in the realm of Carcosse.

I must buy time to find out what Carcosse is really up to.

"I will consider the matter," Aidan said. "In the meantime, you've had a long ride. Take your ease with us tonight. Connor, see to it that man and mount are fed and comfortably housed. We'll continue our business in my office."

❖ ❖ ❖

At this hour, the embers from the morning fire in Aidan's office were banked but still glowing. He stood before it, legs braced, hands spread wide. He turned as Connor entered and latched the door behind him.

"He's settled?" Aidan asked.

"A bit too nervous to properly enjoy his meal."

Aidan lowered himself to a chair before the hearth and gestured for Connor to take the other.

"Your thoughts on the message?" This was an old habit of theirs, for Connor to shave away the superficial aspects of a problem.

"This—I suppose you might call it a joke," Connor said, stretching out his legs. "It doesn't even pretend to be a sincere request for compensation. No man would consider paying such a sum and there's no evidence here to back it up. What exactly is the point? To insult us? What does he expect?"

"He expects me to refuse, of course. That's what a sane man would do." The answer came too easily. The situation was more complicated than a meritless claim. Between them, he and Connor would get to the bottom of it.

"That goes without saying," Connor said, thoughtful. "But what is he playing at? Why make the demand at all? What does he *want*?"

"This might be a prelude to something else. I can't offhand think what that might be."

"Nor I." Connor shook his head. "How will you answer?"

"If nothing better occurs to me overnight, I'll politely acknowledge his concerns, offer my commiseration on the loss of his cattle, and say I'll look into the matter."

Connor sat up straight in his chair. "You cannot mean to venture into Carcosse territory so soon after a cattle raid."

"A *reported* cattle raid," Aidan said, half-joking, half-grim.

"*Vai dom*, it's my duty to advise you regarding the prudence of any action. I tell you now that what you propose is foolhardy at best."

There it was, the old frankness, the openness that Aidan had missed these last tendays. Not merely duty, Aidan thought, but loyalty of the heart.

"Your objections are noted," he said with a nod and a slight smile. "Under other circumstances, that would be the end of it. This time, the matter is a bit more …" He paused, weighing his words. "The place described by the messenger, where the cattle were said to have been taken, lies in an area that was once claimed by both our realms. My father annexed it when I was a boy, and so it has been ever since. It's not just the cattle at stake, it's ownership of the land itself."

"In other words," Connor said, "*Dom* Merryl is in effect laying claim to that strip of border."

"That's the size of it. Here, I'll show you—"

Heaving himself out of his chair, Aidan went to the shelves that held maps, some dating back a century or more. He found one detailing the borders and unrolled it on the desk. "This is an old map, drawn up before my father claimed the land. Now the boundary line would be *here.*" He tapped the parchment with one finger. "And, near as I can figure, the cattle were reportedly *here,* clearly on our side."

Connor studied the map. "Merryl Carcosse knows full well that the site lies on our side of the border. He expects you to refuse that outrageous payment. Which brings us back to my question: What is he *really* after?"

"I doubt you and I will find the answer by sitting around discussing it. So in a day or two—once I've had a bit of time to assess my son's burgeoning skills with the wooden practice sword—I'll see what I can find out. I might add, however, that I'm not expecting much."

Connor frowned. "I don't like it, *vai dom.*"

"You've used the honorific twice in one conversation," Aidan remarked as he rolled up the map. He handed it to Connor as if it were an accolade and waited while his paxman replaced it on the shelf.

Connor turned back, his eyes shadowed. "I'm trying to keep you from riding into a trap."

"A *trap?*"

"How can it be anything else?" Connor threw up his hands in exasperation.

"Indeed," Aidan said dryly.

"Do not be lulled into a false sense of safety because this supposed raid took place on our lands. It's as plain as the ears on Durraman's donkey that the terrain is perfect for an ambush. Maybe you're right and Carcosse expects you to disregard him. But suppose that he claims a raid to lure you in? He will know you're coming, and his men will be waiting for you."

"I understand your concerns. At the same time, we must consider that there is more at stake here than a fake cattle raid." Aidan began pacing, using movement to help him gather his thoughts. He trusted Connor to understand that he wasn't speechifying, he was working his way through a knotty problem. Connor was his conscience, his sounding board.

"The day of the small family-run estate is passing," Aidan said. "We stand on the brink of an age of kings. Victory leads to the lust for more territory and more subjects. This cycle of aggression and retaliation— where will it end? When we and our children have soaked the earth with our blood?"

"I pray Aldones that day never comes," Connor said in a thick voice. "As do I."

A succession of unreadable expressions passed over Connor's face. Not for the first time, Aidan wished he could sense what his friend was feeling. He himself had more than a touch of telepathic talent, enough to pass the Gift to his children, but had never learned to use it.

"Of course, it's a trap." Aidan halted his pacing. "Or if it is not, I must prepare as if it were one. I cannot ignore the accusation, but I must find out what Carcosse is up to—by seeing what he does next. There will be a *next*, I'm sure of it. I aim to draw him out. Otherwise, I leave myself blind to his true aims."

"You'll go well-guarded." A command, not a statement. "And you will send out scouts well in advance. *And* you will hold back part of your force in case the main body is taken by surprise."

"I rely upon your recommendations, and I will go further. The more I think about it, the more I think this is but the opening gambit in a game of power, with the ultimate goal of avenging the Carcosse losses two generations ago. So I will not only take your precautions, I will make my own. You are to put our pledged fighting men on alert. Contact Berrin Valdes, who served my father, and persuade him to come out of retirement to prepare the troops at the mustering place."

"Aye, I remember him," Connor said with a wry smile. The old general had been a stern taskmaster for them both when they were young. "I doubt he'll be able to resist training up another generation."

"They'll be the better for it. Meanwhile, make provisions here that will not alarm my lady wife or daughters. This is a precaution only—I do not want tongues to wag needlessly. Finally, I will summon the circle at Alcabra Keep. If worst comes to worst, I dare not risk them becoming an asset of war to be seized or destroyed. I especially do not want to risk the new *laranzu* from Neskaya falling into Carcosse's hands."

And not only the Neskaya wizard …

Connor stood very still, barely blinking. Aidan noted the effort it took to mask his worry, not for himself but for Neave. The plan had been for her to join the circle folk at the Keep for continued training.

"If Carcosse means the worst," Connor said, "this castle will be as safe as anywhere. We must ensure that remains so."

"Indeed. One thing more before you go. Or two, rather. The spies you have placed in Carcosse's stronghold, have they said anything about a circle owing fealty to him? And if so, does he have the capability of deploying *laran* in battle?"

"I have not received such a report, but I will inquire. It will take time." Connor meant avoiding unnecessary chances of a missive being intercepted. "And the second matter?"

Aidan raked his fingers through his hair, betraying an inner disquiet at entering morally suspect territory. "If I am not at home when the Alcabra folk arrive, and if they have not already done so … they are to investigate both offensive and defensive military uses of *laran*. The workers at Neskaya are pioneering weapons created using the powers of the mind, as well as the direct application of psychic force. My circle—" with a slight emphasis on the word *my*, "—now includes a *laranzu* from Neskaya, brother to the Alcabra Keeper. With Zandru's luck, that may prove an advantage, should the situation with Carcosse come to armed conflict."

Color drained from Connor's face, except for two spots along his cheekbones. Aidan needed no *laran* to tell his paxman was no longer surprised, he was *appalled*.

"My lord, you cannot be serious. Such a thing—"

"I am in deadly earnest," Aidan cut in. "This whole affair may turn out to be a misunderstanding and a bit of bad blood from a generation ago. But if it is more, if Carcosse means to test my weaknesses as a prelude to an attack—and if he has *laran* armament of his own—I dare not do less. I must use every weapon I have or can create. The fate of Hastur and the lives of everyone, within these walls and outside, depends on it. Do you understand me?"

"Understanding is not required," Connor murmured, "only obedience."

"Yet I would have it."

"I am at your service in this, as in all things." Connor's words came slowly. "Forgive me if I spoke out of turn."

Aidan clapped his paxman on the shoulder. "You speak out of love for me and all Hastur. Please believe that I, too, speak out of love."

After escaping from the solarium, where she'd spent the better part of the afternoon stabbing her thumb with a needle, Leora headed back to her room. She'd had her fill of sitting demurely and never hearing a word of anything interesting. Her mother and Jessamy were like matched dolls with their neatly arranged dark hair and their endless chatter.

She slipped through the door to the back stairs, used primarily by the household staff, up a flight and then along the narrow servants' corridor.

A trap?

The words popped into her mind. She was so startled, she almost lost her balance.

Words in her mind … but not *her* words. Not *her* voice.

No, that was impossible. How could it be? She knew about telepathy. What Comyn child did not? But she had never thought *she* might have it. When she was ten, she'd been tested by a *leronis* from Alcabra Keep. Neither she nor her older sister, Jessamy, had any detectable *laran*. The *leronis* had said it was too early to be sure in Leora's case, but Mother had refused to follow up. It was enough that Neave, Leora's older stepsister, had talent enough to train at the Keep.

If it were not telepathy … She must have overheard someone else speaking.

Her skin turned clammy. Dizziness swept through her. She bent over, retching, as the grayness in her vision faded.

A trap—what did that mean? Was this old shortcut a trap? Or was someone setting a trap? For *her*?

She held her breath and listened. This corridor ran behind her father's office. Now she caught the sound of men's voices. Her father sounded upset—at *Connor*, with whom he never got angry. This was bad, really bad.

Heart pounding, Leora raced down the stairs leading to the central hall. The sound of her hammering pulse filled her skull.

A trap, Connor had said. And Father had agreed.

The hammering of her pulse filled her skull.

Father is riding into a trap.

A pair of maidservants, brushing out the carpet that ran down the center of the hall, looked up at her as she headed toward the wing housing the family quarters. Hurrying on, she neared the T intersection where one corridor led to the daughters' rooms and the other to the master suite and Iain's chamber. The girls' rooms were arranged along a single corridor, with Leora's and Sharina's next to each other and Jessamy's further down. Neave's was at the far end.

A trap? What should I do? I can't just do nothing. *But I wasn't supposed to hear that!*

Dashing around the corner, Leora collided with Neave and fell into her older half-sister's arms. Where they touched, a jolt like lightning flashed across Leora's skin. For an instant, she felt Neave's *presence* in her mind.

Neave pulled back, brushing her hands on her skirts as if her fingertips pained her.

"I'm sorry—" Leora began.

"What has distressed you, *chiya*?"

"Nothing, I'm just out of breath from the stairs."

"You've been eavesdropping—" Neave gave her a piercing look, "—on Father. And you didn't like what you heard."

"It was an accident, I never meant— Wait, how did you know?"

"When we touched, I picked up a fragment of your thoughts. Skin-to-skin contact enhances telepathy. I thought you knew that."

Telepathy, so that's what it was?

Leora's vision wavered. She felt sick to her stomach. She reached out to steady herself against the wall. Neave put an arm around her shoulders, carefully placing her hand on the fabric of Leora's dress.

"You poor thing," Neave said, "you've had a fright. First, you overhear politics you're too young to understand, and now a big sister you barely know reads your mind."

"I'm not too young to understand that Father is riding into a trap! Only—I don't know what to do about it."

"Father is far too wily to be caught in a trap, and Connor would never allow him to do anything rash."

"I feel like a goose," Leora confessed, "all ruffled feathers and honking."

Neave laughed. "You spoke from your heart, *chiya*. To you, it's new and terrifying. I cannot say with utter certainty that Father will return, for I have not the Gift of seeing the future—"

"Blessed Evanda! Is there such a thing? I thought it was a myth."

Neave regarded her seriously, "It's not something we Hasturs have ever had to contend with. Some of the Aldaran folk are said to be able to glimpse what is to come, or so Melanie says, but the Gift is erratic and unreliable. The visions may or may not come to pass, and the uncertainty has driven more than one of them mad."

"Then I would rather not know."

"Nor I. I would rather make my own future, wouldn't you? Or rely on common sense to tell me what is a reasonable outcome. So I believe that it is *unlikely* any harm will come to Father. And the more fool Lord Carcosse if he tries."

◆ ◆ ◆

The family gathered for dinner in the usual cozy room instead of the chill, echoing hall reserved for formal feasting. The chamber was not far from the kitchen, so the food was still hot. It was plain, everyday fare that had been stored over the winter, except for the boiled spring greens. As usual, Neave was not included in the meal. Leora missed her, although until today they had never been close.

After everyone had been served, Father announced that he would be gone for a tenday or two. The entire table turned to look at him, from Mother, sitting in the place of honor beside him, to Iain, who was all of eight winters old. Sharina stared, her mouth open, but Jessamy's lips pressed together and her brow furrowed.

"Come now, why the long faces?" Father said. "I'm sure you will all find ways to amuse yourself without me. Although *you*—" turning to Iain, "—must practice with your wooden sword every day to show me how much you've improved when I return."

"I will, Papa!"

"Excellent! While I am gone, you must obey Connor as you would me."

"And what does *Connor* have to say about your leaving?" Jessamy spoke up.

Leora knew perfectly well what Connor had said, but why was Jessamy interested?

"Hush, daughter!" *Domna* Graciela favored Jessamy with a scowl.

"What your father and his paxman say to one another is private."

"Rest assured, my lady wife, I am perfectly capable of discerning which conversations are suitable for sharing with my children and which ought to remain confidential." Father's perfectly polite expression belied the gently mocking undercurrent of his words.

Graciela inclined her head as if she hadn't noticed the subtle jibe. "Are we permitted to know the reason for your absence?"

Father's jaw clenched visibly as he chewed on a piece of meat. It was tough, since the cattle had not yet fattened on summer's pastures. The family waited in silence as he finished.

"I know how quickly gossip spreads and how easily a simple fact can be distorted. And if I know you girls, you will fill that void by concocting a story far more dramatic than the truth. It's this way: I'll be investigating a complaint from our neighbor, Lord Carcosse. I have every hope it can be resolved."

The cattle raid.

"None of you have cause to worry," Father continued in a reassuring tone. "Connor and I talked it over, and he is arranging for my protection, so there should be no concerns regarding my safety. Does that satisfy you, Jessamy?"

"Father, I am sorry. I did not mean to question—"

"Whatever you determine needful is quite sufficient," Graciela interrupted.

"I am happy that it meets with your approval," Father said wryly.

"Of course, you must do what you think is best," Graciela went on. "However, the roads are not yet dry, and all manner of incidents may hinder your journey. Should you be unexpectedly delayed, you may not return for the Midsummer Festival preparations. There is always much to do, and it's a time when the entire household traditionally comes together to celebrate. Can this matter not be put off until afterward?"

Father's expression remained as pleasant as before, but Leora sensed a flare of irritation as vivid and fleeting as if she had felt it herself.

"I am afraid it cannot," he said. "I may be master of many things, but in this case, I am time's servant. Before you protest further, my lady wife, no, this cannot be delegated."

"Forgive me, my lord husband," Graciela said. "I meant no disrespect."

"And none is taken," he replied.

That ended the discussion. An uneasy silence settled over the rest of the meal. Leora could not bring herself to eat more, and fortunately, Mother was too preoccupied to chide her.

Aidan halted his horse and surveyed the terrain before him. Spring greenery draped the hills, although snow still lingered in the shadows. It had rained the night before, but the party had been prepared for that. Each dawn seemed a little brighter, each noon a little warmer, as the planet tilted toward the red sun. Each day strengthened Aidan's belief that no enemy force lay in wait. He'd followed Connor's plan, sending out scouts and holding back a portion of his armed riders. Day after day, the scouts had reported nothing more threatening than evidence of an old wolf kill.

Aidan's captain, a man named Hjalmar who had come down out of the Hellers a decade ago and sworn himself to Hastur service, signaled for the riders to dismount and stretch their legs. Aidan remained mounted for the sake of the longer view. His strong dun gelding, heavy-boned enough for light draft work and indefatigable on the trail, lowered its head and blew through its nostrils.

One of the scouts emerged from the line of scrubby trees along the ridge and trotted toward Aidan and Hjalmar. Aidan recognized him, a man whose father had served his own father.

"It's Regan, isn't it? From Deer Creek village?" Aidan asked. "What news?"

Regan's weather-roughened cheeks flushed with pleasure, for this was the first time Aidan had spoken directly to him. "I arrived three days ago, as ordered, and kept myself out of sight. There's no sign of armed men in that direction." His gesture encompassed the hills to the south. "Not a whiff of camp smoke or hoof print or bent twig. My life on it, there's no one up here, at least not now."

"Someone's been here and has left, you mean? How long ago?"

"I found clear signs of cattle and their keepers yonder," Regan continued, indicating the dell ahead. "Not recent. The droppings were dry, and many footprints of wild creatures overlay those of the cattle. By my reckoning, the cattle had been gone two and a half, maybe three tendays ago."

"Were there any signs of who might have taken them?" Aidan asked.

"A few prints and dried horse droppings, too trodden-over to make out the number."

"Horses out here?"

"Poor quality beasts they were, my lord, little bigger than ponies." Regan sucked air through his teeth, a country mannerism indicating disapproval. "The prints were small and narrow. And unshod."

"Sounds like outlaws, too poor to feed their families by honest work," Hjalmar commented.

"Aye," Aidan said, nodding. "Desperation leads men to lawlessness."

If so, the fault lies in part with me, he thought, *that I did not attend to their misery before this. I've been so caught up in my own affairs that I have neglected those in my charge.* He wondered if Carcosse had the right of it, that poor men living on Hastur land had taken the cattle to feed their families.

Aidan turned again to the scout. "Could you determine which way they went?"

"Aye, the tracks were clear." Regan hesitated. "But there were things that did not sit well with me."

If I am to make decisions based on this incident, I must be certain. "I'll inspect the site myself."

"As you see fit, *vai dom*," Regan said. "I would caution you to not trample on the ground there. I did not have time to inspect the area for older, fainter tracks, and those might be easily destroyed."

"Then we will take only a minimum of men. Hjalmar, I'll want two of the best fighters. You remain here with the others, holding this position."

Hjalmar took hold of the reins of Aidan's horse. The dun gelding lashed its tail, shifting against the restraint. "I urge you to reconsider this action, my lord. We don't know what awaits. There could be an ambush, and you will not be well-defended if you proceed with so few."

"So I have been warned," Aidan said. "Connor will have my head if anything happens to me."

"No, my lord. He will have *mine*."

That he would, indeed.

For a moment, the two men locked gazes. Aidan had been raised to expect loyalty, to command it. But this devotion went far beyond duty; Hjalmar, like Connor, spoke frankly. Boldly. That took courage. Another master might call these men insubordinate, but Aidan knew that Hjalmar spoke out of love, even as Connor had.

"Very well," Aidan said, taking a deep breath. "We shall inspect the site together, but carefully."

The entire party proceeded to a spring-fed pool surrounded by the hillsides green with new grass. A soft breeze blew from the south. Between the ample forage and the water, the place seemed ideal for grazing cattle. Hjalmar deployed the riders in a defensive formation around the pool, with lookouts scattered even more widely.

Aidan dismounted and paced out the site, keeping to the harder ground to avoid disturbing the tracks. As Regan had described, hoofprints led to and from the edge of the pool, yet only a short distance away, the ground was almost untrodden and still covered with grass. In each direction, coming and going, the depressions showed the same amount of erosion, even those overlapping each other. They must have been made around the same time.

Aidan ran his hands lightly over the crumbling surface of the soil, trying to piece together the scene. The brief contact between his bare skin and the soil felt electric. As if the earth itself were speaking telepathically to him, images began to form in his mind.

The cattle had been herded here for water … they milled around … and then returned the way they came …

Aidan stood, brushing the loose soil from his hands. Why bring a herd here and then drive them off a short time later, when there was good grazing at hand?

"It looks to me as if drovers brought in a few head of cattle, milled them around in a small space to make it look like the herd was considerably larger, and then moved them out again," he said to Regan.

"Aye, indeed, that's my thinking as well. The numbers didn't make sense, if you catch my meaning."

"Smart lad. Perhaps the answers lie with the herd. Show me the way they went."

Regan pointed out a trail leading away from the site. It ran flat for a distance before disappearing over the weathered rock of the far hillside. Aidan mounted up with the others, riding beside Hjalmar, and they set out again.

◆ ◆ ◆

Rain began an hour before dusk, a sleety downpour typical of spring in the mountains, and a fitful wind sprang up. The horses trudged on with lowered heads and tails clamped to their rumps, and the men wrapped themselves in their cloaks. They made camp in the shelter of a stand of pitch pine. Aidan's knees ached from the cold. His one luxury was a tent of his own, which granted him a measure of privacy.

Despite his weariness, he lay awake for what seemed like hours. His thoughts went to his family and the castle folk. He found himself longing for Fiona-Maria, his first wife. Their marriage had been a happy combination of prudent political alliance and incandescent romance. For years, the loss had been so poignant that he could not bear to look at their daughter, Neave. Along with her psychic Gift, she possessed her mother's beauty. Instead, when faced with an impossible situation, he'd determined to send her to Alcabra Keep, and already he regretted the lost years of her childhood.

It was not too late for his second family, though. Graciela had been a measured choice, and as the years and children increased, respect had grown between them. He'd developed an appreciation for her skills; she was an impeccable if emotionally distant chatelaine for his castle.

What children she had given him! Iain, of course, as promising an heir as any man could wish for. Jessamy, dark-haired and conventional like her mother. Leora with her independent streak. And little Sharina, a spark of elfin enchantment. Eventually, there would be grandchildren, and he looked forward to doting upon them.

But first, he thought as sleep overtook him at last, this business with Lord Carcosse must be managed. The staged 'cattle raid' didn't appear to be a trap. That should set Connor's mind at ease. A ruse, then? For what purpose? Perhaps the cattle themselves would reveal the answer.

◆ ◆ ◆

Aidan emerged from his tent the next morning to find the rest of the encampment eating and the pack animals almost ready to go. His aide offered him a mug of *jaco* and a serving of jerky-laced trail porridge that, by some miracle, was still hot. He ate hastily and mounted up.

The last clouds of night's rainfall drifted away on the gentle breeze. Birds sang in bursts and the horses plodded along, heads swaying, ears relaxed, tails swishing an occasional fly. As the land rose, their route wound between low hills.

Toward dusk, when inky shadows wreathed the eastern hills, they came upon a trampled spot with the usual cattle droppings. A chill wind sprang up, promising more rain. Regan paced out the site and reported this was where the herd had passed the night, the animals bunching together. He'd found tracks made by unshod horses around the periphery.

"How far ahead?" Aidan asked.

"Four or five days, my lord. I'm sorry, I can't say for better certain. This nightly rain muddles the tracks."

"Time is our adversary now," Aidan said.

The next day, they moved more quickly, following the contours of the hills. By the time the light was too poor to continue, they reached a place where the herd had rested. Here a spring supplied water and nourished a stand of ambernut trees. Aidan had loved them as a boy, but at this stage, the poisonous compounds in the husks rendered them unfit to eat.

Rain began to fall as the men were tending their horses, setting up the tents, and gathering fuel. Dinner was a cold affair, since the only fallen wood was wet and half-rotten. The trees protected them from the worst of the elements.

Aidan sat with the men, laughing at their jokes and joining them in song.

I've been a wild rover for many a year, he sang,
And I spent all my money on women and ale,
But now I've returned with gold in great store,
And I never will play the wild rover no more.

And it's no, nay, never
No, nay, never, no more,
Will I play the rover
No never, no more.

The men whooped in appreciation, Regan among them.

"If I am ever dispossessed of lands and title, I'll earn my bread as a bard," Aidan joked.

"We pray that day may never come, *vai dom*," said Hjalmar. Several of the men cheered.

"You've had enough of my croaking, lads," Aidan said. "I'm off to bed."

Calls of "Rest well, my lord!" followed him to his tent.

Several days after Aidan's party had departed, Leora surrendered to duty. Her mother had made it clear that she expected Leora to participate in needlework along with the women of the household. On a day like this, Leora didn't mind. The solarium was warm and bright, capturing the early spring sunlight. The furnishings had been chosen for the ladies of the castle and everywhere displayed the artistry of their handiwork. Besides the finished tapestries, fireplace shields, and pillow covers, several musical instruments sat waiting, for it was their habit to play or sing as they worked.

Lady Hastur sat at a free-standing frame that held a partially finished wall hanging. Her lady-in-waiting, Estella, wound a skein of gray wool. Jessamy, haloed in a pool of sunlight, was knitting socks on double-pointed needles.

Leora went to her mother and kissed her on the cheek. "What work shall I do today, Mother?"

"You might begin by giving Estella a hand. Winding always goes more smoothly with two."

Leora brought up a chair facing Estella and held her arms out. Estella looped the skein over Leora's hands, straightened out the strands, and resumed winding the ball. While she worked, talk resumed. They'd been complaining about mending holes.

"Holes in the linens," Jessamy grumbled dramatically. "Holes in the socks, so we must knit more of them. Holes in the—I don't know what else, but I'm sure the list of things with holes in them must be a long one. Sister, since you're almost done with winding, don't you want to knit socks with me?"

"Or sit by me and work on this hanging?" Mother said.

"Given the choice between wall hangings," Leora said, "which are pretty to look at, and socks that will prevent frostbitten toes next winter, I'll take the socks."

"You are quite right," her mother said. "Even in summer, exposure to cold can be serious." With a sigh, she added, "We must also make up more arnica salve. Our supplies are running low."

"All the more so since Father plans to recruit several hundred more men," Jessamy said. "In case Lord Carcosse is planning something dastardly."

Dastardly? Who would have guessed that Jessamy would ever use a word like *dastardly*?

Wait—"recruit several hundred more men"?

"Jessamy, you are not to repeat idle gossip." Mother's tone was sharp.

"It's not *idle gossip*," Jessamy whined. "*Connor himself* told me."

"How many times must I remind you? Do not tell falsehoods and do not make excuses. If Connor deemed it necessary to speak about the matter to anyone other than your father, he would have entrusted the information to *me*, the lady of the castle, and not a girl who clearly has not yet learned discretion. *How* you came by this ridiculous notion is not the issue, only your wagging tongue. Especially when it pertains to men's affairs."

Jessamy dropped knitting into her lap. "I don't see why we can't talk about what's going on."

"Because it is not proper for women to engage in idle speculation."

"What happens to Father—to Connor—to *Hastur*—affects all of us! If there's to be a war, don't we have a right to know? To prepare ourselves?"

Leora stared at her older sister, who never talked back to their mother. What had gotten into her? And Jessamy had mentioned Connor twice in as many minutes. What was going on?

"My darling," Mother said, more quietly now, "men and women live in separate worlds. It is how we are made. If war with Carcosse comes in our time, as it did in the time of your grandfather, the women of Hastur will meet it as we always have, with courage of the spirit instead of the body. Meanwhile, there is nothing to be gained in gossip, only needless agitation and impaired digestion."

"It isn't fair," Jessamy said. "Why can't we talk about it? We have as much right to shape our destinies as men do. This—" she indicated the knitting in her lap, "—is hardly a significant contribution—"

"Enough!" Mother was the mistress of the castle—the *vai domna*, the high lady. Jessamy gave her a mutinous glare but kept silent.

After an awkward pause, Leora said, "Is that what Father has gone to do, then? To prevent a war with Carcosse?"

Jessamy jumped in before Mother could answer. "Why is it all right for *Leora* to ask about what Father's doing but not me? It's not *fair*."

"Life isn't fair," Mother said severely. "That's not a justification for unladylike behavior. From *either* of you."

"I thought everyone knew he's investigating Lord Carcosse's complaint about the cattle raid," Leora explained.

"*Cattle raid*?" Estella gave a little shriek and then cringed before Mother's reprimanding look. Jessamy frowned.

Why, oh why could she have not considered for one moment before she let slip the cattle raid? Father had deliberately *not* mentioned it at his last dinner.

"Your father's mission may pertain to a cattle raid or it may not," Mother said. "Aldones knows there have been enough of them over the years. You must learn to cultivate patience. Your father will tell us whatever we ought to know."

"Well, he's not here, is he?" Jessamy said. "He can't very well forbid us from discussing matters that concern us, too."

"I can—and *I do*. We've heard enough on this inappropriate subject! Leora, you are not to blabber about matters about which you know nothing. Jessamy, I expected you to be a better influence over your sister, not egg her on to behavior unbecoming the daughter of a noble house. It is not seemly for a girl of marriageable age."

Cheeks flaming, Jessamy picked up her knitting.

For a time, the only sounds were the faint clicking of needles and an occasional sigh. Leora took one of the balls of yarn she'd wound and began casting on the cuff of a sock. She wanted to talk more with Jessamy, but not under Mother's watchful eye.

"All right, my darlings, that's enough for today." Mother shook out her fingers as she got to her feet, leaving Estella to tidy up. "You're free until dinner, although I expect you to behave decorously while I am not here." She swept from the solarium.

Jessamy tucked her knitting into her work basket, set it on the shelf, and then left. Leora followed her to the family wing and up the stairs.

"Hold up!" she called as Jessamy was just about to open her bedroom door. "I want to hear what you had to say."

"You see what it's like," Jessamy burst out. "Every time I try to talk about something serious, Mother acts as if I've been caught by a Ghost Wind and am spouting gibberish."

Leora refused to be diverted. "You said Connor told you Father has gone off to investigate. What else did he tell you? Did he say anything about it being a trap?"

"A trap? No, why would he think that?"

The door to Sharina's room flew open. "What's going on? I thought you were doing needlework with Mother."

"As *you* should have been," Jessamy said.

Sharina flushed. "It's not my fault! I had a tummy ache."

Leora faced Jessamy, who was often dismissive but rarely mean. "Lay off her, will you? She's done nothing to *you—*"

"For Evanda's sake, will you keep your voices down?" came from the end of the corridor. Neave stood there, hands on her hips.

"What's *she* up to?" Jessamy sneered. "Butting into things that are none of her concern!"

Evanda's grace, she's in a foul mood, thought Leora. Had all this talk of Connor— and father and a trap—*and Connor*—poked a tender spot?

"If you want to carry on," Neave said, coming toward them, "please do so where you cannot be so easily overheard. The racket you're making can be heard halfway to the Wall Around the World."

"This is a *private* conversation." Jessamy folded her arms across her chest.

Neave ignored her. "What's the hubbub about?"

"The cattle raid," Jessamy said at the same time as Leora burst out with, "Lord Carcosse's dastardly plot!"

"*What* cattle raid?" Sharina asked. "*What* plot?"

"The one you're not supposed to know about?" Jessamy turned to glare at Leora. "But that now everyone does?"

"Oh, *that* cattle raid," Sharina said.

"It's got to be a trap," Leora explained.

"*What trap?*" Sharina wailed.

"You think I made up Father preparing for war?" Jessamy tossed her head. "Connor told me, so it must be true. He tells me many things. We have an *understanding.*" Without waiting for a reply, she flounced into her room.

Leora put her arm around her younger sister's shoulders. Sharina was still a child, after all, with a child's fears. "Do not let Jessamy's words trouble you. Father is doing his best to keep us safe, as he has always done."

Sharina blinked back tears. "I'm afraid something bad will happen to him."

"As we all are," Neave said in a reassuring tone. "He has come through worse perils than this, I promise you."

"Let's go to our rooms," Leora murmured to Sharina. "I'll braid your hair with the blue ribbons I promised you."

With a last sniffle and a brightening smile, Sharina allowed herself to be led away.

◆ ◆ ◆

As for Connor …

Ah, Connor, Neave thought as she made her way to her father's office, where she knew he would be. *Why could you not have been someone else, or I born into a different family?*

Neave felt Connor's presence from halfway down the hall. It wasn't a tele-pathic contact. If he had *laran*, it was so deeply buried that neither she nor the *leronis* from Alcabra Keep could detect it. The connection that ran be-tween them was intense and visceral. It had been so from the moment she'd looked into his eyes and saw a reflection of her own hopeless passion. Now she paused outside the door, his nearness like a fragrance in her mind. She closed her eyes, willing herself to ignore it.

Silence. Patience. Purpose. Let everything else be as if it had never existed.

The latch lifted from inside. Then it swung open and he stood there. She couldn't breathe. Her heart sounded too loud in her ears. He took a step back, indicating that she might enter. As she did so, she passed within arm's length of him. The heat of his body touched her face. He closed the door and she turned toward him. They were too close.

It was a mistake to come, she thought. *Why could I not let the matter rest?*

The room teemed with ghosts of the last time she'd stood here. Her father had sat behind his desk, his expression growing ever grimmer as she'd opened her heart to him. Hope had driven her to him, hope that faded as she stumbled to a halt.

"I understand your feelings," Aidan had said in a voice like flint. "But what you ask is impossible. It should have been *unthinkable*. I cannot have Connor as both paxman and son-in-law. As my aide, he is invaluable to me. Nor will I throw away the potential alliances from your advantageous marriage."

"Then I will never marry," she'd thrown back at him, and stormed out of the room.

As ill luck willed it, she had stumbled, tear-blind, into Connor's arms.

"*Preciosa*," he had murmured into her hair. "What we have, we will always have. Matters could not have gone otherwise. Your father has no choice."

"Are you defending him?"

He'd pulled away, eyes locked on hers. "The world goes as it must, not as you or I would have it. And I will always defend him, with my life if need be. You know this, or you would not love me."

She could not bring herself to say, *You are my father's paxman, as I am his daughter. Our hearts are not entirely ours to give.*

A tenday later, her father informed her that he had arranged for her to study at Alcabra Keep, permanently.

Thrusting the memories aside, Neave managed to keep her hands at her sides as Connor walked around to the far side of the desk, placing a physical barrier between them.

"How fare you, my lady?"

She made a dismissive gesture. "I've just spoken with Jessamy. She fancies herself in love with you. She hangs on your every word and gloats about your—how did she put it?—your *understanding*. You must not lead her on like this. She is not the easiest person, but she does not deserve to be deceived this way. The situation is impossible. It must end."

Connor drew back, clearly startled. "*Damisela* Jessamy? I've barely exchanged two sentences with her since Midwinter. Why would she say a thing like that?"

"Why would she lie?" Neave countered. "Something must have passed between you. What did you say?"

"You know me better. I would never betray Lord Hastur's trust. And with a child whom I barely know."

"*She* seems to think you know each other very well. And she is not a child but a young woman of noble birth who has reached marriageable age. The truth, now—did you tell her that my father intends to raise an army against Carcosse?"

"I, what? An *army*? Did she say that?"

"She did! And with such glowing confidence in your intimacy that I wanted to—never mind what I wanted."

"*Preciosa*, are you jealous of your little sister?"

She forced herself to stand still. *Silence. Patience. Purpose.*

"I am *not* jealous. It is not that. Please don't change the subject." Neave took a breath. "We are talking about Jessamy's feelings, not mine. A paxman cannot court his lord's daughter. You know that, and I know that. Apparently, Jessamy does not. She and I are not close as sisters ought to be, but I would spare her the heartbreak if this goes on."

Connor fisted his hands and then released them. "I see now where she might have gotten such a notion. For a tenday now, she's been following me around like a lost puppy, always asking questions. As a member of my lord's family, I owe her every courtesy. Otherwise, I would never— Neave, please understand. I could not dismiss her out of hand."

Neave's anger dissipated in a heartbeat. "You never meant to deceive her with an affection you do not feel?"

"No! I never meant to lead her on or give her a false impression of our relationship. I will behave with more discretion from now on. If she does not take the hint, I will speak to Lady Hastur and let her handle the matter, rather than embarrass the young lady."

"I see. Thank you. I could not ask for a more gracious reply." Neave turned to leave, then hesitated. "Is there any truth to Father raising an army? About a possible war with Carcosse?"

"Jessamy wanted to know where *Dom* Aidan had gone and whether he was in danger. I meant to reassure her that he would be well-guarded. I don't recall my exact words, only that he took an adequate force with him. How she leaped from that to preparations for war, I have no idea."

Neave's cheeks went hot. "How could I think you would betray my father's trust? I don't know what is wrong with me. Please forgive me."

He crossed the distance between them. She thought he might hold out his hands to her, which she could not bear, but he did not.

"There is nothing to forgive." His voice was soft. He was the lodestone of her heart. "You spoke out of your care for your sister, and for that I honor you. You are also worried about your father's safety. We all are. He is cunning and experienced, not easily tricked. He has taken every reasonable precaution. Be content with that."

He knows more than he tells, and he is not as confident as his bold words indicate, Neave thought. But there was nothing to be gained by belaboring the subject. At least, Connor would now do his best to discourage Jessamy's fantasies.

They were still standing uncomfortably close. Words echoed in her mind: *A paxman cannot court his lord's daughter.*

She stepped away, her gaze downcast so she need not see the longing in his eyes, the wish that the world were different—

And flinched at the sudden, sharp rapping at the door.

"Come," Connor said, his tone crisp. A couple of steps took him behind the desk.

The door opened and a page rushed in, stammering out the news that another messenger had just arrived.

6

Connor watched Neave disappear into the shadowed interior of the castle. She seemed even more remote than ever, wrapped in the mantle of Hastur pride. That made it easier to remain while she walked away. It had been folly to hope for anything more.

Lorcan appeared a few minutes later, but not with the expected news from the spies Connor had positioned in Carcosse Castle. For that, he must be patient. Instead, Lorcan reported that the rider, Kavan of Deer Creek Village, waited in the guards' room. He added that the messenger insisted on seeing only Lord Hastur.

Connor went down to find two men-at-arms drinking *jaco* and playing at castles. A young stranger in a coarsely woven jacket and breeches, and rope-bound shoes instead of riding boots, sat on a bench in front of the fireplace. He jumped to his feet at Connor's entrance.

"M'lord!"

"Not *my lord*," Connor said. "I serve Lord Hastur as his paxman—you know what that is?"

"His Voice?"

No, but that would do. "I act in his name when he is not here."

Connor poured himself a mug of *jaco* and one for the boy. He cut a couple of slices of bread, smeared them with soft chervine cheese, and carried the plate to Kavan. For a few moments, the two sat together, eating and sipping the steaming brew.

"You hail from Deer Creek?" Connor said.

"Tis a smallish village, much like any other, I reckon. Close by to forest. Groves of nut-trees and hardwood, not pitch pine that goes up in flames every year or two. Folk harvest nuts and farm goats."

"Then it is not unlike the place where I spent my early years. One of my first duties was as goat-herder."

"Mine as well." Kavan was beginning to relax now. He must be half-famished, by the rate at which he devoured the food.

"I remember dreaming of all the adventures that awaited me beyond the village fences," Connor said. "Deer Creek, that's where Regan hails from. He's a scout for Lord Hastur. Do you know him?"

"He's me cousin on our da's side."

"Yes, I see the resemblance. Is it the family tradition to serve the Hastur Lord?"

Kavan's eyes brightened. "That it is, four generations now. I was to join the scouts last year but me da cut his foot bad while harvesting firewood last winter—'twas a raw one, that—and I couldna be spared."

"That shows commendable loyalty to your family. When you are free, I am sure Lord Hastur will welcome your service." Assuming an air of unconcern, Connor turned his gaze to the fire. He'd established a camaraderie with the young man—barely more than a boy, really—and knew enough about the gentling of young horses to back off.

He did not have to wait long. Kavan covered his face with his free hand.

This was not what Connor had expected. "Lad, what ails you?"

"Oh, m'lord, I've failed in me duty! The first task I was given—not herding goats but something powerful grave—and I've come a cropper!" Now that the dam of silence had broken, Kavan was almost prostrate with guilt.

Connor resisted the impulse to put his hand on the boy's shoulder. "Surely it can't be as bad as that."

"What's the use? Me honor's broke for sure!"

"Then there can be no harm in telling me," Connor said.

Kavan's next words came all in a rush, without a pause for breath. "I shoulda done that right off! I only thought—me grandda, who's headman of the village, he said to take the message as quick as quick may be and to give it to Lord Hastur's own hand—and I thought—all I thought was that you weren't *him* and of course, I couldna give it to the lady—and here I've wasted all this time, and now what happens is sure to be me fault!" He buried his face in his hands.

Connor hardened his voice. "You made a mistake, an error in judgment. The best way to fix it is to deliver the message *at once*."

Kavan lifted his head, cheeks dripping. Sniffling, he dug into the leather scrip at his belt, extracted a wrinkled, folded piece of paper, and held it out.

Connor accepted the missive. "Do you know what this says?"

"Nay, I canna read. But it's to do with the outlaws. Come down from higher in the Venzas this season, they did. Past times, they'd run off a few goats now and again, but nothin' more. Last two-three tendays, though, one run-off after 'nother. A coupla steadings farther out been burned—"

Burned? Goat thieves, like cattle rustlers, rarely struck human habitation. Armed resistance, or even vociferous unarmed protest, usually discouraged attacks. Ordinary robbers were loath to destroy livestock and dwellings.

Burned, the boy had said.

Connor unfolded the letter. The writing was awkward, the letters crudely shaped. That was to be expected from a headman who had been taught long ago and had little occasion to practice since then.

He tucked the letter into the inner fold of his vest and stood. "This letter is not overlong and you may remember things that are not noted in it, details that might prove crucial. When you have eaten and rested, I will have a scribe attend you, so that we may record everything you say. The more information we have, the more complete our understanding. We must not judge ahead of time what is important and what is not."

"N-no, m'lord."

◆ ◆ ◆

Connor lowered himself into his accustomed chair in Aidan's office and tried to imagine his lord and friend sitting on the other side of the desk. The image would not come. The air in the study tasted stale, as if the space had been carefully dusted but long disused. It lacked the familiar, lingering presence. He wished he had a trace of *laran*, which would allow them to speak mind-to-mind across the leagues. There was no one else he could consult.

Burned, the boy had said. And likely seen it with his own eyes.

Aidan trusts you, he reminded himself. *He's heeded your counsel many times in the past. Think what advice you would give him now.*

With that thought in mind, he bent to the letter.

To Lord Haster, it read. *This be writ by Steffin, headman of Dere Creke vilage. I send this by my boy Kavan, who can tele of its truth. This snowbreke we have had steadins burnt, tho not so far the vilage itself. They been gettin worse and closer. Two night ago, Hamal and his sons fought raiders off and kilt one. Hamal say he rekon the man as one of Lord Carcose's. He worked as stableman to Lord C and knew him. To this I canna swear. By yr oath to us, send us aid, we beg. And quick.*

—Steffin, by my hand

My boy Kavan is a good one and tells true.

Connor let the letter fall on the desk. A pattern of raids, commanded by Lord Carcosse! No wonder the boy sounded so desperate.

At the very least, Connor thought, he must investigate. He must also be prepared to take action to protect the village and its environs.

It is *a trap.*

Connor had used those very words, believing the cattle raid was the set-up for an ambush. Now an equally chilling possibility occurred to him. He got up and began pacing. A pattern took shape in his mind: the cattle raid as a ruse to draw off the castle's armed men. Carcosse gambling that with this new calamity, more men would be sent, and in a different direction. That would leave Hastur Castle dangerously under-protected. Thanks to Aidan's foresight, a word would summon reinforcements already readied.

At the same time, he dared not ignore the request—the *plea.* These were Hastur folk. Aidan owed them protection just as they owed him obedience and service.

He forced himself to sit back down at the desk, this time not in his usual seat but Aidan's.

"*Vai dom,*" *he imagined himself saying from the chair opposite him.* "*What are your orders?*"

For a long moment, he sat in silence. Then memories rose in his mind: Aidan's face, creased with thought. His voice. His words.

He took out a sheet of paper and began writing.

◆ ◆ ◆

An hour later, Connor went to the solarium in search of Lady Hastur. There was no requirement for him to advise her of his plans. He did so out of courtesy and to prevent another round of gossip. It was one thing to have young women passing tales of imaginary romances and quite another to encourage rumors that, true or false, might endanger the people he was charged to protect.

One of Lady Hastur's maids met him at the door. "Oh! *Mestre* Connor!" She seemed disconcerted by his appearance at a traditionally feminine venue.

"Good day, *mestra*. Is your lady within? And might I have a private audience?"

"I shall inquire." Through the closed door, women's voices reached him, and then the maid gestured for him to enter. "My lady will hear you, but it would not be proper—" she bobbed a curtsy, "I shall remain just inside the door."

As far as he knew there had never been any gossip about him and *Domna* Graciela, nor had either of them, by glance or gesture, behaved with anything less than the strictest propriety. Still, given Jessamy's story, caution in the form of an impeccable witness was prudent.

He stepped into the sunlit solarium, taking in the tapestry frame, the chairs and divans and upholstered footstools sized for a woman's smaller frame, the potted plants beginning to flower, the cushions bright with their own embroidered gardens. It was, all in all, a feminine sanctuary.

Graciela greeted him with a half-smile that did not reach her eyes. "Connor, this is an unexpected visit."

He bowed. "My lady, I apologize for the intrusion. I would not have disturbed you without cause."

"Very well, then." She sat straighter in her chair, composing herself. "I am listening."

"It has to do with the matter *Dom* Aidan went off to investigate a tenday ago."

"He was following up on a complaint from our neighbor, Lord Carcosse." Her expression shifted to one of concern. "Has aught gone amiss?"

Connor raised his hands in reassurance. "Nothing like that, *vai domna*. The last message from him was that all was well."

"I am relieved to hear it."

"The initial grievance concerned an alleged cattle raid," he explained. "At the time, there was a question about whether it had actually happened or was a deception."

From the glint in her eyes, she understood the implications. He paused for a moment in case she should have something to say, but when she did not, he went on.

"This very day, I received a letter from one of our villages in the Venzas. It lies in a forested region of no particular strategic significance, its primary source of income arising from the harvesting of nuts."

"Nuts are a valuable food crop," she remarked. Provisioning the castle, making sure everyone had enough to eat through the long, cold winters, fell to her as chatelaine. Whatever else might be said about her, she took her responsibilities seriously. "Go on."

"Steadings nearby have been raided and burned," he replied, "and the headman believes the village itself is in imminent danger. He says the strikes were carried out at the command of Lord Merryl Carcosse."

Graciela paled, although her composure did not waver. "Do you believe these charges?"

"I do, *vai domna.* If Lord Carcosse did not order these raids himself, then men under his command acted on their own and he *should* have known."

"Lord Carcosse may be many things," she said dryly, "but *incompetent* is not among them."

"No, my lady. Not that I have ever heard."

Graciela met his gaze levelly. "What is your assessment of the situation?"

"We cannot know Lord Carcosse's true intent, but I believe he sought to draw off a portion of our armed defense."

"That seems a reasonable conclusion to me, as well. Continue."

"Now we have this second action, designed to provoke our response, sending away *more* of our forces. We face a dilemma, whether to dispatch an inadequate party to the aid of Deer Creek or to lower the castle's defenses, perhaps to a dangerous level. You see the conundrum, my lady?"

"If we abandon Deer Creek, we break faith with the people who look to us for protection in exchange for their fealty. If we do not, we are left vulnerable to a direct assault."

Aidan would have said very much the same thing.

"What is your advice?" she asked.

"Not my advice, but Lord Hastur's. He knew Carcosse might try something like this, and that we dared not wait for his return."

"No, indeed. This offense must be answered, and speedily."

Connor explained that before Aidan departed, he had begun the assembly of a fighting force. "I will proceed with the muster. I will also send a small, swift force to Deer Creek, but I will retain enough fighters to hold the castle for a limited time. If we are attacked before the army can assemble and Lord Hastur is delayed, we may be hard put. A messenger must be dispatched to inform him of this latest development and speed his return."

"*Mestre* Connor, are you asking my permission to do these things? You do not need it, you know. My husband has bestowed all the requisite authority on you." Her breath caught in her throat, but she mastered herself.

"There are other precautions to be taken," he said. "Lord Hastur gave instructions to summon the Alcabra circle. I understand that *Damisela* Neave was to join them at the Keep, but that is now too dangerous. The circle is a valuable asset and must not be placed at risk. Lord Hastur may choose to command them in battle if these skirmishes escalate into outright warfare."

"Is that possible? Another war?" Her voice rose in pitch, and for the first time, she did not seem in complete control of herself.

"Lady," he said, trying to sound reassuring, "in these times, anything is possible. It is better to be overly cautious than to be caught wanting."

She nodded, her color returning. "My husband did well to place his trust in you."

With a bow, he left her.

Leora answered her mother's summons, unsure what she would find. It was unusual for all the sisters to be called to the solarium at once, and rumors had been flying about the castle. Sharina took Leora's hand in damp fingers, looking as if she were about to burst into tears. They knocked and went in.

They were not the first to arrive: Jessamy and Neave had already taken their places. There was no sign of the dreaded needlework, and Mother's tapestry frame had been moved to one side.

Once they settled, Mother began. No argument, no discussion, no response was required or even allowed. Leora sat quietly through descriptions of plans, the dispatch of a party to defend the villagers and how Connor would prepare the castle for attack, and a message to be sent with all speed to her father—

Somewhere between one moment and the next, she was plunged from subdued astonishment to frantic, splintered thoughts.

No, I can't stay here—not when I must see him every day—it's impossible!

Leora reeled under the onslaught. With an effort, she remained in her seat and upright.

No! I cannot bear it!

Stop it, Leora pleaded mentally. *Oh, please make it stop!*

Stop? The word echoed in her mind, her thought and yet not her thought.

She glanced around the room, unable to believe how *normal* everything looked. Her mother was still speaking—something about the *leroni* from Alcabra coming here instead of Neave going to them—and her sisters were listening politely, hands folded on their laps.

All of them.

And yet one of them had *heard* her. One of them had blasted out fury and denial and despair.

Neave! It had to be her.

Neave turned her face toward Leora, eyes widening.

Sweet Evanda, you heard *me?*

The room began to spin. Nausea brought the taste of acid to Leora's mouth. She forced herself to think. Should she try to "send" a thought message to Neave? How? Or pretend nothing had happened and wait for a moment to speak privately—

Queasiness whirled together with vertigo and a sickening, clammy feeling in her belly. The room slipped sideways and she found herself falling into a chasm of gray ice.

◆ ◆ ◆

Neave glared at her stepmother. *What do you mean, bring the Alcabra Keep folk here? I am to remain home? Father promised—no, it's impossible!*

Words could not express the emotions raging through her. The anguish. The loss. The fury.

She didn't know who to throttle first—Connor—or her father for being absent—or Lord Carcosse for provoking this stupid argument—or her mother for going along with the plan—or Jessamy for her stupid, childish gossip.

She was alone, without ally or hope.

She could not bear it.

Stop it, came a mental voice bearing the unmistakable stamp of untrained *laran. Oh, please make it stop!*

The telepathic contact startled her out of her furious thought. She came back to her physical self with a jolt. Her mother was still prattling on—

Neave!

Leora?

Her half-sister had *laran,* she was sure, but she'd supposed it to be a minor Gift, not this voice ringing through her mind like a silver bell—

Sweet Evanda, you heard *me?*

Leora went pale and slid from her chair onto the floor. Sharina screamed. In the commotion that followed, Neave crouched beside Leora. Leora's eyes rolled up in her skull, crescents of white through partly opened lids. Her arms and legs twitched once, twice— her body convulsed. The back of her head struck the carpet with a *thunk!*

Whimpering, Sharina clutched Jessamy, while Jessamy just stared. Graciela sent Estella to the kitchen for a restorative.

Neave turned Leora on her side. *At least I can prevent her from choking.*

As soon as Neave's hands touched bare skin, their telepathic bond intensified. The link was so powerful, it stopped her breath in her throat. Leora glowed with powerful, untrained *laran*.

Blue-white power rushed over Neave, threatening to unmoor her.

I am Neave Hastur, daughter of Aidan Hastur and Fiona-Maria Aillard. This is my place, this is who I am. I am a leronis *as well as Comynara.*

The wild currents abated enough for Neave to focus on her sister's mind. She concentrated on the energetic patterns of her sister's body, the sullen, stagnant nodes.

Neave had not yet finished her training as a healer—a monitor, it was called, skilled in the use of *laran* to assess and treat ailments. What she'd been taught came back to her in a rush.

Her laran *has overloaded her channels. Here—and here—*

"Sweet Evanda!" Graciela's voice trembled with shock and dismay. "This is no ordinary fainting fit. What's wrong with her?"

"It's threshold sickness," Neave responded without taking her focus off Leora.

"How can that be? She was tested—"

Neave blocked out the rest of Graciela's protest. Leora was old for the psychic upheavals that often accompanied the awakening of *laran* in puberty, but the Gift sometimes manifested late. And she had no doubt at all about her diagnosis.

"Leave me be, stepmother. I know what to do. But—if there's any *kirian*, bring it."

Drawing out the silken pouch holding her starstone from where it rested between her breasts, Neave dropped the stone into the palm of her hand. It flared into brightness. With her inner vision, she sought the pattern within the light, one that had emerged the first time she'd held it. The starstone focused and magnified her native *laran*. She'd keyed into it, so that stone and mind became mirrors of one another, inextricably linked.

Aiming her thoughts at the dully pulsing nodes in Leora's body, Neave carefully untangled the stagnant energy. Moment by moment, they began to flow more freely. Sullen brown shades gave way to healthier, brighter hues. Blood flow returned, bringing physical warmth.

Satisfied, Neave withdrew from Leora's mind. When she returned to her body, she was shaking with fatigue. *Laran* work drained physical as well as psychic energy. All she wanted was sleep, but she'd need to replenish herself with sweetened foods or risk her health.

"There's no *kirian* in the household medicinal pantries," Graciela said. "The last batch was years old and had gone bad. I believed we did not need more." She did not add that *kirian* was difficult to make and had few uses other than for the maladies of telepaths, being made from the psychoactive pollen of the *kireseth* flowers. Even the ignorant knew that exposure to the unseasonably blooming plants resulted in the madness called the "Ghost Wind," which few survived with their minds intact.

The Alcabra folk will have a supply. At least, Leora is out of immediate danger.

"The main thing now," Neave said, "is to keep Leora warm and to urge her to eat when she is able."

Graciela listened—at first grudgingly, then with a morsel of respect— as Neave explained the plan of care. Graciela had Leora carried to her room and tended to, then sent Estella for another platter of pastries for Neave. Wide-eyed and unprotesting, the other sisters left the solarium at their mother's command.

"I should go, too," Neave said, "to look after Leora." When she got to her feet, her knees shook. She sat down heavily in a chair.

"Nonsense," Graciela said, taking a seat beside her. "You are clearly in need of care, as well. Ah, here is the food. Thank you, Estella. You may leave us now."

Neave occupied herself with honeyed spiral buns, reflecting on this unwonted kindness from her stepmother.

"I know little of the development of *laran* or the ills that attend it," Graciela said, her tone quiet, almost shy. "I had an older brother, Turlach. He would have been heir, but he died of threshold sickness before I was born. Of course, since I was a girl child, it would not have been such a calamity if I had suffered the same illness, but as it turned out, I seem to have very little *laran* and I made a smooth passage through adolescence. Or as smooth as any girl. I think—" she tilted her head to one side, her gaze turning inward, "that it pained my parents to even breathe the word *laran*, particularly my father, who took Turlach's death hard. Then when you became ... troubled, and your father summoned a teacher from Alcabra Keep, I was content to leave him to it. I feared—I would have been of no use to you."

It was as close to an apology for neglect as Neave expected.

Several days brought Aidan's party to an expanse of rolling pasture. To the south, a ribbon of brightness marked a stream. A hawk soared overhead. Before long, they came upon a settlement, primarily a communal living and working space of the sort often found in this area. The practice of many families sleeping and eating together under the same roof was a bit old-fashioned, but countryfolk still held to it.

A villager, gray-haired but robust, emerged from the lodge. He paused, his gaze fixing on the Hastur colors. His face paled beneath his ruddy beard. Then he pulled himself together visibly. A half-grown girl and an elderly woman, wiping her hands on her apron, came to stand beside him. He put his arm around the child's shoulders protectively.

Aidan, thinking that the presence of so many armed men might intimidate the villagers, signaled a halt. He rode on alone, keeping his hands away from his weapons. "Good man, I bid you a fair day."

"My lord Hastur!" The man fell to his knees. Behind him, the old woman and the girl bobbed awkward curtsies.

Since when did his countryfolk react to his presence with terror? He swung down from the saddle and went up to them. "Be at your ease. I mean you no harm."

The man hung his head and would not look up. "We are yours to command. What more would you have of us?"

What more?

Someone has demanded a great deal of these people in my name, or they would not be terrified.

Then: *The stolen cattle did not come from Carcosse lands. They came from* here.

Hjalmar managed introductions. The man's name was Orrim, headman of the village. The old woman was his mother and the girl, one of his granddaughters.

Aidan entered the lodge, accompanied by Hjalmar and Regan. The interior was clean and light; instead of bare earth, the worn wooden planking was scoured white. An earthenware pot simmering on the central hearth gave off the aromas of wild onions and herbs. A babe slept in a nearby cradle.

Aidan lowered himself to the one solid chair, with Hjalmar and Regan flanking him to either side. Orrim stood before him. "Tell us what happened here, for it was not on my orders."

"*Vai dom*, men came to our village. They wore Hastur colors. They said they spoke for you, that you—you *required*—our cattle. When we protested that a levy was never in our fealty, they said old oaths no longer held. They—they drew steel upon us. We are farmers, not warriors. We could not—" he paled, "dared not—"

"Say no more." Aidan's hands tightened into fists. "It is wise to know when to fight and when to yield. Goods and livestock can be replaced, crops can be re-sown and dwellings rebuilt, but no one can bring back the dead. There is no stain upon your honor."

Orrim thrust out his chin. "That is all very well, but when next winter comes, how will we feed our children?"

Anger flared in Aidan, that his adversary—*his enemy, now*—had shown such little care for these villagers. It had taken courage for Orrim to speak as he had. Courage, or desperation.

By Aldones, these are my *people!*

"Your families will not starve," Aidan said, his jaw tight with anger but not at these villagers. "I give you my word."

"The word of a Hastur," Orrim murmured with a touch of awe.

Aidan shrugged off the reverence. He didn't want it. He hadn't done anything to earn it. He and these villagers were bound by tradition and oaths to mutual responsibility. It was his *duty* to protect them.

"We will pursue those who have taken your cattle," Aidan said. "If possible, we will restore your herd to you. If not, I will make good your loss."

"My lord, I dared not hope for so much. You—you *believed* me. I am shamed that I doubted you."

"Think no more of it. Tonight we will rest here with you. We will not ask for food, only water and firewood if you can spare it. And a place to set up our tents. Hjalmar, see to it."

With those words, Aidan strode out of the lodge. He was perilously close to revealing how angry he was. At Carcosse. At himself. At their fathers and grandfathers. These people had suffered enough without being drawn into whatever was coming. War, once likely, now seemed certain.

The next morning, Aidan's anger had not abated. It had chilled into something he dared not look too closely at, lest it consume him. The matter of the stolen cattle must be settled. Then he would deal with Carcosse.

They broke camp under a bright, cloudless sky. While the men were packing up and Aidan was finishing his third cup of *jaco*, Headman Orrim presented a youth to act as a local guide and identify the cattle when they were discovered. The boy was about Leora's age, with the gangling height of recent growth and a bit of dark fuzz along the jawline. He carried a cloth backpack with a rolled-up blanket and a stout walking stick that could also function as a staff for defense.

"This be me grandson, Derry," said the headman. "He's but a cowherd, yet old enough to have sense. He's a hard worker and true to his word. He'll not lead you astray."

Shifting from one foot to the other, Derry refused to make eye contact with Aidan.

"I thank you, and you, too, young Derry, for your service," Aidan said. "Hjalmar, see if your men can lend this lad a mount."

One of the men brought up a pony, a pack animal pressed into service, with only a halter with a lead line and a pad held in place by a woven surcingle. Derry's face lit up when he understood this was to be his steed. He stroked the pony's forelock, crooning softly, and then vaulted onto the animal's back.

The party retraced their path toward the line of hills. Regan took point, ensuring that they were not veering off-track. Derry seemed very taken with the scout, always a pace behind to watch him work. When they stopped at midday, Regan remarked that in time and with the right mentor, the boy might become a fair scout. Derry hunkered down a short distance away, straining for every word from his newly found idol, and blushed deeply.

Ah, youth, Aidan thought, and wondered if Iain was also that impressionable. He hoped not. Still, Derry was a likely lad, a lad such as Connor had been when the elder Lord Hastur had taken him in and educated him. Iain was too young to need a paxman but eventually he would, and who better than someone raised alongside him, someone who had learned to love him and whom he trusted?

I shall see how Derry fares on this mission. There would be time enough for decisions later.

After a time, Hjalmar suggested a rest, and Aidan agreed. The party dismounted and checked their girths and the feet and legs of their horses, then allowed them to forage.

Derry came up to Aidan and stood, shifting from one foot to the other. He kept his gaze downcast, although he clearly had something he wished to say.

"All right, lad. What is it?"

"M'lord—*vai dom*—is there aught I might do?"

"Why, take your rest, like we all are."

The youth looked disappointed, just as Iain might have. Aidan imagined his son saying, *"But I'm not tired!"* Aidan would reply, *"Of course not, a strong lad like you."* Then he thought of what they might encounter. The cattle thieves might be armed and expecting trouble. If Carcosse had set a trap, it was likely. He must keep Derry well away from any fighting.

Aidan handed the dun gelding's reins to Derry. "Mind you water him well. I'm counting on you."

Derry looked thoroughly enchanted with his new responsibility. "I will, m'lord!"

Aidan climbed one of the slopes, high enough to see the trail leading back to the village. He found a smooth, level stone big enough to perch on. The sun had left it warm and dry, but he could not relax. His thoughts were drawn to what lay ahead. Being in a battle personally did not dismay him. He had fought many times, both while his father was alive and since his inheritance. He remembered the nerves before the first encounter and how all notions of how things might unfold got swept away.

… Pulse rampaging, mouth dry, sweating fingers gripping sword hilt. War cries, horse surging beneath him, vision blurring in billows of dust. Adrenalin surging through his veins, nerves lit up as if by lightning …

Screams. Blood.

Much later, pain. Bodies of men he knew, still. Oh, so still.

Not Derry. Not if I can help it. Not Iain.

The sound of galloping hooves drew his attention. On the trail below, a rider burst around a brush-overgrown corner. Sun glinted on the blue and silver of his jacket. Aidan scrambled down the slope to where his men waited just as the rider arrived.

The rider reined his horse to a halt. "Lord Hastur! Is he with you?"

"I'm here."

"My lord, I come from the castle with orders to deliver this to your hands only." The rider reached into his saddle bags and took out a message scroll, which he thrust at Aidan. Sweat lathered the horse's body and the lines of fatigue marked his face.

Aidan accepted the scroll. "Aldones's grace, you've ridden long and hard. Hjalmar, see that man and mount are given water and food, whatever they need."

"My lord, the message is urgent," the rider protested.

"I can see that. I can also see that you and your horse are nigh exhausted and will serve no one if you founder."

"I will see to it." Hjalmar gestured for the rider to come with him.

Connor would not have sent a courier with such urgency unless something dire had happened. A death in the family? A natural disaster? Some new perfidy by Lord Carcosse?

He sent a silent prayer to Aldones, although Zandru of the nine frozen hells, each one colder and more wretched than the one before, or even Naotalba, Daughter of Darkness, might be more fitting.

The seal was his own, entrusted to Connor during his absence. Inside the vellum envelope, he found a letter in Connor's distinctive hand.

The letter was direct. The village of Deer Creek had been attacked by Carcosse's men. Reading on, Aidan nodded in approval of the measures Connor had taken, sending aid to Deer Creek as best he could to maintain the castle's defense, as well as the measures Aidan had put into motion, signaling the muster of troops and summoning the Alcabra circle to Hastur Castle. Connor concluded by asking if Aidan wished any further action taken.

So, Carcosse has shown his hand. First the cattle, now this.

He means to divide my forces. Another diversion will come soon.

He had promised Orrim that he would return the cattle. No matter what the difficulties, he had given his word. Connor would see to the safety of the village.

Deer Creek … The name mentioned in Connor's message was familiar. Oh yes, it was the place that Regan, the scout, hailed from.

The rest break was over and men were readying their mounts when Regan rejoined them. Aidan met the scout apart from the others for privacy. "I received word of your village. Deer Creek, is it not?"

"Aye, that's the place."

"That messenger—" with a nod toward where the tired rider was seated, sipping hastily brewed *jaco*, "—brought a report from my paxman at Hastur Castle that your village has been attacked by Lord Carcosse's men. We had word from Steffin, so he at least is well."

Emotions flashed, clear and raw, across Regan's face—shock, distress. Anger.

"If you wish to return home, you may," Aidan said. "It is difficult to be away at such a time. But I urge you to consider. First, your headman's plea has not gone unanswered. My paxman has sent aid, more hands—and swords—than any one man can offer." Relief shaded Regan's features, tentative yet. "Second, I must get this business with the cattle settled as speedily as possible. You are not my only scout, but you are by far the best. I will not command you to stay," he repeated. *Only ask.*

Aidan could almost hear Regan's thoughts: *M'lord could have kept silent, not told me. Could have forbid me to go. Could have broken faith with my kin.*

"'Tis enough for now," Regan said in a voice gone hoarse with emotion. "I'll do me best so we can all go home as soon as may be."

"I will not hold you a moment longer," Aidan replied.

Before moving on, Aidan composed a reply for Connor and furnished the rider with a fresh mount for his return to Hastur Castle.

◆ ◆ ◆

The route took Aidan and his men higher into the hills, gently sloping terrain. Soon, they looked down on a shallow valley at a dozen or so rangy, rough-coated beasts. A bull lifted his head, trailing ropy grass from his jaws. The shadows under a nearby copse might be a campsite for cowherds watching over the stolen beasts.

Relief buoyed Aidan's spirits that he'd found the cattle after so short a search. After returning them, he would be free to return home for the next encounter with Carcosse—one that would be on *his* terms.

Derry nudged his pony to the fore. Aidan asked, "Are those your village's cattle?"

"I can't swear to it on me life, m'lord, not every single one. That bull, Thunderer he's called, on account of when he runs. I'd know *him* anywhere.

He chased me and me brother out of the pen when we was too young to know better. Caught me brother with them horns and left a scar—see here, like this, on his arm." Derry sketched a line just below his shoulders.

Aidan smothered a laugh at the youth's earnestness. "That's all right, lad. I believe you. Now, what is the best way to get those cattle heading home, do you think?"

"See that there cow, the one with the white on her face? She's the queen cow. Give me a rope and I'll lead her, and they'll all follow."

"Even the bull?"

Derry gave Aidan a look that meant, *Especially the bull.*

Derry and one of the men with experience with cattle trotted down the hill. The bull made grumbling noises and pawed up clods of earth before lowering his head to graze. Ignoring him, the lead cow ambled forward, head swaying and tail swishing lazily. Derry got down from his pony and wrapped his arms around the cow's neck. She stood like a rock, jaw working side to side. He slipped the rope around her neck. For a moment she resisted, then with a sigh, she followed as he jumped back on his pony and led her away.

Hjalmar directed his men around the periphery of the herd until they formed a semi-circle around the herd, facing the trail. "Slow and easy, now. Don't spook them."

Derry led the cow toward the hill, talking to her. She ambled along, apparently happy to keep him company. Whistles from Hjalmar's men got the rest moving. The bull rushed past the lead cow, almost knocking over Derry's pony.

The narrow trail forced the cattle to go single file. First came the lead cow, with Derry urging her on and pulling on the rope. Then another, following placidly. And another …

It was taking longer than Aidan liked to get them out of the pasture. Too many things might still go wrong. The cowherds might notice the herd moving. Aidan preferred to spirit the cattle away without a confrontation—

Without warning, the bull snorted and tried to dodge sideways. Hjalmar spurred his horse to intercept him. The bull wheeled with surprising agility and headed back toward the pasture.

"Cut him off!" Aidan shouted.

Two of Aidan's men positioned their horses in the bull's path. They waved their arms and yelled. The bull lowered his head and raced toward them.

Turn! Aidan didn't know if he were sending a prayer to Aldones—or Zandru, or any god that might be listening—or to the men—or to the bull itself.

Turn!

A sensation swept through him—not vision, not sound, not ordinary human perception. He could no longer feel his own body, mesmerized by the looming collision. He found himself in *another* body—

Eyesight blurred, colors shifting. Powerful muscles drove him forward, fueled by territorial instinct.

Turn … echoed through his awareness.

The humans on their horses scattered before him. He glimpsed the other men, the whip-men. Two of them burst from the shade beneath the trees, running hard to cut him off.

A red haze engulfed him. He knew their smell, their raucous voices. *Their whips.* He gathered himself and barreled toward them.

*Turn…*No, he would *not* turn aside, not until he had gored and trampled and beaten them down. Not until the field was bare of invaders, the field that was *his* as the cows were *his* as the sky and grass were *his*.

The whip-men scrambled out of his path, one in either direction. He pivoted, aiming for the closer one. The man swerved, but he could not change directions so easily, not with his bulk and momentum. He raced past, dug his hooves into the grass, and circled back. Several of the men-and-horses broke away from where they'd taken the cows—*his cows*—and sprinted toward him. He slowed, searching for a target and confused by all the movement—

Aidan jolted back into his own body, still mounted on the dun gelding. Hjalmar yelled at the top of his lungs as he circled his horse around the bull. While he distracted the bull, his men pulled the cowherds up behind their saddles and raced back toward the trail, the bull on their heels. At the base of the hill, the riders separated, shouting and waving their jackets. The bull shot between them and lunged up the hill.

Hjalmar reined in his horse in front of Aidan's. "My lord? Are you well?"

A tremor passed through Aidan's muscles. "You acted quickly. Those cowherds owe you their lives."

"They moved fast enough once the bull's temper was up," Hjalmar replied with a touch of dryness. "Now let us see what they have to tell us."

His men forced the captives onto their knees. They wore rough-spun, worn clothing. Under the sheen of sweat, their faces were weathered like leather. The younger wiped tear-streaked cheeks with a tattered sleeve.

"I have a question for you," Aidan said. "Think carefully, because if you lie, it will be the last words you ever utter. Who paid you to steal those cattle?"

The younger cowherd hung his head. Aidan fixed his gaze on the older man and held it until the man looked away, flushing deeply. In their faces, he saw—or perhaps *felt,* the way he'd *felt* the bull—a flare of despair, a jabber of frantic thoughts.

It's the Hastur Lord, oh truly we are dead dead dead, we are dead no matter what we say. Lord Carcosse willna lift a finger to save us.

Carcosse, Aidan thought, triumphant. *Now I have my proof.*

"Don't bother with a lie," Aidan growled. "My men saved you from the bull. Guilty or innocent, your lives are mine to do with as I choose. I could end your miserable existence right now. I would have the right of it and none here would gainsay me. Well? What do you say to that?"

The younger began snuffling and mewling, too overcome for words. The elder lifted his head.

"'Tis not for the likes of us to expect mercy from a great lord. You bid us go here or do that, and we mun do it. You take and you *take*—if you take our lives as well, what can we do? What difference makes it how we answer? Come winter, our little ones will starve all the same."

Aidan thought of his own family—of his Iain, his joy and hope, and of his daughters, of Neave still at home, and Jessamy and Leora and Sharina, and of Graciela, whom he would miss even if there was little love between them, and also of Connor, whom he did love. He thought of what he would gladly do to keep them safe.

Carcosse, he thought again. *To these men, poor and desperate, there is no difference between us.*

This has to end.

"What were you to do with these cattle?"

"Watch 'em, my lord, for all that we failed. Until our master sent for them."

"Lord Carcosse?"

"Aye, him."

The dun gelding shifted under Aidan, sensing his unease. "They belonged to men like yourselves, men who sought only to provide for their families. Without the herd, their families will fare poorly, if they survive next winter's snows at all." As much to himself as to the cowherds, he added, "Where is the justice in that?"

There was no answer, of course.

"Tell your master that Lord Aidan Hastur has taken back his own, as I will do every time he steals from me and my people."

To Hjalmar, he said, "Set them free. We will waste no time lingering here." He spurred the dun gelding up the slope after the retreating cattle.

Leora floated in a sea of gray light, broken in places by darker, colder tides. She had long since lost all sense of direction, as well as the passage of time. Currents tugged at her, eroding her borders, layer after layer. When she tried to move her arms and legs, the edges of her body dissolved into mist. She felt herself stretching into a gossamer membrane, breaking apart into ribbons that twisted and tangled …

Calm yourself, breda. The voice was familiar through the odd reverberations. *All will be well. I am here with you.*

You—who are you?

No answer came, as winds of light seized her.

Then she stood on a great plain, golden grasses rippling in the wind. Overlaid on it, the distant, transparent form of a tower. Blue light shimmered around it like a halo. She had never seen such a place in her life, and yet it called to her.

It felt like home.

◆ ◆ ◆

The glare was too bright. It stung her eyes. She thrashed, searching for escape. Her arms and legs met resistance. Her body pressed against a surface that yielded slightly. Her eyelids parted, sticky with residue.

She struggled to focus. She knew this place, and yet everything seemed strange. The bed on which she lay. The tangled sheets. The dresser. The chest at the foot of the bed. The walls and chair, and even the ewer and basin atop the dresser.

"She's awake."

She recognized her bedchamber and her mother's voice, reedy with tension.

"Allow me to examine her." Neave, stern and determined. "As I told you, this is threshold sickness."

Mother: "Very well."

Brow furrowed, Neave bent over Leora and stroked her brow. "No fever and no chills, either. That's a good sign. How do you feel? Can you understand me?"

"I don't know. What am I doing in bed?" Leora tried to sit up, but the effort was too much. "Ay, me! I'm as weak as a babe. Have I been ill?"

"Yes, dearest, you have," Mother said.

And I fear you are yet far from well. Neave's words echoed through Leora's mind. *Until the folk from Alcabra Keep arrive, I have no* kirian *to ease your symptoms.*

"What did you say?" Leora asked.

"Only that you have been ill," Mother said.

"No," Leora said, "Neave, you said something about Alcabra and *kirian.*" *You heard me?*

When Leora nodded, the motion of her head provoked a rush of nausea. She curled into a ball, gagging and retching. The currents of light flowed through her, stretching and compressing her body. Through her misery, she felt a cool, wet cloth being pressed to her forehead.

"Deep, slow breaths," Neave said. "That's the way."

Go away, Leora thought.

"That would be even more dangerous," Neave said. "You need a focus point to keep you from drifting. Open your eyes and look at me."

Leora tried, but the brightness of the room made her eyes water painfully. She tried to burrow under the covers. "Go *away.*"

"She's raving!" Mother's voice had a curious echo and sounded far away.

Hands jerked the covers aside. Leora gasped in the cold air of the room. Fingers dug into her shoulders and turned her around.

Neave glared at her. "Let's get you up and walking. Estella, can you support her on the other side?"

"Don't—*wanna*—" When did Neave become so *mean*?

When did you become so stubborn, little sister? Or so heavy?

Dragged upright between her sister and her mother's lady-in-waiting, Leora managed a few steps. A fire had been lit in the hearth, spewing forth brightness. The flames lured her with their intoxicating movement.

"Don't look," Neave ordered. "Turn around and keep moving."

Back and forth they went, from bed to door to dresser and back again. Before they'd finished the second circuit, Leora was able to carry most of her own weight. By the third time, or perhaps the fifth, her vision cleared and her stomach felt less queasy.

"I don't like this," Mother said, her voice rising in volume and heat. "The child's shaking like a leaf. She should be in bed."

"Walking will help the threshold sickness," Neave said. "It stabilizes the balance centers."

Mother and Neave went on bickering, or so it sounded to Leora. She couldn't follow everything they said. Suddenly, her legs gave out from under her. She staggered, almost falling. Estella caught her and eased her onto the bed.

"*Do* something!" came her mother's voice.

"I've done everything I know!" Neave replied.

"—excuses—not good enough! Your responsibility—the only one who knows anything—always hated your sisters—jealous of them—"

No, Leora thought. *That's not true.*

The voices receded into mumbling and then into rushing and roaring, like a cataract.

◆ ◆ ◆

There's nothing more I can do, Neave thought. *It's my fault. If only I hadn't blasted through her defenses! I knew she had* laran. *I knew it! I should have been more careful.*

There was no cure for the past but to behave better in the future.

Neave left the family wing and wound her way to the second floor, emerging onto a balcony overlooking the main gates. If she craned her neck, she could see the old Western Tower, built centuries ago as part of the original castle. It had been in use as recently as her grandfather's time. From her vantage, she could see the main road as well as the village with its vegetable plots and livestock pens, fields of ripening barley, and distant lines of forest. The trees around the original castle had been cleared, either for fuel or to ensure a line-of-sight for defensive purposes. The far-off Venza Hills appeared as a bank of purple-gray mist.

Neave's eyes burned. She told herself it was from staring into the distance against the brightness of the day. Longing shook her, to be away from the castle and Lady Hastur's vitriol, not to mention the daily reminders of her heartache. She blinked, her eyes cleared, and there, where the road curved around a line of trees—

A rider. Two—three—more! And chervines bearing bulky packs.

The Alcabra circle! They were yet too far away for telepathic contact, but she hoped—she felt sure—it was them.

She raced down the stairs as fast as she dared. Her heart pounded and she was breathing fast by the time she burst through the castle doors toward the great gates. A guard stationed on either side called out, "*Damisela*! Is aught amiss?"

In the curve of the road, she spotted the foremost rider, a woman in a wine-colored cloak. Instantly recognizing Melanie Dellerey, her friend and teacher, Neave sent out a silent greeting. Melanie responded by urging her horse faster. A short time later, she halted inside the gates. Lorcan emerged from the castle, flanked by a pair of his assistants.

"I'm so glad to see you!" Neave cried. "Your coming is most timely."

"This is a warm greeting, indeed!" Melanie kicked her feet free of the stirrups and jumped to the ground. She was a few years older than Neave, with the bright red hair, freckles, and wiry frame common among those with *laran*.

The remainder of the party clattered into the yard, led by Raymond MacAran, the Keeper of the circle, and a man who could have been his double. Both were in their mid-thirties, red-haired, with broad cheekbones and snub noses. Neave had studied with Raymond, but this second man was a stranger.

"Enter and be at peace among us." Lorcan bowed to the new arrivals and directed his people to take charge of their animals.

"We thank you for your hospitality," Raymond spoke in an easy, open manner. "*Mestre coridom, Damisela* Neave, allow me to introduce my brother, Luis-Jorje MacAran. And here is Derik Gonsalves, our matrix mechanic."

Derik was an older man with a quietly competent air. "I'm happy to see you again, *damisela*."

"You remember our little Callista," Raymond went on, indicating a willowy strawberry blonde, perhaps fourteen years old.

"Please—could we save the pleasantries for later?" Neave said. "My younger sister is desperately ill with threshold sickness. She's had two seizures and is now in a coma."

Derik said, "I'm so sorry."

"I've done all I can for her," Neave rushed on. "No one else knows how to treat it—and we don't have any *kirian*—so please, come quickly!"

"Say no more," Raymond said. "Melanie, you are our most skilled healer. You must go to her."

"Of course," Melanie said. "There's a vial of *kirian* with the medical kit in my saddlebag."

"I believe these are yours, *vai leronis*." Lorcan held out the saddlebags, from which Melanie withdrew a pocketed leather case.

Neave hurried back into the castle with Melanie at her side, medicine kit in hand. As Raymond had said, Melanie was a talented healer with experience in the treatment of threshold sickness. When Callista's *laran* had awoken, she'd started setting fires with her mind. With wildfires an ever-present threat in forested areas, such a talent could result in the loss of human lives as well as timber. Melanie's care had seen the girl through the worst of it.

Leora lay as Neave had left her, with *Domna* Graciela and Estella hovering over her.

"They've come," Neave said, panting. "Stepmother, this is the *leronis* Melanie Dellerey, our healer."

Melanie gave a half-curtsy, one suitable for a woman with status and authority to her elder. "*Vai domna*, may I be allowed to examine the patient?"

"Yes, of course." Graciela moved away from the bed, her expression a mixture of caution and relief.

"You and your attendant must leave us now," Melanie said, but not unkindly. "*Laran* work can be unsettling to those unfamiliar with it, and it might be dangerous if you were to interrupt my concentration."

Graciela's mouth opened and a flush rose to her cheeks. Neave suspected that no one had ever spoken to her in her own household with such a lack of deference.

Melanie added, "I do not say it lightly, Lady Hastur, and I intend no insult. My concern is your daughter's welfare."

Graciela drew herself up. "No offense is taken. You shall have everything you require." She left the room, Estella close behind.

Melanie poured a measure of *kirian* into the empty cup on the nightstand. An aroma filled the air, fresh and clean but with a sharp edge. She drew out a silken pouch on a cord around her neck and tipped her starstone into her bare palm. It flared into blue-white brilliance. Knowing better than to focus on another's starstone, Neave lowered her gaze.

"Take out your matrix, Neave," Melanie said. "I may need to draw upon your *laran*, depending on what I find." With that, she closed her eyes, directing her focus inward.

A moment brought Neave into resonance with her starstone. She dropped her psychic barriers. Leora's skin thinned to transparency, revealing the glowing channels that carried *laran*. From her training as a monitor, Neave recognized the dull, sullen reds and browns where psychic energy stagnated. Shades of gray shrouded Leora's mind. Melanie reached out, probing. Neave felt a shiver, an unnatural chill, through their joined minds.

Darkness flooded her—through her link with her sister—gradually giving way to gray, unending, featureless gray devoid of warmth. There was little to mark the passage of time. Gradually, patterns of shadow emerged from the colorless firmament, shifting from light to dark. She drifted on them—

Without warning, tremors shook the gray, wave after jarring wave, shot through with blue-white lightning—

"She's seizing again!" someone shouted from far in the distance. *Melanie.*

With a shock, Neave found herself back in her own body.

"Drink." Melanie lifted Leora's head, holding the cup to the girl's lips. Leora struggled, sputtering, before swallowing.

Again. This time, Neave heard the command in her mind, shimmering with blue light. She added her own power to it. *Drink. The* kirian *will help.*

Leora's throat opened up and the potion flowed into her.

Gray evanesced into black, and the last of the *laran* bond dissolved.

◆ ◆ ◆

After Leora settled into a deep, natural sleep, Melanie turned to Neave. "You did well, but now you also need rest. And something to eat, preferably sweet."

"You taught me well," Neave replied with a weary smile. "But—"

"Go! Go! I'll sit with her and make sure all is well."

Neave closed the door behind her and stood for a moment, her back against the wall, and closed her eyes. The muscles of her legs trembled. Melanie was right, what she needed now was food. She headed toward the stairs that would take her to the level of the kitchen.

She was so preoccupied, her mind divided between concern for Leora and what she needed to take care of herself, that she didn't watch where she was going. At the landing halfway down the stairs, she collided with Connor, who was coming up. She lost her balance and fell into his arms. The rush of emotions—hers, his—almost brought her to her knees, but he held her up.

"I'm so sorry—clumsy of me—"

"Neave! Are you unwell? Is it your sister? Lorcan told me she's had a bout of threshold sickness. Has she taken a turn for the worse?"

Neave lifted her hands, *Slow down!* "I—I don't think so. I hope she's over the worst, but it's too soon to tell. I just left her, and the *leronis* Melanie was tending her."

"Then she is receiving the best possible care." He moved away, putting the length of the step between them.

"I suppose I have you to thank for that." It was almost physically painful to admit to being in his debt. "I mean, for Melanie and the others being here instead of back at Alcabra. So that—" she stumbled, "—they might help Leora when I could not."

"I asked them here according to Lord Hastur's instructions."

"I'm so sorry, I'm not thinking straight." The timing was wrong. How could he have known? She started to move past him, then hesitated. "But why did you, then?"

Connor held himself very still. "The reason I gave Lady Hastur was for their protection during this ah, difficult time with Carcosse."

"You're saying it's not the whole reason?"

"Certainly, it's important to safeguard those under Lord Hastur's rule. The circle folk are not just subjects, however. They represent a vital asset."

Neave startled, not sure she'd heard correctly. "An … asset?"

"A *military* asset," he said, his tone grim.

What possible military advantage could Alcabra provide? As far as she knew, none of them had any skill at arms. Then she remembered overhearing talk during one of her visits to the Keep, a phrase here and there, the conversation quickly broken off at her approach, and Melanie saying, "Whatever can hurt, can also heal."

She went cold inside.

"Your father did not wish you to be exposed to ideas that might distress you," Connor said after a moment.

"Like that I myself might be turned into a weapon?"

He was silent for a handful of heartbeats. Then: "What do you know about *laran* weaponry?"

"I have heard of poisons produced in the same way healing medicines are," she said, slowly putting together the picture. "What else is possible, I do not know. Tell me, is it more than just talk? Have *laran*-produced weapons been used in combat? Would Father expect the circle—me included—to create such things if the worst comes to pass?"

"As far as I know, we are not at the point where such weapons might be called for." Connor made a gesture intended to be reassuring, but it fell short. "Please, *carya*—I beg your pardon, I misspoke—*damisela*. Set your mind at rest. I opened this conversation only because you have always wanted to know the truth. I would not have you believe the sole reason I brought the Alcabra circle here was the security of these castle walls."

She heard the concern behind his words—the love—yes, it was love and nothing less—and she could not be angry with him. But he had not answered her question.

"I ask you again, have such weapons been used in war? And how likely is Father to do so?"

Connor met her gaze levelly. "Yes, they have. Neskaya Tower are investigating a method for projecting the illusion of fire into the minds of soldiers—flames as high as this castle if the reports are accurate. They have used the same technique to make water take on the appearance and smell of blood. I do not believe it is practical yet or— I see I have shocked you."

"Not shocked. Surprised, I suppose."

"I should not have inflicted such horrific details on you. You asked—I only meant—" A shadow passed over his eyes. "It was an inexcusable lapse in judgment on my part. I crave your pardon."

She felt his guilt like a pulse of pain and ached to ease it. When she spoke, her words came out gentle, as if no power she knew could keep the love from them. "Thank you for your honesty. You spoke from your care for me. And your respect, too. Your faith that I am capable of understanding troubling ideas."

Neave's words, meant to reassure, produced no apparent effect. Connor looked as stricken as before.

"I would not see you suffer because you treated me as a resourceful and competent adult," she rushed on. "To me, that is a wonderful thing. Should the matter be brought to my father—and *I* certainly will not mention it—I will tell him it was my doing. That I *commanded* you to tell me."

As his gaze locked with hers, the shadows fled and his eyes filled with liquid light.

I want, I want, sang her heart.

In that silence, she knew that he would never be Jessamy's, regardless of whether she remained here or went to Alcabra.

She said, her voice thick with emotion, "By sending for the circle, you saved my sister's life. *That* is what matters now."

Not the only thing, his eyes said.

"You were always—" and here he hesitated, "your father's daughter."

She turned away. "Let us both pretend we never had this conversation."

Over the next tenday, Leora made a steady recovery and the Alcabra circle settled into the quarters assigned to them by Lady Hastur. Their rooms were in the guest wing, the women and the men separate. These chambers were for those of lesser status, such as holders of smaller estates who owed fealty to Hastur. If any of the circle took offense at being treated as elevated servants, they made no complaint. The chambers were comfortable enough, although not luxurious. As Melanie pointed out when Neave grumbled at their treatment, space had been limited back at the Keep.

"There's so much *room*!" Callista added. "Here we can sit in the garden courtyards on a fine day or run downstairs to the kitchen anytime we're hungry!"

Melanie had given Callista a mildly scolding look after the girl set fire to the clothes chest in their shared room. Callista claimed she'd been having a nightmare, and Melanie remained adamant about the renewed need for self-control exercises.

"Well," Callista said in a chastened tone, "maybe not *anytime* we want a treat."

At this, Neave laughed. Callista sounded so very much like her youngest sister, Sharina.

The matter of a place suitable for matrix work remained. Neave accompanied Raymond and Melanie to make their request of Lady Hastur, who received them in the solarium.

"Very well, what more do you require?" Graciela's tone was formal with a hint of frost, as if the hospitality already extended in the form of shelter and food was sufficient.

Neave bristled. Had her stepmother forgotten the crucial role Melanie had played in saving Leora's life?

"We are grateful for your welcome," Raymond said smoothly. "You have been generous and gracious, truly a high lady, *vai domna*. We cannot pass the days in idleness, living off your largesse. There is work to be done, beginning with training the *damiselas*—" with a delicate hint at the needs of both Leora and Callista. "To accomplish this, we need a relatively isolated chamber where we will not be interrupted or subject to the strong psychic vibrations of others. We work primarily at night, so we should not disturb the normal operations of the castle. We do not wish to burden you."

"The means to make yourselves useful is by no means an unreasonable request." Graciela's manner shifted, more open now, almost friendly. "I will see what can be arranged …"

Pausing, Graciela rubbed her swollen knuckles. Neave had never noticed the early signs of arthritis before. Why should she, so infrequently in her stepmother's presence? Yet now she felt a breath of pity and wondered what might be done to ease the pain.

"I know just the place for your workroom," Graciela said. "There is a disused office in an older part of the castle. You will bother no one there."

Neave knew the place. The staircase leading to that chamber was frequently used by servants seeking a bit of privacy for courting. Apparently, Graciela neither knew nor cared.

Raymond brushed his fingertips across the back of Neave's wrist, a telepath's light touch. *What's the matter? Is there a problem?*

An image sprang to Neave's mind, one he'd surely pick up—the circle deep in rapport, silent and still, barely aware of the external world—until a kitchen maid and her swain, thinking this part of the castle unoccupied, fractured their concentration. In response, she felt Raymond's flash of dismay. The low-level telepathy of ordinary minds was distraction enough, but nothing like the violation when the minds of the circle were open and vulnerable.

"Would it be possible to lock the bottom of the staircase?" Raymond asked. "To prevent an inadvertent disruption?"

Graciela looked skeptical. Before she could speak, Neave dived into the pause.

"I have a better idea. The Western Tower!"

"My dear, it's entirely unsuitable," Graciela said. "The tower was abandoned in the time of my late father-in-law. I'm quite certain that it's thick with cobwebs."

"Cobwebs and disused furniture can be remedied with polish and feather dusters," Neave said, warming to the notion. "The roof is still sound and there's a fireplace that might be made usable again. And, stepmother, we will do the work ourselves, so you need not trouble the household staff on our account."

"A tower …" Raymond repeated, his expression thoughtful. "Yes, that might serve us well."

"Very well, you may have the tower." Graciela rose to indicate the audience was at an end. "But do not complain to me when you sneeze from the dust."

Neave and Raymond left the solarium with the appropriate homage.

Well handled, he said telepathically. *I hope we won't regret it.*

It's perfect, I promise.

He wasn't convinced. *"Abandoned" does not bode well for the soundness of the roof. How do you know it won't leak all over us?*

Because, she replied with a grin, *I've been sneaking up there for a spot of solitude for years.*

Leora followed the members of the Alcabra circle into the tower chamber and gazed around. Instead of cobwebs and gloom, candles set in wall sconces filled the space with warm light. Outside the mullioned windows, mauve Idriel glimmered in a sweep of stars. Neave had taken charge of the renovation, gathering together the furnishings, including the round table that had been her mother's, chairs and benches, a sideboard, and a deep-hued carpet that had long been in storage. Needlepointed pillows cushioned the seats, gifts from Lady Hastur. The smells of furniture polish and lavender hung in the air.

"It's perfect," Callista murmured.

This is my place, Leora thought, *and these are my people.*

"What shall we begin with?" Derik said, caressing the carved back of a chair before lowering himself into it. "With what task shall we inaugurate this place?"

"By all means, let's accomplish something instead of standing here, admiring it all," Luis-Jorje said wryly.

And I will be part of it! Leora could not suppress her excitement. "I have been practicing my exercises, so I am ready to join the circle."

Raymond gave her a kindly look. "Tonight you will serve as our monitor." He gestured to a chair set to the side.

"But that's *outside* the circle!" Leora tried not to sound like a petulant child, but the words just popped out. Callista was already seated at the table. *It isn't fair!*

Melanie turned to Leora from where she'd seated herself beside Callista. "Without a monitor to safeguard our physical well-being, not to mention our minds, matrix work can be dangerous. You will be our guardian, our protector, and that is very important."

Derik added, "We would not trust just anybody to do it."

"Well, then." Leora sat down, determined to do her very best.

When everyone was in their places Raymond placed a tray containing bowls and glass bottles on the table. "Tonight, we will be fabricating a small quantity of healing powder. The raw materials are arrayed before you."

"Healing powder is all very well," Derik said with a faint frown. "But in this case, may I conclude its choice arises from the possibility of injuries sustained in conflict?"

"Perhaps," Melanie temporized, "but it will also be useful in a household this size."

"Oh, yes!" Leora spoke up. "People are always cutting themselves in the kitchen or stubbing their toes. Or getting splinters."

"Pray Evanda it will never be needed for anything worse," Callista murmured. Since her first fire-starting accident, she had worked hard to keep her talent under control.

"Then let's begin," Raymond said.

Leora freed her newly acquired starstone from its wrappings and focused on it as she had been taught. The boundaries of her mind softened. She floated in an ocean of blue-tinged radiance, apart from the circle but yet at one with it. It felt as if she held them all, linked together, within imaginary hands. Already she sensed their heartbeats, their breathing … the easing of muscular tension as they adjusted their posture.

Once the circle achieved unity, she sensed Raymond directing their psychic energy into manipulating the assembled materials. First the contents of one bottle, then another, particle by particle, one small change in molecular structure led to another. A severing here, a linkage there … until an entirely new substance was created.

How long the process took, Leora could not tell. The slow, sure currents of *laran* through the glowing blue mist never changed their hypnotic rhythms. All the while, she monitored the physical well-being of the workers. There was so much to keep track of! Each time she checked, all seemed to be well. Even Callista, the youngest and least experienced, floated in the circle's rapport.

Leora became aware of Luis-Jorje's thoughts. He was still part of the circle, still pouring *laran* energy into the tapestry of energy his brother had woven. But there was something distinct—*separate*—in his mind. His focus divided between the task of the circle and something else. A pattern, but not the one used to produce the healing powder. A molecule altered here, a bond shifted there … the new formula took shape. Now Leora sensed Neave's reaction, too, both surprise and alarm. From Neave's thoughts, Leora understood that the new substance would not promote healing. Instead, it was designed to stop the transmission of currents along nerves and energy channels. Into Neave's mind came images of muscles spasming, uncontrolled vomiting, and a heart stuttering into immobility. Leora recoiled, although she could not have said if the reaction were her own or her sister's, so closely were they connected. The bonds between Neave with the rest of the circle wavered—

Neave ... Leora formed the words telepathically. *Are you all right? What should I do? Do you want to stop?*

No, sweetling. I am just ... surprised, that is all. Do not fret over me. I shall be well enough in a moment or two.

Neave concentrated on finishing the healing medicine. As she did so, her mind reassumed its previous calm. Leora returned to her work as monitor, but Luis-Jorje's formula remained in her memory.

At last, Raymond signaled a halt to the session. The bonds joining the circle faded as the flow of power from their minds slackened. Leora came back to her own body. On a glass dish set in the middle of the table sat a mound of blue-tinted powder, tiny crystals to soothe and combat infection, speed the knitting of torn tissues, and restore healthy blood flow.

The chamber had gone cold. Despite Leora's oversight, everyone's muscles were stiff. Around the table, the circle stretched and rose to their feet. Leora arched her back and rolled her shoulders, her joints popping. Her stomach rumbled.

Melanie turned to Leora with a gentle but weary smile. "You did well tonight, *chiya*. We could not have completed this night's work without you."

"Oh!" Leora glowed with pleasure.

Luis-Jorje picked up a tray of honey buns and dried apples from the sideboard and offered them, starting with Leora and Callista as the youngest.

Nibbling on a honey bun, Leora caught the way Neave locked gazes with Luis-Jorje, but the look he gave her in return was unreadable. As he held out the tray, Neave grabbed his arm, a breach of manners among telepaths.

"What was that design in your mind?" Neave said. "A template for a poison?"

"Anything that can heal can also harm." His tone was light, almost casual, as he removed her hand. "It is only a matter of degree."

"Everyone, be sure to eat enough to replenish your energy, and then sleep as much as you can," Raymond said, addressing Leora in particular. "It's important to take good care of ourselves."

Residual rapport shimmered between the brothers, who were clearly as close as Leora and Neave, if not more so. Raymond said to Neave, "Do you trust me?"

Leora's breath caught in her throat. *Raymond knew.*

We were supposed to be making healing powder! Neave said silently. Her gaze flickered to Luis-Jorje. *But* he *had something else in mind, something deadly. For what purpose? A murder weapon? Against who—my father? Our enemies?*

I swear upon my honor that nothing we do is against Lord Hastur's interests. Raymond replied. *I will answer your questions. Do you really wish to hold such a conversation where your young sister might overhear?*

Neave wrestled her temper under control. "When?"

"When you have rested and replenished your energy. I ask again, do you trust me?"

It took Neave a moment to search her conscience. "I do."

That was all very well, Leora thought. As for herself, she did *not* trust Luis-Jorje after what she had seen in his mind, and she doubted that her sister did, either.

Neave received her answers when the circle gathered again in the tower workshop, all except Callista and Leora. She took her place between Raymond and Melanie. Luis-Jorje, opposite her, held a small box between his hands. She had never liked him and now she did not trust him, but she did not want this meeting to turn into a confrontation. For good or ill, she and Luis-Jorje were members of the same circle. He was a skilled *laranzu* and she, a novice.

Raymond began. "Neave, I want to reassure you that everything we do is by the command of Lord Hastur. All of us are oath-bound to his service."

"We have sworn fealty to your father and must follow his commands, just as you do, as his daughter," Melanie added, her voice gentle.

Neave's first thought was that she would *not* obey her father if she thought he was wrong, but he was her father. He had once indulged her as his child. If she were a *leronis* in a circle sworn to him, she might—she *ought to*—lose that privilege.

"Please go on," Neave said, her voice thick.

"*Laran* can do many wonderful things, but it can also be deadly," Raymond explained. "We can make a medicine to heal wounds, but we can also make one that produces festering sores that never close over. Or, in this case—" indicating the box his brother held," —one that interrupts the flow of energy along nerves, which in sufficient exposure can stop a man's heart."

"We are not trying to hide anything from you," Luis-Jorje said. "I sought only to discern whether this circle was capable of a more complex chemical synthesis." He indicated the box. "This is a sample of the poison, a template if you will."

Neave's mouth went dry. "Is it safely contained?"

Luis-Jorje pushed the box across the table toward her. "Try opening it."

The box was wood, unadorned except for a carved leaf on one side. A hairline crack separated lid from body, although there were no discernible hinges. With shaking hands, Neave applied pressure, pushing the lid upward. Nothing happened; she might as well have been attempting to pry apart a solid piece of wood. She tried several times more, with increasing force, but the result was the same.

Luis-Jorje took the box back. On one side, so small she'd missed it before, was a tiny starstone. He telepathically sent a pattern of syllables into the stone. The lid opened with a faint click. Immediately, he closed it and sent a second mental sequence.

"It's a telepathic lock," he explained. "Only someone with the key—and the ability to send it—can open the box. So yes, it is safe."

"The healing powder and Luis-Jorje's poison are not the only things we can create using *laran*," Raymond went on. "The folk at Tramontana are studying the chemistry of fire-fighting chemicals, using starstones linked together into a matrix screen."

"Surely that's a good thing," Neave said.

"That's a *life-saving* thing," Raymond replied. "But those same formulas can also—theoretically—produce an unquenchable fire that eats through wood and metal as well as flesh. It's only a matter of time before someone perfects the method and devises a delivery system."

"Pray Aldones that time never comes," Derik murmured.

"Such things lie within the purview of neither Aldones nor any other god," Luis-Jorje countered. "They are strictly human endeavors. Ours to create, ours to control." The exchange had the feel of an ongoing debate.

"You are saying that *laran* isn't evil in itself, any more than a length of steel is," Neave said to Raymond. "Anything—a hawk, a sword, a boiled egg, for all I know—can be misused."

"We know, for example, that *laran*-Gifted workers, whether single or in a circle, can affect the minds of others—enemy soldiers, for example— to terrible effect," Raymond answered. "We can cast spells that create blindness or terror, or that cause men to mistake their comrades for their enemies. You see how effective such things might be during a battle?"

Father knew about this, Neave thought.

Lord Hastur is not the only Comyn leader interested in laran *weapons*, Luis-Jorje said.

Who else? Neave demanded.

Luis-Jorje did not respond.

Heart-sickness passed through Neave. She felt naïve and stupid. *Laran* had opened a new world for her, a landscape of the mind as well as an escape from her stepmother's casual scorn. How could she have possibly learned about weapons of the mind?

And Leora, must she lose her innocence, as well?

"The younger ones must be given the chance to mature before their Gifts, as well as their consciences, are put to the test," Melanie answered aloud. She shot Luis-Jorje a stern look. "It was a lapse in judgment to visualize synthesizing the poison while Leora was acting as monitor."

"There was no harm done." Luis-Jorje had the grace to look abashed, and his voice held an edge of defensiveness. "She didn't pick up on it, nor did Callie."

"But *Neave* did," Melanie pointed out.

Neave felt a surge of protectiveness towards both girls, especially her sister. She faced Luis-Jorje, her cheeks flaming. "How dare you assume Leora doesn't know? You don't know her the way I do. She has a propensity for ferreting things out. She does her best to not eavesdrop, but I assure you, if she does not already know, she will find out."

Luis-Jorje glared at her. The muscle in his jaw tensed visibly. "What do you propose we do?"

"It would be better to tell both Leora and Callista forthrightly," Derik interrupted. "As Neave pointed out, the girls are old enough to know when something is being kept from them and young enough to come to erroneous—perhaps disastrous—conclusions. We owe them the truth."

"I agree," Melanie said. "The damage is already done. Now we must minimize its effect. We will help Leora and Callista understand and give them perspective, and that is a far better thing than repairing the loss of trust by keeping secrets."

Luis-Jorje regained his composure. "We are all children of our times, and these girls will grow up in the shadows of war."

"Very well," Raymond said. "I agree in principle to not withhold secrets unless it is necessary. As Keeper, it is my responsibility to educate them, and I shall do so. They are also entitled to an explanation as to why they may not directly participate in the conflict. I won't allow that, even if it comes to defying Lord Hastur's commands."

Neave found herself unexpectedly moved by the Keeper's solicitousness for her younger sister and the volatile, adolescent fire-starter. "I will do my part, assuming I am included in any war effort."

"In all honesty," Raymond said, a brief shadow across his features, "I hope it will not come to that."

In all honesty, Neave responded, knowing he could hear her unspoken words, *I am sure that it will.*

Raymond took Leora and Callista aside and explained to them that *laran* might be used in the coming war. Leora felt alternately thrilled and terrified, restive and desperately worried for her father and Connor. In the days that followed, her primary responsibility was monitoring. Forbidden from participating in more dangerous work, Leora and Callista helped to make healing powder and a signal device for use on the battlefield. Small and easily portable, powered by a specially tuned starstone, it was designed to shoot into the air and emit a burst of colored light that could be seen at a distance.

During this time, Leora and Callista spent more and more time together. They often gathered in Leora's room, delighting in speculations on what role they might play if the friction with Carcosse erupted into war. More than once, Raymond had told them, *none*, but that could not quell their imagination. If not this conflict, then surely they would participate in one in the future.

One afternoon when they were alone, Callista said, "I'm *wild* to see what I can do with fire!"

"Hush," Leora replied. "Don't let Raymond hear you or we'll end up locked in our rooms whenever anything interesting is happening."

Midsummer Day dawned, stormy, the wind driving sleet-edged rain. Thunder rumbled in the north. Tonight the family would celebrate Midsummer Festival in a subdued manner, for Lord Hastur had not yet returned.

Leora lay in bed past the usual time of rising, listening to the rain battering against the windows and the muffled sounds of voices. At last, she slid out from underneath the comforter, washed her face, and pulled on a dress.

She opened her door to go down to breakfast. There, on her threshold, sat a basket of mountain peaches and rosalys, decorated with a garland of ribbons. It was the custom for men to present such gifts to their kinswomen and sweethearts in honor of the goddess Evanda, mother of growing things and fertility. For the last few years, her father had left treasures like this for her. She assumed that Connor now fulfilled that role, since Iain wasn't old enough to care for such feminine frivolities.

She took the basket inside, set the flowers in an ewer of water, and braided the ribbons into her hair. As she was doing so, a knock came on the door. When she opened it, Callista stood there, looking forlorn and lonely.

Poor thing, she must miss her family.

"Good Midsummer morning," Leora said, standing back for her friend to enter. "Have some peaches."

"Oh, my. These are like the ones my brother used to pick for us before he … went away." Callista's only brother had been killed in an ambush with a rival family.

The two friends made themselves comfortable, sitting cross-legged on Leora's bed and munching peaches. Leora was glad to make Callista's Festival Day brighter. She could not imagine being apart from her parents and sisters on Midsummer. Callista, in her turn, launched into a series of stories of how her own family celebrated the season.

"Of course," Callista concluded, her expression turning serious, "that was in the *before times*."

Before her fire-starting Gift awoke, she meant. Before her brother died and she was sent away.

Leora took her friend's hand. Warmth—orange light, heat, jagged flames—rushed through her from the contact, but she ignored it. "It's time to start making new memories—"

A knock at the door interrupted her.

"Yes, what is it?" she called.

The door opened and a page stood there. "*Damisela* Leora, I am sent by Lady Hastur to say that you are expected in the family dining room."

"Drat," Leora muttered.

"I'm sorry!" Callista said, at almost the same time. "I've kept you too long."

"No, it's fine. Or rather, this is the best way to begin Festival Day. With peaches and a new sister." On impulse, Leora leaned over and hugged Callista. "I'll see you later!"

◆ ◆ ◆

In the family dining room, a festive breakfast had been laid on the sideboard. Mother was at her usual place, brow furrowed and lips pressed together. Jessamy and Sharina were in their seats but not Neave. Or Iain, who usually breakfasted with his tutor.

"Good Midsummer morning, everyone." Leora went to the sideboard and helped herself to sausages and apple cakes, then carried her plate to the table.

"Good morning to you, daughter," Graciela replied. "What a cheerful greeting! It's a shame your father may not return in time to celebrate with us. We must make the best of it."

Jessamy twisted her head to display the many ribbons braided into her hair. "We have not been entirely neglected by our menfolk."

Graciela went on, "Nevertheless, we will have our usual holiday festivities, both the family and the castle servants."

Leora lifted her head, her fork with a morsel of apple cake poised in mid-air. "And the Alcabra folk?"

"They may indulge themselves with the servants. To intrude upon a family celebration in the absence of its lord would be unseemly."

"That's not fair," Leora muttered. Then, to her mother: "They're far away from their own families and they're my *friends*. Isn't Midsummer a time when we all celebrate together? Can't they join us, just this once?"

"That will be quite enough on the subject." Mother's voice was icy, her eyes like jet. "*We* are your family."

"May I please be excused?" Leora said, her gaze lowered. Further objections would only make matters worse. She had better retreat before she said or did anything unforgivable.

"You have not finished your breakfast."

Leora picked up a piece of toast, trying to project the image of a demure and obedient daughter.

Another conversation began, mostly about the night's events. As was customary, dancing would follow the feast. Jessamy and Sharina could hardly contain themselves at the prospect once they learned that the officers—the well-born ones—were invited. Graciela forbade the younger girls from dancing with men, except for their kinsmen. In Aidan's absence, that meant Iain, who had no interest in dancing with his sisters. Otherwise, Leora and Sharina were expected to confine themselves to women's dances. Maybe, Leora thought, she could sneak away to enjoy the servants' dances with Callista. She wondered if Neave would attend the family feast. Lady Hastur clearly would not object if she didn't.

◆ ◆ ◆

The great red sun was well overhead, warming Leora's shoulders as it burned away the last of the night's chill. The kitchen garden had been her favorite place to play as a child. It brought back memories of a time when the world had felt safe and being caught snooping along the back passageways was the worst thing that could happen to her. As she turned back toward the castle, she heard the brazen tones of trumpets approaching from the main gates, then a clamor of horse's hoofs and men's raised voices. She picked up her skirts and raced to find out what was going on.

The yard teemed with men—men on horseback, men on foot, men leading pack chervines, men armed and laden with packs, and men covered with mud past their knees. Her father shouted orders as he wheeled his horse about. Through the gates, she spied more soldiers.

Aidan swung down from the saddle and handed the reins to a waiting stableman. His face lit up when he saw Leora. Before she could greet him, Connor and Lorcan burst through the castle doors.

"*Vai dom*, welcome home." Lorcan bowed formally. "We didn't know to expect you today, but you will find everything in readiness."

"I never had doubts. Ah, Connor—" Aidan clapped his paxman on the shoulder. "Gods, man, it's good to see you!"

Connor bent toward Aidan, speaking so low that Leora could not catch his words.

She thought wistfully that no matter how fond her father was, he would never treat her in this comradely way, nor would her future husband. Such fellowship was a world in which she had no part, and she did not know if it made her feel more angry or sad.

Aiden straightened up. "We will speak more of this later. For now, I need you to coordinate with Hjalmar—" He gestured toward the uniformed man on the bay. "These men are to go to the encampment. Make sure they have a hearty meal tonight but no wine."

"I will see it done." Connor's tone implied, *They will be well-fed but clear-eyed and ready to ride out at your signal.* Then he headed off in the direction of Hjalmar.

Aidan caught Leora's gaze once more and gestured for her to approach.

"I'm so glad you're back," she said. "And so will Mother be, and my sisters and—oh! Everyone else!"

"I couldn't miss Midsummer Festival, could I? Here, let me look at you. How you've grown!" His tone was light and affectionate, very unlike the way he'd spoken to his men. "You're a young lady now."

"Never mind that! There's so much I have to tell you—"

"And so you shall, at the proper time. Lorcan, have Yosef notify my lady wife of my arrival. I want to wash off this trail grime so I can greet her properly. Connor and Hjalmar will sort out the men and their beasts, but the other business can wait until after tonight's Festival. I trust that you and Lady Hastur have outdone yourselves with preparations."

"Indeed, my lord." With a decorous bow, Lorcan left to carry out Aidan's orders.

Aidan held out his arm for Leora as if she were a fine lady. She placed her fingertips on his forearm. Under his overcoat of Hastur blue, he wore heavy leather arm guards. He patted her hand with his free hand. Together they entered the castle, where he halted.

"Now I must leave you, my dear. Go to your mamma. I'm sure she will need you." Aidan squeezed Leora's hand before heading up the broad stairs that led to the family wing.

Aidan studied his image in the half-length dressing room mirror. He didn't remember so many gray hairs or that grim set to his mouth, yet there they were. No amount of adjusting the velvet jacket of Hastur blue and silver or re-arranging the lace at his cuffs could alter the fact that the war with Carcosse, not yet joined, had already changed him.

Changed all of us. Connor, even though he hides it. Neave, for what I must ask her to do. Graciela, who has had her share of grief. And Leora, who's too young for any of this. Gods, she's still a child—as are Sharina and Iain!

He understood why Leora had been brought into the circle, according to Connor's report. Threshold sickness could be fatal. There must be a way to keep her out of the war, though. And then make a good marriage to keep her safe. A strong husband, able to defend their home. Not right away, for there was the conflict with Carcosse to manage. But afterward … What was he thinking?

Too young, they're all too young.

He settled his jeweled belt and gave the hem of his jacket a final tug. Graciela would undoubtedly find fault, but it couldn't be helped.

Connor was waiting outside, wearing holiday attire. How he found time to execute orders and show up on time, freshly shaven and impeccably dressed, Aidan had no idea.

"Come in, come in." Aidan closed the door, settled in one of the two chairs at the sitting room's fireplace, and gestured for Connor to do the same. "Did you and Hjalmar get everyone settled?"

Connor lowered himself in the chair facing Aidan. The gently flickering flames bathed his face in a ruddy glow. "Every man you brought has been given a meal and an assigned sleeping place. Lorcan and I found room for the officers in the castle barracks, and everyone else is out at the encampment site a day's ride down the valley."

"Excellent!" Aidan clapped his hands together. "Now, then. How are our plans progressing? Have you heard back from your spies at Carcosse Castle? Will Berrin join us?"

"No, and yes." Connor's face tightened into a frown. "I have no reason to assume the worst, not yet. There are a handful of good reasons why a message might be delayed. And yet, I cannot shake the feeling that something has gone amiss ...”

"Let us hope for word soon," Aidan said, striving for a reassurance he did not feel. Connor's words had sent a shudder down his spine. He had no way of telling whether this was a precognitive Gift or merely his own anxiety. Besides, there was nothing to be done at the moment. Sending an additional message could make matters worse. Silence might be their only answer in the end. And there were other questions to consider. "Go on."

"As for General Berrin, he replied almost as soon as he'd received my letter." Smiling, Connor shook his head. "I don't think he waited for the messenger to use the piss-pot before sending him back again. I daresay retirement does not suit him."

"Being an officer is all he's ever known," Aidan said. The thought brought sadness, that a man as loyal and competent as Berrin should know no other life than soldiery and battle.

"Be that as it may," Connor went on, "he has set up in the encampment and is training the mustered troops as they arrive. His account—on your desk, when you're ready to read it for yourself—comments on the deterioration in quality since *he* was a young man. He didn't quite call the men *slothful*, but he implied it."

Aidan felt a chuckle rise in him. "Whatever their present condition, I'm sure Berrin will soon harden them."

"But will it be enough? We've yet to discover the strength of Carcosse's army. Shall I send out scouts?"

"Without knowing where to search?" Aidan shook his head. "Were any of your agents placed so that they would go with the army?"

"I fear not. I managed to place one as a blacksmith's assistant, lowly enough to be hired without too many questions and affable enough to enjoy a pint with the horse handlers. The other works in the kitchen. Several attempts at higher placement failed." Connor's tone shaded toward apologetic. "We had no thought of how things might change with a war brewing. I deemed my sources to be adequate at the time."

In Aidan's mind, Connor had nothing to regret, but saying so aloud would only worsen the paxman's self-reproach. "The lack of foresight is as much mine as it is yours. Neither of us anticipated what has come to pass. Ah, well. We must deal with what the gods ordain, not with what you or I would have."

Connor responded with a wry half-smile. "I very much doubt the *gods* have anything to do with *Dom* Merryl's schemes."

"A hit! I am of your mind in this. Still, we don't know where Carcosse's forces are mustering and I am loathe to spend resources, even as small as a scout or two, on such a slim chance. Speaking of resources, what is the standing of the Alcabra circle? How goes their work?"

"They have established a space in the old Western Tower," Connor said. "I believe they had been creating a sort of nerve poison using the template Luis-Jorje MacAran brought from Neskaya. Neave was concerned about requiring the younger members—Callista and your own Leora—to be part of the creation of weapons, but I believe the issue has been resolved. They have also been practicing *laran* spells that might also be called upon."

Aidan nodded, half in approval, half in grim acceptance. If all went well, neither the poison nor the spells would be needed. Ordinary military strength might suffice. Such had been the case in his grandfather's time and his father's. But he dared not assume that would be the case now.

Once a weapon has been envisioned, a weapon capable of turning a battle with only a small investment in manpower, men would be fools to avoid using it out of an overly scrupulous sense of honor.

If we do not have our honor, what is left?

◆ ◆ ◆

After Connor left, Aidan presented himself at his wife's door. She wore spidersilk in wine-dark hues, slightly worn along the seams after years of use. She'd added a band of lace threaded with gold to the neckline and wore the garnet earrings, part of her dowry.

I should have arranged a gift for her. Perhaps jewelry, gold or copper. The thought came to him that Fiona-Maria had never wanted lavish gifts. She'd been as delighted by a surprise kiss or a fistful of wildflowers as by any precious gems.

Graciela dropped a graceful curtsy. She held out her hand and he turned it palm-down, planting a kiss on the back. The look she gave him was flustered but not displeased. "My lord husband."

"My lady wife. Are you ready to go down?"

"The festivities cannot begin without us," she said.

"Surely, you have preparations in hand," Aidan said in a casual tone. They continued down the corridor, heading for the stairs that led to the great hall.

"Everything is as we have always had it except for the officers, and I must tell you, my dear, the girls are keen to dance with them. I have instructed them as to the propriety of the occasion."

I'm sure you have. "It is Midsummer Festival and they are young. They have my leave to dance with whomever they like, so long as they do not wander off into gardens or shadowed nooks." Surely, Leora and Sharina were too young to be interested in such things. Jessamy, on the other hand, was seventeen and could not be expected to dance only with other women. As for Neave, he must rely upon her honor, and Connor's.

They paused, looking out over the hall filled with merrymakers. Under Graciela's direction, the castle staff had transformed the gloomy, echoing space with greenery and tiny candles. Tables and benches occupied the center of the floor, covered with snowy cloths and set with candelabra.

As Aidan and Graciela entered, the room fell silent. All heads turned in their direction. "Happy Midsummer Festival!" Aidan called.

"Happy Festival, *vai dom*!" they responded in unison.

Aidan took his place at the head table with Graciela at his left, Connor at his right, and the children arrayed to either side. Minor vassal nobles and senior officers filled out the rest of the table. A bevy of servants brought out sliced roasted meat swimming in its juices, disjointed fowls with crackling brown skin, platters of root vegetables, bread, meat pies, egg tarts, and all manner of holiday treats.

The meal progressed, embellished with cheerful banter. Family and guests seemed determined to enjoy themselves. When everyone had finished, Aidan rose, signaling that the tables were to be removed for dancing. According to custom, everyone except those at the head table went to work, moving the tables and benches to the periphery of the room. The musicians, who had enjoyed their festive meal earlier, set up on a balcony. Soon the opening measures of a *promenada* filled the hall. The soloist's flowing, pale hair and colorless eyes indicated strong *chieri* lineage, and the sound of the flute was so pure and haunting that the entire assembly halted to listen. Then the other instruments joined in and everyone took a breath.

Following custom, Aidan bowed to Graciela and extended his hand. Flushed with wine and pleasure, she placed her fingertips upon his. He led her into the center of the hall, where they faced one another, bowed and curtsied, and began the first figure to the applause of the merrymakers. Graciela danced well, the hem of her gown swirling with each shift of direction. Soon other couples joined them, elegantly circling the room. The dance ended with a musical flourish.

Aidan was escorting Graciela to her seat of honor when he noticed Jessamy heading toward Connor. Before she reached him, however, Connor turned and, deftly avoiding her path, placed himself in front of Graciela. With a perfectly executed bow, he asked if he might have the honor of the next dance. Graciela accepted with a genuine smile.

Well done, Aidan thought. *In a single gesture, he gives the lady of the castle the recognition due her rank and avoids the appearance of favoring one of her daughters over the others.* But he could not leave Jessamy standing alone, red-faced and rigid, even if no one else noticed the slight.

Aidan went directly to her, as he had many times over the years when she was too young to partner with any but her kinsmen. Her look of desperation eased when he held out his hand in invitation. "It's been a while since we danced together. When was it? Last Midwinter Festival?"

With a smile only slightly forced, Jessamy placed her fingers on his arm. "No, it was a year ago. Don't you remember, Papa? I had a fever the day before. I begged and begged, but Mother sent me to bed after the feasting."

Those were simpler times, when a young woman's disappointment at not being allowed to stay up for the dancing was the tragedy of the day.

"But you are now a fine young lady and deserve to enjoy the festival. Do not fear, you will have partners besides your old father, more than enough to satisfy your love of dancing."

A series of emotions passed over Jessamy's features. Disappointment warred with determination to behave in a manner worthy of her rank, not like a spoiled child. "But you are more than my *old father*, Papa. You are the Lord of Hastur. I am sensible of the honor you do me."

"You are the eldest except for Neave and therefore take precedence."

"Over Leora and Sharina? Papa, they're little girls!"

He smiled and said nothing. It was just as well that Neave was celebrating with her Alcabra friends. Relations between her and Connor seemed to have settled down, but it would have been a difficult situation, regardless of whether Connor danced with Neave or Jessamy. The household would be less fraught once affairs with Carcosse were resolved, Neave off to Alcabra, and Jessamy with a husband.

Aidan danced with each of his daughters and again with his wife.

Connor played no favorites, going from Graciela to Jessamy to Leora and then an easy dance with Sharina, who was in truth too young for anything but a women's circle.

As midnight approached, the older folk retired and the musicians played more lively tunes: a reel, a jig, a *roundele*, nothing too wild yet, and no sword dances. Aidan, once more sitting beside Graciela, caught Connor's gaze across the room just as one of Lorcan's assistants finished speaking to Connor, clearly about something urgent. And private. An unspoken signal passed between Connor and Aidan. Aidan recognized the nuances of hidden alarm in Connor's face.

Something's happened. One of his agents returned from Carcosse?

Aidan nodded, a short dip of his chin that was then echoed by Connor. *My office. Now.*

Aidan indicated the musicians might now take a short break. "My dear, the rigors of the trail have left me weary," he told Graciela. "Will you retire now or would you prefer to enjoy the rest of the evening?"

Graciela produced a fan from the folds of her gown and applied it vigorously. "Oh! I am not tired. Are you quite sure? It seems a shame to leave so early."

"I would not deprive you of your holiday. Please continue." Aidan bowed to her.

Her answering look was half gratitude, half smothered curiosity. She had never been one to pester him with questions, even if she privately might wonder if there was more to it. He had rarely appreciated her conventional wifely obedience as on this night.

"It is Midsummer Festival, after all," he said, his tone light. "There are but two moons in the sky—" referring to the old saying that no one need remember whatever is done under four moons, "—surely a little license can be allowed."

"I shall do just that. But first I will send Leora and Sharina to their rooms, although I doubt they will sleep before dawn. Jessamy may stay up a little while later ..." Graciela went off in search of her daughters.

◆ ◆ ◆

Aidan went directly to his office. Connor was waiting for him, along with Hjalmar and Tiernan, one of the other senior captains, and a man shrouded in a hooded cloak. Yosef, Aidan's body-servant, attended him. Beneath the hood, Aidan recognized General Berrin Valdes, greatly changed from the powerful, decisive soldier who had served his father. Berrin's face was ash-blotched, his cheeks sunken, and his eyes fever-bright. His plight tore at Aidan's heart.

On impulse, Aidan knelt and took Berrin's hands. The skin felt hot, like burned leather. "Zandru's frozen hells!" Aidan murmured. "What happened to you?"

"*Vai … dom.*" Berrin's words rattled in his throat.

"Connor, we must get him to bed at once!"

"My lord, I thought it best for you to hear what he has to say first," Connor said. "He refused to take his rest until then."

Stubborn old man, Aidan's father had called him.

"Very well." Aidan went to the sideboard, poured a mug of *jaco*, and stirred in extra honey. He placed the sweetened brew into Berrin's hands, folding the old man's fingers around the warmth. Then he took a second for himself and eased himself into his chair. "Please proceed."

Berrin roused with a visible effort. "The mustering place … most of the men … sickened …" He fought for breath. "… a good half of them unfit … a quarter, maybe a third … dead."

"Dear gods!" cried Tiernan, the younger captain. Hjalmar, steady Hjalmar, looked shaken to his roots.

Aidan's mug clattered on the desk surface. By reflex, he managed to keep it from toppling. *Jaco* splashed over the top.

An entire army wiped out, or close enough …

Only Connor did not seem surprised. He must already have heard the news from Berrin, hence the urgency of this meeting.

Aidan swallowed down a burst of hot acid. He dared not allow himself to reveal what he felt. *Shock. Outrage. Despair.* By some miracle, his voice, when he spoke, was steady. "How did this happen?"

"Was it treachery?" Hjalmar said.

Berrin's head shook under its hood. "Poison … not natural … Sorcery."

The two captains muttered prayers of protection and curses against anyone who would so violate the natural order. Aidan silenced their outburst with a gesture. He and Connor exchanged a meaningful glance. This had to be Carcosse's doing.

"Sorcery?" Aidan repeated. "You mean a poison created by the use of *laran*?"

Berrin nodded, a sagging of the head, then a jerk upward.

Aidan leaned forward as if he could peer into the old man's memory. "How do you know? Have you the Gift?" He could not bring himself to add, *And why were you not sickened?* because it was obvious that Berrin had not come away unscathed. The man was near death.

"My lieutenant ... minor *laran* ... sensed it. In the water ... or food ... or rocks. Not sure. Could be all of them. He ... warned me ... almost too late ... then—then he—"

For a long moment, there was no sound beyond the sound of smothered weeping and the hammering of Aidan's heart.

Berrin must be thinking he should have died with his men. Would have, but for the duty of bringing word.

"Tell me—exactly—what happened," Aidan said.

The story tumbled out in broken phrases, often so hoarse and weak, Aidan had to ask Berrin to repeat himself. All had seemed well with the mustered troops. Training was progressing, discipline and skills improving in a manner that satisfied Berrin's exacting standards. Word had gotten out, and new volunteers arrived daily. Some were veterans still able to fight, men whose experience and savvy made up for their decreased vigor. Berrin knew some of them and had no cause to question the others. Aidan heard both regret and self-recrimination in Berrin's voice. It wasn't the old general's fault; anyone would have welcomed extra men under the circumstances, and there was no time to check out each one's story.

As the evening meal approached, Berrin's lieutenant was uneasy without discernible cause. The horses, too, were restless, as if a wolf or a great cat had come down from the heights. Berrin had settled to his food.

"*General ... sir ...*" A hand thrust out to keep Berrin from his cup of water and wooden bowl of grain with a splash of sauce and a hunk of trail bread. A shake of the head. "Something's off—"

From across the camp, a cry of pain had pierced the dusk. Then another—Berrin's camp aides doubling over, clutching their bellies. Berrin glanced up to see a soldier running through a lighted campfire, coat and hair ablaze.

"I t-tried to help—" Berrin stammered. "C-couldn't stand, couldn't see—wild c-colors—blurring sight—belly cramping—"

"It's all right," Aidan said soothingly. "You need not say more."

Berrin's eyes were tear-bright, reddened. "I couldn't save them. I tried. *Vai dom*, I tried."

Aidan felt sick. Sick and appalled and grief-stricken. An army destroyed. An old man forced to bring such dreadful news and at what cost—perhaps even now dying? He placed his hand on Berrin's shoulder.

The bones felt hot and brittle beneath his touch. "It's all right," he repeated. "You have done more than the heroes of old to bring us word. Rest now, for you have earned it."

Carcosse did this thing. What will he do next?

Think, he had to think. He could not afford the luxury of grief, not now. Not when so much depended on his response. Hjalmar and Tiernan looked to him, eyes brimming with loss and desperate hope.

Vai dom, *tell us what to do.* Vai dom, *save us.*

This, from seasoned captains.

He met Connor's eyes, steady and sure.

If anyone can save us, Aidan, it is you.

Aidan straightened up. He felt as if his muscles were moving on their own, shaping his body into the posture of a hero. It did not matter whether or not he felt that way, he must *behave* like one.

"Yosef, see that General Berrin receives the best care. Connor, you have arranged for a chamber and attendants for him? Good. Send the healer—the one who tended Leora—Melanie Dellerey?—yes, and make sure she knows to be discreet, but if she can identify the poison, I must know. Suffice it to say—" now encompassing everyone in the room, "—nothing said here tonight may be repeated except on my orders."

"Understood," came the swift agreement.

Aidan waited until Yosef helped Berrin from the room. "Now, then. Connor, bid Raymond MacAran attend us, but have him wait outside the door until we are ready."

While Connor spoke to the page outside the door, Tiernan said, "Lord, I am uneasy admitting someone unknown to us to these councils."

"As the Alcabra Keeper, he has my confidence," Aidan answered, and was met with a barely disguised look of suspicion and awe. *Sorcerer.*

Yet the circle may be our only hope.

Aidan was beginning to emerge from the first shock. A pattern took shape in his mind, a sequence of actions. Carcosse had thought to lure him from his stronghold, all the while plotting to decimate Hastur's military force. *But I do not know where he is or where he will strike next.*

"We must find out two things as quickly as possible," he said. "One is how many fighting men remain to us, including those gathered here, the survivors of the poisoning, and those who can be summoned at a moment's notice. Berrin may be able to tell us more, once he has rested. Did his lieutenant accompany him?"

"No, *vai dom*," Connor said, using the formal address in token of the seriousness of the situation. "Berrin arrived alone, his horse run half into the ground. His lieutenant stayed behind to nurse those who might be saved."

Hard choices lie before us all.

"Secondly," Aidan said, "what is Carcosse's next move? How much time will we have to prepare?" When no one answered, he continued, "I would have your thoughts on this, expressed freely. None of us holds the key to the future, and yet that future may depend on reasoning this matter out between us. I rely on your judgment as well as your prowess at arms. Speak!"

The temperature in the room seemed to drop. They were all wondering the same thing, Aidan thought: *Are they even now on their way here? If not, where else?*

"What about Colina Doir?" Connor spoke up after a tense pause. "It might furnish a tempting target."

The sources of Hastur wealth, which in turn generated power and influence, arose in part from land and herds, forests and waterways, but also from one of the few gold mines on Darkover: *Colina Doir*, the Hill of Gold. It would be a rich prize, indeed.

In a head-to-head battle, one army ranged against another, Hastur would prevail. It far outmatched Carcosse in military power. By splitting its forces to protect the gold mine, however, Hastur would lose that advantage.

If I were Carcosse, I might feint at an attack on Colina Doir, hoping to force a diversion of strength in its defense. And then attack Hastur Castle itself.

"He knows I will suspect another trap and will not take the bait. No, this—" Aidan encompassed the castle around him with a gesture, "—*this* is the prize he'll come after. I want every man capable of fighting summoned and armed. Draw up plans to repel an attack, taking into account that if Carcosse strikes soon, we may have no greater resources."

Nods of resolute agreement answered him.

"I rely on you for military advice while Berrin recovers," Aidan said to Hjalmar and Tiernan. "Therefore, I appoint you, Hjalmar, as my general. The situation may seem desperate, but we may have another resource."

A tap on the door signaled the arrival of the Keeper. Raymond entered, as poised as ever. "*Vai dom*, you sent for me and now require the skills of the circle. We expected no less when we were summoned here. My brother, Luis-Jorje, joined us from Neskaya Tower, where they are developing weapons and *laran* spells with military applications. One of the other workers was recruited by another lord. I assume that it was Lord Carcosse."

It would explain a great deal. Aidan blessed whichever god had been watching when Raymond persuaded his brother to join Alcabra. Now, with a great deal more luck, they might stand a chance against *Dom* Merryl and his sorcerous poisons.

The circle had already created a stockpile of healing medicine as well as a small amount of poison powder. With more practice, they would be able to create illusions of fire or water having the smell and appearance of blood, or even mindless terror.

"A level fighting field," Hjalmar breathed.

"I urge caution," Raymond said, shaking his head, "for we are not yet in a position to deploy any of these techniques."

"How much time will you require?" Aidan asked.

For the first time, Raymond looked unsure. "That depends. Small quantities of healing powders or poisons can be accumulated over time, assuming the substance is stable, but a focused psychic attack is quite another matter. The youngsters, Callista and your Leora, my lord, are not nearly ready. They're Gifted, no doubt of it, but they're young and impressionable. Untested, although eager. Zandru knows what might happen if their concentration breaks under pressure. I would not ask it of them."

Aidan found the prospect of employing children—*girl* children at that—in battle horrifying.

Connor swallowed. "What about Neave?"

"It would be better if she had more training," Raymond answered. "But she's been working hard and improving. With more practice, I believe she would do well. Regardless, we may need all her strength. Without her, there will be only four of us, not nearly enough to take on an army."

Aidan squared his shoulders. War was abhorrent enough without the need for women and children to fight. But if the realm itself were at stake, they must all do their part. Neave had begged to go to Alcabra. If Raymond thought her capable, that was all Aidan needed. But Leora, his little Leora, was still a child and must be kept out of it.

"Then," he said, shaking off a shiver of premonition, "may the gods grant us the time we need to prepare."

"We will do our best, regardless of the circumstances," Raymond said.

❖ ❖ ❖

Aidan and Connor remained for a time after the others left. They sat in silence, each wrapped in his own thoughts. Embers made soft sounds as they fell away into ash. Night pressed in from all sides.

If only I had not delayed … We might now know—I might have—

I should never have left the castle or given credence to Carcosse's ridiculous 'cattle raid'–if only I had prepared then—

Is there time to send for help? I can claim kinship with Aillard as my first wife's family—but they are too far away. Likewise, Aldaran up in the Hellers.

None of the great houses will come to our aid. We stand alone.

Aidan's thoughts rattled around the inside of his skull like the proverbial boy with a stick and the nest of scorpion-ants. With an effort, he held himself still when what he wanted was to get up and pace, to go down to the practice yards and batter a wooden practice dummy with his sword, or—better yet—jump on a horse and scour the countryside for Carcosse and his men. And none of these things would help except to vent his temper. The real danger lay in moving forward, planning the castle's defense—*leading his men*—with a mind divided.

"What is it?" Connor asked. "Besides everything we have just wrestled with? And all that still lies before us tomorrow?"

Aidan's tension eased in the presence of someone whom he trusted enough to be fallible. He could say things to Connor that he would never allow himself to reveal to his captains. With them, he must always be *Lord Hastur*.

"You are right," Aidan said, breathing relief. "And yet—" Now the dam was broken and words burst forth. "—I cannot let go of the thought that if I had only sent out scouts, we might even now know where Carcosse is." There it was, that kernel of guilt. That fear of having failed.

"And you might not." Connor's tone was both gentle and intense, determined to get his point across. "Do not berate yourself for a decision made in good faith."

"We have to know where he is and how many men he has and when—"

"*Vai dom* … Aidan. Stop."

"We have to know!"

"Listen to me," Connor said, quietly rational. "As soon as Berrin gave me his preliminary report, I posted sentinels along every possible route of attack, even further out than in normal times. There are no guarantees anywhere in life, but unless Carcosse has a flock of gigantic *kyorebni* to drop swordsmen upon us from the skies, we will have advance warning. Every day he does not attack, we will be better prepared."

Aidan took a deep breath, willing Connor's composure into his mind. Panic was contagious, he told himself, and although the worst of his self-doubt was over, its echoes lingered. "All may yet go as we hope, but if it does not … Connor, we must consider the worst situation, that we will have no time."

Connor nodded, his eyes shadowed in the flickering light. The fire was dying down, the candles near to drowning in puddled wax. "I have devised a plan for the women and children of the castle, as well as the elderly and those who cannot fight. Just in case, you understand, praying then as now that we will never need to use it. I conferred with *Domna* Graciela on the details, where each member of the family and staff is to go, and who is to protect them at the last extremity. I will present these plans to you … but not at this hour. Do not insist. For today, you have done all that is prudent—all that is human."

Aidan sat back in his chair. The fatigue of a long day and an even longer night had cast shadows on his thoughts, intensifying all that was ominous. The situation might not be as bad as his fears made it seem. There was hope, after all. "Are you telling me I do not do my best thinking after a long day's ride and an even longer Midsummer Festival?"

"I am *saying* that we have done enough for one night. Today's worries will still be here on the morrow."

As Aidan rose in token of agreement, he reflected on what a superb paxman he had in Connor. And that perhaps he had made a mistake in refusing to allow him to marry Neave.

16

Leora woke to near darkness, every muscle tense. The shutters over her window admitted a faint eastern light. All but one of the moons had set, and that one was the merest sliver. Curled up like a kitten beside her, Callista made a gentle snoring buzz. Since Midsummer Festival night four days ago, the two girls had shared a room and Callista's bad dreams had improved. Much to Sharina's delight, they'd included her in their games. Callista was delighted to have found not one but two sisters, and Sharina's initial jealousy had faded in the thrill of being treated as an equal.

What had roused her? Straining, Leora heard running footsteps outside her door, then shouting, too distant and confused to make out the words.

Heart pounding, she slipped out of bed. The floor was shiveringly cold. She pulled on her indoor boots and an everyday tunic over her nightgown, then tiptoed to the door and lifted the latch. Mother rushed down the hallway, holding a candlestick in one hand and dragging a bewildered-looking Iain with the other.

"Remember your orders! Get back into your room, Leora! And *stay there!*" Before Leora could stammer a reply, Mother hurried Iain away. As heir to Hastur, he must be safeguarded separately from the rest of the family. Rumor was that Mother had insisted on it.

As for hiding in her room … going back to sleep was impossible. She'd end up cowering under the covers like a trapped rabbit-horn. *Oh, this was terrible! Anything was better than not knowing!*

The voices she'd heard on awakening had come from downstairs in the main part of the castle. If she were careful, she might get a look without being seen.

From the top of the stairs, she spotted a flurry of activity down below, maids, manservants, and even one of the men who worked in the stables, carrying pots and baskets and piles of unrecognizable goods. They scurried out of the way as a trio of armed soldiers made for the front doors. Creeping down to the first landing, she spied Lorcan at one end of the hall, shouting orders.

What could she do to help? Nothing. She had no skill in arms or even the kitchen. Yet she couldn't just hide in her room, the way Mother expected. There must be *something* she might do!

For the moment, though, she couldn't stay out here. Any moment now, she'd be caught. *Father will be furious!*

Then a thought came to her: In all the uproar, what must Sharina be feeling? And Callista—she'd left her alone—in a strange castle—under attack!

Sharina first, before she panics.

Leora raced back up the stairs toward her sister's room, knocked lightly, then tested the latch. It lifted smoothly. Sharina was in her bed, buried under bedcovers and pillows.

Sharina poked her nose out. "What's going on?"

"The castle's under attack—" Leora broke off at a great rumbling noise from the direction of the front gates. It sounded like a mountain avalanche, shouting mixed with the clash of swords, the tramping of feet, and the neighing of horses.

With a yelp, Sharina pushed off the covers and threw herself into Leora's arms. She was trembling hard, fighting back tears.

Mother had said to remain in their rooms, but was it truly safe? Was *any* place safe tonight?

Leora stroked her sister's hair. "It's all right, I'm here. I won't let anything happen to you." She sounded braver than she felt, but it was good enough for her sister, who calmed down. "Come on, let's get Callie. She must be terrified, don't you think?"

"Yes, of course!" Sharina wiped away her tears and scrambled into her clothes. "She's so far from her family. She needs us, as her sisters. We must look after her, right?"

"Yes, indeed. Come on, but be very quiet."

The two of them tiptoed along the deserted corridor. The air seemed even more chilly than usual, or was that Leora's imagination? They found Callista tangled in her bedding, thrashing.

"Callie?" Sharina said, but there was no answer, only whimpers.

"I think she's having a nightmare."

"What should we do? Is it safe to wake her?" Sharina referred to the old maxim about not interrupting a person's bad dream for fear that they might never emerge.

Leora reached out to soothe her friend. Before her fingertips made contact with the bare skin of Callista's hand, a spark sprang across the gap.

"Ouch!" Leora jerked away, shaking her stung fingers. Callista struggled upright and stared, wild-eyed.

"It's all right," Leora crooned. "We're here with you, Sharina and I. You're not alone."

"The castle's under attack," Sharina said. "You've been having a nightmare."

Callista said in a hollow voice, "I dreamed this very thing." And burst out crying.

♦ ♦ ♦

"We can't stay here," Leora said once the worst of Callista's storm of tears had passed. This wouldn't do at all. Waiting like helpless chervine foals, not knowing what was going on, at the mercy of any invaders who got this far …

"We need a safe place where we can see what's happening," Leora said.

"How about the Western Tower?" Sharina asked. "It's got a good vantage. A place we feel safe—" with a glance at Callista, "—right?"

Callista said nothing, just stared blankly.

Leora shook her head. "No, sweetling, because the circle will be meeting there." *Doing their part to defend the castle. We'd be in the way, interrupting their concentration.*

"We can *help* them," Sharina said, eyes bright and eager. "Both you and Callie have worked in the circle, and I'm sure I can do something useful. Bring them hot spiced cider or something."

Leora didn't want to rub Sharina's nose in being excluded. On the other hand, her little sister had a point. Raymond had said that the girls were not to fight, but if the fate of the castle and everyone in it was at stake—

—her heart leapt in her throat—

—then he would need every talented mind for their defense. Surely, she and Callista could contribute to the circle. As for Sharina, she could make sure no one interrupted them.

"I think you are right," Leora said, "but once we're in the topmost chamber, you must be very still, quiet as a mouse."

"I promise!" Sharina practically quivered with eagerness.

"Yes!" Callista straightened up, clearly having shaken off the echoes of her night terror, as Leora had hoped she would. "You are exactly right! We must lend what aid we can."

The three girls hurried down the stairs, heading for the staircase leading to the old tower. Andres, the under-steward, stopped for a moment, arms laden with bedsheets, and told them to stay out of the way. Leora held fast to Sharina's hand, squeezing her fingers in warning to stay silent.

Leora promised they would not bother anybody. With a nod, he went in one direction while they headed off in the other.

By the time they reached the top flight of stairs, all three were breathless. As they shoved the door open on its creaking hinges, another racket filled the room, rattling the window. The noise froze them for an instant. As it fell away to a dull roar, they ventured inside.

The chamber was empty.

Leora gazed around the tower workroom in astonishment. Everything appeared tidy. The central table and the sideboard were clean and bare. Even the benches were neatly tucked beneath the table. If the circle had been here this night, they had not left in a hurry.

"Where are they?" Sharina cried. "What's happened to them?"

"I don't know," Leora murmured.

Callista said, "It looks as if they were never here."

"Where else would they be?" Sharina cried. "How are we going to defend the castle without them? *What's going to happen to us?*"

"Father will take care of us," Leora said, more concerned with calming her sister than telling the exact truth. She felt his worry through the walls of the castle. Something bad had happened to the army he was gathering. Or worse.

She shoved the thoughts from her mind. "Let's take a look."

Callista released the window latch and flung it open. They craned their necks for the best view. From here, they could see the roofs directly below and, beyond them, the main courtyard, the interior walls, and the front gates. In stronger daylight, they would be able to make out the road leading up to the castle as well as the surrounding woodlands. Men were rushing about in the yard, and archers along the tops of the walls were shooting again and again. Boys scrambled up, their arms full of quivers. In the midst of it, mounted on a white horse that shimmered in the light, a man in Hastur colors shouted orders.

Father!

"There!" Callista cried, pointing.

A balcony projected from the main part of the castle, overlooking the gates and part of the yard. A group of men and women stood in a circle on the balcony, cradling motes of blue-white brilliance in their hands. Their heads were bent so that their faces were hidden, but she knew who they were. In the back of her mind, she could *feel* their gathering rapport.

I should be with them! But she could not abandon her sister and her friend.

Leora's attention was captured by the woman in a cloak of Hastur blue, a little apart from the others. Neave, it had to be. A glimmering of *laran* skimmed Leora's thoughts, an echo of their deep bond. Leora sensed the others through Neave's rapport with them. She stifled the impulse to respond. It would be dangerous, foolhardy even, to break Neave's focus.

"Why are they down there?" Sharina asked. "And not up here, where it's safer?"

"They might need to be closer," Callista said. "Or they might require a line-of-sight they can't get from here."

Flaming arrows arced over the walls from outside the castle. Some landed in the yard, but one struck a defending archer. Sharina let out a shriek as the archer fell backward, his hair and clothing afire.

Leora's heart was beating so hard, it battered the inside of her chest and threatened to jump out of her throat.

The next moment, the fire died, snuffed out. Through her relief, she sensed a familiar trace of *laran. The Alcabra circle!* But how many arrows could they put out, and how long could they keep it up?

If only Callie and I were down there with them. If only there was some way we could help!

At the outer wall, she could just barely make out ladders being thrown up. Soldiers in Carcosse colors, pale gray and blue, appeared atop them.

Oh, no! Leora was not sure if she cried out aloud.

Men in Hastur blue and silver rushed to beat the invaders off. Meanwhile, more arrows flew over the wall, a dozen—no, two dozen—more—blazing in the night. Some extinguished in flight and others landed on the ground, but not all. The arrowheads seemed to be ensorcelled, the way they ignited whatever they landed on. Fires broke out, there—and there! A shed near the stables went up like a bonfire.

Father was down in the yard, his horse prancing under him as he directed the defense. Leora couldn't make out his words through the din. Women as well as men ran back and forth with buckets of water. Servants and household staff joined the armsmen in putting out the blazes. Two men hauled a steaming cauldron up the stairs and dumped it over the edge.

A mass of gray-and-white clad soldiers advanced along the road leading to the castle. They made Leora think of scorpion-ants, relentless and venomous. At the main gates, the column diverged, some remaining at the gates, others swarming up the ladders.

The men on the walls held their posts, concentrating their efforts where Father directed them. For every ladder the castle armsmen pushed off the wall, three more—five more—appeared. Carcosse soldiers surged over the ramparts. Soon the bodies of the defenders littered the ledge inside the top of the wall and the courtyard below.

Having gained the top of the walls, the Carcosse men moved out in both directions, engaging the Hastur forces. A few had already reached the stairs that would take them down to the courtyard. Father sent his men to contain them, but the defenders were already spread too thin to be effective.

Leora's stomach curdled around a sickening pit. *There aren't enough of us to keep them out, even with the Alcabra circle helping.*

Just then, another barrage of flaming arrows sailed over the wall. They converged, as if guided by a malevolent intelligence, on the balcony where the circle stood. Where they struck, sparks tinged with green and yellow erupted. Leora staggered under an invisible psychic blast. Her core went cold and blinding hot and then blank. Empty.

Dead? Was Neave dead?

No, it could not be true—

—she was falling, falling into an airless, frozen void—

Neave! Neave, where are you?

—she fought to awaken, to breathe in air. To connect with her own body. Something summoned her—a cry of anguish.

Nauseated and trembling with a chill not of the flesh, Leora returned to herself. She was still on her feet, gripping the windowsill so hard that her fingertips had gone numb. Her finger joints throbbed.

Sharina was choking back sobs and pressing her hands over her mouth. Runnels of wetness gleamed on her cheeks. "We've got to hide—like Mother said—" Sharina's eyes were wide and white-rimmed. She looked like a deer surrounded by wolves, searching for a way to bolt.

"We're here, my sister," Callista murmured. "You're not alone." Her face was pale, almost bloodless, but her voice did not falter.

"But what will happen if—if we lose?" Sharina said. "There are so *many* of them."

Carcosse won't execute the women and girl-children, Leora thought.

He'll marry us off … but he might kill Iain— No, not little Iain! It's more likely he'll keep Iain alive as a hostage and then—and then—

Visions rose in Leora's mind. *Connor, lying dead. Father—*

Breda. Callista's mental touch was calm and tender.

If she can be brave, so can I.

Leora put her arm around Sharina's shoulders. "Sweetling, if this tower room is not safe, then nowhere in the castle is."

This was not strictly true. Mother and Iain were now in a strongly guarded place deep within the castle. But Mother had made it clear when she gave Leora and Sharina instructions to remain in their rooms that there wasn't room for everyone there. Leora, thinking of what might befall her little brother at Carcosse's hands, could not argue with that.

Sharina nodded as she wiped at her tears.

"There now," said Callista. "Let us see how the battle goes. There may yet be hope."

Frenzied battle continued on the walls. A ladder fell, only to be replaced by two more. With each sally on the part of the invaders, fewer defenders remained.

A laden wagon came down the road where it emerged from the wooded slopes. As it approached, Leora saw that the wagon was bearing a huge tree trunk. Closer and closer it came, until she realized it was a battering ram.

"They're going to break down the gates," Leora said.

Sharina whimpered, "That will be the end, won't it? There are so many of them."

Leora could not answer. Her throat had closed up. She sagged under the weight of despair. She thought of the circle and how many hopes had rested on them. Of Father on his shimmering gray horse. Of Iain, huddled with Mother in the inmost strong room. Of Neave, who was—no, who *might be* dead.

"It is *not* the end," Callista said with such spirit that Leora jerked upright in surprise. "I can stop them."

"How?" Sharina wailed. "What can we possibly do against a whole army?"

Ignoring her, Callista grasped Leora's shoulders and looked at her full in the face. "I need your help."

Leora dropped her barriers and felt their instant rapport.

My Gift, Callista said telepathically, *is fire-starting. If I set the battering ram on fire—if I get it hot enough to turn it into ash—then they'll have nothing left to use.*

No! Leora replied. *You mustn't! Not after what setting fires has already done to you. Melanie said—*

Do you think I'm not strong enough? You're wrong—I am *strong enough. Your family created the circle that saved me. Lord Hastur gave me a home, and you, my dearest sister-by-choice, how can I* not *do everything in my power to save you?*

It's too dangerous, Callie.

It's up to us, Leora. You and me. We have no other choice. Listen, breda— *we both know that some things are worth the risk.*

Leora thought of her bout of threshold sickness, which she barely survived. She thought of her uncle, her mother's brother, Turlach, who had died from the same thing. Of Neave's mother and who knew how many other women, lost in childbirth. Men risked their lives in battle or against the elements, but so did women. There was no safety anywhere.

An enormous percussive thud issued from the front gates. Leora felt the impact in her bones. She looked out the window. Carcosse men were already hauling the battering ram back, readying it for another assault. Arrows rained down on them from the castle walls, but many of them bounced off the invaders' armored shoulders and helmets.

What are we going to do? Callista went on. *Let those we love perish? I* choose *this risk—just as your father does. They're out there, fighting for us. Can we do any less?*

Callista meant every word, every thought. She was going to set the battering ram on fire, no matter what Leora said or what it cost. The only question remaining was whether she would do so alone and unguarded. Leora had nothing like a fire-starting talent, but she had other skills. Melanie had said what a competent job she'd done as a monitor.

Then do it, Leora told Callista, *and I will keep you safe.*

Boom! came from the gates.

"**W**hat can I do?" Sharina sounded both excited and frightened after Callista explained what she and Leora intended to do.

"Keep watch and make sure nothing distracts us," Callista said.

"But—but," Sharina protested. "I want to *help*, not just stay out of the way. That's for little kids who can't do anything important."

"Fire-starting is not something to take lightly," Callista said sternly. "It would be really bad—as in *people-dying* bad—if my concentration was broken. Do you understand me?"

"Uh-huh." Sharina nodded, for the moment cowed.

"I know it looks boring on the outside, but we can't do this without you," Leora said as gently as she could. "We're counting on you to keep us safe. Can you do it?"

Sharina's expression shifted from stormy to eager. "Yes! Of course, I can!"

"I'm sure you'll do an excellent job," Callista said.

Under normal circumstances, a monitor's job was to ensure that the circle members not be distracted by physical discomfort. Leora couldn't do anything about the sounds of fighting below or her fears about Neave. She would simply have to concentrate twice as hard, both for herself and for Callista. She could do something about the cold. In her work as a monitor, she'd learned how easy it was to become chilled while immobile. The tower room was unheated and the three of them were dressed in ordinary indoor clothing. At least, they weren't still in their nightgowns.

She rummaged around in the sideboard and found thick shawls for all three of them. Sharina was shivering, her teeth chattering as Leora draped the warmest of the shawls around her shoulders. Then she handed one to Callista and wrapped herself in the third. Within moments, the chill eased.

"I'll need line-of-sight," Callista said, "so I'll have to position myself as close as possible to the window. Here, Leora, you stand beside me. And you, Sharina, just inside the door. You can move about a little if you get stiff."

Callista drew out her starstone, cupping it in her palm. Leora did the same with her own, focusing on the blue-white light twisting in the heart of the gem. Preternatural calm settled over her. The noise of the battle and the thunderous shocks of the battering ram faded. As she had been taught, she focused her *laran* into the crystal. She closed her eyes, reaching out to Callista along the streams of energy. It was like seeing double, the image of Callista's physical body overlaid by a tapestry of glowing energon channels. Callista's were unusually bright, orange and gold with a shimmer like silver edged here and there with crimson.

Leora felt the mental shift as Callista activated her Gift. An image sprang to their shared thoughts: a heap of glowing embers flaring into life. Moment by moment, the flames leaped higher and hotter. The dull red of Callista's energetic form intensified, then receded. Leora wished she knew what that meant. She must simply trust that her friend knew what she was doing. Callista had had much more training than she had, and from an earlier age.

Time slowed as the flames grew and grew. Leora sensed Callista gathering her inner fire and calculating the distance and trajectory to the battering ram. Orange shifted to red and then to white, an inferno ready to erupt.

Any second now ...

Callista's energon channels flared to searing brightness. A burst of intense blue-white lightning arced out, fading quickly to dull red.

The *laran* firebolt struck the battering ram. Where it impacted, it fractured. Jagged forks of electric-white brilliance shot out in all directions. Wood ignited wherever it touched. It struck the men carrying the battering ram. Some of them dropped the ram and fell, batting at their smoking clothing. Leora heard their screams with both her physical ears and her mind. The men left standing tried to rebalance the weight, but the huge trunk—now on fire in a dozen places—tipped over and crashed to the ground.

Officers shouted out orders, their voices barely piercing the din. Men and horses wheeled frantically about. Carcosse archers on the ground loosed volley after volley of flaming arrows at the castle.

The attackers managed to heave the battering ram off the ground.

Sections were ablaze now, but not the entire length. The men hefted it and rushed it toward the gates again.

Boom!

The impact shocked through wood and wall and air, followed by the sound of splintering, or did Leora hear it only in her mind? Callista's fire spell had temporarily slowed the assault but not stopped it. The gates could not withstand many more blows. *And then what?*

Callista gripped the windowsill, her fingers bloodless. Her lips pulled back from her teeth. *Laran* surged through her starstone, not the blue-white Leora had sensed before but a river of hot, thick, red-yellow. Callista shaped it like a spear and hurled it down below.

Again, her aim was true. Again, the battering ram went up in flames and more men fell. Shrieks of pain and terror replaced war cries.

Without a pause, Callista sent another bolt, not at the battering ram but at the massed assailants. The power was less focused this time but covered a greater area. Leather armor and living flesh smoked and then ignited. Horses screamed in terror, even those that were not directly hit. They reared and bucked, throwing their riders.

More energy shot from Callista's mind, this time aimed outside the walls. Fireballs mushroomed where they struck, hurling flaming spheres high in the air, to plunge down on the Carcosse soldiers. Their screams melded together into a single, inhuman sound of agony.

Callista laughed, high-pitched and eerie.

With her expanded senses, Leora sensed motes of life energy winking out—the archers! And then another, a *laran*-Gifted mind—a flash of violet-white brilliance. *Fading now …*

Leora wrenched her attention from the battle to her friend. Callista's energy channels seethed, sullen and murky. Blood-dark red flowed like liquid metal. Spots of brown shifted to lethal black that surfaced and then slowly dissolved.

For a dizzying moment, Leora remembered the sensations of her near-fatal bout with threshold sickness. She felt chilled, nauseated. Then she'd had Neave and the circle to rescue her. *Neave—pray Evanda Neave is still alive!*

Now she was alone. *She* was the one who was supposed to make sure nothing happened to Callista.

Leora dropped out of rapport. The glowing patterns of stagnant rust and black faded from her mind. Her vision steadied. Warmth rushed through her core.

You are the monitor, she told herself. *Callie's sanity—her very life—are* your *responsibility. You must find a way because there is no one else.*

"Callista." Leora tried to speak gently. She wanted to attract her friend's notice but not jar her from her trance. "You've got to ease up, sweetheart."

No response.

"You're in too deep," Leora said, more firmly. "It's not safe. Pull back—just a bit. Please. Do it for me. Just a bit."

Callista did not seem to hear. With a wordless snarl, she hurled another blast of jagged energy onto the Carcosse forces beyond the wall—no, not at the soldiers. At a *laranzu* who stood apart. The fire was so dark, it looked edged in blood.

Leora's vision blurred and her heart stuttered. The entire chamber shuddered around her.

"What's going on?" came a voice across a vast, echoing distance. "Leora? Callie?"

Leora's breath wheezed in her lungs. Acid clawed the back of her throat. She was trembling so hard, she could hardly keep her feet. Grabbing hold of the windowsill with one hand, she reached out hesitantly to Callista with the other. She couldn't reach. Her fingertips barely brushed Callista's shawl.

Callie! You've got to stop!

A spark leaped the gap. The electrical shock sizzled along Leora's fingers … up her arm … through her body. Her teeth snapped together. Her muscles twitched, jerking her away. Struggling to regain her balance, she tripped. Her skull hit the edge of the table. Her vision went white for a moment, then she found herself lying on the carpet.

Sharina, on her hands and knees, peered down at her. "Are you all right?"

Leora lifted her head. The movement sent a rush of pain through her temples. She lay flat again, willing the throbbing to stop.

"Callie!" Sharina heaved herself to her feet and disappeared from Leora's sight. "What's going on?"

Leora turned her head to see Sharina dashing toward the window.

"Sweet Evanda!" Sharina yelled at Callista. "Did you do *that*? Did you set all those men on fire—and the poor horses? And the trees yonder? And our gates? Stop! You must stop! Now, before you burn down the castle!"

Sharina reached out—

"No!" Leora shouted. "Don't!"

Sharina grasped Callista's shoulders, fingers pressing through layers of fabric—

Callista turned slightly, just enough so that Leora could see her eyes—

—her eyes glowing, molten red—

—her eyes, filled with fire—

The air burst into flame. Roiling incandescence filled the room. The carpet ignited, spewing forth billows of thick, acrid smoke. Someone was screaming, but the roar of the fire made it impossible to tell who.

Fumes filled Leora's lungs. Coughing convulsively, she curled on her side. Tears poured from her eyes. She could barely see through the swirling smoke. Her skin felt as if it were turning to ash. She grabbed the hem of her tunic and covered her nose and mouth. That brought her a tiny measure of ease. She lifted her head.

"Sharina! Callie—!" She broke off in a renewed spasm of coughing. When she tried to take another breath, her lungs closed up. Her heart beat frantically.

The firestorm was past all control, feeding like rage upon itself.

She had to get out—she would die if she stayed here—but her sister, she couldn't leave her little sister—and Callista—the fire was Callista's doing— if she could only break her concentration—

The screaming broke off suddenly.

Move!

Leora crawled on her belly toward where she had last seen her sister. The carpet around her was burning furiously in patches. Sparks flew in all directions. A cinder landed on her outstretched hand. Shrieking, she jerked back.

Bouts of coughing racked her entire body. It felt as if her windpipe were jarring loose in her chest. She couldn't catch her breath. Dizziness turned her vision gray.

She was a daughter of Hastur. She couldn't—*wouldn't*—give up.

Which way to go?

Somehow she'd gotten turned around. She couldn't tell in which direction was the window and which, the door. The only thing she could see clearly was the carpet in front of her.

Suddenly, flames encircled her in a great whoosh of heat and eye-searing brightness. as the blaze receded, she made out the shape of the table beside the window, engulfed in smoke.

Keeping her mouth and nose covered with her tunic hem, she inched her way to the side of the burning table. Air hunger gripped her. With every breath, she coughed more weakly—she couldn't think—her muscles wouldn't work—the room was going gray—black—

She clung to the last shreds of consciousness long enough to pour her remaining strength into a silent plea.

Neave! Help me!

For a fleeting moment, through the closing dark, she caught a glimpse of a dim gray country and through it, past it, an expanse of golden grasses under a sky so pure it pierced her to the core. Gladness rose up in her, and a sense of welcome. She *knew* this place. It was where she belonged. And then it, too, faded into nothingness.

Fire engulfed her.

Neave struggled free from her monitor's trance like a swimmer too long submerged. Never before had she come out of rapport so suddenly. When she gasped for breath, heat and smoke filled her lungs. Her body convulsed in coughing. Tears blurred her vision, but she managed to keep on her feet.

She fought to steady herself. To make sense of what had happened. One moment, she had floated serenely in the circle, tending to the needs of the others as they blocked the incoming attack, and the next—

She had a vague image of those same arrows converging, sensed rather than seen.

The circle had been sitting on the balcony. There wasn't room for a table. Now bodies lay tumbled like stringless puppets. The chairs were overturned and on fire. In the smoke, she couldn't make out much more. Her heart clenched.

Someone groaned. *Melanie?*

Blinking hard, Neave made her way to the person nearest her. *Luis-Jorje.* He lay on his back, one shoulder of his jacket smoldering. He began rolling on his side to put it out. He saw her and waved her off. Both were coughing too hard to speak, but clearly, he meant for her to help someone else. On his hands and knees, he crawled toward his brother. Raymond was curled on his side, facing away but still alive by the heaving of his ribs.

Neave grabbed the hem of her skirt and held it over her nose and mouth. It wasn't much, but it cut down a little on the smoke. Heart pounding, she glanced around—*Derik? Melanie?*

She spied Derik behind an overturned chair, a shadow of gray-on-gray in the smoke. Raymond murmured words she could not catch, then Luis-Jorje's echoing answer.

Melanie! Where was Melanie? Why didn't she answer?

Neave took a breath, fighting the urge to cough, and lowered the hem of her gown. "MELANIE!"

Eyes watering, Neave was still half-blind. She crouched, feeling with her hands. And touched a form, a body on its side away from her. Her extended fingers met with soft flesh. There was no trace of the energy carried along *laran* channels, not even the sullen burnt-red of fading embers. When she reached for Melanie's neck, she could not feel a pulse.

Her teacher, her friend, the *leronis* who had saved her sister's life.

Dead, how could she be dead?

If it were possible, Neave would have hurled herself into the Overworld in search of Melanie's spirit, regardless of the danger.

Dead … Gods, no!

Neave! Raymond broke through the circle's tattered rapport.

For pity's sake, give me a moment, she pleaded.

There was no answer, only the relentless command. She shoved her grief to the back of her mind.

A blast of blue-white fire curved over the outer wall to land among the Carcosse soldiers.

Neave rocked back, stunned. "What is it?"

Raymond shook his head, *I do not know.* Luis-Jorje said aloud, "None of ours. Even at our full strength, we could not generate such power."

With a groan, Derik sat up. Neave went to him and helped him to his feet. Through the brief contact, she perceived that he was only stunned, not seriously hurt.

"It's Callista." Derik spoke in a low, intense voice. A voice that struck Neave as profoundly sad.

"Callie? How could she—"

"Neave. Derik," Raymond said in a voice that brooked no argument. "We must re-form the circle."

The smoke was lifting now. She saw him clearly, sitting facing his brother. As she opened her mind, she felt their unbreakable bond. Brothers, twins, each highly skilled. Together, immensely strong.

Now linked to them and Derik, Neave felt herself carried beyond the balcony, over the yard where fighting still raged, and over the walls. Raymond and Luis-Jorje shared a single goal, to seek … to find … and now it was her goal, too. Their minds merged, far stronger than the usual bonds of a circle. The ferocity of the brothers' determination ensnared her. She could not free herself.

Then she realized their target.

The sorcerer who had done this—the Carcosse *laranzu*!

She rode with the energy, gathered together by Raymond, shaped by his brother into a weapon more deadly than any arrow or spear. Derik was a rock, anchoring them. With her *laran*, she fed the energy. Poured herself into it. Her awareness narrowed to a single thought: In the Carcosse camp was one who had abused his Gift. Who had killed her teacher. Who would have killed everyone she loved. Who no longer deserved to draw breath.

There!

He stood apart, cloaked in midnight. Colorless fire spewed forth from his raised, cupped hands to create a wide swath around him. Red, the color of fresh blood, pulsed through the light, or perhaps that was a reflection of her fury. It sickened her, repulsed her, and yet she held firm. The Carcosse sorcerer took no notice, he was so fixated on his next attack.

Hold! Raymond's command whispered through her mind. He bound them in a circle and shaped them into a weapon. A weapon far more potent than anything Neave alone could generate. She surrendered her will and poured every bit of her strength into his invisible hands.

A web of their joined consciousness settled over the Carcosse sorcerer. Neave felt the moment when he became aware and then afraid. The gossamer strands tightened into steel. Raymond held the web as the sorcerer descended from fear to terror. And then to the void.

The circle burned the sorcerer's *laran* from his brain.

Neave reeled with the sudden absence of life force. She had seen death before but had never been this close. Never been in telepathic contact with a person as they died. Never desired it so much. Did this make her a killer?

This man killed Melanie, she answered herself. *Could have killed us all. He abused his Gift. He deserved what he sought to inflict on others.*

This is war.

War using *laran*.

Her father had warned her. She'd understood the manufacture of healing powders and poisons. But to kill at a distance, using the powers of the mind—she'd had no idea that such a thing was possible. Or what it would mean, deep in the core of her being.

Luis-Jorje had studied at Neskaya. Neskaya, where *laran* weapons were being developed.

My father sent for him for just this purpose. And once such a thing is done, it will be done again. We were right to defend ourselves.

Raymond spoke a word, and the remnants of rapport lifted.

Then her sight went blind.

Neave, help me!

◆ ◆ ◆

Neave whirled through mists, cold and gray, drawn by her sister's fading call. *The Overworld.* It was perilous for the living to venture here. Yet if Leora was caught in a half-dying state, it might still be possible to summon her back to life.

Neave sent out a telepathic call. *Leora, where are you?*

Chill, dense vapors swirled around her. The surface beneath her feet was smooth. The horizon, what she glimpsed through gaps in the mist, seemed to go on forever. She shuddered in the cold. This was a place that sucked the warmth from the living, the land of the dead.

She'd heard stories of those who had ventured here, desperate for one last word with a deceased loved one, only to be drawn deeper and deeper, chasing phantasms that retreated before them until their worldly bodies withered away.

Leora, where are you?

She took a few steps, then stopped. *Idiot! You have no idea which direction she's gone.*

Then she spotted a slim figure, little more than a child's, with curls like flickering firelight against the gray. The figure turned slightly. Beyond her lay a swath of golden-green under a clear blue sky.

Plains? Why would Leora be drawn there?

COME BACK, NEAVE! COME BACK TO US!

◆ ◆ ◆

Neave lay on the balcony floor, Raymond leaning over her. His expression was one of grave concern. Behind him, Luis-Jorje and Derik knelt beside Melanie's still form. Bits of burning furniture were almost extinguished.

With Raymond's aid, she sat up. Her heart ached, her body responded sluggishly, and all she wanted was to weep, but Leora's mental cry still echoed in her mind. "I must go to my sister."

Wordless, he offered her a hand up. She hesitated for a moment before taking it. As a Keeper, he had always been scrupulous in avoiding casual contact. "Go!" he said.

She stumbled from the balcony. Her feet gathered speed as she scrambled down the stairs. The mental cry had come from the Western Tower. What had Leora, who ought to have been safe in her bedchamber, been doing there?

Struggling to stay focused though her physical senses blurred and twisted, she skirted the great hall. The castle reverberated with the clamor of battle outside. Lorcan's voice boomed over the shouting and clatter. She hurried past maidservants carrying linens for bandages and buckets of hot water, pages with piles of arrows.

Neave tried to shut out the cacophony of thoughts and emotions, but it was no use. Her *laran* barriers were in tatters. Everything had happened so fast, from the moment the Carcosse sorcerer had hurled fire arrows at them to the shuddering abyss of his death. Now she was without defense against ordinary minds, untrained and chaotic—

Her feet froze, anchoring her to the spot. There was Connor, the last person she expected to see. Her heart leaped in her throat. He had just slipped in through the outer doors. His gaze swept the hall. Time slowed. At the exact moment when the crowd parted, their eyes met. He was an island of calm, a haven in chaos. She saw the flash of relief in his face, a mirror to her own.

Before she could breathe, he was beside her. "Your father sent me. To find out—to make sure you were all right. We saw the fire arrows—and we thought—*he* thought." With a visible effort, he controlled his emotions. "Did the circle remove to the tower, then? Beyond the reach of Carcosse's attacks? Did you send the fire bolts into his army?"

"That … that was not us." She forced out the words. There was so much she wanted to say. "Callista—"

"Ah. The little fire-starter."

"—and Leora. Something's happened, Conn. Something dreadful. She— I must go to her."

The light in his eyes shifted. Tenderness wrapped her in softest down.

"Come with me." Carefully not touching her, he headed for the part of the castle that led to the tower. The crowd parted for him. Neave had to half-run to keep up with him.

Trusting to Connor's protection, she reached out telepathically. *Leora?*

No answer came. Unconscious, then. Or … No, she must not allow herself to imagine. Not now. Not after losing Melanie.

As they rushed up the stairs leading to the tower workroom, she caught the reek of smoke. Connor, who was ahead, paused. Terror spurred her on. She surged upward.

The door was ajar, its wood streaked with black. She slammed her shoulder into it, sending it swinging. And stepped inside into an ocean of smoke. Her eyes burned and she could not see through the tears. But then, oh then! As air blew in through the open window, the room came into focus—furnishings she knew so well, now overturned, in splinters, still smoldering. Could anything here live?

Connor cursed softly under his breath.

The air quivered with *laran* gone wild. With madness and frenzy. With death.

Two deaths. Sharina, by the door. Callista, a heap of char and ash by the window—incinerated by her Gift.

But only two. One person still lived.

Neave hauled at the smoking remains of the central table. She knelt beside the soot-covered form and touched it gently.

Leora …

A heartbeat, faint and fluttering. Lungs clogged with smoke and exudate. A mind, buried inside.

"Love, I'm so sorry," Connor began.

"Leora. She's *alive*."

"Avarra's sweet mercy! What must we do?"

"Carry her to her bedchamber. A familiar place will ease her mind when—" *when, not if,* "—she wakes. Bid them take care. She feels no pain now, but her skin will be easily damaged. Lorcan is in the great hall. He will make certain it is done properly. Then—" She rose, brushing soot off her hands, "—fetch my father."

Aidan watched a flight of fire arrows converge on the balcony where the Alcabra circle was working. No ordinary archers, no matter how skilled, could create trajectories so precise.

The balcony erupted in a fireball of green and yellow.

Neave—*Neave*—was up there!

Maybe the circle had been able to shield themselves. He couldn't see through the darkening smoke, not at this angle—

"Connor!" He pitched his voice to penetrate the uproar. "Connor!"

Connor, mounted on a raw-boned sorrel mare, emerged from the confusion. Soot streaked his face. "My lord?"

"Get up there—" with a jerk of his head, Aidan indicated the balcony. "See if they need help."

You mean if they are still alive. Connor spurred his horse toward the castle doors. Aidan watched just long enough to see him throw the reins to a man carrying a water barrel and race inside.

Battle-fever swallowed him. Dust and fumes and shouting—slashing down with his sword as a Carcosse soldier barreled toward him—

Boom! The wooden gates quivered under the blow. Aidan expected to hear them cry out.

Lighting erupted high above him—the Western Tower! Over the main gates it soared, toward the battering ram. From the vantage point of his horse, Aidan spied a jet of flame, dying down, and then another. Screams pierced the din outside. Then those, too, fell away into silence. The battering at the gates stopped. Within the yard, however, fighting continued.

He wheeled his horse around, shouting orders. Summoning his men, giving them heart. Another volley of flaming arrows hurtled over the walls. Many of them fell short.

Boom!

The enemy must have salvaged the battering ram. The gates could not hold. In his mind, the hinges loosened and the heavy wood cracked and splintered. His horse pranced, ears flattened, as it fought the bit. He'd been clenching the reins as if by holding on to them, he could forestall the final, lethal struggle. Better to go down with as many of the enemy as he could—

Another jet of white-hot energy issued from the tower. He threw his head back—*what was going on up there?* The circle must have retreated to a safer location. High up, beyond Carcosse arrows. Exultation surged up in him, bright and singing.

For the first time, hope surged, real hope, not only of survival but of victory.

Another flaming bolt issued from the tower, this one streaked the color of blood. From outside the castle came more screams. Horses, he thought, as well as men. And another, glowing like molten iron.

Blinding light. Searing heat.

Flames shrouded the yard. He could see only a short distance around him now. His horse arched its back, head down, threatening to buck. When he wrenched its head up, it trembled, too terrified to move.

It's an illusion. It's got to be. Smoke choked his lungs. His skin felt fever-hot and dry. *I am not a dumb beast, to be beaten down by sorcery. I will not cower here, penned for the slaughter. By my ancestor, who was Son of Aldones, Lord of Light, I will prevail!*

He throttled the impulse to cough. Forced air into his lungs. Reached for all the command he had ever possessed. *"Hastur! Hastur! To me!"*

Voices answered, "Hastur! Hastur!" Shapes emerged from the fumes. Gray on gray, and white on smoke. Blue shimmered through the whirlwind. *Hastur blue.*

"My lord." A man appeared beside the shoulder of Aidan's horse. Soot and blood streaked his face, but his eyes were clear. Beyond him, smoke thinned. Men gathered, weapons bright.

Glancing up, Aidan caught the fading of the light of the Western Tower. "Open the gates."

Without a pause, the soldier dashed for the gates.

"With me!" Aidan shouted. "With me—charge!"

More and more of Aidan's men converged behind him. With war cries at his back, and chants of *Hastur! Hastur!*, he spurred his horse through the gates.

Outside lay an inferno: Carcosse soldiers aflame, horses throwing their riders. Further up the road, blackened corpses. Bonfires that might have been carts or wagons. Trees, too, burning. Burning. The stench of charred flesh and blood. The moans of the dying.

Here and there, a handful of Carcosse soldiers drew together, back guarding back, swords ready. Hastur men engaged them, but there was little fight left in the enemy, only despair.

Carcosse, where is he?

Aidan urged his horse from one knot of attackers to another. "Throw down your arms! Surrender, and your lives will be spared!"

The Hastur Lord … Murmurs flew through the fighting. Invaders fell to their knees as he passed.

Where is he—? There!

Aidan spotted a cluster of gray and white, ten defenders, then half that. Those remaining fought desperately, throwing away their lives. One fell, and another labored on with blood across half his skull. Hastur men drew in upon them.

Aidan halted his horse a length away. "Carcosse! Save the lives of your men! Surrender to me."

"Never!" The cry was half snarl, half defiance. A cornered beast.

A Hastur soldier parried a defender and thrust. Carcosse's guard crumpled, as if he were already dead. Three left now, only three. Hastur men engaged them, and a path opened between Aidan and his adversary.

Carcosse settled into a swordsman's stance, using a two-handed grip. His sword was a bit longer than usual but well-balanced. Light glinted off the flat of the blade. No blood dulled the steel.

Aidan nudged his horse forward. "It need not come to your death, *Dom* Merryl. We have been neighbors for many years. Lay down your weapon and let us find an honorable peace."

Carcosse deepened his stance. Aidan caught the faint tightening of fingers around sword hilt, one hand on top of the other.

So be it.

He shifted his weight, using the pressure of his leg to send the horse forward. In passing, he could use the advantages of height and momentum, putting his weight behind the strike. The horse, well-trained, went from a near-standstill to a canter. Aidan readied his sword for a downward slash—

—Carcosse swiveled out of the way—

Aidan's horse gave way beneath him, carried by inertia. Then began to fall, as if time had slowed—

He kicked his feet loose and pushed off, tucking into a roll. Came up to his feet. His sword was somehow still in his hand. His horse thrashed on the ground, squealing in pain. It kept struggling to rise but falling back.

Hamstrung. Damn him! Damn him to Zandru's coldest hell!

Aidan circled, keeping well away from the flailing horse. Red rimmed his vision. Fire surged through his battle scream. Fueled his muscles.

Villainous scum!

Carcosse had recovered his balance, but just barely, when Aidan closed with him. Gave way before Aidan's fury. Another blow, aimed at the weak place in Carcosse's armor. Carcosse pivoted, tried to deflect. Slow, too slow—

Contact!

Bright blood high on the gray-and-white sleeve. A leap out of range, Aidan following up. He didn't think what he was doing—strategy—*couldn't* think—slash and backstroke—advance, advance—

Back-footed, Carcosse staggered before Aidan's assault.

Aidan could no longer hear the wounded horse or the other men fighting. His focus narrowed to the man retreating before him, step by stumbling step. The whisper of his blade through the air. The pounding—*hot, red*—of his pulse. The hiss of his breath.

—Advance, advance—

Carcosse stepped wrong, caught himself. Too late. Steel slid past armor to pierce cloth and flesh. The grip and tug as Aidan pulled his sword free. Blood smeared the bright metal.

"Yield!" Aidan cried. "Yield or die!"

With a hoarse, almost animal roar, Carcosse launched himself at Aidan. He swung blindly. Missed. Recovered. Sprang forward.

Aidan swiveled, parrying. Steel clashed. Carcosse's next lunge overreached. Chest and belly open.

Sweeping upwards, Aidan's blade slipped beneath armor. An instant of resistance, then a smooth path. Deep and deep and deeper. He felt the tip connect with bone, with spine.

Carcosse collapsed, knees folding, limp, as slowly as if all the air, all the life seeped out of him. His weight, when he settled on the ground, pulled Aidan's sword from his hands. Aidan stepped forward, balanced still. Looked straight down at his enemy.

Blood drenched the tunic covering Carcosse's armor. More pooled beneath him … so much blood. His eyes were open but not vacant. Not yet. Mouth dropped open, sucking in air. A rattle deep in the throat.

Aidan lowered himself to one knee "Why did you do it?" *It* meaning everything from the sham cattle raid to the siege.

"With—last breath—I curse—your house, your blood—may Naotalba—" The name of the Daughter of Doom, the Cursed One, the unwilling bride of Zandru Lord of Hell, died half-uttered. Crimson froth bubbled on whitened lips.

Pupils went wide and wider, filling eyes with the starless night that was the realm of *La Damnée.*

Aidan stared at the husk of Lord Merryl Zamboro Carcosse, as if by force of will he could wrest answers from the clay-dense flesh, already cooling. Sweat stung his eyes and the cut across one cheek. He had no memory of being struck there. His knee twisted and he landed, sitting in the blood-flecked dust.

Sometime later—a moment, an age—came a gentle touch on his shoulder.

"*Vai dom.*" A voice he knew. Loved.

He lifted his head. The day was too bright. He tried to form words. *It's over. He's dead.* Most of all, *Why?*

Aidan clambered to his feet. His muscles felt stiff and his knee joints crackled, but he was steady enough when he bent to free his sword. An aide in Hastur blue and white, dirtied with mud and smoke, ran up to him with a cloth to clean away the blood. He looked down into the face of his enemy, lips drawn back from teeth in a parody of a death's-head grin. Beyond, the horse was still and silent. Someone must have delivered the mercy stroke, rather than letting the animal suffer.

Connor approached on foot, leading the sorrel mare and a second horse, a bay. He held out the reins of the bay to Aidan.

"My lord." His voice was rough with smoke and shouting, but something else lay beneath those few words. Sorrow, perhaps, or simple exhaustion. Or some greater horror.

"What is it, Connor?" *What's happened? What worse than this?*

A pause, a lowering of pitch, words spoken in intimacy. "My lord, please come with me. This you must see for yourself."

In the yard, staff and armsmen, ostlers and kitchen boys alike were clearing the battle debris. Lorcan shouted orders as he supported a bloodied castle guard.

With Connor at his side, Aidan hurried up the castle steps. Neave waited beside the flung-open doors. Her eyes were reddened and her cheeks, shock-pale. Her hair tumbled about her shoulders in an unkempt tangle. A touch, a breath, a word would shatter her. When she saw him, she inhaled sharply.

Gods, he must look a fright, covered in sweat and blood and dust. Reeking of battle fever.

Aidan moved toward her, then halted at Connor's restraining touch— *Give her a moment.*

Neave struggled visibly to collect herself. She clasped her hands together over her heart as if she dared not let go. A quick, sharp gasp brought a rush of color to her cheeks.

"Father. You've come—you have to see ..." Not waiting for a reply, she spun around and plunged through the castle entrance. Aidan went after her, Connor close behind.

Past the foyer, rows of beds lined the great hall, pallets and folded blankets on the floor as well as proper cots. Wounded men occupied almost all the beds. Muffled groans arose from everywhere. The stench of blood and filth washed over Aidan. From burns, he thought, as well as dreadful injuries. One of Lorcan's assistants and an older woman in black were directing the castle women and boys in a flurry of activity. The assistant rushed forward as a man in a stabler's rough garb half-carried in the soldier Lorcan had helped.

"Alive! *Dom* Aidan's alive!" rustled through the infirmary.

With Aidan and Connor on her heels, Neave crossed the great hall, heading for the stairwell to the Western Tower. As Aidan set foot on the lowest step, a chill slithered down his spine. Halfway up, the reek of smoke clawed at the back of his throat. His eyes watered and he fought to suppress a cough.

Neave paused at the workroom door, one hand resting on the latch. "I wish I did not—" She broke off. "Father, the fire that destroyed Carcosse— it was not our doing. Not Alcabra's. It came from here."

"If not the circle, then who?" He had not thought Raymond and his people capable of it, either. Then a thought came to him: the young girl in the circle, the Storn girl, was said to be a fire-starter. She'd been sent to the Keep for her safety as well as everyone else's until she learned to control her Gift.

Neave's eyes widened, as if she'd read his thoughts. "Callista."

Entering the workroom was like stepping into a furnace after everything within it was reduced to powder. Smoke hung in the air, laden with an acrid reek that made him want to retch. It smelled like charred human flesh. The window had blown open. The walls were scorched black. Piles of whitened ash littered the floor. Here and there, embers smoldered around shards of unburned wood. *This was once a table,* he thought. *A sideboard. The rung of a stool.*

Aidan followed Neave's gaze to two heaps, black like coal. Like death. One lay near the blasted-out window. In the other, near the center of the room, grayish fragments of bone stood out against burned fabric.

"Who?" He forced the question through a throat gone dry. Color drained from the world. "Who were they?"

"Callista—" Neave pointed to the corpse near the window, then the bundle of ash and bone, "—and … and Sharina."

"Sharina?" What in the names of all the gods was *Sharina* doing here? Frost coalesced around his heart.

Neave wasn't finished. When she spoke, her voice sounded distant, as if she called to him across an expanse of ice. "Leora … survived. She's badly injured. Her mind— They've taken her downstairs."

Time hovered from one frozen moment to the next. He heard Connor say something about *treatment* and *leronis* and *another Tower.*

His eyes focused on the remains of the two girls. That was Callista by the window, he told himself. Her hair had been red-tinted gold. She was so young—the soft mouth, the rounded cheeks.

He considered Callista first because she was not his. He could bring a measure of dispassion to examining what was left of her. Not so now. A step, then two, took him across the floor. His knees bent of their own accord.

Sharina's blackened corpse was curled up on her side, knees drawn up, hands—were the finger bones over the skull in a vain attempt to shield her eyes? Or cover her mouth to still her coughing? Smoke had gotten her, but she was still fighting when she lost consciousness. *Please, Dark Lady Avarra, she died peacefully. Not in pain. Not in fear.*

Sharina, my little Sharina.

Were there tears enough in all Darkover's oceans for such a loss?

As if across a great distance, he heard murmuring voices. Connor, then Neave, half-choked with tears, then Connor: *"Later ... let him have this moment ..."*

It could have been Iain, Aidan thought. *Iain, my hope.*

Then, with a soul-deep chill: *Carcosse would have slaughtered them all.*

Aidan straightened to standing. A flame ignited within him. Its light grew with each throb of his stricken heart. It thawed the ice of a moment ago.

"Connor, make provision for the castle folk, men and beasts alike, and those of Carcosse's men who lay down their arms. If they swear loyalty to Hastur, they may retain their liberty. Also, I need the number of our men able to ride hard and fast, and then fight. As soon as can be arranged, I must meet with my captains, Berrin if he is able, and also with the Alcabra Keeper. And Connor ... there was something else. Do not think to shield me. Best that I know it all right now."

Connor glanced from Aidan to Neave's tear-streaked face.

"Carcosse had a *laranzu*," Connor said, "one he bought from Neskaya. The man was known to Luis-Jorje as being skilled but disdainful of ethical restraint."

Aidan felt impatient to plan his next steps. What did it matter where the sorcerer came from or what his name was? Or if a family somewhere would wait for his return? "Did he survive? Need we consider any future attacks by him?"

"He is dead," Neave said in a strange voice, thick with emotion. "But he served his master well. Melanie Dellerey was killed in the attack."

Ah yes, Neave's teacher. The one who saved Leora's life. He remembered her vividly, with her bright red hair and freckles, but most of all, the gentleness of her speech.

"A terrible loss to us all." Words fell short.

Neave responded with a choked-off sob. His heart ached for her. This was his daughter, his firstborn, before him, trembling with exhaustion and grief, and also determination. Holding herself aloof. Aloof and terribly alone. Years of his neglect and Graciela's thinly disguised spite had estranged them. He had lost one child and another might still die. By Evanda's grace, it might not be too late to bridge the gap.

Vengeance can wait a little longer.

Aidan held out his arms and, after a moment's hesitation, she stepped into his embrace. He whispered into her hair, "I'm so sorry, *chiya*. So very sorry."

After a long moment, her shoulders lifted and fell, and she pulled away.

"I would like to see Leora," he said.

"Papa, she's unconscious."

Neave had not called him *Papa* since she was a small child. "Nevertheless. She may not be able to respond, but she will know I am there. Will you take me to her?"

She nodded, drew herself up. "As you wish. But you may stay only a short while. We have no other *laran* healer, and her wounds are of the mind as well as the body. I require privacy and concentration for my work."

He agreed. After sending Connor about his errands, he followed Neave to the family quarters. He had not been inside any chamber in this wing except his own and, on occasion, Graciela's. This corridor belonged to the children.

Graciela's lady-in-waiting stood outside Leora's door, her posture radiating anxiety. Neave entered without knocking. He followed her in. It felt like an intrusion for him to be here.

One of the castle midwife-healers, an elderly woman, rose from her stool beside the bed. She rose, curtsied, and left them.

Leora lay atop a mound of comforters. Blisters pocked the reddened skin on one side of her face and neck, above the downy night dress, and the hair on that side had been cut away. Aidan ached for her, his beautiful, mischievous daughter. He knew from his own experience how painful burns could be.

Neave must have read his thoughts, for she said, "The burns will hurt when she wakes, but they should heal, given proper tending. The more serious injury is to her lungs."

He noticed the rasping sound of Leora's breathing, the soot around her nostrils. On the bedside table lay a bowl of liquid that gave off a pleasant smell, and a stack of towels. Neave dipped a cloth into the basin and gently wiped away the soot.

Leora's chest rose, the movement stuttering, and then fell. The unburned portion of her face was very pale, her lips almost blue. Even though her labored breathing proved that she still lived, it tore at his heart.

If he had not already seen Carcosse die, he would have sworn to kill the man who'd done this.

"Father." Neave's voice was adamant. "Have you seen enough? If so, I must ask you to leave so that I can concentrate on healing her."

"Of course," he mumbled, and left her.

Leora will wake, he thought. *She* must. *Just as the family of Carcosse* must *pay for this.*

They will pay in blood and in fire, in pain and in ice. In the name of Aldones Lord of Light, I swear it.

The midwife-healer was waiting outside the door as Aidan closed it behind him.

"M'lord?" She spoke with a strong country accent. "Is there aught I might do?"

It seemed a waste to keep her waiting just in case Neave needed anything when so many others who were wounded. A castle page could carry messages just as well. He was about to dismiss her to the improvised infirmary under Graciela's direction when a thought shook him.

Graciela …

Sweet Evanda, she doesn't know. Neave and Connor had brought the dreadful news to him first. He owed it to Graciela to tell her in person, and it could not wait.

"Ask Lady Hastur to join me in my sitting room immediately."

The old woman stared at him, clearly disconcerted.

"*Immediately.* Accompany her. She may need you."

With a dip, a gesture at a curtsy, the healer hurried away.

On his way to his quarters, Aidan encountered Connor, as well as Lorcan and half a dozen others with urgent requests. As usual, Connor was in such sympathy with Aidan's thoughts that no explanation was necessary.

The encounters delayed Aidan enough so that he and Graciela, along with the midwife-healer, arrived at his sitting room at the same time. She wore an old gown with an apron and kerchief over her hair but otherwise looked as prim as always.

"My husband," she began as they went in. The sitting room was chill, for no fire had been lit, and there was no attendant. "What—may I inquire what this is about? What would you have of me?"

"Sit down." Later there would be time for comfort, such as he could summon and she could accept.

She sat, the healer standing behind her right shoulder in an unconscious echo of the position of paxman. He remained on his feet.

"I have bad news. You know of the fire bolts issuing from the Western Tower during the battle."

"I may have heard something to that effect—fire arrows and whatnot—but I did not concern myself. Stone walls cannot burn, after all. I was busy securing Iain's safety and then tending to our wounded."

"It is true that Carcosse's archers shot fire arrows over the walls and we were hard set to counter them. No, I refer to a devastating defense."

Her eyes widened. "You mean a weapon wielded by the Alcabra sorcerers?"

"Not … exactly." Why was this so damned hard to say aloud? *One of your daughters is dead, along with a child entrusted to our care, and another lies gravely injured.*

What father could say such a thing easily?

Using simple, direct language, he told her what had happened. Her cheeks paled and her eyes went unfocused, but she showed no other visible reaction. The healer covered her face with her hands, her shoulders quivering silently.

"Neave is tending Leora now," he concluded. "The *leronis* who helped our daughter through threshold sickness was killed during the fire arrow attacks. Neave will do her utmost and asks that we not disturb her."

After a moment, Graciela gave a little shake, as if waking from a trance. "Then there is nothing more that ordinary medicine can do."

"A page will bring word if she needs anything." What a useless thing to say. If Graciela had been anyone else, he would have gathered her in his arms. They would have wept together.

She said, "At least, our son is safe. And now—" rising with a rustle of skirts, "—I must see to those who require my care."

"Will you allow this good woman to tend you?" he asked, indicating the healer with a tilt of his head. "And take a little time for yourself? Surely, others can carry on in your absence."

Graciela had already turned toward the door, but now she glanced back at him. In the unguarded moment, he glimpsed her grief, raw and burning. Then an invisible barricade returned and she continued on her way.

No revenge could mend certain wounds.

◆ ◆ ◆

Aidan paced the castle and its surrounds, assessing the damage, comforting the wounded, and struggling with the urge to retaliate. Had he been able to set forth immediately, he would have done so that very evening. As he left the improvised infirmary, he encountered one harried-looking officer after another, then finally, Berrin. Although moving stiffly, the old general seemed to be recovering from his ordeal. He bowed to Aidan, his expression grave.

"We are all very sorry to learn of the death of *Damisela* Sharina and her friend," Berrin said. "She was a bright flower in these dark times."

Aidan allowed the murmurs of sympathy. He did not want to be reminded that he was human. At this moment, he needed to not be. A human man would grieve. Would weep salt tears.

I must weep fire.

Finally, Connor convinced him to take a meal and some rest. "At this rate, you will be no good to anyone," Connor insisted. "Your people need you."

Aidan began to protest, then silenced himself. "You are right, of course. Send a meal to my quarters. Something simple, soup and bread, if there is any. Whatever's left after the men have eaten."

"I will make sure of it."

With the door to his sitting room closed behind him, Aidan eased himself into his favorite chair. There was no fire, but it did not matter. He closed his eyes and forced his taut muscles to relax. A few minutes of peace were all he needed.

Iain is safe, and Neave. And Jessamy. And my sweet Leora. Ah, Sharina! Yet how many other fathers were now grieving the loss of their sons, sons weeping over the bodies of their fathers …

Carcosse was dead, but it was not enough.

Between the poisoning at Berrin's mustering place and the fire arrows, he had lost too many men to field an effective invading army. How many remained to Carcosse, he did not know. If only he had allowed Connor to send scouts before the attack! He still could, although it would take time to hear back.

Armed conflict was not the only way to defeat Carcosse. He might be able to blockade the castle. That would entail tendays or more of patient watchfulness, waiting for starvation or thirst to weaken his enemy. He had no stomach for a prolonged siege. His place was here, with his family. With his people.

On the other hand, he was no longer dealing with a seasoned adversary. His best guess was that the castle had been left under the command of *Dom*

Merryl's heir, Darren. Darren was no longer a child, but he was young and inexperienced. He would be grieving his father, too. Would that make him more likely to retaliate? Or cowed and dispirited, willing to negotiate? It was worth a try at convincing him of the futility of resistance. Then the siege might be short. But if not …

He had another weapon.

◆ ◆ ◆

Sunset came and went. After comforting the wounded in the improvised infirmary, Aidan returned to his office, now transformed into a war room. The men assembled there rose as one: Raymond for the circle, his cheeks smudged with soot; Connor, as ever a solid rock; Hjalmar and two of his senior lieutenants, but not Tiernan, who was still directing matters below. All of them had the grim mien of men recently engulfed in battle. Lastly, Berrin, wearing ordinary, off-duty clothing. The space felt both too crowded and too empty.

Aidan waved the others to sit as he lowered himself into his chair. A map lay unfurled across the desk; Connor's doing, no doubt. Knives and a paperweight, a chunk of misshapen steel, weighed down its corners. At a glance, Aidan recognized the territory between his home and his enemy's stronghold. A second map showed the immediate environs of Carcosse Castle.

"Thank you all for coming at such a late hour. We have beaten off the enemy. Lord Carcosse is dead and his army decimated, but a lasting victory still lies before us."

"We are at your disposal, my lord," Berrin said in his rumbly voice, echoed by the others.

"Carcosse has made a grievous error," Aidan went on. "It is one thing to fake a cattle raid and quite another to attack my home. My family. My people. I mean to cut off the head of this scorpion-ant once and for all. If I succeed, his heirs will never be in a position to threaten us. This—" he encompassed the castle and its surrounds, the fires that had burned and the blood that still flowed, "—requires no less."

He addressed his war council. "How many able fighters remain to us?"

Hjalmar and his lieutenants consulted briefly with Berrin, then supplied a figure that was greater than Aidan had hoped. A contingent from Berrin's mustering place, survivors of the poisoning, had arrived toward the very end of the fighting.

"They are helping with the aftermath, tending to the wounded, inventorying supplies, and putting out the last of the fires," Hjalmar said.

Aidan nodded. "Be sure they have a hot meal and adequate rest. I want them ready to ride and fight."

"That will require several days," Berrin said, with a slight emphasis on *require*. "A tenday, if possible."

Berrin spoke sense. As in all things, the best solution was one of compromise. Rest and readiness to fight pitted against speed and secrecy.

"Do you mean to lay siege to Carcosse Castle, *vai dom*?" Hjalmar asked in the pause that followed. "Or to draw them out to fight?"

Aidan took a moment to respond. "*I curse—your house, your blood—*" echoed through his mind.

Beware of curses, went the old saying, *lest they turn back upon the one who utters them.*

"Either strategy presents its own particular challenges," Aidan said. "If Carcosse is now weakened, so are we. However, there is another alternative." Throughout the room, eyes brightened with interest. "Carcosse was able to wreak destruction with but a single *laranzu*. We have an entire circle at our service, and therein lies my plan." He outlined a strategy based on the spells that Luis-Jorje had assured him the circle was capable of.

"'Tis a bold move, *vai dom*," Berrin said. The others murmured agreement.

Aidan said, "I intend to allow young Darren Carcosse to surrender. If he refuses, I will end the conflict. Make sure our officers understand the nature of our attack. These *laran* spells may affect our men, as well. Meanwhile, rest, heal, and prepare. When we ride forth, we must have our full available strength."

Once all was in readiness and Leora was deemed recovered enough to be entrusted to ordinary healers, Aidan's army set out for Carcosse Castle. Speed was their ally, but they could cover only so much ground, walk-and-trot, on each long summer's day. There was scant time for grazing, and even with rations of grain, the horses lost weight. Even Aidan's gray stallion grew visibly thinner.

Aidan joined his soldiers in nightly arms practice, pushing himself to even more aches and bruises. By the time they crossed the border, he felt stronger than he had in years.

Scouts brought the news that the castle had been newly fortified. Only the onset of battle would tell whether Carcosse had a circle of *leroni* as well.

The terrain rose sharply into a jagged arm of mountain rock, pierced by a cleft that sheltered the castle. Aiden sent men up hills to either side of the stronghold, keeping out of sight as best they could. The Alcabra circle and their escort took a circuitous route to the back of the overlook, where they would have line-of-sight on the castle. They had previously arranged a signaling device by which Aidan could let them know when to cast their spell.

Once drawn, this sword cannot be put back. This use of laran *will change the face of warfare, not just for us but for our children and their children's children.*

Aidan took the remainder of his force along the direct approach, passing through small settlements, collections of cottages, livestock pens, barns, silos, and gardens. Farmers paused in their work along the rows of vegetables. These were not the enemy, Aidan reminded himself. He prayed they would be well clear of the effects of Luis-Jorje's spell.

Aidan's party halted before the castle. Stone walls ringed the fortress except for where the cliffside protected it. Some sections looked new, and the older ones in good repair. There were no wooden palisades, nothing to burn or batter down. Battlements topped the walls, interrupted by regularly spaced openings through which archers might aim while sheltering from return fire. The gates remained shut, but heads and spearpoints appeared along the tops of the walls.

Berrin reined up his horse beside Aidan. "Much has been done to reinforce the walls. Nevertheless, this place can still be taken. It won't be easy or quick, or cheap in blood."

Aidan nudged his gray stallion forward, halting the horse with his weight at a safe distance from the central gates. *I did not begin this fight, but by all the gods, I will end it. Carcosse will not rise again to slaughter any more of my children.*

"I am Aidan Valdir Hastur, lord of my realm," he called, "and I am here to lay charges upon the heir of Carcosse. I demand that he come forth, that he may hear my complaints and make satisfactory restitution."

A voice shouted back, "We will not deal with one who comes armed to our gates. Send away your army, Lord Hastur, and then we shall consider your request."

"I will not bandy words with an underling," Aidan shouted back.

"Send your army away!"

"Come out and make me—or I will peel away your shell like a river cray and devour you entire!"

For a long moment, nothing happened. The gray horse pranced sideways, sensing the tension, before Aidan settled him with a touch. Then one of the lesser, side gates opened and a mounted man emerged. Two armsmen followed closely, one of them carrying a flag of parley. The man leader was slender, with the barely-formed slenderness of youth. Not yet twenty, Aidan judged, but no longer a child, either. He carried a sword, still in its sheath, and the sleeveless tabard over his armor bore the gray and white of Carcosse. He halted a short distance away.

So this is Darren Conall Carcosse.

Aiden let the moment stretch out, testing the nerves of the youth before him.

"My father isn't available," Darren said. "In his absence, I command here."

"Indeed," Aidan said. Keeping his face impassive, he lifted his voice. "Your father waged war upon me when we had no prior quarrel. He launched an attack not in honor, one army against another, not one *cause* against another, but by deceit and sorcery, raining fire upon women and children."

Darren sat very still, his only response the slight blanching of his cheeks. So, he did not know.

"As you see," Aidan said, "he failed. Your army is destroyed and Lord Carcosse is dead …" a brief pause, a heartbeat only, "… by my hand."

Darren's cheeks flamed, but he said nothing.

"You are Lord Carcosse now," Aidan said, "and you are solely responsible for the fate of your people. Surrender now and spare their lives. I have no quarrel with them. On my word, the word of a Hastur, I will be merciful. Or you can refuse my offer and the calamity that follows will be your fault alone."

To his credit, the youth was well-schooled. His voice did not shake and he held himself proudly. "What terms?"

Darkness lapped at Aidan's heart. Darkness, and flame. Had *Dom* Merryl offered terms before he launched the attack that had slain or injured so many? Would diplomacy bring Sharina back to life? Or Melanie? Would it save Leora?

I must weep fire.

He found his voice a moment later. "I will not bargain beyond what I have already offered, your lives for your surrender."

Darren's response was to wheel his horse and gallop back to the castle. As soon as the gates closed, a volley of arrows flew from the wall above. They fell short of Aidan's position. Nevertheless, Berrin urged Aidan to retreat beyond range.

"Since we cannot be sure of the range of our circle's spells," Berrin said, "we must pull back so we are not similarly affected."

"Pull back? Oh, that'll give yon lordling a thrill," said Hjalmar with a wicked grin. "He'll think he's chased us off!"

Aidan thought the Carcosse boy was inexperienced at war but not foolish. "As long as he doesn't come after us. We need to pen him within those walls for the spell to do its work."

"We'll keep him there," Berrin said, his tone sober. "By your leave, my lord, our men will remain on either flank. At the first sign of bolting, we'll be on them like a falcon on a rabbit-horn."

They discussed the plan for a few more minutes, then Berrin signaled the main body to retreat, which they did in an orderly fashion. Aidan and an aide remained behind.

Reaching into his saddlebag, Aidan drew out the device Raymond had given him. It was a fist-sized sphere, heavy for its size. A wink of blue light glinted in the band formed by twin parallel incisions along its equator. As instructed, he grasped one hemisphere and twisted. The device clicked and the tiny starstone flared into brightness. He hurled the ball aloft. It gathered speed as it rose, passing the limit of his throw.

Up—up—

He followed it with his eyes, squinting against the sun. The device reached its apex and hung in the air, giving off plumes of blue smoke. The smoke dissipated, moment by moment, blown by the wind. If anything was left of the device itself, he could not see it fall. Then he saw the acknowledgment, a flash of blue at the cliff top.

Moments passed in waiting. Aidan could not sense the *laran* spell. Had something gone wrong? Was he beyond the limit of the circle's influence? Or had they not yet begun? Or was everything going according to plan, and the castle defenders were now themselves helplessly caught in delusion-born terror?

Would he find unguarded gates and an easy victory? Or resistance and bloodshed, a long assault, perhaps a siege?

At last, he could wait no longer. He had to find out what was happening. He nudged the stallion's sides. The horse thrashed its tail, restive. Could it sense what Aidan's human senses could not? Regardless, Aidan was determined to investigate. He kicked the horse again, harder.

The gray moved forward, but it was fighting him now—another moment would bring outright rebellion—murderous rage—

In his mind, the gray reared, pawing the air, crashing down and launching into wild bucking—he was a good horseman, but he knew, he just *knew* he'd be thrown—

—and then those metal-shod hooves would smash into his sides—his hands—his spine—with rising panic now, he thought—*his skull—*

Drenched in sudden sweat, he pulled the horse up short. His hands were shaking. His mouth had gone dry, and his tongue cleaved to his palate.

The spell … it must be the terror spell.

With that thought, his fear subsided a little. He forced his fingers to relax on the reins. He'd been sawing on the horse's mouth while digging his heels into the animal's sides. The horse shook its head, bridle rings jingling, and gave a gusty, aggrieved sigh. Aidan sent a silent apology to the horse, which had only been doing its best with contradictory, painful, and increasingly frantic commands.

Barely able to trust himself, he turned the horse away. The gray moved out easily, rising to a trot at Aidan's signal. With each stride, the frightful spell ebbed. Aidan stopped trembling. He could think more clearly, although it took effort to maintain focus. If he had been this badly affected, he wondered, what must it be like for those within the castle? He halted, swinging the horse to look behind him—

—just in time to see the gates open. At first, a crack, a sliver of light. Then wider, open enough to slip through. A man pelted through the gap, then another and another. As the gap grew, bodies flooded out. They darted forward headlong, without any order to their flight. The foremost threw themselves to the ground, where they lay writhing.

Aidan heard their screams, raw and wordless. They echoed inside his skull. *This could have been me!* The enemy was no longer a threat, yet their plight, how the frenzy stripped away their manhood, surely made them pitiable.

Howling like maddened animals, Carcosse men leaped from the walls. Their arms and legs pinwheeled before they crashed. Those still on their feet rushed down the slopes, some falling, others tripping and stumbling in their haste. Some clawed the air, but others looked as if they were gouging out their own eyes.

One of the aides said something about no one deserving such a fate.

No one? The image of Sharina's dead body seared Aidan's vision. Smoke filled his throat and ashes lay heavy on his tongue. If it was wrong to use such a weapon, was it not what Carcosse deserved? Men poisoned, one daughter dead and another who might never recover, a healer slain—these crimes had demanded justice. Retribution. Revenge. He had answered with the weapons the gods had granted him. Now Carcosse had paid the price. Was it not, in fact, a righteous response? History would have the final judgment.

It was over now, at any rate. Not a single one of his men had been killed, and Carcosse Castle was all but taken. Many of its defenders were either dead or maimed by their own hands.

The spell was falling away. He felt its power waning. With every passing moment, he no longer had to fight for control over himself. Now that it felt safe to do so, he moved forward, guiding the gray between the fallen men. Behind him came Berrin and his soldiers.

Bodies littered the ground, corpses with distorted faces and twisted limbs. Here and there, men sat up, blinking in confusion. Others curled in on themselves, moaning and twitching. These were men driven to extremity, helpless in their agony, their minds unmade by a sorcery against which they had no defense.

I brought this about.

"My lord." That was Berrin, riding up beside him. "We must secure the castle before those within have a chance to recover."

"We must make sure that none of these—" Aidan's glance encompassed the field, "regain the capacity to fight."

"They'll be our prisoners before their wits return."

"As soon as is prudent," Aidan said, "send a party to the Alcabra folk. Make sure their needs are tended to, for we owe them this victory."

"I'll see it done, my lord."

24

On entering the courtyard, Aidan saw men lying twisted on the dirt, some still overcome, others sitting up or helping one another to stand. But there were women here as well, and children. Half-grown girls in scullery aprons, boys in stable garb. A woman in housekeeping drab knelt in the dust, her arms around an elderly man, rocking him as he sobbed. Another, gray hair escaping from her cap, stood like a pillar and glared at the Hastur troops while a half-ten of smaller children clung to her skirts. Two adolescent girls tugged at the limp arms of a man in the robe of a *coridom*, pleading with him to get up. To tell them what to do. When they spied Aidan and his men, they cowered, whimpering.

Berrin, in the lead, ignored them. "Find the Carcosse boy! Drag him out if he resists."

"There is no need of that," came a voice, reedy with strain. The young man had been sitting on the steps leading to the doors. He clambered to his feet, holding himself with fragile dignity as he stood before Aidan. Tears streaked his reddened cheeks, and his tabard was creased and dusty. His sword was gone, as were the belt and scabbard. His eyes didn't seem to be tracking properly. Even with the lifting of the terror spell, it must have taken considerable courage to face the enemy that had so easily overcome the castle's defenses.

Seen up close, Aidan was surprised at how young he looked. *He can't be much older than Jessamy.*

"I am Darren Conall Carcosse," said the youth, "and this castle has been given into my keeping. Therefore, in the absence of my father, I speak for Carcosse." His speech lurched from one phrase to the next, each rush of words separated by a pause in which he gasped for breath, struggling to continue. "I have no choice but to surrender to you, Lord Aidan Hastur. I ask nothing for myself, only that you show my people the mercy you spoke of. Did you mean it? Or did that become meaningless when we refused to surrender immediately?"

"I meant it."

A flush suffused Darren's cheeks. Red like blood. *Like blood.* "Do I—I crave your pardon, *vai dom.* I don't know the proper terms." He moistened his lips. "Do I kneel before you?"

"We'll do that at the formal surrender. For now, we need to make sure your people cease fighting, assuming they're still capable, and that all are accounted for."

"I will command them to stop, if you'll permit me," Darren said, his voice cracking. He hung his head. "What—what happened? We were prepared for a siege, yet it ended within the hour. Our very will crumbled away, and we saw—I saw—nightmare visions, like those when I was a child and lay abed with a fever. No, worse. *Worse.* Was that a—a *laran* spell?"

Aidan considered refusing to answer. After all, the boy was now his prisoner and was owed nothing, certainly not an explanation. Yet at that moment, when his victory was complete and his enemy's stronghold laid open to him, he found that his craving for vengeance had eased somewhat. This was not the end, a final triumph. Both realms would continue, but whether with the same simmering feud as their grandparents knew depended upon what he did next.

Could Darren be trusted to honor his pledge? Would he pretend to surrender, only to seize the opportunity to take back what was his? After all, he was *Dom* Merryl's son, tutored in deception and treachery, steeped in his father's animosity. The entire strategy—from the fabricated cattle raid to hiring a Neskaya sorcerer to the attack on Hastur Castle—must have taken years. Had Darren known about it? How could he not? Had he been ignorant or had there been the slightest chance of his questioning the scheme, Lord Carcosse would not have left him in charge.

"Give me your word of honor that you will not attempt to escape or urge others to retaliate," Aidan said.

Darren met his gaze forthrightly. "Readily will I do so."

The capitulation seemed genuine, but too much was at stake to rely on first impressions. Darren appeared to be open and affable, but that might be a carefully coached charade.

Had he been younger or had Iain been older, Aidan would have considered fostering Darren in his own household. At his age and with his parentage, however, it would be too risky. But perhaps, if Darren behaved honorably, there might be another way—if he were true to his word.

There was only one way to be sure. For that, he would need someone skilled in *laran*.

Meanwhile, he would keep the Carcosse heir under close guard.

◆ ◆ ◆

Guarded by four of Hjalmar's best men, Darren mounted the castle steps and loudly proclaimed that Carcosse had surrendered.

"Lord Carcosse is dead! The war is over! I call on every one of you to disarm immediately! Cease fighting!" With his escort, he went throughout the outbuildings as well as the castle itself, shouting orders to yield.

Men lay down their weapons with thinly disguised relief. An older soldier, his uniform sleeve wet with blood, his arm hanging useless, and his face ashen with shock, fought back tears as he struggled to remain on his feet. Darren, standing bracketed between two of his guards, glanced at Aidan. It was a risk, but Aidan wanted to see what would happen. He nodded assent. Darren went to the old man, catching him as he fell.

"It is over, my friend," Darren said. "No more is required of you than to allow your wounds to be tended." Aidan motioned to his men to support the wounded man to the makeshift infirmary, and Darren returned to his place.

Berrin gave orders to round up everyone who still looked capable of armed opposition. Here and there, they encountered opposition. Most of it was ineffective, the men still struggling to regain their mental bearings. The majority heeded Darren's commands. The few who resisted were quickly overcome.

Lady Carcosse, a sallow, cowed-looking woman, and her younger children, two boys and two girls, were brought before Aidan in the courtyard. Aidan would have let them remain in their quarters. Berrin urged otherwise, saying closer confinement was safer. There was a dungeon of sorts, most likely dank and chill and riddled with cobwebs. Here Aidan balked; he could not condone jailing the Carcosse lady and her children under such conditions without imagining his loved ones shivering in the damp.

"House them in servants' rooms, but under guard," Aidan said. They were too intimidated or perhaps too grateful to protest.

"My husband ... he is truly dead?" the lady asked. Her eyes were red but dry. Aidan could not read her expression. Did she mask her grief? Or was she secretly relieved?

"He is, *domna*," Aidan said. "I was present."

"I knew it would come to this! I told him. May that wicked old man rot in Zandru's coldest hell." Then she turned abruptly, snatching hold of her nearest children, and allowed herself to be conducted back inside the castle. She did not look back.

The old man—Merryl's father? Ah yes, the old story of the betrothal feast. If the tales were to be believed, wars had been fought for less.

Aidan said, "Berrin, I will occupy the lord's personal quarters. Reserve the other family rooms for the circle. We owe this victory to them. First, be sure to search the rooms thoroughly."

Berrin offered an abbreviated bow, and if he thought it unnecessary to be reminded of how to do his job, his face and posture gave away nothing.

◆ ◆ ◆

Once Berrin was satisfied that the castle was safe, Darren and his *coridom*, along with his guard, took Aidan on a tour of the premises: the living quarters of the family, the treasury, the barracks and stables, and in particular, *Dom* Merryl's office. Tiernan took charge of safeguarding the treasury and ensuring a proper inventory. A heavy desk and table, bare except for scraps of candlewax and a stray paperweight, dominated the office. Shelves held journals, scroll cases, and stacks of papers. Darren pointed out the castle ledgers, records, and correspondence, everything necessary for the orderly running of the realm. Aidan skimmed through a few.

He set down the ledger he'd been looking at and turned to Darren. "Is this all?" he asked, and read in Darren's face a moment of hesitation, a veiling of thought. He would have mistrusted anything less. He was asking the boy to betray his father's secrets.

"All that my father wished anyone not in his confidence to see," Darren admitted. "He kept his plans and private journals here—" Going to the far wall, he pressed a decorative panel. A door slid aside, revealing a narrow shelf piled with more ledger books and stacks of documents.

Aidan motioned for his guard to bring out a sample of the documents. As he anticipated, they detailed Carcosse's schemes. He found correspondence with the Keeper of Neskaya Tower, offering a position for a *laranzu* with training in military *laran*.

◆ ◆ ◆

Aidan stood on a balcony overlooking the yard, assessing the situation below. The area had been cleared of Carcosse soldiers, and only a few castle folk remained. Beyond the walls, shadows shrouded the eastern sky. Clouds scudded in from the north. He lifted his head, scenting rain on the wind. It was just as well the day's events had come to a close.

On the road leading to the castle, he glimpsed riders, moving slowly. The circle and their guards—it had to be! He sent a quick prayer to whichever god might be listening. A short time later, a young boy—one of the Carcosse pages—brought word that it was the sorcerers from Alcabra.

By the time Aidan arrived in the yard, having exasperated his guards by plunging on ahead without them, the cortege had arrived and one of Berrin's officers took charge. In the gloom and newly lit torches, the riders halted—two men—no, three, one—a riderless horse—another man holding the limp form of a woman in front of him.

Heart in his throat, Aidan rushed to catch Neave as she slid from the horse's back. He pressed her to him, her cheek cold and stiff against his. *Dead? Is she dead?*

Hjalmar reached out to take her weight, but Aidan could not let her go. Sight blurring, he sought one of the others—*Raymond!*

Raymond came up to him, ashen-faced in the failing light.

Gods! They must all be exhausted—to have done what they did—but Neave, Neave—

"She lives, my lord," Raymond said in a voice hoarse with exhaustion. "We were delayed, I am sorry. What we did was almost beyond her power. Now she needs warmth and rest. Sleep."

Aidan shouted orders for the Alcabra folk to be housed in the quarters given to the Carcosse family. "Fires!" he yelled. "Hot food!"

He carried Neave up the stairs and along the corridors himself. He sat with her, chafing her cold hands with his.

"*Vai dom,* come away." Hjalmar, solicitous, stepped into Connor's role, knowing Aidan would heed him when he would no other. "There is a woman whom Raymond examined and found trustworthy. An herbal-healer, he says. Let her tend the *damisela.* You are needed elsewhere."

It was not what Connor would have said, but close enough. Gods, he missed his paxman! And if something happened to Neave and Connor were not here because he, her father and his lord, had forbidden it—*please Dark Avarra, let her live!* He could not face Connor otherwise.

Later, when he was finishing a hasty meal, one of his aides brought word that Neave was sleeping peacefully, as were the others of the circle. Raymond was the last to retire, having insisted on monitoring Neave to make sure she suffered nothing more serious than fatigue and the energy drain of such a huge *laran* undertaking.

Greatly relieved, Aidan retreated to the lord's bedchamber. It had been thoroughly checked by Hjalmar and two of his best men would stand guard outside all night. The space felt dark and close, although it was in truth not small. Age had darkened the furniture, as if shadows clung to the wood grain. A chill emanated from the stone walls, bare except for a few age-tattered weavings. Even the mattress felt old. Flat. He did not care; it was better than sleeping on a bare floor. The sheets had been freshly changed and carried the scent of strawflowers.

At first, he thought he would not be able to sleep, not in this strange bed or in this strange castle. But the day's exertion had taken its toll and at last, he fell into a restless slumber.

Rain lashed the windows, but he dreamed of fire.

◆ ◆ ◆

The next morning, Aidan breakfasted in his new quarters on trail bread, *jaco*, and eggs prepared by his camp cook. Berrin was still cautious about trusting the castle staff. Aidan did not protest. Food was food. Still, from everything he had seen thus far, these people had not loved their lord overly. He remembered Lady Carcosse's reaction and the protective way she had reached for her younger children.

Berrin and several officers joined Aidan, cradling steaming cups of *jaco* in the morning chill. While he ate, he received reports of the progress in fully securing the castle—Berrin's men had found a handful of armed men hiding in a closet—and proposals for occupying the demesne.

"It won't be easy," Berrin concluded, "but it can be done."

That was exactly what the old general had said about taking the castle by force. "It was never my intention to rule two realms," Aidan said, "only to put a stop to Merryl's aggression. I hope to find a way other than executing the entire family and everyone loyal to them. Even with Darren's surrender, we will generate ill will, and that breeds resentment."

"And rebellion," one of the officers added grimly.

"At any rate, we would have to leave a substantial force here and it would not be prudent to split our resources."

"My lord, I am a military man," Berrin said, "and therefore, I think in military terms. I presume you intend a diplomatic solution."

Aidan nodded, a frown tightening his face. "I do not yet know how far Darren Carcosse can be trusted. At the moment, he seems biddable enough."

"So would any young man who has just come through a devastating psychic attack and seen his soldiers driven mad with fear," Hjalmar said. "Not to mention a son in the first grief of his father's untimely death."

"Indeed," Aidan said. "Even a son who believed his father's actions were wrong might seek revenge. And the old feud—how much will that affect him? Will he bring it back to life?"

Berrin spread out his hands. A slight shrug of his shoulders conveyed that the answers were beyond him. "Men can swear, but their hearts may alter with time and circumstances. Oaths are never to be taken lightly, even among men of honor."

Eyes red-rimmed with age and constant vigilance met Aidan's. In them, Aidan read, *I would trust my life to your word, Lord Hastur. But not another's.*

"The question is," Hjalmar said in the pause that followed, "is the young Carcosse heir a man of honor? As his father's son, does he even know what that means?"

"We cannot be sure," Aidan conceded, "but we have the means to look more deeply into his heart. To discern the truth of his intentions and the strength of his commitment. I believe a test under *laran* can determine these things, as far as it is humanly possible."

A ripple of emotion—surprise, disbelief, hope, what more he could not tell—engulfed the room.

"A … truth spell, my lord?" one of the officers asked.

"I do not know that such a thing exists … *yet*," Aidan said. "The Altons claim to have the ability to force rapport. Not reliably, not yet."

From the fleeting paleness of their faces, he saw that his military men grasped the implications. *A sorcerer who could read minds … compel obedience … command a man's innermost thoughts … send an army into certain death …*

And yet, he answered silently, *how is that different from what we did here?*

A vision flickered through his mind of an age beset by terrible *laran* weapons wielded by battling kingdoms. Of unchecked chaos. Shuddering, he turned his attention again to the matter at hand.

"I intend to ask Raymond MacAran or his brother to observe Darren's mind while I receive his formal surrender. It may not be possible, of course, but if it can be done, I believe it is our best assurance."

There were nods all around, except for Berrin, who stirred uneasily.

"What then, my lord? Young Darren may fully intend to keep his promises, but how does that ensure peace for the next generation?"

"By arranging a marriage between him and one of my daughters, and thereby combining our realms into one. His sons, if he has any, will be second only to my own in the line of inheritance."

Berrin leaned forward, eyes glittering. He was a canny and suspicious man who had seen too much of the world's betrayals. "What will prevent his sons from arranging a convenient accident to their rivals?"

"That could as well be the case between natural brothers," Aidan said mildly. In truth, he had considered this very question, and it still troubled him. "We will nurture the bonds with careful education and fosterage so that his heirs will grow up proud to be paxmen and brothers to my own. What more can any of us do?" *Short of slaughtering them all?*

◆ ◆ ◆

Darren's formal surrender took place later that day on the largest balcony overlooking the yard. As many of the castle folk and armsmen as could be crammed into the space below bore witness. Luis-Jorje stood slightly behind Aidan's left shoulder, not behind his right as Connor would have. The other members of the circle were either still resting or tending to the wounded. The event was staged to demonstrate the united acceptance of the surrender.

Darren knelt on the pillow provided by his mother and recited the words of submission. His voice was steadier than on the day the castle fell, and as he gazed up at his new lord, he did not flinch. When he finished, he kissed Aidan's signet ring. There was no applause, only a ripple of silent relief. And worry. Aidan could sense it in the air. None of the Carcosse folk knew what was going to happen next, but at least, the fighting was over.

In the old lord's presence chamber, the gloom, which had previously seemed oppressive, now perfectly suited the occasion. Aidan lowered himself into the massive dark chair and silently blessed Lady Carcosse for furnishing it with new pillows. Then he motioned for Darren to approach. There was no need for Darren to kneel, only to repeat the oath of fealty.

Luis-Jorje took his place behind Darren and took out his starstone. Blue-white light flared, harsh and quick, then died to a mote of brightness. As Luis-Jorje focused on it, the light reflected in his eyes. He glanced up, met Aidan's gaze, and nodded.

"Do you, Darren Conall Carcosse, swear allegiance to the realm of Hastur, and pledge your life to serve it?" Aidan could have used a shortened version of the ritual, but he wanted to give Luis-Jorje enough time for an accurate reading. "Do you swear to defend the honor of Hastur in all just causes and to amend all evil ones?"

Darren repeated the words, phrase by phrase. He began smoothly but soon he was sweating visibly, his face flushed. When he vowed to defend the honor of Hastur, he winced as if in pain but kept on until the end. Aidan held out his dagger, hilt-first, choosing the shorter blade over a sword. Darren placed his hand on the hilt and said in a voice raspy with strain, "All this I do swear, and may the gods strike me down if ever I prove false."

Aidan caught Luis-Jorje's nod. Darren's chest rose and fell, tension draining from him as his color returned to normal.

He still had to receive Luis-Jorje's report, but he was inclined to believe Darren's promise. Taking the oath had not been easy. "Go along now," he said to Darren. "I'll be with you shortly."

Once they were alone, Luis-Jorje related his findings to Aidan. "He is as honest as any man and has more honor than most. He meant every word of it, that much was clear. His feelings about his father are mixed—the devotion a son owes his sire, to be sure, but shame as well. Offer him a different path, one he can nobly follow, and he will prove loyal. I cannot say how he will respond if treated contemptibly, for he himself does not—cannot—know that."

"Thank you," Aidan said, rising to indicate he was finished. "Go, join your brother. Rest if you have need. You have done better than you know."

With an inclination of his head, Luis-Jorje departed. Aidan signaled for Darren to be brought back in. His guards took up their positions just inside the door, eyes vigilant and hands resting on sword hilts. Darren's expression was guarded.

Aidan felt a pang of—not guilt but remorse. "In this conflict between our families, I regret having to take certain actions. This … assessment was one of them. I now have reason to trust you."

Dark eyes glittered. *Was my word of honor not enough?*

"The enmity of the past is behind us now." Aidan allowed warmth to temper his words. "I hope that in the future, we will come to understand one another better."

"I hope so, too. If I may ask, what happens now? Will you occupy Carcosse as a Hastur fiefdom?" *What will happen to my mother? My little brothers and sisters?*

"I have something entirely different in mind. For the moment, you will return with me to Hastur Castle as my guest, not my prisoner. Your mother and siblings will remain here in comfort. One of my senior captains will act as temporary governor until affairs are settled."

Relief spread over Darren's features, and something like hope. "Temporary?"

"Until affairs are settled," Aidan repeated.

Darren took a moment to digest this. "When will we leave—will I have time to say farewell to my family?"

"Oh, not for some days yet." Not until Neave was ready to travel.

Neave recovered sufficiently over the next days to begin working in the circle. Imagining Melanie at her shoulder, guiding her, lessened the pain of grief. She alternated with Derik, who was not yet up to his full strength, in rapport with Raymond and Luis-Jorje, who seemed to have boundless energy. Together they were able to correct the distortions in life energy resulting from the terror spell. Not every patient could be helped. Some were too badly damaged, too lost in the Overworld to return to the living world. Physical damage was less complicated. Often, only skilled nursing and rest were required.

As the great red sun lowered on the western horizon, the circle finished their work on a young Carcosse soldier. He looked barely old enough to fight, and his mind had been so beset by nightmares, Neave had feared he was among those who could not be helped. With the resilience of the young, he had rallied. Blinking hard, he tried to sit up.

"Lie quiet now, lad," Raymond said. "A hot meal, a good night's sleep, and you'll be back on your feet."

"The visions—they're gone!" the young man said. "May the gods bless you all, my lords."

Luis-Jorje smirked, but Raymond said, "*Laranzu'in* is the proper term. We are not noble, although the lady is. She is the daughter of Lord Hastur."

Reddening, the young man attempted to bow to her while staying atop his wobbling cot. "I fought against your father. You could have left me to torment, even death—yet you healed me. Why would you do that? And how is such mercy to be repaid?"

Neave laid a hand on his trembling shoulder. "You and I are not enemies, if indeed we ever were. You are no less deserving of compassion than any of us, do you see? As for repayment, I ask only that you tell the story of the kindness of a Hastur stranger so that in the future, there is no need for swords—or spells—between us."

With a nod and a sigh, he lay back and closed his eyes.

Neave got up, shaky on her feet. What time was it, she wondered, and how long to dinner?

Raymond accompanied her toward the stairs leading to the family quarters. "That was well done. If this is the quality of the Hastur honor, I foresee a time when you will all be peacemakers."

She made a dismissive gesture. "I am no politician and deserve no such praise."

"That is exactly my point."

Shaking her head, she made her way to her suite of rooms and threw herself into a chair. She wondered whose room that had been, with the slightly shabby carpet and the soot-tinged fireplace that was currently cold and drafty.

A short time later, she received an invitation from her father to join him for supper. She found a shawl draped over the chest at the foot of the bed, flung it around her shoulders, and went to his quarters, where she found him seated before a lively blaze. A portable table bore an array of covered dishes. After greeting her and inviting her to sit, he handed her a bowl heaped with beans and parched grain with a splash of sauce.

"It's plain food from our camp supplies, I'm afraid. My people still don't trust the Carcosse cook not to poison us, all the more reason to be on our way home. Oh, and here's some bread to sop it up."

Smiling, Neave accepted the dish and spoon. The food was bland but warm and filling. They ate in companionable silence, two bowls each.

Aidan sat back with a sigh. "I don't need to ask how your day has been, *chiya*. You look as tired as I feel, and twice as satisfied."

"I've been mending the damage from the *laran* spell. If the boy we just healed is an example, half the castle will be throwing themselves at your feet in gratitude before the tenday is out."

"I doubt that. Still, the point is well taken and also pertinent to what I want to talk to you about."

She straightened in her chair. "Oh?"

"The gratitude you referred to, as well as compliance with Darren Carcosse's surrender, may give us a temporary peace. Sooner or later, the old grudges will resurface, if not in this generation then in the next. I cannot leave sufficient forces to occupy Carcosse, nor is it feasible to rule both realms." His eyes took on a faraway look, and she wondered what he was seeing, what future he imagined.

He picked up his goblet and set it down. It was empty, but he did not call for more. "Darren passed Luis-Jorje's truth detection under *laran*. He is neither deceitful nor self-serving. He swore fealty to Hastur sincerely. If I offer him a treaty that would allow him and his family to remain here in their home, on honorable terms, I believe he would accept it eagerly."

"A treaty? On what basis?"

"A marriage alliance."

A marriage alliance?

"… I have given thought to the succession of rulership of the united realms," Aidan went on. "Iain and his sons will be my heirs, not any sons that may result from Darren's marriage …"

Neave's thoughts whirled. Could she have misunderstood? No, her father meant to marry Darren to one of his daughters. Did he mean *her*—is that why he brought it up? It was impossible, surely he must see that! But … she was the oldest, her bloodline impeccable, her Gift established—it was miserable enough to be separated from Connor, but to be forced into a marriage with someone she did not love—how could she bear it?

She must tread carefully now, lest she provoke a futile argument. "All my life I have wished for nothing greater than to be your daughter. Now I have become a *leronis*, a wielder of power. My Gift sets me apart. I will not sacrifice it to satisfy what is expected of young women of my rank." *And I will not be married off for political advantage.*

He had been studying her, his eyes shadowed with—was that kindness? "Be at ease, my daughter. I did not mean you! I am sorry that you thought this was why I invited you to share a meal."

She blinked, barely remembering to keep her mouth from gaping open. "I, too, am sorry. I misunderstood …"

At that moment, she saw him as three different men. The father to whom she owed a daughter's obedience. The war leader, facing one impossible situation after another, searching for a way out of the cycle of violent feuds. And a man in need of someone to talk to, to reason things out with. A man missing his closest friend.

Then the moment passed, and he was saying, "True, it crossed my mind that Darren might make you a good husband. You have earned your place anywhere it is within my power to arrange."

She could breathe again. "I want nothing more than to remain part of the Alcabra circle."

"I will never question that, although it leaves the question of the marriage alliance. Not so difficult, after all. The gods have blessed me with two daughters of marriageable age."

So Jessamy might become the next Lady Carcosse, with all the dignity and authority that entailed. Perhaps having a castle to rule over and a title of importance would make her less pettish. She would likely jump at the chance, but she ought to be given a choice.

"I think you should ask Jessamy what she wants," Neave said.

"I intend to. It would be a good solution for everyone." With a sigh, he added, "I do not know what your stepmother will do without both of you."

"I am sure she will figure something out."

Autumn tightened its grip on Hastur Castle with nightly snow flurries and piercingly clear afternoon skies. Leora felt restless, unmoored. She had not been allowed downstairs during her convalescence. Day by day, the walls seemed to close in on her. On too many mornings, she'd wake to the sound of muffled screams, uncertain whether they were her own or memories of that day in the tower. She did not speak of them, not even to Neave.

Throwing back the bedcovers, she dug in her chest for her everyday indoor clothes. The *linex* underdress had been washed so many times, it was soft on her healing burns. She was taller than when it was made, and thinner, too.

"Young *damisela*, you must rest!" The castle healer-woman stepped between Leora and the door.

Leora was *tired* of resting. It wasn't fair to take her frustration out on the healer, who was only looking out for her. "If I am to regain my strength, I must move about. I will return the moment I feel fatigued."

The healer-woman hesitated. "On your word, then."

Leora went downstairs. She'd heard that the central hall had been turned into an infirmary, but she saw no present sign of it, only servants carrying furnishings back to their original places.

"Leora!" Jessamy turned from where she was supervising the placement of a table. She looked excited, her cheeks rosy, and elegant in a gown of Hastur blue trimmed with silver-edged lace.

Jessamy folded her arms across her chest. "You should be in bed."

"So my nurse said," Leora said, restraining the impulse to roll her eyes. "Is Father about?"

"He and Connor are up in his office. With my husband-to-be."

In one of their healing sessions, Neave had mentioned the treaty that would unite Jessamy and Darren Carcosse. Jessamy, Neave had added, was overjoyed at the prospect of becoming the lady of a grand castle. And Darren was an eminently presentable husband-to-be. However, the ceremony would have to wait until the memorial for those who had died in the attack.

From across the room, one of the under-stewards called out to Jessamy. "I must attend to my duties." She gave Leora another head-to-toe glance. "As for you, it will be your own fault if you make yourself ill by being obstinate. Just please stay out of the way."

Leora scuttled out of the way as servants brought in stacks of long benches. Above her, the musicians' gallery led to a flight of stairs and the balcony overlooking the main gates. From there, she could look over the gates and the road along which Callista's family would approach. Her father had persuaded them to accept his invitation to a joint funeral for Callista and Sharina.

A joint funeral … Callista and Sharina …

The fire-licked darkness that lurked behind Leora's vision stirred. Her muscles tensed and her breath hissed through clenched teeth. That only made the roiling in her stomach worse. Nothing she did helped once those inner fires woke. Then memories would shroud her, leaving her shaking and spent.

Maybe … crept into her mind. Maybe if she went to the tower workroom, she would *see* how it had changed. How the flames and soot and screams happened in the past, not now. She had to do *something*. She couldn't go on, hiding how bad it was.

Resolute, she headed for the tower staircase. No one tried to stop her, although Andres, Lorcan's assistant, paused with a concerned expression and asked if she needed anything.

"Just stretching my legs," she said. "Trying to stay out of the way."

"Oh, it's no trouble at all, young *damisela*. We're all that happy to see you on the mend." He very deliberately did not look at her face, where burn scars laced one cheek and the side of her neck.

The closer she got, the heavier her feet seemed to get. It felt as if a leaden weight dragged her down. She didn't *have* to do this—she could turn around and go back to bed. Throw the covers over her head. But she might also sleep, and then the dreams would return, just as they had each time she'd hoped they'd gone away. It wouldn't be easy, going back into the tower workroom, but *not* facing those nightmares would be worse.

The door at the bottom of the stairs had been replaced with boards fastened with cross pieces and hinged to the old frame. With neither lock nor bar, it was a reminder, not a barrier. She lifted the latch and went up.

Before long, she was panting and her mouth was dry. Her leg muscles burned. Did the reek of smoke still linger? Or only the echo of it in her mind? Stumbling, she reached out a hand to the wall. Bare, blacked wooden stubs marked where a handrail had been. Her fingers brushed the charred wood. Reflexively, she jerked away.

One dogged step after another, she kept on until, heart pounding, she halted. It took an effort to remain there, a quarter of the way still to go. She wanted to race back the way she'd come, holding her breath until she reached the bottom. She wanted to curl into a ball, rather than take a single step. She wanted to scream.

She was a daughter of Hastur. She had set her mind to a task—to face the memory of fire. The terrible emptiness where her friend's mind had been.

She would not back down. She would not—*would not*—run.

She set her foot on the next step, took a breath, and climbed. One step at a time, one breath at a time, she climbed.

At the top, an improvised barrier shut off the workroom. At the sight, her nerve almost failed her. She took a deep breath and rushed up the last few steps, shoved the door open, and stumbled inside.

The room seemed full of light. A half-opened window admitted a fresh breeze without a trace of smoke. There were no ashes, no charred wood, no scorched remnants of the carpet Neave had so proudly supplied. The floorboards had been replaced. Even the furniture was strange, a plain square table and four benches, a fifth against the wall. To all appearances, that horrific fire had never happened. Not here. And yet—

—and yet in her mind, a girl was still screaming. Lungs choked on dense smoke. Fire was everywhere, licking up the walls, flaring up from carpet and cushion, singeing hair and flesh—

Where is Sharina? I have to find her—get her out of here! I have to—

She fell to her knees, pulse racing. Tears stung her eyes.

She's dead, she's dead. Sharina and Callie, both of them, dead … gone … burned. I failed them! If only—

I should have died instead … I shouldn't be the only one alive—

Gray lapped at her vision, closing in until she could no longer see the room or the daylight outside the window. Ice brushed her skin, leaving beads of half-frozen sweat.

The Overworld … take me there … leave me … it's what I deserve …

She staggered forward, not over wooden boards but across an eerie gray terrain. Already, she made out the billowing, colorless mists. Soon they would clear. They would be waiting for her, there in the far distance—

Her foot caught on a lump, rock or root or knot of thickened vapor. She caught her balance. A shimmering blue tower over fields of yellow beckoned in the distance.

Yearning filled her. A name whispered through her mind. *Arilinn …*

Gathering her strength, she raced toward it. The ground gave way under her feet. She seemed to be running on mud, mud that sucked her down with each step. The harder she tried, the less forward progress she made and the farther that elusive finger of blue-white radiance retreated.

She fell heavily, landing on her hands and knees. The tower was no closer. Screaming in frustration, she hauled herself upright and forced her feet to move. Fell again. And again, until she lay on the chill gray surface, weeping helplessly. Her tears felt like drops of ice on her face. All she had to do was let the Overworld have her.

She had been here before. She ought to be wary of this place, but she no longer cared. This time, Neave would not come for her …

Neave.

With the bond between them, stronger than that of most sisters, Neave would sense something was wrong. Even if she did not cry out for her, Neave would know.

And Neave would know everything Leora had hidden from her—the nightmares, the guilt, the impulse to wither away in the Overworld. Neave would do everything in her power to rescue her, even if it meant both of them becoming trapped here.

I have lost my little sister and my friend. I will not let Neave sacrifice herself for me.

With a groan, part effort, part rage, Leora clambered to her feet. *This is a place of the mind, so I must use my mind to escape it.*

Walls of wood and stone, she thought, not formless gray. A window— *there!* Daylight and a patch of blue beyond. Solid floor beneath her feet. With each repetition, the room became solid. When she stood up again in the room that had been scrubbed of every vestige of the fire, she almost wept. There were no answers, no escape for her here. The only alternative was to live.

She turned and went back down.

Neave was waiting for her at the bottom of the stairs. "I had no idea it was so very bad for you." *As your sister and your healer, I* ought *to have known.*

Shrugging, Leora moved to pass by. Her foray into the Overworld had left her shaken. The last thing she wanted was to discuss it, let alone with someone who would know how close to death she had come.

"It's not your fault," Leora murmured.

Neave grabbed her arms, forcing Leora to meet her gaze. "*Fault* and *responsibility* are not the same thing. What happened was not my fault, but it was also not *your* fault, either. Neither Carcosse's attack nor what drove you into the Overworld. I am sorry I have not taken better care of you. It's no excuse to say I have been tending others or that you appeared to be making a good recovery." *I almost lost you.*

Leora's eyes stung. She could not bear the compassion in her sister's touch. What could she say? That she should have stopped Callista from using her fire-gift, and that if she had, Sharina would still be alive? No, she must live with the consequences, with the scars on her mind that mirrored the scars on her skin.

"You need help," Neave said, "more than I can provide."

Leora caught Neave's thought: *Melanie would have known what to do…*

"Leave me alone. I'm all right." Leora pushed past Neave. "Don't tell Father."

Callista's family had braved the worsening weather to bring their daughter's remains home for burial. Aidan invited them to attend a joint remembrance, a kindly outreach for a father who was himself bereaved, and the Storns had responded with equal graciousness.

The funeral party set off for the family graveyard, a pleasant place on a hill not far from the castle. The morning turned gray as clouds rolled in to shroud the great red sun. They went the final distance on foot, following a path marked by chalk-white stones, and stood together at the top of the hill.

It was appropriate, Leora thought, that the only sign of where her ancestors were buried was the irregular mounding of the ground. *It does not matter where their physical remains lie. They have gone elsewhere, to a place where I will journey someday. Perhaps the Overworld, perhaps someplace beyond.*

A wind sprang up, carrying spits of sleet. It tugged at Leora's hair and sent her cloak swirling. Her face went cold and then numb. Droplets ran down her cheeks, as if the sky itself were weeping. But when her father began to speak, a stillness fell upon the heights. The clouds thinned. The sun's brightness burnished his hair.

"Since the days of my ancestors, we have gathered here to bid farewell to those we have lost." Aidan pitched his voice so that all could hear. "Today, one of my own joins them, and although none will know where her physical remains lie, we will always remember her in our hearts." He went on to tell of Sharina's birth and how, from the very first time he had held her in his arms, she had been his love, his darling, the bright star in his life. "Let that memory lighten grief," he concluded, and the assembly echoed his words.

Graciela spoke in a cool, distant voice, as if out of fear that if she once gave way to her grief, she would never be able to put the pieces of her shattered self together. So Leora imagined, but perhaps that was a reflection of her own pain.

"Let that memory lighten grief," Lady Hastur concluded in a hushed voice.

"Let that memory lighten grief," the assembled mourners responded.

Soon it would be Leora's turn. She could not remember a time when Sharina had not been part of her life, her baby sister, always following along and getting into trouble together.

Neave left her side to stand beside their father and offer her remembrances. Then Lorcan. One story followed another, always "Sharina and Leora" or "Leora and Sharina," as if they had been joined at birth and never separated.

Summoning her will, she took her place beside her father. She was trembling so badly, she thought that even the smallest gust of wind would topple her. Memories crowded in—which one to choose? Which one could she tell without breaking down? Already, she was sobbing silently, invisibly.

She thought of Melanie, her healer and teacher, how ill she'd been with threshold sickness, and how Melanie had reached her mind and eased her turmoil. What advice would Melanie give her now? What solace?

She remembered Callista's bright laugh and her delight in her Gift. Gone now, all of them gone, as Sharina was gone. As Melanie was gone.

Her eyes burned with remembered smoke. Pain shimmered through her nerves as her skin charred. She opened her mouth to scream, but her breath caught in her throat. As if it were happening to someone else, she felt her knees buckle, her body sway.

Neave, help!

Was the cry still ringing in her memory, or did she reach out again?

As Leora stood, mute and irresolute, the other mourners searched their memories for a moment of kindness or pleasant encounter with Sharina, and Melanie, and Callista.

At last, everyone who felt so moved had spoken, some of them more than once. The wind returned, blowing in fits and eddies. The party broke up, returning to the base of the hill where their horses waited. Leora, shivering in her cloak, had not been able to say anything. It didn't matter that no one demanded it of her, she *should have* been able to honor her sister, her friend, and her healer. What was wrong with her?

Would it ever be made right?

Aidan remained behind, the first to speak but the last to leave. Neave walked up to him and the two went apart, heads bent together. Even so, the wind carried Leora bits of their conversation

"… must not delay …" Neave said in a low, impassioned voice. "Surely, you must see … her sanity—"

"I had hoped …" came his reply, his voice rough with sorrow, "… keep her with me … longer …"

"… will *lose* her!"

"As you wish, then … after the betrothal … I will send her …"

She was to leave, then. To leave behind father, mother, brother, sisters … everyone and everything she had known. To be truly alone, rejected. Abandoned.

To save my mind … and my life.

She took a breath. The air tasted sweet with hope.

Let that memory lighten grief.

The betrothal of Jessamy Hastur and Darren Conall Carcosse took place a tenday later. Under normal circumstances, it would have been inappropriate so soon after a memorial, but soon the weather would not permit the necessary travel. Every minor lord owing fealty to Hastur had sent a representative. Lady Carcosse and a few of the senior nobles of her court had arrived and the Storns had stayed over. Graciela recruited everyone from the lowest maidservant to Leora in her whirlwind preparations. Only Jessamy was exempt, although she took great pleasure in supervising. By the appointed evening, the great hall and bridal quarters were as gorgeously bedecked as if it were Midwinter Festival. Leora had welcomed her tasks, for the work gave her the sense of being useful.

Earlier that day, Aidan had summoned Leora to his office. She was relieved to take a break from running errands for her mother. The office felt like a haven of quiet after the bustle. Her father sat behind his desk, Connor at his elbow. As she entered, they were laughing, clearly in a good mood. She paused a few steps before the desk, neatened a few tendrils that had come loose from her cap, and wondered if she should curtsy. As a child, she would have walked up to her father for a kiss, but she was no longer a child.

"You sent for me, Father?"

"Please sit," Aidan said. Connor rose, leaving the chair beside him vacant. "Connor, we'll discuss this at greater length later."

"Surely not later *today*." Connor's tone was light, almost teasing.

Aidan responded with a mock horrified expression. "Aldones forbid! I have a daughter to see betrothed, which must surely be enough business for one day."

After Connor took his leave, Leora settled in the chair beside her father's and folded her hands in her lap.

"I am glad to see you so well recovered." He seemed to be studying her. Watching for her reaction? She had no idea what he expected from her.

"Yes, I'm feeling better."

"And the nightmares?"

How did he know? Or that she had to force herself to eat? If her thoughts drifted, the faint reek of smoke would creep back and her heart would race.

"I understand," he said, although she hadn't spoken aloud. "Neave has described your problems. Your burns and … other things, the nightmares I asked you about. I did not take her concerns seriously at first, and for that, I am truly sorry. I'd hoped—wrongly, it turns out—that I might keep you with us for a little longer. I never intended to prolong your suffering."

Leora startled. "Father, none of that is your doing."

"Only insofar as I have failed to obtain proper help for you. Now Neave has persuaded me that your symptoms will persist and worsen over time unless treated. I confess I have little understanding of the sort of wounds she refers to. Bodily injuries are one thing, but damage to a person's *laran* body, if that is the correct expression, is something else entirely."

Emotions roiled up in Leora, a mixture of loss and uncertainty and, rising through it all, hope, sweet and wild. Splashes of vision came to her—a tall building, a room filled with blue-white light, faces she did not recognize and yet who felt familiar—

Her father was talking again. She'd missed a moment of conversation, caught in her visions. "—as soon as your sister's betrothal is sealed and it can be arranged, I will send you to a Tower for treatment and continued training. Luis-Jorje speaks highly of the healing skills practiced at Neskaya. Second to none, I believe were his words. I hope this is something you wish. I'm afraid I have become so accustomed to making decisions for other people's lives that I assumed your agreement. Do I have it?"

Neskaya Tower? She knew nothing of it or the *leroni* who worked there, beyond that their skills were unsurpassed. Whatever else she thought of Luis-Jorje, his competence was beyond question.

A place away from smoke and nightmares. A place for me to become—what?

She thought of the tower of her dreams, shimmering with radiance like blue topaz on fire. Could that be Neskaya? And yet, another name still echoed in her memory …

Arilinn.

She'd never heard of a Tower by that name. It might be all her imagination. *Or not.* If it was a flash of precognition, like the Gift said to be held by the Aldarans, then someday she *would* see it.

Her father was staring at her curiously. "*Chiya*? Is aught amiss? If you would rather remain at home, say the word."

Tears blurring her vision, she shook her head. And threw herself into his arms.

◆ ◆ ◆

A dais with a row of chairs had been erected in the great hall, and bright-colored garlands hung everywhere. Family and guests laughed and chattered around the seating benches.

Leora, wearing her best finery, waited beside Neave and Derik as her father stepped onto the dais. Graciela was already there, as was Jessamy. Opposite them stood Darren and Lady Carcosse. She was thin, her cheeks hollow and pale. She looked worn out by war and childbirth, yet she held herself with pride. Jessamy was radiant in a gown of blue and silver-thread spidersilk, a coronet of costly copper in the shape of starflowers on her head. Leora had never seen her older sister look so happy. Darren, she could not tell. On Neave's advice, she'd locked down her *laran* barriers as tightly as she could. If he did not look joyous, neither did he look displeased.

Aidan settled in his chair, and the other three followed. "Welcome, family and friends." His voice rolled out over the assembly. "We especially welcome those who have been our adversaries and are now our allies, soon to be our kin. The end of this war is an occasion for celebration and a renewed dedication to peace."

A murmur of approval passed through the hall. It wafted over Leora, leaving her untouched. Listening to her father's speech and watching the rapt attention of her family, she felt as if she had broken into pieces. Part of her wore a fine gown with a garland of dried rosalys in her hair. Part was already on the road to Neskaya Tower. But another part still wandered in a shadowy, smoke-filled landscape, searching for the light.

"To secure a lasting peace between our two realms, Darren Conall Carcosse will tonight be formally betrothed to my daughter, Jessamy. The wedding itself will take place as soon as the formal marriage contracts can be prepared." He meant the specification of the dowry and bride price, as well as provisions for the fostering of children in each other's households and the provision that any sons from this union could not inherit the united realms as long as Iain and his sons lived.

Aidan concluded with wishes for happiness and a new age of goodwill and cooperation between the families. Blood ties were the strongest of all, he said, more lasting than any treaty.

The betrothal ceremony itself was mercifully brief. As it was, Leora struggled to pay attention. The two families—Aidan for Hastur and Lady Carcosse as Widow Regent of Carcosse—had already concluded the details and signed the formal contract, so it needed only the signatures of the prospective bride and groom. Jessamy placed her hands in Darren's, and Aidan bound them together with ribbons of blue and silver and gray and white. Then the ribbons were unwound and the Hastur colors given to Darren, the Carcosse to Jessamy. She fumbled, trying to twist hers into her hair, and he stepped in, tying them in a neat bow. She reciprocated by winding his around his upper arm. Congratulations and wishes for a fertile marriage mingled with cheering.

"A good beginning," Leora heard her mother say. "With the approval of both families, surely the gods will bless their life together."

I should be happy for Jessamy, Leora thought. *I suppose it's a good thing she is the one being married off to secure an alliance.* But the shadows still clung to her as if, in some corner of her mind, the war were still going on.

Formalities concluded, servants set about replacing the benches with tables. A separate table was set up at the far end, where the family settled themselves. At a signal from Aidan, servants carried tureens of soup, platters heaped with herb-crusted roasted meat and fowl, bowls of late summer vegetables and glazed fruits, baskets of nut-studded savory rolls and meat buns, pitchers of watered wine and *shallan*, and trays of condiments, enough food to feed the castle for a month.

The family table was soon taken up in lively conversation. Graciela tried to draw Lady Carcosse out, but unsuccessfully. Jessamy asked Darren questions about life at Carcosse Castle. Aidan and Connor talked about light subjects, and below their murmured tones, Leora sensed the comfort they found in another's company. Once or twice, she looked up to catch Neave's glance and wished she could sit with the Alcabra folk. She pushed her food around her plate, unable to eat more than a few bites.

The meal came to an end and everyone rose to allow the servants to clear away the dishes and then push the tables back for dancing. Musicians played the opening bars of the inaugural dance. The newly betrothed couple led off a regal *promenada*. After a few bars, they were joined by the most senior nobles, Lord and Lady Hastur and Lady Carcosse, escorted by General Berrin.

Leora watched with growing discomfort. Perhaps she would be able to slip away soon.

But here was Darren, holding out his hand in invitation. "Come now, it's not improper for us to dance together. We've been introduced and will soon be kin."

Leora racked her brains for something to say. It was difficult enough keeping track of the steps, although she'd been taught to dance as a child, as had every Darkovan.

"Now that you have met Jessamy, do you think you will suit one another?" she said.

He met her gaze with a frank expression before the figure of the dance moved them apart and then together again. "I hardly have a choice in the matter, as you well know. None of us do."

No, none of us.

"*Damisela* Jessamy is intelligent and expressive," he went on, his tone cheerful. "We may not always agree, but life with her will not be boring."

Being married to Jessamy might be exasperating or infuriating or desperately blood-boiling, but it would never be *boring*. And Jessamy had gone out of her way to be amiable to her promised husband. "You will live at Carcosse?"

"That hasn't been decided. I'll remain here until the wedding itself, which won't be until Midsummer. Jessamy and I will get to know each other, tempers will have a chance to cool, and I will contemplate a future in which our two realms are joined into one."

"That does not sound too bad."

"I regret the cost in lives and suffering that it took to arrive here. I—" The dance came to a close, and they bowed to one another according to custom. He stepped closer to her, bending down to speak softly. "*Damisela,* I cannot begin to tell you how very sorry I am about your sister and the other girl."

Caught off guard, Leora didn't know what to say. Her hands twisted themselves in her skirts as if they had minds of their own. When she found her voice, it was thick with unshed tears. "You are not at fault, *Dom* Darren. After all, *you* did not decide to attack us."

"No, but my father did."

She stood utterly still, staring at him. The sounds of music and laughter receded, drowned out by the pounding of her heart. Shadows clotted into darkness behind her eyes.

"It does not matter whether I could have changed his mind." Darren's voice sounded faint, distant. "I did not *try*, and therefore, I share a measure of blame."

Someone was screaming, crying out in wordless agony. The reek of smoke filled her nostrils.

It's a memory, nothing more. It's real, right now. I don't know what it is.

In a panic, Leora sought the nearest way out. Darren was staring at her, his face a mask of conflicting emotions. Did he think she *blamed* him?

"Just—just— Never mind. Forget what I said!" she blurted out. "It's nothing to do with you. Please enjoy the rest of the evening."

Without waiting for his reply, she rushed for the nearest opening between the dancers and fled the hall.

◆ ◆ ◆

Leora was halfway up the back stairs to the family quarters when she heard footsteps below her. She was breathing hard with exertion and remembered trauma. Leaning on the wall, she tried to compose herself. No one must see her in such a state. She must look a fright, and Aldones only knew what Darren thought of her erratic words and graceless departure. She smoothed her hair, feeling it damp with sweat. Her cheeks were even wetter, although she had no memory of crying.

Even as she turned, she felt the gentle touch of Neave's mind on hers.

Chiya, *what has distressed you so?*

"I was talking to Darren—and I couldn't help—and I remembered—" Leora said in between hiccoughs that threatened to dissolve into sobs. "He said it was his fault—because he did not try to stop it—"

She couldn't utter another word. Her throat had tightened up so that only a wheeze came out. Her entire body shook with the effort of drawing in a breath. In a panic, she grasped her sister's hands. Telepathic rapport ignited between them.

And then I was back there—on that day. And someone was screaming— in my mind. Callie, I think—but maybe both of them. Maybe me. I could smell smoke—and I had to get away!

"You poor child," Neave said aloud. "The evening was too much for you, I shouldn't wonder."

When can I leave?

"You know Father. He's thinking he'll have to persuade *Domna* Graciela and who knows how long it will take her to come around. Not to mention making what she considers suitable travel arrangements in the midst of all *this!*" Neave made a vague gesture, encompassing the entire castle.

If I have to remain here much longer—every time I turn around, a reminder—I don't know what—

"It's all right, sweetling. I can't get away or I would offer to take you there myself. But the other members of the circle don't have any specific responsibilities. It would not surprise me if your mother was perfectly happy to get them out of the castle. It won't take much to convince Luis-Jorje. Neskaya was his home for a long time, after all. I'll speak to him, and also to Connor about arranging for an armed escort. A day, perhaps two, should do it. Can you be ready?"

Leora suddenly found her voice. "I'll start packing right now!"

"*No.*" Neave was gentle but firm. "You will start packing *tomorrow.* Right now, you will get some sleep."

INTERLUDE

Midwinter Day

To Lord Aidan Valdir Hastur, Hastur Castle

Consider this a preliminary report on the welfare and status of your daughter, Leora, entrusted to my care and training. Leora came to us severely damaged in mind as well as body. In the first few tendays, it was uncertain whether she would survive with her sanity intact. In particular, her laran *channels had been disrupted by severe trauma and were degenerating instead of improving. Our first goal was to stabilize her. This process has begun. It is too soon to determine when and whether her* laran *will function normally again, given the magnitude of her talent and the seriousness of the injuries. I will keep you apprised as to any significant change in her condition. Secondarily, our healers have started a stepwise process to rejuvenate her burned tissues. We anticipate her physical recovery over the next three to five years, since the damage was not caused by burning, but the deeper layers of skin and underlying tissues were assaulted by uncontrolled, violent* laran.

Leora has settled into our community, again an ongoing process. We hold her in high regard and are concerned for her welfare. I hope that eventually she will not only be restored to health but be able to wield her very considerable Gifts as well. To do that, she must be free from unfortunate reminders of what she survived. Therefore, I insist in the strongest possible terms that communications be kept to a minimum for the next few years at least. Do not send gifts or items of a personal nature.

Mikhail Toman, Keeper

Neskaya Tower

◆ ◆ ◆

Midsummer Festival, Year Two

My dear sister,

Father has said we are not to write to you, but surely enough time has gone by for silence to be hurtful in itself. I am not much for prayer these days, but if the gods are listening, I beg them to guide your way back to health. You are ever in my heart and my thoughts.

As you can imagine, there have been changes since you

left us. Iain has been growing like a jump-up bush, although there is no sign of a beard yet. Jessamy and Darren moved to Carcosse Castle after old Lady Carcosse died of lungfever last winter. Jessamy is pregnant and expects their baby early next year. It will, no doubt, be the most perfect baby ever, and she will make sure everyone knows it. Lady Graciela will make a suitably doting grandmother.

Alcabra is diminished with Luis-Jorje leaving for Tramontana and Derik retiring. I think Derik never recovered from Melanie's death. I am not sure any of us will. I keep thinking I have finished grieving, and then I dream of her. ~~I hesitate to mention my dreams, given what you have been through. Suffice it to say, there are too many ghosts from both sides in the war. Too many accusations for which I have no answer.~~

Raymond returned to the Keep this spring, as soon as the weather made travel possible, along with a handful of adolescents who have demonstrated laran. *He's determined to help them, as there are not enough Towers or places in those we have to train them all. I think my stepmother was glad to see them leave. I would have gone with Raymond, and gladly, but Father had other plans for me. I suspect my stepmother's hand in it, but he will not say.*

So here it is, my big news. I'm being dispatched to Aillard Castle as household leronis *to Lady Bettina Aillard. She is my mother's kinswoman, and so is also mine. My only regret about leaving would be if you returned home and I was not here. The world goes as it wills, and not as you or I would have it, as the saying goes.*

~~*Connor says*~~

Please write to me at Aillard, when you are able.

Your devoted sister, Neave

◆ ◆ ◆

Midsummer Festival, Year Five

My dear daughter,

Keeper Mikhail sent a note that you are in good health and he has no present objections to our correspondence. Perhaps he thinks I can summon a messenger bird at whim! Lacking that, I must rely upon good roads and fast horses while the weather is still clement. We are all merry here at this festival season but miss you. Do the men at the Tower leave baskets of fruit and flowers outside your door, as we do at home? If not, you must imagine a mound of the mountain peaches you used to relish as a child, my gift to you.

Life has assumed a new rhythm, as it must. Jessamy and Darren are with us for the holiday and the place seems more alive than since you, Iain, ~~and~~ were children. Jessamy's boy, Esteban, is as fine a lad as could be, given your mother's tendency to indulge his every whim. I, of course, do no such thing. Iain treats him like a much-loved younger brother. I have in mind to foster Esteban here when he is of the right age in order to nurture the bonds of loyalty and honor.

I have heard from lords at Alton, Elhalyn, and, indirectly, Ardais—your mother's people—and Di Asturien, although they are not enthusiastic—proposing a yearly gathering to discuss issues of mutual interest. Perhaps a council of some sort might use debate and diplomacy to resolve differences. I am unsure of whether this is a prudent thing for all of us to be away from home at the same time, or where it might take place. Thendara, perhaps? Alton proposed meeting at his seat at Armida, but no one else seems willing to cede that much advantage. I do not know how a truce would be arranged to prevent sabotage or a surprise attack, but it is good we are considering it.

One thought that might persuade me is if we can agree upon policies for the education of young folk with laran. *Lord Elhalyn is very much in favor of that, but I am not sure whether the others agree.*

When you can travel again, you will be most welcome here at home.

Aidan, Lord Hastur

P.S. Your mother insists that I add this. Jessamy is with child again and the midwife suspects twins. I fear the castle will soon be overrun with wee ones.

◆ ◆ ◆

Midsummer Festival, Year Seven

Dear Father,

Thank you for writing to me over the years. I know that Mikhail, my Keeper, has been protective of me, but I missed you all very much, especially once I was over being so very ill. I cannot thank you enough for sending me! I have become close with my friends and teachers. Mikhail started me on lessons almost from the first. Simple things like lighting a candle or moving small objects with my mind. Once I keyed into my starstone in the third year I was here, I was allowed to work as a monitor. As you may remember, Melanie was the one who first taught me. I feel sad that I cannot tell her how far I've come. Some days, I still miss her very much.

I love Neskaya and I love the work. It feels as if my Gift is a fine horse and being part of a circle is putting it through its paces. You will be glad to hear how strong I've gotten.

Thank you, also, for your invitation to come home for the festival. To be blunt, as so many Tower folk are, I would rather stay here. Not only are my skills improving, I am doing valuable work. I do not want to interrupt either. Perhaps in another year or two, we can discuss the matter. You are my father and liege lord, so if you command it, I must come. But please, Papa, please let me stay here as long as I may.

Give my love to Iain, who must be a grown man now. And to my little nephew and twin nieces. Jessamy must have her hands full with them! And to Mother. And, of course, your dear self.

Yours,

Leora Hastur, leronis

◆ ◆ ◆

Undated, Year Nine

To Neave Hastur, *leronis*

Aillard Castle

Breda,

I owe you a thousand apologies for not having written sooner. I had so many things to tell you, things I was afraid might cause you hurt, and I did not have the words.

In the first couple of years at Neskaya, I was still very ill in mind as well as body. The nightmares, flashbacks, and panic spasms intensified once I stopped fighting them. Mikhail Toman, the Keeper here, said he would catch me if I fell—if I allowed myself to experience all the feelings, and that is what happened. The more things I remembered and felt, the more I healed. He started training me as soon as I was able, saying that strengthening control over my laran *was integral to my recovery.*

I have come to see that grief is not an enemy, it is a measure of the love we once shared. As for the men who died in the laran *assault at Carcosse Castle, you are worthy of forgiveness from their ghosts—and from yourself. Even as I am for the fire at home.*

Now comes one of the things I was afraid to tell you—Neave, you cannot imagine how glorious it is to nourish the core of my laran, *to channel it through my starstone—the starstone that is a unique reflection of my mind—and to accomplish so much! I went from the early work of monitoring and simple healing tasks to taking my place as a matrix mechanic in the circle. And now! Just yesterday, Mikhail asked me to take on the work as under-Keeper! To learn to gather the psychic energies of the entire circle into a single, interwoven whole and then direct that energy as I choose!*

Is it too painful to hear how far I have come, and that I have been given the opportunities you never had? Please say you are glad for me, and not jealous. I owe you my life and my sisterly devotion. I could not bear to hurt you.

As for other news, we have had word from Luis-Jorje at Tramontana. I wasn't surprised to hear he'd left Alcabra. He was always too ambitious to remain under Raymond's more moderate rule. Father wrote to say that Derik died last spring from a seizure of the heart. I was sad to hear it. I remember him as a gentle, kind person. Alcabra is going to need two or three more workers or else disband entirely. Father must allow Raymond to test young people from families known to have laran. *If he doesn't—well, that is his responsibility if he wants*

a circle under his command, not anything you or I can change.
  Adelandeyo, *my dear sister,*
  Leora, under-Keeper
  Neskaya Tower

PART II

Ten Years After the Hastur-Carcosse War

29

Spring came late to Neskaya. Snow still lay thick and fell nightly on the peaks. Sitting by the narrow window of her room, watching the great red sun lighten the sky to the east, Leora reflected that at home, in the Hastur realm, the first crop of barley would already be green. Blossoms would cover the apple trees in the castle orchard and the brambleberries along the roads. The cooks would be using the last of the preserves from the year before, carefully setting aside enough for tartlets for the children. She remembered the smiles that accompanied those treats almost as fondly as the pastries, and wondered who would be begging for them now. Iain, at eighteen considered a man, would doubtless think he was too old. Jessamy's eldest, Esteban, who'd be around eight now, would carry on the old custom, or the twin daughters, two years younger. She couldn't recall both girls' names, only that one had been named for Sharina.

Enough! It was past time to be up and about her duties. She slipped on her fleece-lined boots, tied a shawl crosswise around her chest, and went down to the kitchen. A cold morning's work lay before her, one that called for a hot breakfast.

In the kitchen, laughter and warm air wafted over her, bringing the aromas of sausage, herbs, and *jaco*. A trio of young apprentices trotted about, clearing away dishes and replenishing food on the side table. Catriona, one of those under Leora's tutelage, flashed a smile as she set a jar of honey on the table.

Leora helped herself from the pot of oat porridge, liberally laced with nuts and dried fruit, poured herself a mug of *jaco*, and slid onto the bench. Across from her, Ilona, one of the matrix mechanics of her circle, nodded to her in between bites of nutbread smeared with soft cheese.

A little further down the table, Padraik met her gaze. His eyes were almost colorless yet filled with light, the first thing she had noticed about him. He'd come to Neskaya from a circle no bigger than Alcabra, out by the Temora coast.

She turned to the young woman beside her. "Long night?"

"Aye, and a cold one." Mirrian feigned a shiver, although her eyes were bright. She was a talented monitor working in Mikhail's circle, and she'd been up all night. "I'll be glad when winter is over."

"Come now, Mirri, 'tis but a brisk spring morning," Catriona teased in her lilting brogue.

Mirrian laughed. "Not by Valeron standards. You know the old saying about the *cralmac* who tried to eat an ice melon out of season—"

"Not that one again!" Padraik held up on hand in protest.

"But it's a *good* story."

"One we've heard, what? a hundred times now?" Doranna paused on her way, arms cradling bowls of chopped onions and redroots for making soup. She was the oldest person in the Tower, once a powerful matrix mechanic but now mostly retired from circle work and employing her energy in organizing the needs of the Tower.

By the time Leora finished, the members of her circle were readying themselves for the day's work. It wasn't usual to do heavy *laran* labor soon after eating, but they needed the daylight.

Wrapped in the fur-lined cloak that was a gift from her father, a knitted cap pulled low over her head, and mittens swathing her hands, Leora stepped outside. Night's chill clung to the age-weathered granite walls of the original tower. When it had been built, it had soared above the village of the same name. The village had grown into a town and then a small city. Neskaya Tower had originally housed a small circle, plus the occasional Gifted youngster learning to master their *laran*. A single workroom, placed above the living quarters and classrooms, had been adequate. Now, with the Tower community grown and an increased number of students, the old structure was too small. Only Mikhail and Leora, as Keepers, had rooms to themselves, and the students and apprentices slept in bunks, four or six to a chamber. More than that, they had neither the space nor the staff to train the youngsters that came to them.

Well, she thought as she crossed the courtyard, that would soon change. The new tower was already half-built, a graceful structure of dimly glowing blue stone.

As she approached, she caught a hushed, urgent conversation between

Verity and one of the men. Verity was of a noble family, although nothing to compare with the Hasturs, and the senior member of Leora's circle. She had already been working in a circle when Leora arrived.

"… only reason she was made Keeper is how *important* her father is…"

Heat rushed through Leora. She'd heard rumors of Verity's jealousy but had dismissed them as the sort of gossip that thrives in closed communities. Certainly, no one had ever dared to say something like this to her face. Composing her features, she approached the work area.

"A fair day to you, *vai leronis!*" one of the villagers called.

Leora waved back with a grin.

"You shouldn't encourage them," Verity said, her voice almost a hiss. "They should address you with proper respect as *vai tenerésteis*. I question the wisdom of allowing them to become overly familiar with our work. Proper reverence for *laran* and its capabilities, even fear, dare I say it, is better."

And that, Leora thought, carefully shielding her mind so that no hint of her disapproval seeped through, *is yet another reason why you ought never be put in a position to decide such matters.* She gave Verity the same smile she accorded to the others, Ilona, Julien, and Rosmerta-Anne, the latter being on temporary loan from Mikhail.

Mikhail's circle had been hard at work the day before on a stack of blocks for the new tower's walls. When Leora laid her palm against the topmost block, the stone hummed to her. She sensed the pulverized starstones, too small and poor in quality for other uses, that permeated the native granite. The crystalline powder produced unique psychic properties while giving the blocks a characteristic faint blue glow. Luis-Jorje had been part of the research team during his time here. The new tower was the first successful use of his method. The work was as exacting as it was exhausting, as the mixture of stone and crystal must be precisely balanced and the individual stones shaped to fit so closely that not even the blade of a knife could pass between them.

"Verity, you will be our monitor today," Leora said, remembering her rebellion when, ignorant of its value, she had deemed that work of lesser prestige.

"But—yes, *vai tenerésteis*."

Verity would do an adequate job, perhaps a good one. She wasn't incompetent, just full of herself. If all went well, she would recognize the importance of safeguarding the welfare of the entire circle. This was not a demotion but a trust.

And a test.

Leora favored the others with a bright smile. "Shall we begin?"

They arranged themselves in a rough circle, with Leora facing the pile of blocks and the unfinished wall. On her signal, they took out their starstones, holding them in bare, cupped palms. Every Keeper had their own way of connecting to their circle. Some heard a chorus of voices in harmony. Others envisioned a tapestry of luminous, multi-colored threads. Leora pictured a river of light, growing ever stronger as more rivulets of psychic energy joined it. She wrapped the glowing stream around the topmost stone. This first block would be the trickiest, so she went slowly, testing its weight.

Lift … keep it level … steady …

The block hovered a hand's width above the one below. Leora fluttered her eyes open to check the alignment. A single brief glimpse satisfied her. Slowly, she lowered the block. So exact was the orientation and so precise her control that the top blocks slid into place without a sound.

A vision flickered across the back of her mind … a tower of the same luminescent stone against a field of golden grasses, a place of learning and refuge, welcoming generation after generation of talented youngsters …

I could build such a place. I could be its Keeper.

The first block having been set, the circle fell into a rhythm. Each new block added to the wall's height and solidity. The wall glowed in her mind as it glowed in the outer world, a place of beauty as well as strength. A place of learning. Of peace. A place that might stand for generations to come, an enduring testament to what disciplined, *laran*-Gifted minds could accomplish.

The circle lifted block after block, positioned them with meticulous precision, and lowered them into place. Leora lost herself in the soaring joy of shaping *laran* into useful work.

She sensed a hesitation in the flow, an obstacle. The lapse was so brief she could not be sure it had happened. But no, it *had*. And in that flicker of a moment, she knew why: The monitor's focus had faltered.

Ilona, one of the younger workers, gasped for breath and let out a soft cry.

Verity! Damn her!

Leora split her focus. Part of her mind held the circle steady while the other centered on the monitor. Hastily, Verity sent soothing energy to support Ilona. A heartbeat later, maybe more, power flowed easily along Ilona's channels.

With an inward sigh, Leora dissolved the circle. Her eyes opened—a flash of the sun's brightness—the blue glow of the remaining stones—the members of the circle—*her* circle, *her* responsibility.

Ilona was pale, although steady enough on her feet. "I don't know what happened." Ilona was talking too fast, gesturing with her hands. Her eyes had too much white in them. "Everything was fine, and then—I'm so sorry, Leora! I must not have been strong enough. It won't happen again. I'll try harder—"

"It is not your fault." Leora swept aside Ilona's excuses. "You must go to the infirmary to have the matron check you out. Julien! Go with her."

She sent a silent message to Doranna. *Ilona has become overtired. I'm sending her to you now.*

I'll be waiting for her, came the healer's calm mental voice.

Rosmerta-Anne lingered while the rest of the circle dispersed, all except for Verity. "How is she?"

"Doranna will make sure it's nothing more than overexertion," Leora replied. Her heart was beating too fast. The red glow of anger pressed on her. That Verity would, even for a moment, fail in her duty towards another *leronis*!

"Is there anything I can do?" Rosmerta-Anne persisted. She was Ilona's closest friend.

"You can take care of yourself," Leora said. "Get something to eat and a hot drink. You could also ask Catriona to have the kitchen send up something. I'll be in my chamber shortly."

Rosmerta-Anne headed back to the Tower in a swirl of skirts, leaving only Leora and Verity at the construction site.

"It's too cold out here and not nearly private enough for the conversation you and I need to have," Leora said. Verity would not meet her gaze. "We'll talk in my chamber." It was the one place they would not be overheard or interrupted.

The two returned to the Tower in silence. A pair of students, sitting cross-legged on the common room hearth, looked up. At Leora's stern expression, they hastily returned to their own business.

Leora closed the door to her chamber and lowered herself into the one good chair. Verity remained standing. A moment later, Rosmerta-Anne arrived with a tray of the usual sweet pastries and a jug of steaming *jaco*. Leora poured two cups and handed one to Verity. As Verity cradled her cup in her hands, a little of the taut pallor left her face.

"Verity, do you know why I asked you here?"

Verity looked acutely uncomfortable. "Because I didn't …" Her voice trailed off.

Leora felt sorry for her. *She knows she did wrong and that I have every right to scold her. Until now, her talent has insulated her against her shortcomings.* There was no point in humiliating Verity, making her even more unsuitable for circle work. Fear made a poor taskmaster in a Tower.

"Because you did not do a careful job in monitoring the circle, as I explicitly asked you to." Leora pitched her voice to be both gentle and firm. "And then, because you were not safeguarding her, Ilona became exhausted. I do not think she has any lasting damage, but she *could have.* You owe amends to her and the others, not only to me."

Verity looked away, hunching her shoulders. "Are you going to dismiss me?"

Leora let the moment linger. "When I first worked in a circle, I thought monitoring was beneath me, too. Then I realized that without a conscientious monitor, nothing can be accomplished. The *leronis* who saved my life and was my first teacher was a monitor, none better. *You* were our protector, the guardian of our physical and psychic well-being. Do you understand me?"

Mute, Verity nodded.

Now came the most challenging part. "Do you resent taking my commands because I am younger and newer to the Tower?" Leora said. "It's not a matter of *prestige* but of aptitude and mental strength. We cannot choose the talents we are born with, only how we use them for the benefit of others." She caught the flash of—was it hope?—in Verity. "Then no, I will not dismiss you. Gifts such as yours are too precious to waste. But I want you to consider what I have said. There are no small tasks in a circle. Every one of us is vital to the work."

Verity lifted her head. Her eyes were bright, but no tears marked her cheeks. "Thank you, *vai tenerésteis*. I will take what you have said to heart."

The next morning, Leora donned her warmest cloak and stout boots, and headed for the town of Neskaya. One of the oldest settlements on Darkover, it had grown over recent centuries. The original structures had been added on to, so that the upper stories leaned toward each other like old friends eager for gossip.

A short walk took her to the central market, where the city opened up to the sky. The place bustled with craftsfolk in their stalls, shopkeepers, and children, whooping as they chased one another or played with hoops and sticks. Men in furs guided shaggy chervines between carts piled with spring vegetables, barrels of pear cider, and sacks of rye and barley. Women in shawls picked over the last of the ice melons and haggled over pots of honey.

Leora paused at a food stall, where roasted nuts gave off a savory smell. "How much?"

The vendor, a grizzled man with swollen knuckles, shook his head. "For you, *vai leronis*, a gift."

Leora recognized him as one of the first patients she'd treated. By the deftness with which he worked, his fingers were still free from pain. "This is your livelihood. I must pay like everyone else." She held out a few coins.

"No, no, I canna take that." He filled a cone of folded leaves with nuts and held it out to her.

It would be unkind to refuse his gratitude. None of us fare well when we have nothing of value to offer in return.

As she continued her stroll, people moved out of her way with gestures of respect. As a healer, she had earned her place among them. As a daughter of Hastur, however, she would have been set apart. Her father might be loved but he was also feared, and that uneasiness would extend to her. As a child she'd had little awareness, but now …

Why is the past in my mind?

A ripple of psychic warmth rushed over her. Her feet stilled on the paving stones.

Padraik.

With a smile, she turned. Like her, he wore ordinary clothing, a padded jacket instead of a cloak, his fire-bright hair bare.

Padraik was not her first lover, although he was the first she truly loved. She'd waited until she was eighteen, older than most of the students, before experimenting. Doranna had furnished her with the necessary information to prevent pregnancy and then became a confidante during Leora's first encounters. And then, Padraik.

Wordlessly, she slipped her free hand through the crook of his elbow. His arm muscles tightened in response. She held out the nuts. He took them.

We could hold an entire conversation like this, she thought.

He grinned impishly. *What would be the fun of that?*

If only I'd been able to do this as a child … Leora slipped her hand from the crook of his elbow and rubbed her arms. She wasn't cold.

What troubles you, preciosa? he asked silently.

"I find myself thinking about my family. I haven't done that in a long while. I was very young when I left home."

"Does that trouble you?"

They paused to allow a laden cart to pass. In the other direction, a girl of a dozen winters was attempting to teach a puppy to walk on a leash, much to the amusement of a gaggle of younger children.

"I know what you're asking," she said carefully, "whether my family line carries the Gift of precognition."

"It might not be common knowledge, even within a family," he remarked. "Not everyone speaks of such matters freely. The Keepers at Nevarsin have begun maintaining records of the Gifts in the various Houses."

She raised an eyebrow. "I did not know that."

"Nevarsin has been keeping records for—I don't know, ten years, at least," Padraik said. A brisk breeze gusted, tousling his hair. He squinted up at the sky, deepening the lines around his eyes. "Now there is talk of arranging marriages between those with the same Gift to make it more powerful and transmitted more reliably to the offspring."

Leora imagined her mother demanding what right had strangers to pry into private affairs. Her family would likely object to their lineage being recorded in such a manner. It would be akin to scrutinizing the bloodlines of horses or hunting dogs. Then she thought of how her father had arranged a marriage to bring an end to a feud. A worthy cause, but what next? Would the day come when women were traded like bloodstock for the Gifts their children might bear?

"I repeat, what is the matter?" Padraik pulled back, a gesture more felt than actual movement. "*Preciosa*, have you been having nightmares again?"

A calming breath allowed her to collect her thoughts. "None that I can remember. I just—something's going on. Something impending. I can sense it." Her father had told her that he sometimes *knew* when something was wrong.

"You are safe here among us," Padraik said, clearly misunderstanding her intent. "Safe at home."

Home. For a decade now, Neskaya had been a place of shelter and healing. It was where she had learned to fully use her *laran*. Where she had fallen in love. Where she had carved out a place for herself, based solely on her achievements. But was it *home*?

They passed beyond the market district, wandering along crooked residential streets. Winter's chill still clung to the shadows beneath the overhanging eaves. She caught the mingled aromas of bread, honey, and spicebark, used to make fragrant pastries. Behind thick glass windows, someone was playing a plaintive air on a flute.

"Let's go back," she said. "I'm getting chilled."

He gave her a sideways glance. *You, who never complains of the cold?* But he said nothing, only walked companionably at her side.

At the Tower gates, a caravan of a dozen laden beasts was being unloaded under the watchful eyes of mounted guards. Their tabards of Hastur blue and white glimmered in the dusk.

"Gifts from your father, I'll warrant," Padraik remarked.

Leora felt irked, rationally or not, at the reminder of her special status at Neskaya. From time to time over the last ten years, her father had sent goods to the Tower: finely woven wool and *linex*, food staples, and luxury items like sweet, mildly alcoholic *shallan* and small metal tools. He meant well, saying they were "for the comfort of my daughter," but such things implied a debt.

Leora's gaze lit upon the rider who was clearly in charge. Mounted on a heavy-boned gray, he leaned over in the saddle to speak with Doranna.

The older woman, noting the approach of Leora and Padraik, turned and pointed.

"I will leave you to deal with your father's emissary," Padraik said.

Will I see you this evening?

He shook his head. "My circle is on rotation for shaping stones tonight."

She let him go, feeling vaguely guilty that she had kept him from the rest needed for a night's demanding labor.

He knows his own limits, she reminded herself. *No one* forced *him to spend the afternoon with you.*

The Hastur man swung down and, handing the reins of his horse to one of the baggage handlers, approached Leora. He bowed to her, a subtle reminder that she led two lives, one as *leronis* and Keeper, the other as her father's daughter. She did not curtsy in return. Keepers did not curtsy.

"Be welcome to Neskaya Tower," she said. "I don't know your name." Not, *I'm sorry, I don't remember you from ten years ago when I was still a young girl.*

"Derry, *vai damisela.*"

No last name. A villager or herdsman, then, come up through the ranks by hard work and merit. He was young for an officer, no more than her own years. *Derry …* She'd heard that name long ago.

She forbore from correcting his form of address. He'd meant to be respectful. And he really was very young.

"Will you—" she began, thinking to invite him inside for a hot drink, then realized that he could not abandon his duty to see the goods carried in, and his men and animals settled for the night. The Tower had originally included a chamber for visitors, but it had been taken by students. There was no possible way of accommodating the number of guards her father had deemed necessary.

"I hope you will catch me up on the news from home, once you have discharged your responsibilities," she said.

"With pleasure," he replied. Leora didn't think his cheeks could get any duskier. "Once I have—I beg your pardon, I should have presented this letter from your father straightaway." He fumbled in the scrip at his belt and brought out a packet. "I did not expect—I mean—"

"What?" Had this youth expected her to grow horns like one of Zandru's demons or to be withered by her work?

"So—" He stumbled to a halt, but not before she caught his thought, *so beautiful a lady.*

The praise stung. She wasn't accustomed to being admired for her appearance, only for her skills. Her mother would have approved, although perhaps not of the impertinence of this young villager-turned-officer in daring to think it.

Mother? Sweet Evanda, I'm thinking of home yet again! Mere coincidence, or a presentiment?

After Derry returned to his duties, she remained for a moment, gazing at the packet in her hands, and fought against the feeling that her life had just changed beyond her control.

In the privacy of her room, Leora examined the packet. The outer wrapping was of oiled *linex*. Inside lay a letter, bearing the imprint of her father's signet ring. It opened with a formal greeting, then a warmer expression of wishes for her well-being.

> *It has been too long since we celebrated Midsummer Festival together as a family. The latest communications from both you and Keeper Mikhail Toman have detailed your remarkable recovery from both your physical injuries and those resulting from the terrible events of the Carcosse war. Since then, our efforts in ensuring that another conflict never comes to pass have been successful. The initial surrender has generated a robust peace, in no small measure due to the marriage between Darren and Jessamy. Their children carry a dual heritage and shared allegiance to Hastur, thus ensuring reconciliation and amity between the two realms.*

Leora set the letter down on her lap. The style of the letter was stilted, lacking the warmth of his previous letters. *What was going on? More like, what did he want?* She took a deep breath and read on.

> *Important matters have arisen that require your presence at home. Derry will ensure your safety for the journey.*
> *The family looks forward to you joining us this season, as do I,*
> *Aidan Valdir, Lord Hastur*

There it was, the meaning clear. The letter was about more than the family celebrating Midsummer together, news about the alliance, or plans for Jessamy's children. It amounted to a demand. A summons.

She very much did not want to go. She had not set foot in Hastur Castle since the war … since the fire.

Memories clawed at her. Screaming, her throat raw with smoke and strain, the noise of furniture crashing, the reek of skin crisping in inferno heat. Laughter, high-pitched and eerie and utterly mad. Crawling along the floor, seeking refuge from the acrid smoke, of reaching, reaching for the light. The silence where so many minds had been. And falling, falling into the chill gray of the Overworld.

Breaths … she cautioned herself. *Measured, deep breaths.* Drawing upon her years of Tower discipline, she repeated the calming drill. *Heartbeat … slowing … Muscles … relaxing …*

Her vision cleared as she regained control. She wished for a reason to refuse her father's demand, but no honorable course presented itself. Her father was not only her parent but the head of her house to whom she owed fealty. She had no choice.

Leora began her farewells and explanations that same day, starting with Mikhail. He was senior to her as Keeper and in most matters the head of the Tower. Both his rank and common courtesy required her to inform him first.

He listened, his face grave. "Are you willing to return home as a dutiful daughter, even if it means giving up your place here?"

Leora heard the affection in his voice. *He is like a second father to me. How I will miss him!*

"I do not see any alternative," she admitted, sending the harmonics of regret through their telepathic rapport. "I wish there were more time to prepare, but my father expects me to return promptly."

As she left Mikhail, she prayed to whatever god might be listening that her sojourn would be a short one.

In the kitchen she found Doranna and some of the younger folk, finishing their afternoon tisane. Keeping her tone light, she announced, "I will be returning home for Midsummer Festival, so you will have to enjoy the festival without me."

"But you will be coming right back, won't you?" Ilona asked anxiously.

"Oh, no!" Catriona cried, and someone else burst out with "You cannot leave us!"

Doranna rounded on them. "Can you not see how difficult this is for Leora without your wailing and weeping? None of us is truly at liberty to choose the path of our lives—not you, not I, and certainly not a daughter of Hastur. Nevertheless, we are always able to behave with dignity and honor."

"But she might never—" Mirrian protested.

"*Exactly*. And how will your doubts change the situation?"

Murmuring, the youngsters fell silent. Mirrian hung her head. Verity looked stricken.

"Does Mikhail know?" Ilona asked.

"Of course," Leora replied. "I would not have said a word to you otherwise. You should feel free to tell others. It isn't gossip if I give you permission. As to when I shall return—" *or if,* "—that is not within my power. If I can, I will. You all—you all are my family."

"As you are ours," Ilona said as the others murmured agreement.

"Enough of this! Go prepare for the night's work," Doranna said.

The younger *leroni* filed past Leora on their way out, some with tears in their eyes, others silently saying, *Adelandeyo.* Walk with the gods.

Doranna was the last to leave. "Hurry back to us. We will miss you."

"And I, you," Leora replied with a fond smile.

There only remained Verity, standing in the shadow of the doorway. "Is it—do you have to leave because of me?"

There was no arrogance in Verity's troubled gaze, only fear and self-doubt. And the tiniest germ of hope.

"No, it's nothing to do with you," Leora said gently. "It's family business. My father has summoned me, although he has not said why."

"I see. And how long will you be gone?"

You heard me say I did not know. Ah, there was more behind the question than a simple request for information. Verity was unsure of her place in the Tower.

"We've gotten accustomed to having two Keepers," Leora said. "Losing me, even if only for a season, will make more work for everyone. Mikhail cannot do the work of two Keepers. I wonder if the prudent thing is to train another under-Keeper, don't you agree?"

Verity's shoulders tensed, but she kept her expression neutral. She seemed determined to prevent revealing even a hint of jealousy. "It would seem so."

"Have you considered putting yourself forth as a candidate?"

"I— Is such a thing possible? I thought it was up to the senior Keeper to appoint an under-Keeper. I never—no, that is not the truth. I *have* thought about it. I thought I was *entitled* to it, after all my training. And … and how good I am. But then, after the incident with Ilona, I realized I am selfish, as well. Overconfident. The very fact that I *expected* to become a Keeper made me unfit. I could not see my shortcomings."

"You accepted my rebuke in good grace. It's clear you have been examining your motives."

Verity startled, then looked both pleased and contrite. "I don't understand. Are you saying—do you mean—do you think I could train as an under-Keeper?"

"I cannot say," Leora admitted. "I have never evaluated a candidate for under-Keeper. Yet the question is worth asking. You are talented and capable. It will do no harm to ask as long as you are willing to accept the answer, even if it is one you do not like."

Verity murmured, "Thank you."

Leora thought of Neave and her dreams of a life in a Tower. Had she once aspired to be a Keeper? What a waste it was to relegate her to the everyday, solitary tasks of a household *leronis*.

Drawing the conversation to a close with a few words of encouragement, she left to begin packing.

◆ ◆ ◆

At the end of a long day, Leora forced herself to eat a proper meal in the near-deserted kitchen before dragging herself upstairs to her chamber. She crawled beneath the comforter—

Only to find that her bed was already occupied. Padraik rolled on his side to face her, catalyzing their rapport.

"I knew you'd be tired," he murmured into her hair. *And cold.*

She wriggled closer into his embrace. *I'm not cold now.*

And fell asleep. And dreamed of the first time they'd met, of the light in his eyes that seemed to encompass more brilliance than the sweep of stars and more depth than the sea off Temora. Of the way he'd touched her the first time they'd lain together, of how the barriers of skin and thought had dissolved so that each experienced what the other was feeling. Of how her heart had opened to him, as his to her.

Leora roused when he slipped out of bed shortly before dawn. The scent of his skin lingered on her pillow. She washed and dressed with a vague sense of regret, wishing they had made love.

She entered her parlor to find a hot breakfast waiting on the table beside the lit fireplace. *I am three people. I was a girl in my father's house, ignorant and innocent, and I can never go back to that even if I wanted to. Then I was a poor, broken thing beset by dreams of fire and death. Now I am a woman with power of my own, and desires. Who will I be when I leave here?*

You will be yourself, she imagined Padraik's mental voice, *ever and always the woman I love.*

But was love enough?

Leora stood at her window, wrapped in an old shawl, watching the dawning sun edge over the jagged ridge to the east. The sky shimmered, more gray than pastel, but within the hour, richer tones would wash the sky. Breakfast would be served for those who'd worked through the night, loaves fresh from the ovens, boiled eggs, and pots of porridge. Food and laughter and always the communion of minds.

So much to love, so much to lose.

She pulled on her everyday tunic that had once been dyed green before time had faded it. She loved its softness, like an old friend wrapping her in its arms. Her mother would be appalled.

The kitchen was almost empty, except for Derry and one of Mikhail's apprentices, a russet-haired lad with an empathy for winged creatures. The boy rose from where he'd been sitting, freckled cheeks going red. Leora was seized with regret that she would not get to witness his talent blossom.

"Good morn," she said to Derry as she picked up a squashed seed cake and poured a mug of *jaco*. The lone apple at the bottom of the bowl had a bad spot. She made a face and put it back.

Derry said, "Eat hearty, *vai damisela*."

"If we are to travel together, you must call me Leora, as everyone here does. It's my name."

"'Twould not be proper respectful. You are my lord's daughter."

'Twould be common sense! But she refrained from saying so. The poor boy, if a young man her father had entrusted with her safety could be called a *boy*, was bashful enough already.

As she finished eating, Derry carried his plate to the sink. "We'll go as soon as you're ready."

"Of course." She summoned a smile. "Everything is packed and waiting."

She went upstairs to fetch her baggage. Her saddlebags sat, neatly packed, on her chest. But here were a cloak and outdoor boots, glossy with water-repellant polish, as well as a cap of fuzzy rabbit-horn yarn, a pair of mittens, and a woolen riding skirt, split for ease, with suede panels on the insides of the thighs. They had been left here while she was at breakfast, as well as the silver brooch in the shape of a *kireseth* blossom. That must be from Padraik. And the rest—from Ilona, with touches of Mirrian and Verity.

Gifts—*goodbye* and *I love you*—presented with quiet respect for her privacy.

Tears prickling her eyes, she changed into the traveling clothes, picked up the cloak, slung the saddlebags over her shoulder, and went downstairs.

Outside the front door, robed Tower workers parted for her, silently enveloping her in warmth. She slowed her step as she passed each familiar face. Padraik, a smile hovering over his lips. Mikhail, solemn as ever. Doranna. Ilona and Catriona, Verity. Julian and the others. There was no need to speak. Everything of importance had already been said.

Her father's entourage waited in the yard, holding the reins of their horses and the lead lines of baggage animals. Tails swished lazily, and here and there a horse pawed the pavement.

Derry swung into the saddle, signaling the others to do the same. A young woman of Leora's age was already astride a sturdy chervine, bulging canvas bags tied to her saddle. A smile spread across her features, strongly reminiscent of Doranna's.

"M'lady," the young woman said with a dip of her head.

"I'm sorry, should I know you?" Leora asked as one of the guardsmen held out his hands for her saddlebags and secured them to a pack animal.

"Name's Duna." She elongated the vowel so that it sounded like *Doooona*. "The *leronis* Doranna yonder is me cousin's aunt, and she sent me to tend to you."

Doranna would think of such a thing, Evanda bless her!

"I'm glad to have you," Leora replied. In the past ten years of Tower life, she'd not had to worry about the proprieties of a woman traveling alone with a group of men, even if they were loyal to her father.

Waving aside Derry's offer of assistance, Leora gathered the reins in one hand and fistful of mane in the other, and swung into the saddle. Her split skirts settled neatly to either side.

They set off at an easy pace with Derry in the lead and Duna riding beside Leora, with the other guardsmen arrayed to defend them. The chervine's legs were a good deal shorter than those of Leora's horse, but they went slowly enough so the difference did not matter. Leora tried to relax in the saddle, but it seemed her body had forgotten how. She knew how to manage a horse but had not ridden in years, and she hoped she would not be too sore the next day.

◆ ◆ ◆

When they stopped the first evening, Leora tried to not groan as she dismounted. Like everyone else in the Tower, she'd tried to keep in shape when her schedule permitted. An occasional ride on one of the Tower's few horses or a stroll through the village had not prepared her for a long day on the trail.

When Leora attempted to stand on her own, pain shot through her muscles. The insides of her thighs felt as if they were on fire. Her knees wobbled like jelly.

"M'lady, our tent is ready," Duna said, kindness in her voice. "One of the men will look after the horse."

"It isn't right," Leora said, trying to ignore the pain. "I should be responsible—"

"Just one evening, then. I've got something that'll ease you summat."

Once within their shared tent, Duna extracted a stoppered bottle from her bags. Its contents smelled of joint-ease and other, less familiar herbs. After making sure the tent flap was securely fastened, she coaxed Leora out of her skirts and applied the liniment sparingly to the painful areas. The balm felt fiery, causing Leora to draw in her breath sharply.

"'Tis fierce at first," Duna admitted, "but 'twill fade anon."

"It's— Oh!" Leora exclaimed as the warmth of the balm penetrated. "It's feeling better already." She had learned simple herb lore as a novice, but the *leroni* at Neskaya relied on *laran* healing whenever possible. She vowed that next time, she would be better prepared.

After a simple meal and preparations for the night, which included arranging her boots to prevent them from becoming nests for scorpion-ants, Leora snuggled under the blankets. One moment, she was shifting about, trying to ease her hips against the hardness of a single blanket on the ground, and the next, she drifted through a misty, halfway place, neither waking nor sleeping nor the Overworld.

She dreamed of Padraik and of trying to get home, but whether that home was Hastur Castle or Neskaya or that other place—a place of golden grasses waving in sweet summer winds, from her childhood visions—she could not tell.

◆ ◆ ◆

The road led through small villages where they encountered farmers with laden carts pulled by chervines and an occasional herdsman with his dog. It wound along the open, wind-swept slopes before descending through groves of pitch pine and blackleaf. Eventually, meadows opened out, bright with sun and songbirds. The territory through which they passed became more and more familiar. The contours of the land stirred Leora's memories, the shape of the hillsides and the smell of the breeze, even the hues of the wildflowers. Her spirits rose, but also her sense of dread.

Hastur Castle appeared in the distance near the end of a day's travel. A patchy wind sent the blue and silver banners fluttering. Within those stone walls, the memory of smoke still clung to the air, to the stones. Smoke and tears and terror.

I will not dwell on the past, but neither will I shrink from it. I am a daughter of Hastur, a trained leronis. *A Keeper. I will face my fears.*

They came down from the hills, following the main road to the castle, where the gates opened to receive them. Leora's parents and Iain waited on the castle steps. Connor stood at his usual place at Aidan's right shoulder, beside Lorcan, who was even grayer than Leora remembered.

Beaming, Aidan came toward her. "Daughter, what a joy it is to have you with us again."

Leora slipped her hands into his. This was not the Tower, where even a casual physical touch was shunned. This was family. This was home. She felt the warmth of her father's skin, the calluses, and the knuckles swollen with arthritis. The vitality of his grip.

"Oh, my darling girl!" Hands fluttering, Lady Hastur swooped down to embrace Leora. Then, drawing back: "Blessed Callista, how you've grown!"

Leora noticed the frosting of gray in her mother's hair, the lines around her eyes and mouth, and the sagging of the skin of her neck. Ten years had passed, but they had not made her mother any less fretful.

She cannot help being what she is, Leora thought.

Iain came forward, grinning. His chestnut hair tumbled over shoulders made muscular from hours on the training yards. The eyes that met hers were gray and steady.

Leora noted Lorcan supervising accommodations for her escort, with special care for Duna. Stable boys led away the horses and pack animals.

Graciela insisted on conducting Leora inside. "Was your journey arduous? We'd planned to have a quiet family dinner for your first night home, but of course, if you are fatigued, I will have a meal sent up to your room. You'll have ample time to meet our other guests at the Festival banquet and then the ball."

"After the first few days, I did not find travel overly tiring," Leora replied as they passed the exterior doors. "The weather was splendid for the most part. The captain of my escort was a personable young officer—Derry, do you know him?—and for a lady's maid I had a capable village woman. She not only saw to my comfort, she turned out to be an excellent trail cook. All in all, the journey furnished me with many amusing stories. Perhaps I'll have the chance to tell you some of them."

"I've had your old room made over," Graciela said as they reached the level of the family residences. "I hope it pleases you. I had no idea what you're accustomed to."

"I'm sure it will be fine," Leora said, thinking that it was bound to be more luxurious than her chamber at Neskaya.

The hallway was much as she remembered, except the carpet was new, a tree pattern in shades of blue. Passing the room that had been Sharina's, Leora felt a pang. Her feet slowed. Grief took her by surprise.

Her mother, unaware, continued to Leora's old room and flung the door open. "Here it is! I hope you will find it adequate."

Leora went inside. The proportions of the room, and the shape and position of the windows were all as she remembered, but nothing else was familiar. The bed was wide enough for two, with a headboard carved into garlands. An armoire and chest decorated with the same bell-shaped blossoms comprised the rest of the furniture.

What am I to do in such a room? She could hardly fault her mother for having no idea what she might prefer. This was a child's room … or one for two children. *Ah, that makes sense. Jessamy's daughters, when they visit.* The clues were everywhere.

A tap on the door heralded a pair of maidservants with an ewer of warm water scented with rosalys petals, towels, and a tray bearing an assortment of mountain peaches, spicebread, and a pitcher of *jaco*. Graciela oversaw the placement of everything, then said, "I'll leave you to settle in and will send word when dinner is ready."

Alone now, Leora lowered herself to the bed. Her mother was trying so hard. Did she feel guilt for Sharina's death and Leora going away? Would

Graciela see the absence as exile when Neskaya Tower had been a life-saving sanctuary? Again she thought, *My mother is who she is,* and felt sad that the ten years had not given Graciela any deeper understanding.

I will not be here any longer than I can help. I will return to Neskaya, my true home.

She sprang to her feet at yet another tap at the door, this time Duna with her saddlebags.

Duna looked around the room, her lips pursed. "Fancy, this."

Leora set the saddlebags on the foot of the bed. "Is there anything else? Are you being well looked after?"

"Ach! Fancy place, this," Duna repeated. "D'you want a proper lady's maid, then?"

"Gods, no! I never had a servant at the Tower and can manage well enough on my own."

"Oh, I see that, aye." Duna began unpacking. "You manage so well that you'd leave all the wrinkles 'til the last moment." She held up the single decent outfit Leora had brought. The tunic and underdress had originally been dyed green, now faded to gray. And, indeed, they were rumpled.

"Shall I take this down to the laundry, then, and see what a little steam can do?" Duna said.

Leora sighed in surrender.

The corners of Duna's mouth twitched as she carried the tunic and underdress away. The room seemed empty, almost desolate, without her presence.

Answering her father's summons had been the occasion of coming home. Now that she was here, Leora had her own business to attend to. She made her way down one corridor and along another servants' passage until she reached the base of the old tower.

The beams of wood across the door had been fastened on, but the nails were rusty. A few determined jerks freed them. Darkness flowed from the opening. She inhaled, her nostrils flaring, but there was no reek of soot or char. No taint of singed hair. Of flesh crisped and blackened. For an instant, she almost lost her nerve.

Was she torturing herself, probing an old wound to see if it would still bleed?

Old wound? Old embers, more like.

Holding one palm horizontal, she summoned a ball of faint, ghostly blue light. She was one of the few at Neskaya who could create it. It wasn't very bright, and she could not sustain it for long. For the moment, it would be enough to *see by*.

A rope had been threaded through rings set into the stone of the wall. She made out the lowest stair, and then the next.

Up, and up …

Was the air here staler, with a lingering acrid odor? Or was that simply the result of a stairwell long closed off?

A stair creaked ominously as she stepped on it. The wood gave way beneath her. The ball of blue light winked out. She grabbed for the rope, but it came away in shreds. Scrambling for balance, she caught herself against the wall.

The intensity of her panic caught her aback. Her breath came in gasps and her pulse rocketed through her skull. Standing there in the dark, her fingers pressed against the stone, she felt like a child dragged into an old horror-dream. If she ran away now, she would admit the grip those terrible memories still held over her.

In … Out. … Slow the heart. Focus the mind.

Sharpen the will.

When she stretched out her hand again, the blue light was brighter than before.

The walls, illuminated by the ball of blue light, showed greasy, grayish streaks. The air tasted sour. Musty. As she climbed, the streaks darkened and blended into one another. Ahead lay the landing that led to the tower workroom. The rock surrounding the opening was completely black. Nothing remained of the door leading to the workroom. It gaped before her, a void. A maw to swallow her up.

My fault echoed through her skull. *I didn't stop it … I couldn't. My fault.*

Standing on the threshold, she clenched her fists so tightly, her nails dug into her palms. The physical pain mirrored the agony in her mind. Then, as if Evanda herself had wrapped Leora in grace, the pain lifted. Her fingers relaxed.

She stood in a hall of mirrors, each one casting back a different image. Here she was as a carefree child, there an adolescent near death from threshold sickness. Here—and it took a moment to look carefully at this one—the girl who had been dragged, near death, from this very room. Here the grieving teenager.

Here the *leronis*, gaining in skill and sureness.

And here the Keeper, mistress of her own conscience. Commander of her own life, answering to no man.

Not even my father, for all that I love him. Love, not obedience.

None of what had happened here had been her responsibility. Not the war with Carcosse. Not her burgeoning *laran*. Not Callista's headstrong nature or her volatile fire-starting Gift. Not Sharina's insistence on being present when Callista defended the castle. Those choices had not been hers to make.

I wish Callista had chosen otherwise. I wish I had been able to persuade her. I wish Sharina had stayed behind.

Leora had been a child, and she had lost her friend and her beloved younger sister. It was possible to feel regret and grief, and to know at the same time that none of this was her fault.

Her mind still reverberating, Leora headed in the direction of the family dining room. As she passed under an arch between one hallway and another, she failed to see Connor, hidden until they were almost upon each other. He reached out to steady her, and his fingers curled around her forearm. *Laran* impressions flooded her. On the surface, surprise and apology, but surging up from beneath came a clear thought—the girl he remembered had grown into a woman—a woman who reminded him of her sister—

Leora caught images of Neave's face, her shifting expressions, the curve of her lips, the brush of her hand against his, the sweetness of her breath, again her eyes flashing in temper, her voice soaring in song—

—and then a rush of such longing, such heartache, that Leora, overcome, wrenched her hand away.

He loves her still. His heart has never ceased to yearn for her.

Leora took a step back, slamming her telepathic barriers tight.

"Are you all right?" he asked. "I did not injure you?"

"No, of course not. I'm only a little surprised. It was my fault entirely."

He offered her a courtly bow and the hint of a smile. "You have been gone for a long time if you have forgotten that such a mishap is *never* the lady's fault."

At this, she laughed.

He glanced down at her. "It is good to see you cheerful."

"I was rather …" she hesitated, searching for the right word, "… grim when I left for Neskaya."

"Your father acted out of love for you."

She'd forgotten how close Connor and her father were. "I am grateful that he sent me to the only place where I might find healing both of mind and body."

"I am happy to hear it. I was on my way to the family dining room. Would you care to accompany me?" He stepped back to allow her to precede him.

She inclined her head in acknowledgment and said, her tone deliberately light, "So is this to be a gala occasion? A grand family reunion for the Festival?"

"Alas, no. I am sorry to tell you that *Domna* Jessamy has been forbidden to travel by her midwife. Her husband will not leave her side, as is proper." He did not sound in the least distressed.

"I understand they're devoted to one another." Leora slowed her step, as they had almost arrived at the family dining room. "Who would have thought it, the way they were brought together?"

"They had as good a chance at happiness as any other couple, embarking on their lives together without any forewarning of one another's shortcomings." Connor spoke with a hidden intensity that left her wishing for telepathic contact. Was it sorrow? Or envy? He bowed Leora into the room, where her parents and younger brother stood around the fireplace, and then left, closing the door behind him.

Leora remembered family meals in this very same room. Likely at this very same table. It had been set for four in an informal style, she noticed with relief. A pair of servants stood beside the inner door.

"Sister, you've come!" Iain performed a precise, formal bow, showing off his mastery of the nuances of courtly greeting. He looked as if he would like to hug her but was trying to behave in a more dignified manner. He was well-grown, a young man rather than a boy, with his mother's dark hair, a dimple at one corner of his mouth, and a pleasing baritone voice. He seemed a bit full of himself but with such goodwill toward the world and delight in seeing her that she could not hold it against him.

"Little brother," she replied and was answered by a disarming grin.

"Come and sit down," Graciela said as she gestured to the servants to bring out spiced wine. "We are so glad to have you home again."

Does she think I intend to stay? flared in Leora's thoughts. She kept her voice carefully neutral. "I am happy to see you, too, Mother."

"So now you are home again," her father said, "and that must be very strange after so long. We've all changed a great deal. Jessamy is married and a mother three times."

"So you said in your letters. Also they are the most admirable children ever born, am I right?"

Aidan chuckled. "I do believe so."

"They are very fine, if a trifle spoiled," Graciela said, although her words carried no reproach.

"And who has been doing the spoiling?" Aidan teased.

Leora relaxed in the easy banter between her parents. Iain gave her a slantwise look that conveyed his own opinion of doting grandparents.

"And as for you, my Leora," Aidan said, "you left here a little girl and have returned a grown woman. A *leronis*. What has your life been like at Neskaya?"

Leora paused as a servant brought out a tureen of vegetable soup and baskets of bread. She definitely did not wish to talk about how ill she'd been when she'd arrived at Neskaya. Or the soothing touch of the healers' minds on hers, slowly peeling away layers of horror and grief.

Or her first stirrings of sexual awareness. Her first infatuation. The first time she'd embraced a lover. And then Padraik. These memories, too, were hers alone. Her family had no right to any of them.

Her parents were well into the meal, leaving her with the impression the question had been a polite conversation opener, not genuine curiosity. Iain's expression, however, reflected a hunger for stories of life beyond Hastur's walls.

"Perhaps the best way to explain is to tell you about my work. We've been constructing a new tower." She described the process of shaping and placing the blocks using only the power of the mind. "We must fit the blocks so closely that not even a blade of grass can pass between them."

"I have heard of this craft," Aidan said, "but I had no idea you were engaged in it."

"I do not think it proper for a daughter of Hastur to be doing menial work as if—as if she were a stone mason," Graciela said, holding out her wine goblet to be refilled. "Those are worthy trades for common men, not a noble lady such as yourself. What are they thinking, these Tower folk, to require it of you?"

"They do not *require* it of me," Leora answered. "It is my *choice*. You make it sound as if such work is beneath me, but the opposite is true. All honest work is honorable, and none so much as that which uses our talents to the fullest."

Graciela sniffed. "I don't know where you acquired such notions. We believed Neskaya Tower to be a place of decorum or we would not have entrusted your welfare to them. I see we were mistaken."

"My lady wife, we were *not* mistaken," Aidan said in the brief pause when she drew breath and Leora stared at her, appalled. "Quite the opposite. Leora has returned to us, not only healed but grown, a lady in her own right."

Color rose to Graciela's cheeks. "Your pardon, my husband. You are quite correct. The folk at Neskaya have done wonders for our girl. Leora, do not take my words amiss. I spoke out of concern for you, nothing more."

Perhaps she has *changed*, Leora thought. It would cost her nothing to be gracious in the face of her mother's struggles to understand a life so different from her own.

"Of course, Mother," she said with the most sympathetic smile she could manage. "How could you know of the work of a Keeper? It must be very strange to you, so unlike your own skills."

"Yes, that is true," Graciela admitted with a sigh. "I confess I followed very little of what you just said."

"Tell us more!" Iain said eagerly.

Leora searched her memory for an amusing detail or anecdote. "My friend, Padraik, who is a matrix mechanic—that is, a highly skilled circle worker—he hears the stone *singing* in his mind, and when he and the circle sing *back*, the stone shifts to come into harmony with their intent."

"The stone singing inside the mind of a man." Aidan shook his head, bemused. "Iain, what do you think of this? Would you like to train for it, like your sister?"

"I think we live in a very strange world, Father. I am just as glad, though, to not sing to rocks. I can't imagine how that might be done."

"Iain!" Graciela exclaimed.

"It's all right. I understand what he means," Leora said. Whatever her younger brother's talents, a passion for psychokinetics was not among them. "We don't have to do everything equally well. I would be hopeless at swinging a sword, and if I am not mistaken from the state of your shoulders, you have spent many hours on the practice fields. Much like your needlework, Mother, for I confess that my stitches have not improved over the years."

"I don't expect you've been practicing much." Graciela made an indifferent gesture. "I suppose all this will make an interesting story to tell your children."

My ... children?

"That is a topic for another discussion," Aidan said, casting a severe look at Graciela. "For now, we are here to celebrate the Festival. Let us simply enjoy one another's company."

Leora could not bring herself to make polite small talk after her mother had hinted why she'd been summoned home. Living among telepaths, she'd come to rely upon truthfulness. Her friends at Neskaya did not always share their intimate concerns and politeness required respect for privacy, but to continue—how had her father put it?—*enjoying one another's company* struck her as deceitful.

"I'm sorry, Father. I'm fatigued from my journey and I am not good company. Perhaps we might continue our visit tomorrow?"

"Of course, my darling, you need your rest," Graciela said.

Iain scrambled to his feet, Aidan rising more slowly.

Aidan held Leora's chair for her.

"Tomorrow, then," he murmured. "Come to my office after breakfast and we will talk, you and I."

Leora agreed and left the dining room with a Keeper's icy dignity. She felt as if a sword hung over her head and there was no escape.

She did not return immediately to the chamber that had once been hers but wandered the less-frequented corridors of the castle. The courtyards tempted her with their gardens of night-blooming flowers, but she could not be certain of finding solitude there. She wanted to go home. Home being Neskaya Tower. Home being Padraik and Doranna and even Verity, who for all her faults was *one of us*.

The next morning, after breakfast in the kitchen with the amused cook who remembered a small girl stealing honey buns, Leora went to her father's office. From inside came the sound of two masculine voices, their tones easy and conversational. Even without *laran*, she would have recognized them.

She knocked and waited until the door opened. Connor stood there. She greeted him courteously, wishing him a fair day. "I've come to speak with my father. Would you be so kind as to ask if this is a convenient time?"

"Leora?" came Aidan's voice from inside. "Daughter, come in. Come in!"

Connor slipped into the chair beside the desk at Aidan's right side, a paxman's place. Aidan gestured for Leora to take the other unoccupied chair. "Please be seated."

This is not a friendly chat. It's a negotiation. So be it!

Gazing back at him, she realized that, for all his fierce intelligence and trappings of authority, her father had aged over the last decade. He was still vigorous, but silver glinted at his temples. Lines bracketed his eyes and mouth. The skin beneath those piercing gray eyes sagged, as if he had passed too many sleepless nights over the years.

This was her father, whom she dearly loved and whose love she never doubted. She never wanted either love to change.

We must not become adversaries, no matter what comes to pass.

"You must have had a very good reason for your invitation, beyond the simple wish to see me again," she said gently.

An expression flitted across his eyes: *I have never ceased to miss you, my Leora.*

Nor I, you, she answered in her own heart.

"Once the world was a less complicated place," he said, his tone shifting to oratorial. "In that world, I would have tended my lands, decided disputes among my people, married, and raised children, and lived to see them and their children happy and secure. But the world goes as it will, and not as you or I would have it."

He meant that neither one of them was truly the ruler of their fate. He sounded as if he'd rehearsed the words, thinking each phrase through.

"We have not been blessed to live in *ordinary times*. Everywhere we see feuds springing up like tinderweed, igniting into warfare or festering like that nasty trouble between the Ridenows and the ruffians on their borders. Most of these problems we can do nothing about, but from time to time, one arises that we *can*."

He paused, watching her to make sure she understood. When she nodded, he went on, "Hastur is at peace with its neighbors, by the blessings of the gods. Carcosse flourishes, as do Jessamy and Darren and their children. These children will inherit two lands bound by friendship and blood."

"You see this harmony as enduring?" she said.

"I do, and an example to follow. I see others in my position seeking solutions before conflicts erupt into violence," Aidan said. Connor nodded in agreement, his expression grave. "One such realm is linked to us by bonds of marriage instead of blood. I speak of Aillard, the family of my first wife."

This surprised Leora. "Neave's mother's family? Are we at odds with them? How did that come about?"

"At odds?" He shook his head. "No, quite the opposite. Since Fiona-Maria's death, I have remained on cordial terms with her family. The Aillards are close allies, and in today's world, we may need them. They may call on my aid, even as they would if my wife were still living. Now they face a difficult situation with their neighbors, the Lindars. Lord Aillard has appealed to me to intervene before frictions escalate. To avoid a war like the one we went through."

He was choosing his words to remind her of what she had survived. What they both had lost. Why open the conversation this way? Did he mean her to play a part in this peace-making? She needed more information.

"What is the cause of the dispute?" she asked. "And how long has it been going on?"

"The quarrel reaches back at least five generations," Aidan explained, "long enough that no one now living can say for certain what the original issue was. Resentments can linger long past their beginnings, as we saw with Carcosse."

"Sometimes they die down on their own, with neither side the poorer," Connor said. "But this is not the case. There has already been one bloody altercation that only by the blessing of Aldones did not erupt into widespread violence."

Into war, you mean.

"We must heal this rift before it gets any worse," Aidan continued. "The present truce is fragile."

Leora shifted her weight in her chair to signal that she was open to hearing more. "Go on."

"The war with Carcosse ended with an alliance by marriage between the heir to Carcosse and one of my daughters." His voice was level, his gaze unwavering. "I would make the same kind of bond between Aillard and Lindar. Lord Octavien Lindar is a widower with an heir, Kennard, as well as a younger son and two very young daughters. The Aillards, however, have two sons but no living daughters. You see the problem?"

In an instant, revelation struck. A dozen clues crashed together in her mind. She glanced at Connor and read the truth in the tightening around his eyes.

"You are bound to the Aillards …" she said, turning her gaze once more to her father, "and *you* have a daughter of marriageable age. Me."

Eyes shadowed, he nodded. "You have always been quick of wit."

She dismissed the compliment. "It was not hard to figure out. First your letter, talking about marriages and alliances. Mother confirmed it with her comment about children."

"Ah, yes." A smile lightened his features. "You can hardly fault her eagerness. She loves coddling Jessamy's children and will do the same to Iain's when it is time. And yours."

Leora forced herself to answer calmly. "Father, it is no business of hers—or yours—whether I bear children. Or marry, for that matter. You have not considered *my* wishes. *My* dreams. *My* hopes for my own life."

"You mean as a *leronis*. Like Neave."

She lifted her chin, certain that he would understand, and noticed that Connor was sitting very still, his face giving away nothing.

Aidan's expression reflected the care with which he chose his next words. "Daughter, I am glad beyond words to see you restored to health. I will be forever grateful to the folk at Neskaya for that. My greatest hopes in sending you there have been fulfilled. It was necessary to give you training to preserve your sanity. I accept that. But it was never my intention that you be established there permanently, as a Keeper or anything else."

Circumstances change. People change. I changed.

"Why must *you* be the one to solve this problem?" she demanded. "Let the parties involved find another intermediary or some other solution! After all, the Aillards are related to you by marriage, not blood."

Aidan frowned. "That is true. I could disavow my obligations to them, but I will not do so. Even if I did not hold my first wife's family in high esteem, the matter goes beyond a single treaty."

"How so?" Leora asked, genuinely puzzled.

"In appealing to us, the Aillards have placed themselves in our debt," Connor put in.

"I wrote to you about the formation of a council of Comyn lords," Aidan said. "It is on the cusp of becoming a reality, in no small part due to my efforts. Since the Carcosse war, no one has dared challenge us. I want more than fear and intimidation for Hastur. I want respect and influence. I want the word of a Hastur to carry weight throughout Darkover."

"That's … I had no idea you were so ambitious, Father."

"This is not *ambition*!" His voice rang through the room. "*Ambition* is what drove Merryl Carcosse to deceive, manipulate, and then lay siege to us here. My goals are different. I want this new council to be a place where disagreements can be peaceably settled. Our world is changing through political alliances, yes, but more significantly, the uses of *laran* and the training of those who wield it."

Leora's head spun. He meant weapons but also beneficial techniques. Healing. Fire-fighting chemicals. Better ways of constructing buildings. And what more might the future bring? Managing storms? Sending messages over long distances? Communicating with birds and beasts?

Or even more terrible ways of slaughter?

Her father saw his part in the Aillard-Lindar treaty as nonnegotiable. She would not waste breath to change his mind. But surely, there might be an alternative to what he proposed for her.

He'd spoken of a daughter of marriageable age. Actually, there were two eligible Hastur women, Neave being the other. But if she suggested Neave as another choice, that would amount to sacrificing her sister, to whom she owed her life. Even if Neave were acceptable despite her age, such a marriage would forever separate her from Connor.

Her mind raced to the moment she'd run into Connor and his mind had been open to hers. *He loves her still. His heart has never ceased to yearn for her.*

She could not propose Neave as a substitute.

"Surely, there must be another acceptable candidate," she said. "That way, you could keep the benefits of my serving at Neskaya. For instance—could you not betroth Iain to one of the Lindar daughters? They may be young now, but so is he. Children grow. The years will give them time to get to know one another."

"That is not possible," he said in a tone that conveyed he had already considered and rejected the idea. "Iain is my heir and cannot live anywhere else, certainly not at Lindar Castle, and the Lindars will not consider an alliance with Aillard if their daughter lives here."

"One of Jessamy's twins?" Leora heard the rising desperation in her voice.

"Daughter," Aidan said, leaning forward across the desk, his expression intent. "I have thought of that. I have racked my brains for another way. There is none. Think what another war would mean. We survived the battle with Carcosse. You know the cost."

Children maimed and dead, answered her memory. *Smoke and screams. Burned carcasses that were once men and horses.*

Then he said softly, "I would not part with you for any lesser cause."

Leora weighed her dreams against the memory of Sharina's dying cries and the longing in Connor's heart. In a moment of sudden, heart-wrenching clarity, she found her hopes unworthy.

As a daughter of Hastur, I am bound by duty.

"What you say deserves careful thought." She hoped he could not hear the sorrow in her voice. "A response to such a weighty proposition ought not to be given lightly."

"I have not given them an answer," Aidan answered, his tone grave. "I told them that the decision was not solely mine. However, it must not be delayed overlong. The current truce is precarious and might fracture at the slightest perceived offense. We must resolve the situation speedily."

"Very well, then." She rose, her skirts swirling around her. "You will have my answer after dinner."

◆◆◆

Leora could not bring herself to return to her chamber. She wandered from one area of the castle to another. The family residence held too many echoes, too many reminders. Instead, she peeked into the hidden passage that she'd used for childhood adventures. How long ago that had been! Sharina had been her constant companion then, but the memory brought no solace.

From the musicians' gallery, Leora watched Lorcan's assistants and a small horde of maids and footmen prepare for Midsummer Festival. Once the activity and color, the bright ribbons and vases overflowing with flowers, would have filled her with anticipation. Now they heralded a celebration she did not know if she dreaded.

Outside her mother's solarium with its door of honey-pale wood, she paused. From within came women's laughter and a gentle arpeggio played on a *ryll*. All she had to do was lift the latch and enter. There would be sunlight, warmth, and inconsequential conversation. Her mother would be delighted.

Is this what I would be choosing?

There must be a third path, neither the cloistered Tower nor a conventional marriage, but she did not know what it was. Not yet. But where to seek the answer?

It was impossible to think here, within the confines of memory and stone. The air was too thick to breathe. She went down to the stables, where she had one of the castle horses saddled for her. The old chestnut gelding was as placid as any used to teach young children. She reined it onto the main road from the gates and nudged it with her heels. It shifted into a lope, so easygoing she felt each separate hoof strike the ground.

She reached the curve in the road where the hill hid the castle from view. At a shift of her weight, the horse slowed to a walk and then halted.

Within her, a voice wailed, *It isn't fair! I'm a Keeper. Doesn't my father realize what that means? Such a Gift ought not to be tossed aside, and for what? A political treaty?*

Kicking her feet free of the stirrups, she slid to the ground. Her mind churned with questions she could not answer. Wasn't she entitled to the life she had worked so hard for? Didn't she have value in her own right, not just as a thing to be bartered away, no matter how noble the cause?

And hadn't she already given her heart?

Ah, Padraik …

No, she answered herself, that world was behind her now. Her father's summons had brought it to a decisive end. A summons she had answered, had *chosen* to answer.

The last ten years had not been truly hers. It belonged to someone else's life. Her future lay elsewhere.

And yet … in the far corners of her memory, a Tower beckoned. Blue-white radiance filled the windows. Around it stretched a sea of golden grasses, waving in the breeze.

Arilinn.

She *knew* it, the way she knew the beating of her own heart and the light behind her dreams. Was she called to give it up, too? Did it call to her from the future?

Or was this marriage alliance the path that would lead her there?

The chestnut stood like a rock, the only movement the occasional flick of an ear or swish of its tail at an errant fly. Turning, she laid one cheek against the coarse-haired neck. Pressure welled up in her chest, threatening to close up her throat. Her skin felt hot. She could not weep, not when her duty was clear. Honor ran in her blood. *The word of a Hastur* applied to her as well as her father.

The horse blew gently through its nostrils, rousing her. She straightened, wiped a few stray hairs from her cheeks, and patted its shoulder.

If this is to be my lot, I will accept it on my own terms.

◆ ◆ ◆

Leora returned to her father's office at the appointed time. Her eyes were dry, her posture proud. As before, Connor sat beside Aidan's right side. The room seemed unchanged, as if time had been frozen, waiting for her answer. She sat down at her father's invitation.

"I have listened," she said, drawing a deep breath. "And in return, I expect that you will listen to me, as well."

A trace of surprise passed over Aidan's face. "Are you attempting to *bargain* with me?"

"You are asking me to leave the Tower and the work that has given meaning to my life. You propose that I marry a man I've never met for the sake of a political goal. I owe you much, as lord as well as father, but my gratitude is not limitless."

"You want something in return for agreeing to this alliance." A statement, not a question.

"I have … requests."

"You mean conditions?" Aidan exchanged a glance with Connor, and Leora sensed his approval: *She is a true Hastur.* "Very well, let's hear them."

"First, I will be under no obligation to make a final decision until I have met Kennard Lindar. Our temperaments may not suit. He may expect me to be conventional, obedient to his whims. Let me be clear: I will *not* bind myself to a soul-blind tyrant, not for all the treaties in the world. He must take me as I am, a Keeper who has laid down her office but not her wits. It would be better if he saw my experience, *laran* talent, and judgment as assets."

"He would be a fool to think so little of you," Aidan said. "Love comes in different forms, and some would say the kind that grows slowly out of mutual purpose and respect generates a lifetime of happiness."

Leora thought of her parents, who tolerated each other at the best of times. "I have no illusions about a grand, passionate romance being the only basis for marriage."

"I would not see you unhappy in your marriage, yet first impressions are not always reliable. Many unions that begin for reasons other than personal attraction end up in contentment and even affection."

If Kennard had a reputation as a drunkard or a womanizer, Aidan would not have proposed the match. Still, in the matter of a lifelong commitment, she would follow no one's judgment but her own.

"I would like to create my own 'first impressions,'" she said, her head high. "I will be the sole judge of what is acceptable to me. Before we go any further, I would like to meet Kennard Lindar. In fact, I insist upon it."

Returning her father's gaze, she added, "There is no point discussing the terms of the marriage contract if we cannot stand one another."

Aidan's eyes widened slightly. "Very well," he said after a moment's consideration. "You make a persuasive argument. Is that all?"

Her gaze returned to Connor, whose devotion to Neave had never wavered. She'd kept her *laran* shields raised, so now she sensed no emotion behind his painfully neutral expression. He might not approve of what she was about to do, but at least he would have a choice, which was more than he had now.

"One more thing." Rising, she placed both hands on the desk so that her father was forced to look up at her. "You will agree that should they both wish it, you will allow Neave and Connor to marry."

Silence condensed like nightfall. Leora sensed the riot of confusion and hope in Connor's mind, even through her mental shields.

Aidan wet his lips. "That's … unexpected. I will need to think—"

"No, you do *not* need to think!" burst from her. Shaken by her momentary lapse in self-control, she reached inside for calm and lowered her voice. "I am not saying they *must*, only that you will not forbid it. The matter ought to be theirs to work out. Not mine. Not yours." She straightened up. "There is enough sorrow in this world without keeping apart two people who were once so clearly devoted to each other."

Aidan was weighing how to respond while carefully avoiding even a glance in Connor's direction. Connor had gone so tight-faced that it was a wonder he could breathe.

I do not want to lose you— Aidan seemed to be saying.

I would never ask it— from Connor.

But I cannot even ask what he wants—

My service is yours—

How will I manage—

I dare not hope—

Her affair with Padraik had been so simple in comparison, shaped only by mutual desire.

Aidan said in a husky voice, "If this is something both Connor and Neave desire, I will not forbid it."

A flare of joy burst from Connor's unguarded mind, closely followed by doubt. Neave herself must be part of the decision, and she had gone to Aillard Castle years ago. No one, least of all Connor, could be certain of her feelings.

Leora allowed herself a brief smile. She had bought two people she loved the chance to work matters out for themselves. If she herself had no such freedom, at least she had given them this much.

"Then I will meet Kennard Lindar with an open mind and a willing heart," she said. "When can that be arranged?"

"I expect him and his entourage, as well as a representative of Aillard, to join us for Midsummer Festival Night. They sent a message that they expect to arrive a few days before."

Leora folded her arms across her chest. "You were very sure of my answer. I might have refused to and then where would you have been? To have all these people come all this way?"

Warmth shone through Aidan's smile. "I was sure. Sure that you would give me an honest chance to make my case. We have been apart for many years but at one time, we understood one another very well. You have learned many things at Neskaya but not, I believe, anything that could change your inner nature. I expected that you would remain the same open-minded, independent person. I am certain you will judge *Dom* Kennard fairly."

Leora could not speak. Her heart was in her throat. At that moment, she loved her father more than words.

"I look forward to meeting *Dom* Kennard." She inclined her head. "Father. Connor. Since we agree, I bid you good night." And swept from the room.

With dawn came relief, a weight lifted from Leora's shoulders. Gone were the questions about why her father had sent for her, and gone the struggle, the indecision. She would meet Kennard Lindar as she had promised, with clear sight and an open mind. She no longer saw the castle as an abode of ghosts and shadows. In this place that was no longer her home, she was treated as something between a prodigal daughter and an honored guest. Everywhere she went, she encountered smiles and cheerful greetings. She felt free to wander as the fancy took her.

She spent mornings in her mother's solarium, listening to music and joining in the singing. She played castles with her father, the two of them laughing over funny stories. The old cook remembered her well, serving her favorite treats at bedtime while she perched on a stool in the warm, snug room and listened to castle gossip. She watched Iain practice with his sword, cheering him on like an overfond older sister. In the stables, she played with the newest crop of puppies and fed apples to the old chestnut.

All the while, Leora pretended this was only a holiday visit, a time of garlands and baskets of fruit left outside bedroom doors, of feasts and dancing. She amused herself with thoughts of future festivals, of watching Iain grow to full manhood and marry, of meeting Jessamy's children. But when she thought of having a brood of her own, the air turned chill, as if a cloud had come between her and the great red sun. And she would think, *I'll deal with it later.*

Two days before Midsummer, she made her way to the old tower workroom. She could no longer smell the lingering reek of smoke, only the staleness of a room long closed, even though she'd opened the shutters to let in fresh air. She twirled a length of ribbon around her fingers, blue and gray, and thought that no matter what happened next, these would always be her colors. Hastur would always be her name. If she married, she would take her husband's name without surrendering her own. Surely, there were worse fates than being *Domna* Leora Hastur-Lindar. Even if it was a mouthful.

Even if she would much rather be simply *leronis*.

In the distance, where once an army had appeared, she spotted a cloud of dust and mounted horses. Banners glinted in the sun, blue and orange for Lindar, scarlet and gray for Aillard. Eager voices shouted from the yard below. Although Leora could not make out the words, she understood them.

"They're here! They're here at last!"

"Look at their horses! Their bright cloaks! Their pennons!"

The party rode through the gates, a bustle of riders and pack animals. Connor would be down there, greeting the newcomers, and Lorcan and his people organizing escorts for the nobles to the guest chambers, unpacking baggage, and seeing after the animals and servants. She would meet her betrothed-to-be in a short time with proper introductions, not with him dusty and tired from the trail. Best to give him the time to put on his best appearance.

Avarra's grace! She hadn't packed anything remotely suitable. She didn't *own* a ballgown. Maybe Neave had left one behind—*Mother would know.* It would have to be hemmed and was probably the wrong color, but it would be better than her Tower clothing.

Leora headed for her chamber. As she approached, walking down the familiar corridor, she sensed Duna's presence within. She stopped at the sight of the gowns spread across her bed. One was a soft green with a bodice covered in lace and full skirts split to show the underdress in a contrasting, darker hue. And the other— She drew in her breath at the spidersilk that caught the light in rainbow shimmers. The sleeves were full, falling halfway to the knee. Silver embroidery set with tiny crystals framed the low neckline.

"Oh," she said. "Oh, my. Duna, did you— Where did these come from?"

Duna pointed to a folded envelope on the pillow.

Leora picked it up and read,

> *My beloved daughter,*
> *When I held you in my arms for the first time, I dreamed*
> *of your wedding day. Then, when you were injured so badly*

and had to go away, I set aside that dream, as I put away these gowns I sewed for you, silently instilling my blessing into every stitch. Now Evanda has truly blessed us. You have returned to health and, I hope, the prospect of the happiest day a woman can know.

Wear them with my love and hope for a lifetime of contentment.

Graciela Hastur-Ardais

Leora stared at the letter until Duna, coming to stand beside her shoulder, cleared her throat. "They're from my mother. I think she's had them since I was a baby. She must have been terribly disappointed at how long I stayed at Neskaya Tower." *And would still be there, were it up to me.*

"They're very grand," Duna said in a hushed voice.

"Let's hope they fit," said Leora.

◆ ◆ ◆

That night, Leora dined with her family, happy to share a quiet meal before formal introductions and dancing. The conversation was light, touching mostly on the evening's events.

After the meal ended, the family rose, heading to their separate chambers to prepare. At the door, Leora caught up with her mother.

"Thank you for the gowns. I am overwhelmed. I've never owned anything so fine."

"My dear, that may be all very well for your Tower where no one cares what you look like, but all that is about to change. You are no longer a child but a grown woman. You represent Hastur, and we are for all practical purposes royalty. Your appearance and demeanor must honor your house and also the man you would wed."

Leora let her hand fall from the door latch. "He will be marrying *me*, not the dress."

"This union will benefit his people. The Lindars badly need this alliance." Graciela's expression hardened. "Do not shame him. Show him, in adornment and speech, in look and action, that you will uphold the treaty."

Is that what you did when you married Father? But Leora could not bring herself to ask the question aloud. It was mean-spirited, beneath her.

"I'll send ladies to help you prepare," Graciela went on. "Then, when everything is ready in the great hall, Connor will escort you downstairs, where your father and I will be waiting. After that, our guests will enter, you'll be introduced, and we'll have suitably dignified dancing. Go on now, get along! I'll see you soon." With that, she planted a quick kiss on Leora's cheek.

When she arrived at her chamber, Duna was waiting, along with two of the ladies who normally served her mother. The silver-gray gown had been put away, but one of the ladies slipped her arms under the green and held it out. "Please try this on, *vai damisela*, so that we can make any minor adjustments."

Leora could not summon an objection. These women were doing their best for her, after all. She let them measure the gown and sat still while they brushed her hair and arranged it in elaborate plaits. Just as she set her feet into the most comfortable of the selection of dancing slippers, there came a tap at the door.

Connor looked very fine in a formal suit of blue and silver, every hair in place, a ceremonial sword at his hip. He bowed, unsmiling, and gestured for Leora to precede him. Even without telepathy, she could tell how angry he was.

She said, "I am sorry to have caught you unawares earlier. It was never my intention to cause you distress."

"I did not ask you to intervene."

"I cannot believe that your feelings for one another have changed."

He halted, his posture rigid. "You have put me—put both of us—in an impossible position. Everything that stood between us—every objection, every scruple, every oath—none of that has changed. We had, in our separate ways, made our peace with this reality: A paxman cannot court his lord's daughter. A lord's daughter cannot take her father's paxman as a lover. That is the way of the world. Now you have stirred it up all over again. Do you have any idea how much pain this will cause her?"

She stared at him, appalled by what she had inflicted on two people she loved. For Connor to reveal his feelings like this was a measure of his anguish. "Is that truly the way of it? I—I didn't realize. Should I speak to Father? Rescind my condition?"

"No," he said, his voice now gentle. "You meant well, and you thought you were doing the right thing. How could you have known? Neither of us ever confided in you, at least *I* did not."

"I'm so sorry."

They had come to a halt halfway down the corridor leading to the stairs. "You are no longer the little girl I used to know."

"That little girl has grown up and is now accustomed to giving orders," she said. "As a Keeper, I am accountable only to my conscience. It cannot be otherwise. There is a crucial difference between authority and responsibility. You cannot have the latter without the former."

"If you marry Kennard Lindar, you must give up being a Keeper. I think you will make a formidable chatelaine, and I pity any who mistake you for being meek."

They were almost at the great hall now. One door stood ajar so that the strains of a sweet melody reached her. "Will you dance with me this evening?" she asked. "I could use a friend."

"No matter what happens, I will always be yours."

◆ ◆ ◆

The great hall had been decorated with traditional greenery, ribbons, and flowers. The music fell silent as Leora and Connor entered. Moving at a dignified pace, he guided her to stand before her parents. She inclined her head, then dropped into a curtsy. A Keeper did not bow to anyone, but she might as well get used to it. Aidan motioned her to his side, opposite Graciela. Connor took his place just behind them.

The musicians struck up a fanfare and the visitors entered. The man at their head—who must be Kennard Lindar—was young, within a year or two of Leora's age. Next came an elderly man in Aillard colors, whose curly beard softened his cragged features. To the other side and slightly behind came a lanky man about Connor's age, his sallow face marked by jutting black brows, in Lindar blue and orange. Both men wore medallions on copper chains as badges of their offices. The tension between them hung in the air like smoke. All three halted in front of Aidan and bowed, the young Lindar less deeply.

As he straightened up, his gaze met Leora's. For a moment, her breath froze in her lungs. If she had been anyone else, she would have been lost at the first sight of him. He was the most beautiful man she had ever seen. The symmetry of his features was marred only by the slight imperfections that lent them greater character. Nothing about him, not the red-tinted gold of his hair nor the lines of his cheek and jaw, nor the width of his shoulders, the lean-muscled waist, or even the poise with which he held himself, was exaggerated. Every feature was in perfect balance.

"I am Kennard Lindar, son of Lord Octavien Lindar and heir to the realm. I present myself and these emissaries at your invitation, Lord Hastur." He indicated the lanky, sallow-faced man. "May I present also

Mestre Rannirl Cornwell, my father's paxman." And now the elder, "And *Mestre* Finn Anndra-Rufoso, who will speak for Lord Kermiac Aillard."

"You are all most welcome," Aidan replied warmly.

The musicians took up their instruments again. Leora remained at Connor's side as her parents, as lord and lady of the castle, led the first dance, a stately *promenada*. Halfway through, other couples joined the doubled ring circling the room.

Kennard approached, bowed, and held out his hand. "*Vai damisela*, may I have the honor of this dance?"

Leora placed her fingers on his hand and they joined the other dancers. It felt odd to be dancing with someone she'd barely been introduced to. As a child, it had been proper to dance only with her sisters. Then at Neskaya, she knew everyone through the intimacy of telepathy.

"We are strangers to one another," she said, breaking the silence, "but with time and goodwill, we may become easy in one another's company. Neither of us chose this marriage, yet it need not become a hardship. Do you agree?"

He looked startled, although his step did not falter. "You consider this marriage a sacrifice?"

"You do not?"

Leora detected a faint movement in Kennard's jaw. His manners were impeccable, his expression pleasant but impersonal. But in that single, unguarded instant, he'd clenched his jaw.

Now that *is interesting.*

"I consider …" He hesitated, a flush creeping over his cheeks before he regained control. "I consider that my responsibility is, first and foremost, to my family."

"And mine is not? Kennard, you will relinquish nothing except the choice of a wife, and who of noble birth truly has that? You will still enjoy the privilege of rank, you will live in your own home, surrounded by your people, and you will become Lord Lindar after your father. I, on the other hand—"

"You were a *leronis*, I have been told."

I was a Keeper!

Now he looked at her directly, as if seeing her for the first time. Had he picked up her unshielded thought? "I confess I did not expect to find you so … forthright. Rannirl said—but Rannirl would have said anything to ensure my happiness. He has known me since I was a child."

"He is a friend, then, as well as your father's emissary?"

"Indeed."

She thought for a moment. "If I am not what you expected, then what did you think to find?"

"I don't know, in truth." A smile touched his lips, a trace sad or perhaps regretful. "Someone dowdy. Disappointed. Even bitter."

"Someone sent away to a Tower and out of sight of the world, you mean?"

"I suppose." The dance was coming to an end, the music swelling to the final cadence. "You must tell me about it sometime." But he did not mean it.

One musical number followed the next: a reel during which she sat on the side with her mother, another *promenada*, this time with Connor, then a women's dance. Next came a couple's dance, in which Aidan partnered her.

"My dear, you look extremely well," he said when a figure brought them close enough to converse.

"Mother outdid herself with the gown, but it's more likely the exercise. I have always loved dancing."

They circled away from each other, past the next couple, through a complicated weaving pattern, and back again.

"I saw you dancing—and talking—with Kennard," Aidan said. "He was properly attentive to offer himself as your partner for the opening *promenada*."

"You want to know what I think of him," she said, carefully modulating her tone. "I find nothing objectionable. Nor he in me, as far as I can tell."

Aidan nodded, acknowledging that very little could be gleaned from a few comments exchanged on the dance floor. At least, his expression conveyed, neither of them had taken an instant dislike to the other.

The dance ended. As Aidan was leading her to a seat beside her mother, Iain came up, looking splendid in his holiday finery.

"You cannot refuse me a dance, big sister," he said with a bow.

"Indeed not," she said.

He offered his hand with an exaggerated and utterly charming flourish. "My quest is to convince you that I am equally proficient on the dance floor and the sparring yard."

I've barely gotten re-acquainted with him, and I miss him already!

She focused on the dancing, matching his athletic maneuvers as best she could in layers of skirts and a bodice that was too snug to take a full breath in. Afterward, he fetched her a cup of sweet, lightly alcoholic *shallan*. They stood together, sipping their drinks and laughing at her tale about Duna's capacious bags holding as many items as Fra' Dominic's pockets, when Kennard came up to them.

"We ought to dance more than a single dance," he said.

Between the lively ease of being with her younger brother and the effect of the *shallan*, Leora was in a playful mood. "Ah yes!" she exclaimed, passing the back of her hand across her brow in the manner of a traveling player, "I fear we *must!*"

At Kennard's stricken look, she relented. "Let's enjoy ourselves. I now know you dance well, so I need not fear for my toes."

The dance was a lively one, leaving neither time nor breath for words. Leora was breathless by the time the music swirled to a halt. "I must sit the next one out. Go, get me a drink—but no more *shallan!*"

When Kennard returned with two goblets of herb-infused water, she patted the chair beside her and insisted that he sit beside her. If he wasn't going to talk, she decided she must take the lead.

"*Dom* Kennard, do you dance much at Lindar?"

"We do, indeed, although not with such elegance." His glance encompassed the decorations, the musicians, and the swirls of color and brilliance of the dancers. "My home is nowhere near as grand as this."

"Nonetheless, it may be my home, as well, so I am sure I will come to love it. Tell me about it."

"It's the only place I've lived, so what can I say?" For the first time, his expression was open, his love for his homeland evident. "It's small but beautiful. There are fields upon fields of tallgrass. In the fall, right before harvest, the air smells like musty perfume."

Images rose in her mind, plains covered by ripples of green—or could they be gold?

On impulse, she asked, "What color is the grass?"

He gave her a curious look. "Green in the spring, but dun—almost orange—as it ripens. Why do you ask?"

For a heartbeat, all she could do was stare at him. Was this the place of her dreams? A place where she envisioned a Tower?

And was this marriage the road that would lead her there?

The moment stretched out and soon would verge on rudeness. She had never shared her dreams of Arilinn with anyone, let alone this young man she'd just met. For now, they must remain private.

"Just wondering," she murmured. "It is of no importance."

Shrugging indifference, he handed his empty goblet to a passing servant. "Would you care to dance again?"

In truth, she would rather find a quiet place to sort through her thoughts.

"I think I'm overtired from all this—" With a gesture, she encompassed the room. The exuberance had drained out of the evening and most of the older people had retired or were sitting down. "I must speak with my father. I bid you a restful night."

She did not add that she intended to sign the betrothal documents. Having met Kennard, she'd found him personable enough. She saw no reason why they might not get along and even become fond of one another. That was of little importance now. Her doubts had vanished the moment Kennard had described the fields of golden grass.

Leora stood at her window, wrapped in an old shawl, watching the dawn. Aidan was pleased when she announced that, having met Kennard Lindar, she was now prepared to agree to the alliance. After a late breakfast, everyone concerned met in his presence chamber, first Leora, then Aidan and Connor. A short time later, Kennard entered, along with the Lindar emissary, Rannirl, and Finn for the Aillards. When they had all greeted one another and taken their places, Connor brought out the betrothal documents and handed them around. Once the treaty was signed by the couple as well as the emissaries, it would bind the two realms to a transitional cease-fire until the wedding itself, which would seal the permanent alliance between their realms.

Leora read through her copy, sifting through the formal legal language. She suspected her father's guiding hand in the terms. The lords of Aillard and Lindar wanted this agreement to work, and the document did not take unfair advantage of either side. Nevertheless, she made a few suggestions for minor changes, mostly clarifications. These were accepted without objection.

As for the rest, she didn't care whether her children's names were to be hyphenated as Hastur-Aillard-Lindar or what dowries her husband would bestow upon their daughters. She found herself indifferent as to when the wedding would take place—by summer's end—or where—Lindar Castle, by complicated legal reasoning not Aillard, as neither participant was of that family, and not at Hastur Castle, since even though Leora came from a higher-status family, she stood in proxy for the Aillards—or who would attend—

Connor would serve as her father's representative. *Oh, excellent!*

"My lords," Leora said. "I am satisfied that this treaty has been constructed with thoughtfulness and care for the parties involved. I will agree to its terms."

"*Damisela* Leora, we thank you," said *Dom* Finn, followed closely by his counterpart.

Kennard bowed to her with a mixture of genuine respect and sadness. "You lend us grace, my lady."

"Let us hope the gods grant grace to us *all*," she said. "Give me the pen."

She signed each copy, as did Kennard and the two emissaries. There it was, her name by her own hand. Her life would never be the same.

Kennard came to stand before her. "I hope you will be happy at Lindar." Again, she caught a tinge of sadness, fleeting and wordless. Did he mean that although he wished for her happiness, he had given up hope of his own?

We do this for our people … for our children and their children's children.

"With this treaty to guarantee peace, may we all prosper," Rannirl said, oblivious to the slight pause. "*Dom* Kennard and I will depart as soon as may be to inform my lord and to prepare your welcome."

"And we will escort you to Aillard, which is much nearer to Lindar," said Finn. "We will be neighbors as well as allies, and hope to celebrate many festivals together over the years to come."

"Indeed we shall!" said Rannirl, sounding buoyant.

As for Kennard, he said nothing more but returned to his seat to listen silently while the others discussed the schedule of travel.

♦♦♦♦

37

♦♦♦♦

Kennard and the two emissaries, along with their respective corteges, departed shortly after the betrothal treaty had been signed. Leora joined her father in bidding them farewell from the castle yard, with a vague feeling she could not quite put her finger on. Disappointment? Frustration? Perhaps even regret. She'd barely been introduced to Kennard and their interrupted conversation left her with a hundred questions. She sorted through the trousseau her mother had put together, she packed and unpacked, she rode one horse from the stables after another to see which one she preferred, and she engaged Iain in round after round of castles, playing so recklessly that his defenses crumpled.

Late on the last afternoon she was to spend at home, she found her mother sitting alone in a garden courtyard, wiping away tears. The sight took her aback, for she could not remember seeing her mother cry. She lowered herself to the bench.

"What has distressed you, Mother? What can I do?"

"Oh!" Graciela wiped her eyes with the hem of her sleeve. "I don't know what's come over me. I always expected to attend your wedding, but I never thought—Well, with Jessamy it was different, you know. The alliance was between us and Carcosse, so the ceremony was here." She sniffed. "When you were so badly hurt and we feared—not that you would not survive— of course, we knew that after the first tenday or so, but that you would be changed. Marred. Disfig—" She broke off, her cheeks darkening.

With pain? Or shame for what she was about to say, that her daughter might be so scarred as to be unmarriageable?

After a moment, Leora said in a soothing voice, *"Disfigured."*

Graciela lowered her gaze.

"No one cared about my scars at Neskaya," Leora said.

At her mother's silent nod, Leora took her hand and squeezed it gently. "That is all behind us now. Were it possible, I would have been glad to have you at the wedding. We must visit, both here and there. Kennard tells me that the Lindar lands are very beautiful. And of course—" she forced herself to keep smiling, "—when there are grandchildren, I count on you to indulge them as much as Jessamy's."

"My dear girl." Graciela blinked hard through her answering smile. "I have not always been as understanding a mother as you deserve, but your father and I have always loved you."

"And I, you." Leora put her arms around her mother. The two of them remained so as the shadows lengthened.

◆ ◆ ◆

Leora set out from Hastur Castle on a bright morning, accompanied by Finn Anndra-Rufoso and his entourage, Connor, Duna and one of her mother's maids, and a retinue of armsmen, baggage handlers, a cook and staff, everything necessary for the comfort of a lady. As a consequence, their progress was slow.

She rode beside *Mestre* Finn through gently sloping hills. He inquired how she fared, whether the journey was too taxing for her.

"No, not *too*," she said. "I became accustomed to travel from Neskaya to my home with far rougher accommodations. It took a while for the saddle soreness to pass off, but I had Duna to tend me—" with a glance over her shoulder at her friend, "—and she is wise in such matters."

Finn shifted in his saddle, his joints popping audibly.

"Perhaps you might like to try Duna's salve, too," Leora said.

"I would consider it. To be frank, I had not expected so practical a lady."

Leora laughed. "Are ladies supposed to be such helpless creatures that we cannot manage a few aches and pains?"

They rode together in silence for a time. When the conversation resumed, it turned naturally to Aillard and its folk. Finn was a cousin of Lady Bettina Aillard and had kin there, two daughters from a deceased wife.

"It must be a comfort for you to have one another so close," Leora said.

"It is, indeed. Valentina is a great comfort to me."

"I have been looking for the right opportunity to ask you something. Living at Aillard Castle, you must know my sister, Neave."

"I do," he replied, "for I have lived at the castle for these past five years. *Damisela* Neave is a gracious lady—"

"No, no, *Dom* Finn, flattery and platitudes will not do! Neave would scold you, were she here. Is she happy at Aillard? Has she made it her home? Does she find her work as a *leronis* satisfying?"

Finn said, "I cannot speak for the lady's happiness, only the pleasantness of her manner as far as I have been able to observe. Several years ago, she ministered to El Chico—Beysel Aillard, the younger son—when he was ill."

"Then I am happy she has been of use, as I know she must be." With that, Leora let the subject drop. She found herself looking forward to the reunion with her sister.

A line of brightness marked the distant Valeron River. The terrain changed as they angled toward the river, becoming marshy. In a bend of the river stood a fortress whose stone walls glimmered in the slanting sun. Tilled fields, farmhouses and barns, and a sprawling village flanked the castle to the landward side, extending along the river with piers and a fleet of boats. The river formed a natural defense on three sides. The flags flying from the topmost towers and parapets of the castle bore the scarlet and gray feathers of Aillard.

Connor called a halt as a half-dozen riders emerged from the castle gates. At his command, the armsmen took up defensive positions.

"My lady," the senior armsman said. "Please remain where we can best protect you."

"Is this necessary?" Leora said. "Surely we are expected."

Finn's expression tightened. "In these times, we cannot be too careful."

"The feud with Lindar, you mean?"

"That …" he hesitated, "and other dangers on the road."

The riders drew almost upon them, cutting off further conversation. "Ho, travelers!" called the foremost, a captain by the badge on his shoulder.

"Ho, the castle!" Connor called back. "We come from Hastur!"

Finn nudged his horse. "Aillard!" he called out, throwing back his cloak to reveal his emissary's sash in gray and scarlet.

The castle riders pulled their horses up. "You're right welcome, *Mestre* Finn,—" to Connor, "—my lord. And ladies." His eyes lit upon Leora, unmistakable with her mass of copper-bright hair that had, as usual, come loose from the clasp and curled around her face. "We rejoice at your arrival, *vai damisela.*"

"I am happy to be here," Leora replied.

The road to the castle ran along a causeway to a raised portcullis.

Overhead, pennons in the colors of Aillard, Hastur, and Lindar snapped in the breeze. Close up, the ramparts looked new, and everything along the approach revealed recent efforts to strengthen the castle's defenses.

Preparations for war. A war that her marriage would prevent.

Their horses clattered through the gates into a cobblestone yard. A man in *coridom's* robes who might have been Lorcan's older brother hailed them. "*Vai damisela,* my lords and ladies, it is my honor to welcome you to Aillard Castle."

The welcomers standing before the castle steps included a lady of Leora's age, a younger man who was most likely the *coridom's* assistant, … and Neave.

Leora jumped to the ground and rushed to her sister. Their outstretched hands met, catalyzing rapport. Leora saw herself reflected in her sister's mind—

How well you look, and how strong!

Was that a trace of wistfulness in Neave's thoughts?

Have you been happy here? Or lonely without anyone to speak mind-to-mind?

Neave answered aloud, "We must find time for a good, long gossip. I want to know everything!" Her gaze lit upon Connor as he emerged from the bustle, handing his reins to an ostler.

Go to him, Leora said. *He has something of importance to tell you.*

Neave startled, her eyes widening. "What do you mean?"

Leora's reply was interrupted by the *coridom's* assistant giving directions for the disposition of the baggage, the tending of the animals, and the housing for the men. Duna and the maid took charge of Leora's jewel chest and disappeared around the side of the castle to the servants' entrance.

Later, Leora promised Neave.

The *coridom* motioned the arrivals toward the open doors. "If you will follow me, I will see you conducted to the guest quarters. Lord and Lady Aillard will receive you officially at dinner."

The young woman introduced herself as Valentina Anndra-Rufoso—*Ah, Finn's daughter,* Leora thought. "*Vai damisela,* I am happy to meet you. I hope you will be comfortable among us." Her voice was an alto, low but sweet, her movements graceful, and she met Leora's gaze without artifice.

"I am sure my sojourn among you will be agreeable, *Damisela* Valentina— or is it *Domna?*"

A hint of rose swept across Valentina's cheeks. "I'm unmarried, my lady."

Ah, but you wish to be.

"All this," Leora gestured back toward the steps and the welcome party, "is very different from my previous, quiet life. I do not wish to be a burden, although I understand the intention is to honor the alliance."

"Some noble ladies have very romantic notions about marrying solely for love." Valentina flashed a shy smile. "Or so I understand."

Something was going on here, although Leora did not understand what.

"The entire castle has been abuzz with preparations for your arrival," Valentina went on. "Everyone's anxious to put on their best face. I hope that doesn't make you feel uncomfortable." She turned to Neave. "I have been charged with escorting Lady Leora to her chambers and seeing to her comfort. Perhaps—would you care to accompany us?"

"Thank you, *Damisela* Valentina," Neave said. "I have duties that cannot wait. Leora, I will see you later."

"Yes, please," Leora said. "We have a great deal to catch up on."

Valentina led Leora into the interior of the castle, which was more spacious than the Hastur home, one section sprawling into the next. Architectural details and decorations with the repeated theme of the red and gray Aillard feathers drew Leora's eye as they went through the entry foyer to the magnificent hall beyond. At the far end of the hall, they went up a grand staircase and down a long, carpeted corridor.

Valentina threw open a richly paneled door. "This suite is to be yours while you are with us."

Beyond the parlor lay a sleeping chamber and a dressing room. "We didn't enjoy such luxury at Neskaya," Leora reflected. Combined, the rooms could have housed a half-dozen Tower workers.

Valentina opened a door at the far end of the bedroom. She stepped back to reveal a tiled bathing chamber dominated by an enormous tub, filled with steaming, herbal-scented water. "I thought you might wish to bathe after so long a journey. As soon as the sentry spotted your party, we began heating the water."

Leora's muscles melted at the sight. Every bit of trail grime and dust reminded her that she had not had a proper bath since leaving home.

"Shall I send in the maids to help you?" Valentina said.

"No, please! I can manage quite well. Only—" Leora lifted her arms, indicating her equally dirty travel clothes, "—if someone could see to cleaning these?"

"With pleasure. I'll lay out a fresh gown for you."

Alone in the bathing chamber, Leora eased herself into the tub. The water was pleasantly warm and the mild soap, lightly scented. She sank deeper, wetting her hair and allowing the heat to soothe her aches.

I must not fall asleep ...

... Leora jerked alert at a tap on the door and recognized her sister's *laran* signature. Neave slipped inside, lifted the pile of towels on the chair beside the tub, and sat down. For a long moment, neither said anything.

Neave uttered a soft cry. *Whatever possessed you to do such a thing?*

"You've spoken to him, then." Leora sat up with a splash.

"He was very angry at you at first—I'm sure you know that. He has so much pride, perhaps too much. So strong a sense of honor. His family was poor, and he had to earn everything in life. Accepting a favor like this—"

"You don't have to explain," Leora broke in, sending more waves around the tub.

"Nonetheless, it was a courageous thing to do, standing up to Father like that. I will always love you for it, no matter how it turns out."

Leora stood up, grabbed the towel Neave held out for her, and began drying herself. "Do you think you can find a way?"

"I honestly don't know." Sadness tinged Neave's voice. "Father was so set against it for so long. He wouldn't even talk about how Connor might serve as paxman if we were married."

"But he agreed to let the two of you decide," Leora said. "Hand me another towel for my hair, will you? It seems to me—" the towel muffled her words until she got it properly wrapped, "—if the two of you lived at home, maybe using one of the guest suites rather than the family quarters, he wouldn't lose his paxman and Mother won't be *too* outraged."

"That might take some persuasion," Neave said, managing a smile.

"You'll manage, I'm sure of it." Donning the thick, soft robe, Leora finished rubbing most of the water from her hair, leaving a bushy mass of curls. "Oh, dear! It will take forever to comb these tangles out."

"Here, let me. I promise to be gentle." Neave sorted through the items on the cabinet and found a wide-toothed comb.

Leora sat on the chair, her back to Neave. "Please tell me, how have you fared here? Truly? Will you be pleased to leave it?" *If everything works out with you and Connor?*

"I have been well enough. I have a comfortable home with those I call kin. If I have not been accorded the status of a full member of the family, well, that is nothing new. *Domna* Bettina has been far kinder and more hospitable to me than *Domna* Graciela ever was. Valentina, who is in a similar circumstance, has become a good friend. And from time to time, I have had useful work to do beyond stitching pillow covers. El Chico—Beysel, that is—was never in any mortal danger from threshold sickness, but he was ill enough to alarm his mother, and after all *Domna* Bettina had done for me, I was glad to set her mind at ease. So you see, dear sister, there is no reason to pity me. I have done well enough."

But you have not been happy.

Neave paused in combing Leora's hair, her fingertips resting lightly on Leora's shoulders. *I cannot fool you as I have myself.*

I am a Keeper—was a Keeper. I am used to hearing the truth behind the words. Just so long as you do not fool yourself any longer. Or Connor.

"There! Your hair will do very well for tomorrow." Neave seemed eager to change the subject of Connor. "Shall we take a look at the contents of the armoire?"

"We shall, but only if you promise to find Duna and make sure she's comfortable. I came to see her as a friend, and I would not want her to feel forgotten."

◆ ◆ ◆

Before dinner, Lord and Lady Aillard welcomed Leora in an informal parlor where she immediately felt at ease. The ambiance of functional, slightly worn comfort reminded her of her father's office but without the desk and bookshelves. This was a room that was lived in by people who were not afraid of scuffing the carpet or letting the dogs curl up on the divan. There were, in fact, two smallish, shaggy dogs who jumped up from where they'd been lying before the hearth and milled around Leora, stumpy tails wagging.

"Down! Down, you rascals! Let the lady catch her breath!" *Dom* Kermiac was old enough to be Leora's grandfather, gray-haired and stocky, his temper revealed in the set of his mouth and the lines of tension between his brows. Nonetheless, his tone was warm as he sent the dogs back to their beds and turned to Leora. "Don't mind them. We all spoil them shamelessly."

"I like dogs, and yours are very friendly."

His answering smile erased the marks of worry on his face. He had no discernible *laran*, but his essential good nature showed in his expression. "I hope you will enjoy your stay with us."

Leora decided she liked him. "I am sure I shall," Leora said. "Everyone has been very kind, and it's a pleasure to see my sister again."

"Ah yes, Fiona-Maria's girl. Tragic loss."

Domna Bettina, Lady Aillard, came forward with a kindly smile. She looked too young to be the mother of Neave's mother, Fiona-Maria, so Leora assumed she must be a second wife. Her manner conveyed wit, humor, and quiescent *laran*. "Was your journey very arduous? We had planned a quiet family dinner, but if you are fatigued, I will have a meal sent up to your rooms."

"After the first few days, I did not find the travel overly tiring," Leora said, discomfited by being fussed over. "Only a short time ago, my father summoned me home from Neskaya, so I was accustomed to hours in the saddle. By now, I feel like a seasoned traveler."

"In my day, young Comynara did not leave their parents until their weddings," Kermiac said.

"My dear, have you forgotten the circumstances?" *Domna* Bettina said. "In agreeing to the marriage with the Lindar boy, she hardly had a choice."

"True, true," he admitted. "Well, *damisela*, I pray this marriage foretokens an age of goodwill between our houses."

A servant appeared in the doorway.

"Ah! Dinner is ready. Shall we proceed?" Bettina led the way, her fingers resting on her husband's elbow.

Late summer flowers, orange conelillies and false aster, brightened the dining room, and an aromatic incense added to the fire sweetened the air. Neave and Valentina were already standing on one long side of the table, *Mestre* Finn and Connor on the other. They bowed or curtsied at the entrance of the Aillards. Connor's expression was somber, as befitting his role as the Hastur representative, but his eyes were soft. Neave nodded with a fleeting mental touch that conveyed all Leora needed to know.

At Kermiac's signal, everyone sat down. Leora's place was between her hostess and Connor. The food was simple, although there was more meat than Leora was used to at Neskaya and the seasonings were unusually spicy. After the first course, her appetite waned. It would be unthinkably rude to fall asleep over her soup. Its warmth spread through her, soporific. She struggled to remain alert. She could not afford to miss any mention, no matter how subtle, of the conflict with Lindar.

Fortunately, she was not expected to say much. Bettina skillfully guided the conversation through a variety of light topics, touching on the weather, the condition of the roads, and the early harvest. Valentina spoke little, perhaps due to shyness, and Neave glowed with happiness.

As the hour wore on, talk slowed. Leora found it harder to pay attention. At Neskaya, she would have gotten up and gone to bed, knowing that everyone would have sensed her sleepiness. At Hastur Castle, she owed no one an explanation. But here? She must behave in a dignified manner, no matter what she felt.

The main dishes were removed and the servants brought in platters of honey-dusted nuts and pastries iced in fanciful designs. There was more wine, hot this time and very sweet, as Leora discovered with her first sip. Even that much was enough to make her head spin and her muscles feel weak. Hurriedly, she set down her goblet.

"I'm so sorry! I must be more fatigued from the journey than I realized. I'd best go lie down, if you will kindly excuse me."

"Of course, you must rest. I look forward to getting to know you better. Please feel free to call on me tomorrow morning in the solarium." Bettina gestured to Valentina, who rose immediately to accompany Leora back to her chamber.

While it was convenient to not have to find her own way back through the maze of hallways, Leora found Valentina's company a strain. The younger woman struggled between the composure suitable to a lady-in-waiting and an inner turmoil. It wasn't her fault she had no psychic barriers and that Leora was a strong telepath.

They arrived at Leora's suite, where a tray containing a beaker of chamomile tisane waited on the sitting room sideboard. Valentina poured a cup of tisane and offered it to Leora.

"What do you think of your promised husband?" Valentina said, standing while Leora sank into the fireplace chair. "The Lindar party stayed here some tendays while Lord Hastur was brought in to negotiate. He seemed to me in every way admirable—kind, intelligent, with a sense of humor, and not given to imposing his opinion on others. Oh, and an excellent dancer."

A streak of mischief prompted Leora to say, "You *liked* him, did you?"

"I confess I did." Color rose to Valentina's cheeks. "Very much so! Who would not? Leora, I do not think your family could find you a better husband."

"Hmm, yes."

So much made sense now: Kennard's unhappiness and Valentina's. Her yearning. His resignation. The way she'd blushed when she said she wasn't married. And now he and Leora were betrothed. She didn't love him and he didn't love her, he loved Valentina, who adored him. What bad luck! And there was nothing to be done about it. Leora had given up her life at Neskaya, the peace alliance relied on her father's reputation, and if she refused to marry Kennard for romantic reasons, she'd likely start the war they were all trying to prevent.

She wished there was something to say to Valentina to ease her heartache. If they had been at Neskaya, they would have been able to speak mind-to-mind, heart-to-heart, but even then without any hope of a different outcome.

"My lady?" Valentina leaned toward Leora with a worried expression. "Oh, I am so sorry! I have deluged you with idle chatter after you said you were tired."

"Do not fret about it. We can resume the discussion later if you like."

Valentina looked relieved. "Then I will bid you a fair night and sweet rest."

◆ ◆ ◆

Refreshed after a solid night's sleep, Leora had just finished dressing in one of the plainer gowns from her mother when Valentina appeared, accompanied by a maid bearing a breakfast tray. After last night's light dinner, Leora had a hearty appetite.

"Lady Aillard said I might visit her this morning," Leora said, brushing the last crumbs of toast from her fingers. "In her solarium, yes? Would you show me the way?"

Valentina was delighted to be of use. "Lady Aillard is to be found there most mornings. She doesn't like to be disturbed, but for you, I am sure she will not mind."

Leora expected a gathering like her mother's, women occupied with needlework, music, and gossip. When she stepped into Bettina's solarium, sunlight streamed through the dimpled glass, but half the room was so filled with greenery as to resemble a miniature, indoor forest. A central aisle led to a bay set into the interior wall, where scrolls were tightly crammed into bookshelves. Bettina sat at a desk angled to take advantage of the light. A man bent over a slanted writing desk, scribbling away as Lady Aillard dictated. Two others, Finn and a man Leora remembered from her brief passage through the entrance hall, occupied chairs a little distant. At Leora's entrance, they rose, although the secretary kept writing.

Lady Aillard looked up. "My dear, what a pleasant surprise."

"Did I misunderstand your invitation?" Leora said. "I can return when it's convenient."

"Nonsense! This tedious business has eaten up enough of my morning." Bettina dismissed her secretary and attendants.

"Would you like me to remain?" Valentina asked.

"No, my dear," Bettina said. "I would like to get acquainted with *Damisela* Leora. Go see if any of the other guests need you."

Valentina curtsied prettily and left the room. If she resented being dismissed like a servant, she did not show it.

When Leora had seated herself in a comfortable chair adjacent to the desk, she addressed herself to Bettina, explaining her desire for a better understanding of the situation with Lindar. "It will allow me to advise my promised husband wisely."

"That is good of you," Bettina said, "but I know no more of the matter than anyone living, and less than some. In the end, does it matter how the trouble started? With this alliance, we relegate it to the past. Your concern does you credit, but you must fix your attention on the problems of today. Aillard and Lindar have an accord. It will not magically cure the ills of yesterday, but it is a beginning."

Leora knew a polite refusal when she heard one. Perhaps Lady Aillard was right and it was better to look ahead than to rehash the past. "You mentioned a tedious business—is that one of the ills you spoke of?"

"I was referring to the Ridenow mess. Where they got the impression we would step in on their side, I can't imagine. We have no alliance with them, nor are we likely to make one."

"Surely you could offer advice?" Leora said. "Based on your experience making peace with Lindar?"

"The situations are nothing alike, as I'm sure you—oh, you *don't* know. Well, I cannot fault you for that. Local troubles are not generally known." Bettina did not add, although she clearly meant, that Leora had been cloistered in a Tower.

"The short of it," Bettina went on, "is that the Ridenows have a bunch of lawless ruffians on their borders. *Kiharim*, the outlaws call themselves. No one knows where they come from. They're said to have an exaggerated sense of honor and to be so hot-tempered that the slightest perceived insult sends them into a killing rage. At least, that's what the Ridenows claim. Zandru only knows the other side of the story."

"They sound truly dreadful," Leora said, since a response seemed to be called for. Silently, she wondered whether Lindar might become dragged into this dispute and how she might avoid it. "What can be done?"

"I might suggest simple tolerance or negotiation or drawing a line and getting the parties to stay on their side of a border zone," Bettina went on, "but the Ridenows have already tried these things and failed. There's no point in *my* saying so, telling them what they already know, and every risk that if I do, the Ridenows will decide I am secretly involved. I suppose they thought Aillard would make a better ally than Lindar, who are their nearest neighbors. Here at Valeron, we've had very little to do with the Ridenows' affairs, thank all the gods, and I've had my hands full enough with this treaty with Lindar without incurring an imaginary obligation elsewhere."

"I can see that," Leora said. "Not every problem requires us to take action."

"Exactly. We have only so many resources and so many areas we can work effectively in. Best to take care of our own, I say, and leave others to do the same."

"What about Lindar? Surely a dispute on their borders is a legitimate concern."

"If you and Kennard have any sense, you'll stay out of it, too."

Leora thought that she and Kennard would have more than enough to do, ensuring the alliance with Aillard flourished, but she thought it better to say nothing.

They talked for a while longer, mostly about domestic matters, before turning to plans for the wedding.

Dusk gathered, heralding the swift Darkovan night, when a messenger from Lindar galloped up to the gates of Aillard Castle. Leora was down at the stables, chatting with Beysel, the younger son, about which horse she was to ride. They hurried to find out the news. The Aillard *coridom* ushered the rider quickly to Kermiac's presence chamber. Connor was already there, along with Finn. Leora slipped in just as the door closed, Beysel at her heels. Kermiac was just settling into his throne-like chair.

"This must be important," Beysel whispered. "Look at how dirty he is." He indicated the rider's dust-coated blue and orange.

The Lindar rider bowed to Kermiac. "*Vai dom*, I bring news from Lord Octavien Lindar. The weather along the Blackstone Hills has turned unseasonably cold. Normally, late summer travel would be safe enough, but autumn will be upon us early. Lord Lindar cautions against delay, lest the wedding party run into weather so bad, they are forced to turn back."

Kermiac's eyes widened, although he showed no other outward sign of dismay. Finn startled visibly, all but losing his composure. Bettina entered, moving briskly but with decorum. Kermiac whispered to her. When she straightened up and took her place behind his right shoulder, her composure was flawless except for a slight pallor around her mouth.

Leora needed no explanation of the seriousness of the message. If the wedding party were forced to turn back, the finalization of the treaty would have to wait until next spring, once the winter snows had thawed. A delay that long might well imperil the alliance. All the diplomacy and sacrifice would be for naught. She heard her father's voice in her imagination, insisting that the treaty was too important to risk. *It must be finalized!*

Kermiac began, "We are indebted to Lord Lindar for his warning, which we will heed with all due haste. For now, take your ease with us. You will be our guest, with accommodations and food worthy of the seriousness of your mission." He gestured to his *coridom*. "See to it. And send our fastest rider with a reply to expect the wedding party as soon as may be." With that, the assembly dispersed.

Connor paused beside Leora. Their gazes met in silent accord. "Can you be ready?" he asked.

"I could be ready yesterday," she said, keeping her tone light, "but we ought to plan for colder weather, just in case. Warm clothing for everyone and extra grain for the animals. Please consult our travel guides about other preparations."

"I will. Do you know the Blackstone area?"

She shook her head. "I wasn't aware of a stretch of mountains in that direction. Must we pass through them?"

"Not in the normal course of travel." Connor held the door, motioning for her to exit before him. "They lie to the north of our road. They are not what one thinks of as hills but a stretch of arid, deeply eroded rises marked by ridges of harder stone. The guards captain here thinks outlaws have hidden there from time to time, although there have been no recent reports. The land isn't good for much else except sending storms down on the lower terrain, where our road will take us."

"They sound positively grim."

"It's just as well we will avoid them."

◆ ◆ ◆

The wedding party set off early on the second day with two additional baggage animals, sturdy plains chervines capable of carrying heavy loads over rough terrain on sparse rations. Leora had argued for a smaller group, able to move rapidly at need, but Kermiac, Connor, and their travel guide, a grizzled man named Pietro, overruled her. Bettina insisted on a nobly born female attendant, which meant that Neave was to go, too, along with Duna. Connor made no objection.

Once the great red sun had cleared the horizon, the air warmed and only a few gauzy clouds drifted across a piercingly bright sky. Pietro rode in front with Connor and one of the guards, then Finn and the women, bracketed by other guards and followed by the pack animals. The day being fine, the women sang as if they were enjoying a pleasure outing.

When they were a little past halfway to Lindar, their route led across a flat area with widely spaced copses of spindly trees, where the ground underfoot was more sand than earth. To the north, a range of low, broken hills angled toward their route. When Leora asked, Pietro identified them as the Blackstone Hills.

Full night descended while they were still moving, and the vast milky sweep of the galactic arm leaped into overhead view. A wind gathered, carrying a chill edge. Everyone was tired, the horses especially so. The terrain had offered only sparse, leafless bushes that provided no shelter, but by the last ruddy beams of sunset, they made out an outcropping of jagged rocks halfway enclosing a pool of scummy water and a copse of spindly trees. Rather than risk injury by continuing in the dark, they made camp. About half the trees turned out to be dead and dry enough for firewood. It was difficult to set a cooking fire in the increasing wind, although Pietro kept trying. He scowled at the women and ordered them to take shelter.

Leora, Neave, and Duna ducked inside the tent they shared. The sides flapped on their stakes, adding to the noise of the wind.

"Shoulda asked me," Duna grumbled as she dug around in the packs that had been deposited on the floor of their tent.

Leora pulled out the two thickest blankets. "I'd bet you could produce a hot meal in a blizzard."

"Don't tease, m'lady."

"Not teasing," Leora answered, belying her words with a laugh. "Just an indication of how much faith I have in you."

Neave hunched over, chafing her hands. "I could use a cup of something hot."

"Come on, let's snuggle together for body heat," Leora said. Look, I've got blankets. Lie down and I'll put them around both of us."

"Aren't you c-c-cold?" Neave said.

"Not as much as you are. Duna—?"

In answer, the tent flap crackled as Duna crawled outside.

Leora lay on her side, arms around her sister. Outside, the wind whipped, vibrating along the canvas of the tent. Her bones thrummed with it … no, there was something more, something … distant, weaving in and out of her awareness.

Was it her imagination? Or a trace of precognition?

She remembered her father's offhand remark about his sense of disquiet in the face of oncoming danger. When was that, in the days before the Carcosse attack? She wasn't sure.

She tightened her hold on Neave, who had stopped shivering, and now drifted into sleep. And woke to the sound of Duna's gentle snoring.

Neave was deeply asleep, her breathing slow and deep. Leora sat up, pulled her boots on by feel, and crept from the tent. One of the guards on watch outside her tent came alert.

"*Vai damisela.*"

"I couldn't sleep."

"All's been quiet."

Rubbing her arms, Leora lifted her face to the sky. Mauve Idriel and pearly Mormallor, two of Darkover's moons, shone against the diamond-studded galactic arc, bright enough to see by. The shimmering beauty took her breath away.

A heavy stillness lay on the camp. The wind had died down. It was cold, but not bitterly so. Dawn was still a few hours away.

A muffled sound reached her ears. She peered into the inky distance. The tents of the men and the tethered animals made ghostly shapes against the night. A horse moved restlessly, its halter rings jingling. She shivered, suddenly chilled.

Something's out there.

She turned back toward the guard. "Have you—"

An animal's scream shocked through the night, abruptly cut off. She startled, whirling to seek its source.

Not a horse. One of the chervines?

"Attack!" The guard's sword rang as he pulled it from the scabbard.

A furred body the size and general shape of a man hurtled out of the darkness, then another, and another, yowling and hissing. Leora couldn't see them clearly. They converged on the camp from different directions.

Men burst from their tents. She recognized Connor among them, his sword in hand. Blades clashed, metal on metal.

Leora's muscles tensed, knees slightly bent, ready for action. Her heart hammered in her ears—

One of the furred creatures whirled away from the fighting to face her. Green, vertically slitted eyes glinted in the dim light. Hooked claws extended.

Catman!

The camp roiled with bodies, blades glinting—wordless shrieks—war cries—

Connor jumped between Leora and the menacing catman. He brought his sword around in a diagonal slash. The catman leaped nimbly away, but a second rushed them. Connor pivoted, parrying and driving the second catman back. Shadows closed in on them and Leora couldn't see what happened next. She couldn't hear through the screams—that one a human cry, this a horrendous screech. That the whinny of a terrified horse.

Neave! She was alone in the tent, except for Duna. Duna had a knife!

Leora threw a hurried glance over her shoulder as she lifted the tent flap. Neave was struggling upright, muzzy with sleep. "Wha—?"

"Under attack. Catmen, I think."

A chervine bleated in agony, quickly dying into a rattling groan, followed by a shriek—human or animal or catman, she couldn't tell.

"They're after our beasts!" Duna's indrawn breath sounded harsh in the closeness of the tent. She lifted the flap.

"No, you can't!" Neave cried, reaching out. "It's too dangerous!"

Duna paused, a silhouette against pale starlight, and was gone.

"*Come back!*" Neave yelled.

Leora grabbed her sister's shoulders. "We have to help."

"How?"

Leora sensed her sister's enduring anguish from the Carcosse war. Sweet Evanda, she'd been part of the Alcabra circle when Melanie was killed. She would have felt her mentor's death as if it were her own. Later, at the enemy's castle, on their father's orders, her circle had created that terrible, mind-crushing spell. It was a miracle that Neave's mind had not broken.

There must be a better way to use our Gifts. For now, let it be benign.

Light? A floating, luminescent globe? It wouldn't be very bright but enough stronger than moonlight that the guards could see to fight. It might take the catmen by surprise. Second thought, there was too great a chance of blinding the men. But *fire* …

Quickly, Leora explained what she meant to do.

"You can't—" Neave protested, panic strident in her voice.

"I *can.*"

This is not our home, burning. Leora silently reassured her sister. *This will be a natural fire, nothing more. Trust me. I know how to do this. And you know how to feed me the power to do it.*

Neave drew a shuddering breath and nodded.

The two took out their starstones and sat, facing one another. Establishing rapport was the most dangerous part. Their intense, inward focus would leave them oblivious to what was happening outside. Working as quickly as she dared, Leora melded their *laran*. Neave followed Leora's lead except for an instant of resistance when Leora first made contact. That vanished as they came into rapport, a seamless, effortless harmony that went back to their first psychic contact when Leora was only a child. But she was an adult now, a trained Keeper, and the trust flowed in both directions.

Holding their mental contact, the sisters emerged from the tent. The clamor seemed far away, muted. Leora concentrated on the pile of wood. She extended her mental senses, testing its dryness, reaching for the energy stored contained in bark and heartwood and deeper, into the chemical bonds.

Steady … steady … There!

She sent a pinpoint beam of energy into where the spindly kindling seemed most flammable.

Whoosh!

The kindling burst into flames. Within a heartbeat, the flames spread to the larger pieces of wood.

Hold … hold …

Blue sparks sprang from the burgeoning fire to land on the nearest catmen. The creature went berserk, hissing and spitting. It stumbled, landed heavily, and thrashed on the ground, where it clawed frantically at the patches of burning fur. A human guard shuffled back, one arm raised to shield his face from the blaze. An instant later, a catman lay twitching on the ground, its shriek suddenly cut off. Trailing smoke and the stink of burning fur, another followed its packmates into the night. From a distance came the vanishing sound of cloven hoofbeats.

Leora heard her name being called through the smoke and dying screams. Slowly, she dissolved the rapport with Neave so as not to cause a shock. Hands touched her. She blinked, and her vision came into focus. *Duna.*

"It's over, m'lady." Duna bent to wipe the blood from her knife on her hem. "They've gone."

Connor emerged from the fire-licked darkness. Blood gleamed on his sleeve and spattered the side of his face, slick in the reflected firelight.

He's not hurt …

With a sob, Neave threw herself into Connor's arms. Leora turned away to give them a bit of privacy. Her heart pounded with adrenaline from the fight. She could barely feel her feet on the ground. Her thoughts felt preternaturally sharp.

The fire was burning high and hot, but it wouldn't last long. She spotted bodies, both clothed and furred, and a larger form on the ground near the picket line. She counted Connor and Neave … Duna … two men, no three. The third was Finn, still on his feet and holding a blood-smeared sword.

He spied Leora. "By the gods, you're alive! We've got to get you under shelter."

If I had stayed inside the tent, where would we be? "I'm not finished," Leora looked pointedly at one of the fallen guards, who let out a groan. "This man needs my help, and there may be more. Duna?"

"Aye, m'lady?"

"Would you search for the wounded? Finn, we'll take one of the tents as an infirmary, the largest. Where's the captain? Neave … I'm sorry to interrupt, but your healer skills are urgently needed. We must assess who is in most need of care."

As Neave pulled away from Connor, he gave Leora an appraising look. "It seems you have everything in hand. You are indeed a daughter of Hastur."

I am a Keeper, or was.

Connor scoured the camp, assessing the results of the fight, while Leora and the other women searched for survivors. The first was the man who'd cried out. One sleeve and half of his jacket were sticky with drying blood. As she knelt beside him, Leora feared that he was already beyond her help. Placing one hand on the unbloodied side of his body, she examined him using her *laran*. Bright, pulsing lines marked a slash across his upper chest and a gash beneath the collarbone. The underlying rib was nicked and fragments had been driven into the lung. At least, not all the blood was his. Of the remaining two, the Aillard captain was dead and the unconscious guard had a puncture wound deep in the angle between neck and shoulder that gushed weakly and then stopped. Leora felt the fading energy of his last moments.

Finn arranged one of the men's tents as an impromptu infirmary. He'd managed to dig out a pair of torches. With the help of Duna and one of the surviving guards, Leora brought the badly wounded man to the tent. Neave and Duna set about tending the less serious injuries.

Healing was one of the first skills Leora had learned at Neskaya. She had joked to Mikhail that the practice benefited the healer as much as the patient. When she dissolved the rapport, she felt calmer, more sure of herself. The guard slept soundly. He would live.

Leora emerged from the women's tent the next morning into shivering cold. After downing as much dried fruit as she could stomach the night before, she'd fallen into a dreamless sleep. Drawing her cloak tighter around her, she joined Connor looking over at a row of bodies. Two men, laid out straight and covered with their cloaks. Three catmen with prominent, sharp claws, short blades worn in a sort of baldrick, and an unpleasant, musky odor. The large body she'd noticed the night before was one of the horses. Pietro knelt beside the carcass, cutting off slabs of meat. The lone chervine stood beside the two remaining horses, bleating piteously.

Leora looked to Connor, who had cleaned the blood off his face but not his jacket.

"How is Neave?" he asked.

"Still asleep. She needs it, but she'll also need to eat soon, as will I." She didn't explain. "What—" she gestured to the bodies, "—what are we going to do?"

"Our situation looks bad, I'll admit," he said. "The catmen killed or drove off almost all our animals and we're down to Finn and Pietro, plus four guards, one of them too injured to fight. He'll have to ride."

She laid a hand on his forearm and felt his intact vital energy. "I'm glad you weren't hurt. Neave would never forgive me."

"Surely, none of this is your doing. She was here of her own choice."

To be with you. No … to be with me. Between the loss of energy from fire-making and the cold, she couldn't think clearly.

"What's to do?" Duna came to stand beside them, holding another load of branches.

"Can you get some food going?" Connor said. "And *jaco*, if possible. We can't stay here long, and we'll have to decide what to do about the bodies."

"Aye," Duna said, and headed off to the tent where the food was stored.

In short order, Duna produced a hot meal, along with heavily sweetened *jaco* and trail bread slathered with honey, which she first offered to Leora and Neave, and enough porridge laced with shreds of dried meat to go around. Everyone ate silently at first, but as the *jaco* warmed them, their energy returned.

Finn drained the last drops of his drink. "Under normal circumstances, we would carry our dead back home for burial, but I do not see how that is possible. Bevan—" the injured guard, "—cannot walk, no matter which way we go—back or onward. Perhaps he could share one horse and the ladies the other."

Leora said, "We can walk, provided the pace is not too fast. The more important issue is how we will manage with only one pack animal." She looked to Connor for his response.

"There can be no question of returning to Aillard," Connor said. "That would delay the wedding until next spring."

"Which we must at all costs avoid," Finn said. "We must simply forge ahead as best we can."

Pietro cleared his throat. "We cannot carry enough supplies to finish the journey, even divided among us all. Food and warm clothing are heavy, but water and tents are more so. It will take us longer since we must walk instead of ride."

"Just to be clear, you are saying that we will run out of food before we reach Lindar?" Leora said. *Not to mention becoming ill or exhausted from the cold nights.*

Pietro nodded. Finn looked dubious until Duna said, "Aye, that's my thought, too. What must we do, then, if 'twill be a calamity if we go back and we risk not arriving at all if we go on?"

She was answered by general murmuring of consternation. One of the guards, speaking under his breath, said the dead captain was the lucky one. His fellow hissed at him to hold his tongue.

Connor rubbed his chin, then winced and moved his hand away. "Pietro, is there no other, shorter route? One that would save enough time for what we can carry to hold out?"

"Here's the thing." Pietro gestured, making an oblique intersection with his hands. "We came this way, south of the Blackstones, a'cause of the weather turning bad. There's a route what cuts across here— We'd risk cold for sure, but if the snow holds off and we push on, I'm thinking we could make it. My da took me through there a time or two. I reckon it well enough."

Finn looked hopeful. Even the pessimistic guard brightened. Looking thoughtful, Duna said to Pietro, "Would take some doing, that, but I'm thinking you and I could sort it. Everyone'd have to carry their share—" with a hard look at Finn, "—and we'd need a share of luck."

"Luck and skill are the right hand and the left," Pietro replied.

"It seems we have no choice but the hills," Connor said. "Pietro and Duna will organize what to carry. The rest of you men will help me bury our dead. The trowels we use for latrines are not ideal, but they will do for shallow graves. If we don't waste time, we'll have enough daylight to cover a fair distance today, even on foot."

Everyone set to work, no one voicing objections to Connor's orders, not even Finn.

Leora held the casket containing the jewelry gifts from Aillard, including the pearls her mother had bestowed upon her. Neave came up to her.

"What are you going to do with that?"

"I'm not sure. If we were set upon by human thieves with so few to defend us, they would take this."

Neave looked grave. "It's too heavy to carry and too bulky to conceal. Yet what else can we do but leave it with the rest of the gear?"

"Let's bury it. Next summer, we can come back and dig it up."

"That's optimistic."

"Not really. I have to think everything will turn out in the end. Neskaya taught me that even the darkest times come to an end."

"I'm sorry, I didn't mean to bring up painful memories," Neave said. "You are right, though. We cannot see the future, especially when times are difficult. Not even those with a precognition Gift can tell what will come to be. You taught me that, Leora. I couldn't see any way Connor and I could be together, but you changed everything."

"And your caution is welcome. We'll bury most of it and keep out a few pieces in our belt sashes for just-in-case." Leora slipped her hand through Neave's elbow. "Let's ask Connor for one of those trowels. Do you see anything we can use for a marker?"

◆ ◆ ◆

By the time the great red sun neared midday, every person had a pack with as much as they could carry. The wounded man, Bevan, was not strong enough to sit unaided, so he and Finn shared a horse. Connor designated the other horse for a scout on a rotating basis since they were entering little-known terrain. The chervine carried mostly food and water, plus a single tent.

With Pietro in the lead and Connor on the horse scouting ahead, the party set out, angling toward the Blackstone Hills. Leora and Neave took their places after Pietro and one of the guards. Gradually, the exercise calmed and revived her. She'd been accustomed to walking around the village of Neskaya, albeit without a pack on her back. As her muscles adjusted to the weight, she settled into a rhythmic stride. She focused on the line of jagged, yellow-streaked gray rock ahead, occasionally glancing at her companions. Neave was pale but keeping up. Behind them came Duna, striding along without difficulty under a load equal to that of the men, and then the chervine, the horse with its double burden, and the rest of the guards.

After a couple of hours, Pietro called a halt at the edge of low, rising mounds. From here, Leora saw a low plateau in which millennia of hard rain had cut drainage channels, separated by steep ridges.

Neave set down her pack and stretched. Her spine cracked audibly. Sighing, she peered at the heights ahead. "I would not like Connor to hear me say so, but the prospect of climbing those is … daunting." *He would try to protect me, to lighten my load and carry it himself or lay it upon someone else.*

"I think you're doing fine," Leora said aloud. "If we keep our spirits high and help one another, our journey will soon pass. And think of the stories we will have to tell!"

Neave favored her with a crooked grin. Duna, squatting on the ground beside her pack, said, "Umph!"

Dusk came early as the sun dipped behind the westward rim. Pietro led them along a gully with steep, eroded sides and a floor wide enough for two to ride abreast. As soon as they were well inside the gully, the wind died down. The air seemed warmer. They set up camp in the lee of a rock face, with the women in their only tent. Although the vegetation was sparse, they gathered enough for a small fire. Duna took over the evening meal. No one cared how it tasted, as they were all eager to fill their bellies and fall asleep.

The next morning, they scaled the ridge for better visibility. They had not been traveling long when Leora felt a shift in the air. Adjusting the straps over her shoulders, she paused to peer skyward. Slate-dark clouds were gathering along the northern heights.

"That storm is headed our way." Neave followed Leora's gaze. "But how fast ... and how much rain will it dump on us?"

"Let's pick up the pace," Connor called from the front of the line, "and keep an eye out for shelter."

Hour by hour, the clouds thickened. Looming overhead, they blocked the sun. The temperature dropped. A chill wind that carried moisture and a tang of ozone whipped the blood to Leora's cheeks. Light flashed deep inside the clouds. Her anxiety grew. Too many things could go wrong, weather and accidents, a rock slide ... a lightning strike on their exposed position. She wished she had a stronger weather sense, as the Aldarans were said to possess. Or that there was a way to use *laran* to send a storm elsewhere.

"Connor?" she called. "Should we find a way down?"

Cra-a-ck! shot through the sky. Leora flinched at the sound. Connor's horse whinnied and danced sideways, dangerously close to the rim. Then came another peal, deafeningly sharp, and a muted rumbling on the heels of another, more distant flicker. Connor shouted a reply, but thunder drowned him out.

With a whoosh, the rain came down.

Within moments, Leora was soaked—hair, face, skirts, boots. *And cold!* The rain chilled like melted snow. Neave was trembling, frantically wiping the rain from her eyes.

They couldn't stay here. Yet which way to go? Leora couldn't see the edge of the ridge. One wrong step, one momentary loss of balance, would send them plummeting.

"We've got to get out of this rain!" Finn shouted. "—the women—"

Deafening thunder cut off his next words. Coruscating light blinded Leora for a moment. She couldn't feel her skin. It had gone numb, frozen—no, not frozen, burning. The downpour cloud was not water but *smoke*—

No!

I am not a child. I am not trapped.

She tilted her face to the skies. *Cloud, not smoke. Rain, not tears.*

Leora no longer felt chilled. Droplets sizzled as they touched her skin. She drew Neave close and flung the edge of her cloak around them both. Her body heat quickly warmed the thick wool.

"Pietro!" came Connor's voice, commanding but calm. "We need a way down!"

Pietro yelled back, his words lost in the tumult, and someone else answered—the injured guard, Leora thought.

Duna shouted, "Turn the chervine loose!"

"What? *No!*" Finn sounded horrified, and Leora couldn't blame him. "It's got our food, our tent!"

"Never mind," Duna cried as she grabbed the chervine's lead line and yanked it free.

The stout, wooly beast rushed past Leora, almost knocking her off her feet. It trotted toward a notch in the ridge and jumped off the ridge trail.

"Follow it!" Duna cried. "Hurry!"

"Go!" Pietro called. He'd gone further along the ridge and was heading back toward the others.

"Come on," Leora said to her sister. "I'll go first, so I'll break your fall if you slip."

Neave made a *tsk*ing sound. "Don't you dare."

"What are you waiting for? *Go!*" Duna grabbed them each by an elbow, spun them around, and shoved them toward the downward path. Finn came next, with Connor on his heels.

Descending as carefully as she could, Leora slithered on the water-slick rock. Every few steps, her soaked boots slipped. A few times, she skidded a short distance and came to rest, heart hammering and muscles quivering. In places, the angle was so steep and the footing so uncertain that she had to hold on to the jutting rock to keep her balance.

The rain slackened for a moment, still heavy but no longer a deluge. Leora glimpsed the far end of the V-shaped gully. The near side was mostly bare rock with ferns rooted here and there. Patches of moss added to the slippery footing. On the far side, however, the slope was shallower, cut by striated, fractured ledges. Water pooled on the horizontal surfaces, tumbling from level to level in cascades. Greenery covered slope and ledge. Bushes, mosses and low-growing plants, and scraggly vines—were those trees? Her heart rose. If they could get across, they might shelter there.

She pointed. "Look!"

"Yes, we see it!" answered Connor. "Keep going!"

"I'll go next," Neave said. "Don't come sliding down on us."

In the lead, Leora started downward. To her dismay, the thread of a path disappeared into a tumble of broken rocks. The chervine perched on the largest, bleating piteously.

She took one small downward step and then another, feeling for a secure foothold before shifting her weight. Almost at the bank, she paused. A swift-running stream ran along the bottom of the gully. She couldn't tell how deep it was. Water slammed against the rocks. Her heart sank at the prospect of wading across. She searched in both directions, upstream and down, but could not see a safer crossing. They must hazard it.

Neave was a little behind her, then Duna, Finn, and Connor. Pietro and the wounded guard were even higher. There wasn't enough room on the bank for them all, and going back upslope was nigh impossible. She had no choice but to go on. To lead them all.

If only she had a walking stick or staff—

Just then, as if in answer to her thought, the stream ebbed, revealing a broken branch caught in the rocks near the bank. Leora waded in after it. The water was even colder than she feared, and she almost lost her balance. She crouched, wrapping her hands around the branch. Spray drenched her face. She sputtered, but she didn't let go.

"Come back!" Neave called. "Don't take a chance!"

"It's not worth the risk!" That was Duna. "Let another of us—"

"I'm all right!" Leora clambered back onto the bank to examine her find. The branch was bent in the middle and too long, but better than nothing.

She was about to test it in the stream when Connor called, "Wait! I'll help you!"

"Don't you move!" Neave yelled at Leora. "We'll all go together!"

Leora stepped back onto the bank and waited. With Connor holding Neave's arm and Leora steadying herself with the branch, the three began crossing the stream. Duna followed, balancing with the capacious bag tied over her shoulders.

Toward the center, the current got even stronger. It tugged at Leora's legs like a ravenous thing. Her staff slid over the bed and almost sent her to her knees. Then the end caught between the rocks. Rocks shifted under her. She held on hard as the water battered her legs. Neave lost her balance, but Connor pulled her up.

At last, the swell passed. Breathing hard, Leora got her footing back and kept going. They were almost at the far bank now. Just a little more…

A rumble rolled down from the heights. Then the rain, which had let up, fell with renewed force. Leora half-crouched, bracing herself. She gripped her staff. Her stance held firm, but she couldn't remain here for long. One wrong step might topple her.

"We've got to keep going!" she said.

"Hold on—!" Connor cried.

A thunderous boom cut off his words. Leora flinched reflexively. She hadn't seen a flash. Had she missed the lightning? Where was it coming from? She glanced upstream—

—to see a wall of water rushing toward them.

"Go! Go, go, *go!*" Scrambling and sliding, she made for the far bank.

Neave, please be behind me! Duna! Connor, keep them safe!

She dug in with her staff to propel herself. She couldn't stop, not even when she reached solid ground. *Higher! She had to go higher!*

Leora labored on, using her hand and staff as well as her feet. Her breath was like fire in her lungs. She slipped and fell, landing hard on one knee. Pain shot up her leg. Water sluiced over her. It spurted up her nose, filled her mouth. In a panic, she levered herself up with the staff and kept on. And on—

—until she reached a ledge running parallel to the stream. She scrambled onto it and threw herself into the shelter of the trees. Once she stopped moving, her legs folded under her. Her chest heaved, sucking in air.

Connor was helping Duna and Neave up the last stretch, one on each arm. The three reached the ledge. Neave bent over, braced on her knees. She made an *I'm all right* gesture at Leora.

Leora staggered to the edge and looked down. She swore under her breath, words she'd learned at Neskaya but would have never dared to use at home. The rest of the party was divided, with Finn in the lead, arms outstretched for balance. He'd nearly reached the far bank and was about to clamber out. The horse and its rider were half-way across. Two of the other guards had grasped the horse's tail to pull them along.

Too far, they're too far …

The flood raced toward them, dashing up the sides of the gully, a wall of white and mud and froth—

Whoosh!

—with a deafening roar, it hit.

Water blasted through the gully. She saw the horse go down, then men and low-growing trees—gone in an instant, leaving only a cataract of white. The tumult of its passing was so loud, it drowned out all other sound. No screams, only a deafening roar.

Heart pounding, fighting back sobs, Leora watched as foam and spray shot over the rim of her ledge. She heard—or sensed through her *laran*—Neave sobbing.

The swell ebbed after only a few minutes. The flood itself continued down the gully, leaving tangled debris in its wake. There were no bodies visible in midstream … but there, on the opposite bank—a figure on his belly in the mud and stones, struggling to pull himself up. Water lapped at his legs. He collapsed in the silt. She couldn't see if he was breathing.

"Help him …" Leora's voice sounded rusty to her ears. "We must … do something …"

Connor took hold of Neave's shoulders. "I've got to go back. I don't know if I can save him, but I must try."

Neave clung to him. *No … don't leave me …*

"Let him go, lass." That was Duna, her voice kind but her face grim.

Connor looked from Neave to Leora. "I'll come back for you." Lifting her chin, Neave let go.

He hurried down the slope at breakneck speed. Just as he reached the near bank, the waves receded. Without hesitation, he waded in. He moved on a slight diagonal upstream so that he faced the current. Sliding one foot at a time, he advanced by small, careful steps.

He was halfway across now … still moving—

—Neave gave a smothered cry—

—another step, the edge nearer now …

Connor splashed onto the far bank and crouched beside the fallen man. Hooking his arms under the man's shoulders, he dragged the man up toward the opposite slope—

—just as the flood surged again.

Neave screamed, "No!"

Leora caught sight of Connor's head above the raging water before it covered him over.

No no no no no!

Her breath congealed in her chest. She couldn't look away. He had been close, *so close.* This could not be happening. She kept staring, her eyes spilling over with tears.

"Connor!" Neave screamed. "*Connor!*" She started toward the edge. Duna caught her arm and held her back from plunging into the flood. Leora turned her sister around, her back to the flood, and hugged her tight. Neave's body rocked with her sobs.

Against all hope, as if her will held power over water and wind, Leora made out movement in the rocks upstream. A swell over jutting stone? No, the water was draining away. Muddied gray … and Hastur blue.

"Neave! Neave, look! He's alive!"

"Avarra's grace!" Duna said in a breathless voice.

Neave lifted her face, her tears mingled with rain, and looked where they pointed.

Connor, it *was* Connor. He lay, chest heaving, hands twined in the jacket of the man he'd pulled from the flood. Gathering himself, he flipped the other man on his back. The man's legs were still in the water, but Connor had a firm hold on him.

Finn, it must be Finn.

Through her relief, Leora reeled under a sickening thought. If the flood surged again, it could sweep them both away.

Another man rushed down the slope, stumbling and sliding but never losing his balance. *Pietro!* He reached Connor and Finn. The next moment, he'd helped Connor out of the water and the two of them were hauling Finn free from the stream. Connor collapsed against a vertically cleaved rock. Blood shone on half his face, quickly rinsed away.

Neave cupped her hands around her mouth and shouted his name. The din of pouring rain and the turbulence of the wave on stone swallowed her voice. She yelled again. And again, until Leora feared she would exhaust herself when she needed all her strength. Gently, she drew Neave into her arms.

"It's all right. He's alive, that's what matters. He's a hero. You know he's a hero." Leora repeated the soothing words. "He saved Finn. He went back and saved him. And he has Pietro with him. He'll be all right, my darling. They'll be all right."

Leora led Neave deeper into the shelter of the trees. Duna dug around in her bag and drew out a cord and a length of oiled cloth, which she strung from the lowest branches. The shelter was crude but would keep off the worst of the rain.

Neave refused to get inside, despite shivering. Her lips had turned blue and her skin was pasty white. "I can't—what if he—"

"It will do him no good if you get so chilled you become ill," Leora insisted. "Come on," she urged, putting her arm around Neave's shoulder. "At least, we'll be out of the wind."

In the closeness of the tent, Duna handed round a supply of dried fruit mixed with pounded nuts. Leora drew Neave close and wrapped her cloak around both of them. Neave softened against her and stopped shivering.

After a time, she heard Pietro's voice, faint above the sound of the water. "Hoy! Hoy!"

Duna ducked outside the tent. "Leora, you need to hear this."

"I'll come, too," Neave said. "I want to know what's going on."

The three women stood on the ledge, looking across the subsiding flow. Connor was on his feet, standing beside Pietro and waving madly. Finn sat propped up against the vertically cleft stone.

"I'm—all—right!" Connor called.

"Oh!" Neave gave a hiccoughing sob.

"—broken leg—" Connor gestured to Finn. "We'll have to wait—the storm—carry him—"

Pietro said something to Connor. The two men conferred for a moment.

"We'll make—our way—to—" the next word sounded like *Lindar*. "You go—separately. Don't—try—cross! Too—"

Too dangerous.

Pietro yelled, "Follow river—upstream—end of hills. Head southeast—take road—village—crossroads."

"He means for us to go on by ourselves." Neave turned wide eyes to Leora. "I—how can I leave him?"

"How can you *not*?" Leora responded. "He almost died saving Finn. Do you want his effort to go for nothing? The men can take their time, but *I* have to get to Lindar. I can't do it without you."

"Together, we can do it," Duna said staunchly.

"Neave, I need you with me on this. It will take all of us, working together." Leora searched her sister's face. "I will not force you, but in this matter, I have no choice."

Understanding dawned in Neave's eyes. Squaring her shoulders, she faced the river. "I will see you—at Lindar!" she called. "I love you!" Then she turned back to Leora and Duna. "Let's pack up. We still have a ways to go."

Following Pietro's directions, the three women made their way upstream, keeping to the ledges as best they could. The rain let up, becoming only scattered showers punctuated by bursts of sun. The riverbed angled toward the heights, forcing them onto higher and higher ledges. After a few attempts at conversation, they trudged on in silence. Better, Leora thought, to save their breath for the journey.

They reached the summit to find a smear of crimson along the western horizon. By this time, it had stopped raining entirely. Inky shadows stretched from the east, heralding the swift Darkovan nightfall.

"What do you think, Duna?" Leora set down her pack and rubbed her aching shoulders. Everyone was tired and hungry, and trying hard not to complain, but the wind was making her nose run. "Shall we go on while there's light or look for a place to camp?"

"I'd be fine with staying right here," Neave said. "My blisters have grown blisters."

"Walking in wet socks," was Duna's assessment. "By me, we've come far enough. I'm thinking the rain'll hold off for a bit. We have enough day left to find a place out of this wind. Tomorrow, if our luck holds, we'll have a fair view of where we are."

In reply, Leora picked up her pack. Duna took the lead down a path leading roughly southeast, as Pietro had counseled them. The wind died down as they descended. They reached a little bay, bounded by weathered rock on two sides, with a central tongue of flat rock. Rainwater had collected at the lowest place. Mosses and low-growing herbaceous plants surrounded the pool, along with a stand of sallows. Broken twigs lay in heaps at their roots, evidence of prior dry spells. Duna cried with delight when she saw them. Within a short time, their tent was drying in a small, bright fire.

Leora and Neave sorted through the contents of their packs, using the flat rock to lay out things that were still wet. "I just hope it will all dry overnight," Leora said.

"Even if it doesn't, I can't complain," Neave said. "I'm no longer walking and oh! That fire feels good!"

"It won't burn for long," Duna said. "Little better than kindling, this is. Still, a brightness of the spirit can't harm."

Leora laughed. "Have you got anything to eat in that bag of yours?"

"Aye, although naught to cook it in. Me pan went with the chervine." Duna heaved a dramatic sigh over the loss as if it were a personal affront. She handed round more of the fruit and nut confection, as well as soggy trail bread. Then, to the surprise of Leora and Neave, she brought out a couple of light, warm shawls knitted from the undercoats of chervine kids.

"Should we—" Leora's jaw cracked as she yawned wide, "set a watch?"

"Who's volunteering to stay awake?" Neave said. "You? I'm so tired I couldn't, even if I wanted to."

"Rest easy, lasses," said Duna. "I'll sit up for a bit. I'm thinking there will be a grand show of moonslight on clouds after all that rain."

Wrapped in the shawl under her damp cloak, Leora fell asleep almost as soon as she closed her eyes. She woke briefly, after how long she could not tell. The air seemed preternaturally still, with no hint of a breeze in the little bay. Ice clouds haloed the moons Idriel and Mormallor. The multi-hued light was barely enough to see by, but she made out Duna, sitting watch.

Safe, she thought. *We're safe.*

For now.

◆ ◆ ◆

In Leora's dream, the night lay still around her. Four moons cast the road in a shimmering monotone. Closer and closer came hoofbeats, yet though she strained, she could not make out the oncoming riders. Then, carried on a newly sprung wind, came the sound of men's voices. They called to one another in a language she could not make out, only its urgency. Nearer and nearer they came, louder and stranger.

Then she saw, silvered on the road, pale men on pale horses. Colorless hair flowed down their backs in long tangles. Their clothing was unfamiliar, like cloudy tatters. The swords they held were curved, not the familiar straight blades.

Just then, the lead rider wheeled his mount in her direction—

She sat bolt upright, her cloak falling away. Her heart thudded and cold sweat dampened her face and neck. The eastern sky glimmered with approaching dawn. Duna was snoring.

"Leora?" came Neave's whisper. "Is aught amiss?"

"A dream, that's all. Go back to sleep." *If you can.*

◆ ◆ ◆

Something was chewing on Leora's hair. At first, she thought it was a particularly vivid dream. Or Neave tickling her with a grass stem. Wrinkling her face, she pawed at it. Her fingers met something soft and wet … and wooly. With a start, she jerked upright. The tent had been taken down and was neatly rolled up. A chervine stood over her, chewing placidly. It reached for her hair again. She swatted it away.

"Miserable beast! Stop—"

Duna was standing behind it, hands on hips. "Thought that'd rouse you."

"How long has it—why didn't you wake me?" Leora asked, feeling peeved. "Never mind. Neave!" She nudged her sister with one foot.

Neave flounced onto her other side. "Too early …"

"*Neave!* You've got to see this!"

Neave opened one eye, then sat up with a gasp. "It's—it's—"

"It's a bit o' luck, that's what it is," Duna said. "Now, you tether yon beast while I unpack. With a bit *more* of that luck, there'll be dry clothes and me cook pans undamaged."

The chervine seemed very happy to see them. It kept trying to nibble fingers and hair while Duna unpacked it. Leora discovered a shallow gash and swollen tendon in one of the chervine's hind legs, which Duna tended with her salve. Neave helped with gathering more sallow branches, setting a fire, and boiling water from the pool in one of Duna's pans. The aroma from the steeping *jaco* made Leora want to swoon, and the taste was better, even unsweetened, which more than made up for the bland parched-barley porridge.

Once the sun was full up, they returned to the ridge crest for a view of the territory between the Blackstone Hills and Lindar. They were almost at the southeastern border of the Hills. Eroded sides gave way to gentle slopes. From there, sparse low wooded areas bordered expanses of drier, flatter terrain.

"I think I see a road." Squinting against the morning's light, Neave pointed. "See down there? It looks as if the path we're on, if you can call it that, joins a road. It should lead us to the town Finn mentioned."

"You've good eyes," said Duna.

Greatly heartened, they began their descent, leading the laden chervine. Toward the end of a long day, they spotted the expected crossroads village, composed of a half-dozen buildings of sunbaked brick. Pole pens held horses and chervines, as well as a few goats and ungainly long-necked beasts.

"Careful," Duna cautioned as they neared the outskirts. "We know nothing of this place, and we are three women alone on the road."

Leora set aside her longing to inquire after an inn. "We're almost out of food. I do not see that we have much choice but to resupply here."

"Aye, that's the right of it."

"Horses?" Neave asked. Duna's salve had eased her blisters, but she still limped toward the end of each day's travel.

"Bed and bath?" Leora looked pointedly at her trail-stained garments. Her skin was reddened from tendays outdoors, and her lips chapped. "I've got a few pieces of jewelry. Could we sell those or use them for barter?"

"Show me," Duna said. She picked out the smallest and least valuable, a ring of antique design set with a tiny river-opal, and tucked it into her belt. "That'll do. But let me do the talking and the buying. You both canna but sound like fine ladies, and I'm thinking them yonder will see you as sheep to be fleeced."

They entered the village square. Near the center sat a well, its water spilling into a long trough. A man with a weather-beaten face held the leads of a pair of draft chervines as they drank. He gave the women a sidelong glance. Unease prickled at Leora. She felt the suspicion rolling off the man's mind like smoke.

Duna placed herself between the drover and the other women. She glared at him, hands on hips. "What're you gaping at, you old *cralmac*?"

"Nuthin.'" The drover hurried off, muttering under his breath and dragging his chervines away before they had finished drinking.

On the far side of the well stood a two-story combination tavern and trading post, backed by outbuildings and the livestock pens they'd spotted earlier. Cloth awnings shaded the side looking out on an open-air market. The cries of vendors hawking their wares mixed with laughter, chatter, and a skirling tune from an unfamiliar bowed string instrument.

Neave glanced longingly at the merriment and Leora would have followed her over, but Duna stopped them with a look. "Inside, first. You two wait by the door."

Inside the trading post, dense shade blinded Leora until her eyes adjusted. She made out a bar and tables. She sniffed, smelling something alcoholic and slightly sulfuric. *Beer that's gone bad. Ugh.*

Duna headed for the room beyond the bar, where crates and barrels, bolts of cloth and canvas, and covered vats were stacked. Shelves behind a counter held covered baskets and pottery jars from palm-sized to almost too big to lift. Beyond them, Leora spotted saddles and other gear.

"I've never been in a place like this," Neave whispered. She and Leora remained just inside the door as Duna had bidden. "I've only heard about them."

Duna sauntered up to the counter. A sun-dark woman in a pocketed canvas apron, graying hair tucked into a headkerchief, greeted her. After a deal of pointing and back-and-forthing, Duna laid the ring on the counter. Her posture said, *How much for this?*

The shopkeep's focus sharpened. She leaned forward, eyes gleaming in the shadowed light.

She will try to get the most profit from it.

With an exaggerated lift and fall of her shoulders, Duna shook her head and scooped up the ring.

The response was swift, *I'll offer more.*

It's probably worth more than this entire town. Was the piece so valuable it would tempt a buyer to cheat or, worse yet, send ruffians after the seller in the hopes of finding more? Surely, Duna was savvy enough to detect a trap.

At last, the shopkeep grinned. They shook hands, and when Duna dropped her hand, the ring was gone. The shopkeep called out and a young man with the same cast of features came out an inner door. Together, they piled up small sacks and other items.

Duna returned to the sisters, her expression satisfied. "Drove a hard bargain, that one, but she's honest. There's traders to take your trinket off her hands for a pretty profit." She passed a handful of coins to Leora. "Our situation's none too bad. We're on the road for Lindar, for one thing. We've two horses, although how broken-down's anyone's guess, and their tack, and food and a change of clothes such as women here wear. And—a room. And a bath."

"Duna, you are a wonder!" said Leora.

"That is as may be. Me cousin's aunt, your *leronis* Doranna, she'd have my hide if anything happened to you. Now let's see what the market has to offer. Yon shopkeep'll bring our goods to the room. Her man runs the tavern and will have a meal sent up."

The three of them strolled through the square, where vendors squatted on blankets behind piles of greens and globular, pink fruits. The man from the well lounged in the corner, watching the women.

"Sweet melons, try my sweet melons!" The woman vendor took out a knife from the folds of her robes, cut one of the fruits, and held out the slices. "Try them, you will see!"

Leora accepted a chunk and bit into it. The melon smelled like peaches and cinnabark. Tart juice squirted into her mouth. "That's marvelous! Neave, try it. We must get some of these."

Catching the gleam in the vendor's eyes, Leora realized she ought to have kept silent. Undoubtedly, they'd pay more due to her eagerness. When Duna inquired about the price, it seemed entirely reasonable. Leora listened to a few rounds of bargaining before breaking in.

"We'll take six."

The old woman handed over the melons, adding a twine bag in which to carry them and a pair of shriveled cittries.

Duna sniffed in disapproval. "We dinna have to pay so much."

"A few extra coins mean little to us and much to her. It was worth it to see a friendly face."

"Friendly, bah! She knows well the haggling art. We'll be wanting them coins yet."

That might be true, and Leora *had* agreed to defer to the older woman's experience. There was nothing to be done about it now. "Duna, do you know why that man was staring at us? He was suspicious, but there was something more. Fear, I might have said. But of us?"

"Superstitious basdert," Duna muttered. "We're strangers, 'tis all."

"I think we should ask the melon vendor. She seemed kindly disposed and this place makes me feel … uneasy."

"Yes," said Neave.

When they asked, the old melon vendor spat and made a gesture with her fingers, warding off evil.

"Bad man! Very bad! Steal from you, steal! Or sell to—" the old woman used a phrase that sounded like, "woman-catchers."

Woman-catchers? Wife-catchers?

Leora softened her *laran* barriers. The old woman was agitated, but there was no deceit in her. She was fearful—and here Leora caught a fleeting image of horses galloping in the night, men with long, straw-white hair, and a woman's fading scream. Whether it was from rumor, legend, or the vendor's personal experience, she could not tell.

She laid a hand on Duna's shoulder. "Let's go back to the tavern."

The shopkeep showed them to a narrow, dusty room with a single glassless window that let in a breeze. There was one bed, a pallet laid over leather straps on a frame. After so many nights sleeping on the ground, both the pallet and the wood floor looked enticing.

"Do you know—" Leora addressed the shopkeep. "The melon-seller in the market spoke of women-catchers. What did she mean?"

"We do not speak of them, the wild men—the *kiharim*," the shopkeep responded, lowering her voice as if to avoid speaking evil. "They come, they take for wives, for slaves, who knows? I say, let them stay where they are, wild lands for wild men. Keep to the Ridenow, I say, and leave us alone!"

For someone who said she did not speak of them, their host said a surprising amount. Leora had no idea what *kiharim* meant, but the name *Ridenow* sparked a memory, something she'd heard Lady Aillard mention about problems that realm had with lawless neighbors. Cattle raids were one thing, as she well knew. But *wife-stealing*?

Let the Ridenows deal with these *kiharim*. Soon she and her companions would be safe at Lindar Castle.

◆ ◆ ◆

The two horses Duna had bargained for didn't look like much, with bony withers and cow hocks, uninclined to go faster than an amble. Duna urged both Leora and Neave to ride, insisting that she was well enough walking. "The horses'll carry my share, and I'll tend to this beastie," with a fond pat on the chervine's nose. In return, the chervine butted her lightly. Leora said they'd take turns.

The morning was pleasant and the road, easy. They passed other travelers, farmers with hay-laden carts, families with laden chervines, and a boy and dog herding goats with long, scraggly fleece. At midday, they stopped to rest and water the horses. Duna brewed *jaco* that she'd acquired from the trading post, with bread from the same source, still soft from yesterday's baking. They pushed on, constrained only by the leisurely pace of the horses, until the sun dipped toward the west. They ate a good dinner that night and curled up in their blankets around the dying embers.

Leora gazed up at the glittering stars and listened to the sounds of nightbirds and insects. Once or twice, a shadow passed silently overhead. It was a natural hunter of the wild, she thought, nothing more.

Days passed. The landscape grew wilder, sere and windswept. Birds were fewer, heard mostly at night. They spotted antelope and, once or twice at a distance, wild cattle. Then the land began to climb, rocky outcroppings jutting above flinty ground. The road wound through the hills, then emerged into a crossroads. Here it branched, one fork toward arid wasteland, the other disappearing into rock-strewn hills. Scrubby trees and a crumbling rock wall ringed the clearing.

"Let's give the horses a breather," Duna said, dismounting. The chervine, which showed no sign of weariness despite its heavy pack, butted her hip. When she rubbed its forehead, it tried nibbling on her sleeve.

Laughing, Neave slid to the ground. "Leora, you look fair done in. You must ride next time."

"I will not argue with that." Leora looked around for a comfortable place to sit. Swaths of low-growing brush had been torn up, revealing gravelly soil beneath. Clumps of horse dung lay half-covered by grit.

What had happened here?

Despite the stillness of the air, a chill brushed the back of her neck. She unfastened the neck of her jacket. Her starstone warmed as it touched her palm. Closing her eyes, she focused her mind through the stone onto the residue of energy … swirling, invisible, yet now coming clear … the ghostly echoes of shouting … a scuffle … boots in dirt … a woman's scream … a cloak swinging, catching on a thorn-laced branch …

She tucked her starstone back into its pouch and jerked the drawstring tight. "Duna? Neave? We must not linger here. It's not safe."

"I don't like this place, either," Neave said. Her horse sensed her anxiety and threw up its head with a snort. She patted its neck, murmuring soothing words.

"Hunh!" Duna paced the clearing. Crouching down, she held up a scrap of dark green fabric caught on the thorny underbrush.

A slithering sound reached Leora's hearing. Wind over sand? A small creature, digging its way into safety?

Shouting erupted from all sides. Deep voices, men's voices. Men burst into the clearing, roiling—

—Neave's horse reared—men rushed toward her—

Duna spun around to grapple with one of the attackers—

Fast. It was all happening too fast.

A horse jinked sideways—she threw herself out of its path—hands grabbed her—tripping—

—losing her balance—

—falling—

A hood slipped over her head. She could not see, could barely breathe—

—the air stinking of sweat and unfamiliar animal stench—

Something hard collided with her head and darkness took her.

Nausea and a throbbing head brought Leora to muzzy consciousness. She couldn't see—was it night? She struggled to wake up, but her senses were muted, as if she had suddenly become half-blind, half-deaf, half-dead. Was she sick—delirious with fever? She tried to sit up but her arms refused to move.

She opened her mouth to call for help. Only a whimper came out. She remembered hitting the ground, then a hood coming down over her head. Then nothing. She was lying on her side on a hard, lumpy surface—where? The last place she remembered was the clearing.

With an effort, she found that she could move, although only a little. She was not paralyzed, as she'd first feared. Her hands were bound behind her back and her ankles tied together, restrained but not immobilized.

"Hello?" she called. Her voice sounded muffled to her ears, her tongue so thick she could barely form the word.

"L-L-Leora! Evanda's b-b-blessing, you're ali-i-ive!" Neave's voice echoed weirdly. Cloth rustled nearby.

"Yes, but I don't—" Syllables jumbled together in Leora's mind. Her voice did not seem to belong to her. She had the sensation of being only partly in her body.

She managed to force out, "Where are we?"

"Y-y-you know-w-w no-no-no m-m-more than I-I-I," Neave said. "I-I-I assume you're also h-h-hooded and tied? I-I-I think we're in a t-t-tent. As near as I can reckon, we've b-b-been here for two days."

Two days!

"Who—who has taken us?"

"Don't talk. They'll hear us."

"Who is *they*?" Leora said, more whisper than speech.

"Quiet!" snapped another voice, a woman's but harsh like that of a *kyorebni*, a scavenger bird of the heights. She spoke with a strong accent, one Leora couldn't place. Then came more sounds of fabric sliding one layer over the other and the scuffling of feet.

"Who—" Leora began.

A blow caught her on the side of the head, sending sparks through her vision. Her neck snapped. She sprawled on her back, her shoulders wrenched under the weight of her body.

"Quiet." Again, that raptor-hoarse voice.

Her ears filled with a rushing, chaotic tumult of noise. It felt as if the bones of her skull had fractured, splintering. Heat swept over her skin, the next moment followed by icy chills. Tremors began deep within her body.

Something was very wrong with her.

She forced herself to lie still, breathing as shallowly as she dared.

Please, let the spasm pass.

Her shivers eased, but the next moment, a renewed wave of nausea took her. Sour bile filled her mouth.

Am I delirious? Dying?

She was not in the Overworld, the land of the dead, that much she knew.

A sickness? An injury to her brain, a concussion …

In the darkness of the hood, pinpoint lights danced in her vision, leaving trails of glowing smoke that curled into uneasy shapes. They caught her attention, pulling her along. The trails merged into a luminous fog in which almost-recognizable shapes emerged and then dissipated. She watched them, fascinated. They reminded her of her adolescent threshold sickness.

Move about. Don't let yourself drift.

Focusing on her starstone would soothe her mind and normalize the flow of *laran* energy. She was seized by a sudden craving to hold the gem. If only she could reach it! The spidersilk pouch hung on a cord between her breasts. With her hands bound behind her, that was impossible. Shift though she might, she could not feel the small lump over her breastbone or the faint resonance through its insulating silk. She tried to sense it with her mind and felt nothing.

Nothing.

Tried again, and to her horror touched only an aching void.

Panic clawed at her. *They have taken it!*

Oh gods, I'm going to die—I'm going to die!

She wrestled her panic under control. She *wasn't* dead. *Think!*

Her captors had taken her starstone … but they had not unwrapped it. They had not *touched* it. If they had, she would be in shock or worse. Insane or dead. Only a Keeper could safely handle another person's starstone.

Once, when she was newly come to Neskaya Tower, one of the novices had foolishly attempted a prank with another student's stone. The victim, hemorrhaging from eyes and ears, had died the next day. The senior Keepers had modified the prankster's brain, burning out his *laran* centers. His family had come to bring him home, she remembered. She also remembered the deadness in his eyes, the flat, gray light. She had thought, *I'd die if that happened to me.*

But that hadn't happened to her. She felt weak and disoriented, beset by hallucinations, that much was true. Her thoughts were muddled and slow, but she could still think after a fashion. She could feel her body, more solid now that she focused on it.

She forced her breath into a slower, deeper rhythm, calming her thoughts.

Neave?

There was no response. She sent out the silent call again with no result. Neave might have been too overcome by what had happened to focus or they might be too far apart to form a psychic link. Or she herself might be too befuddled. Or telepathic contact might be impossible without her starstone.

Breathe … don't give in to panic.

It was difficult to breathe in the suffocating darkness of the hood. She determined to endure it as best she could, letting her body recover from being knocked unconscious, and wait for an opening. Her shoulder joints ached from the strain, and she could not find a position that did not hurt.

One question after another rolled about in her mind. Their captors must be the *women-catchers*, so who were they? Where had they taken her? Where was Duna—had she evaded capture?

When will they take off this gods-forsaken hood?

Eventually, her mind and body shifted from craving rest to enforcing it. She drifted into an uneasy, dreamless slumber.

◆ ◆ ◆

She awoke with a mouth lined with lint, a pang in her bladder, a now-familiar dullness in her mind, and no idea how much time had passed. The hood clung to her face. Her skin felt clammy, as if she'd been ill but now her fever had broken.

She lifted her head, wincing as the movement sent a jolt of pain through her temples. "Hello? I need to use the latrine."

When there was no answer, she called again, more loudly. Footsteps approached. Cloth rustled and a burst of cooler air swept across her skin. Hands fumbled at the cords around her ankles. Claw-hard fingers scooped under her armpits and hauled her to her feet. The pain in her shoulder joints stole her breath. She could barely stand, between the rush of dizziness and returning circulation and the stiffness in her knees. A palm between her shoulder blades propelled her forward. She stumbled, fighting for balance.

"Please—" she began.

A second blow knocked the air out of her lungs. She went down to her knees, her head whirling.

"Up!"

Shove—forcing her onward. *Air, open air!* Shove—another lurching step.

Since sight was denied her, she relied on her other senses: the hammering of her heart, the sour taste in her mouth. And sounds, the snort of a horse and men's voices, speaking low and rapidly in a dialect she wasn't familiar with.

"Here." *Kyorebni*-voice again.

"I don't understand—"

"Make water here."

"What? I need my hands free. I need to see."

Kyorebni-voice cuffed her on the side of the head. Sickly pain reverberated through her skull. "Here. Or not. Quick!"

Leora had no assurance of any privacy from the men but every certainty that if she said anything more, she'd be struck again. At least, the men's voices had receded in the distance. Bending her knees, she grabbed the fabric of her skirt and hiked it over her hips. Removing her lower undergarment was much more difficult. She fell on her buttocks several times in the process. By the time she had done the best she could and given in to the overwhelming pressure in her bladder, she felt utterly humiliated. And that, she thought as she re-adjusted her splattered clothing, had been the point of being treated like this.

I am a daughter of Hastur, and I am a Keeper. With my starstone or without it, I will not be broken by petty torments.

Neave—she might have been subjected to the same abuse. And Duna? Her heart ached for them, but there was nothing she could do. She must bide her time while regaining her strength.

Instead of being taken back to the tent, she was left standing where she was. She tried a step, but an iron grip on her shoulder held her fast.

A horse approached, identifiable by its hoofbeats and earthy smell. A man said something unintelligible. Rough hands spun her around. She swayed, then regained her balance—a good sign. The worst of the disorientation had passed.

Her hands were untied and then re-bound in front of her. The pain was so intense that her shoulders felt as if they would pop out of their sockets. Someone grabbed her from behind and slung her, face-down, across a saddle. Blood pounded through her skull. Someone grabbed her ankles and tied them tight enough to hold her in place as long as she didn't move around too much.

Submission means survival.

The horse began to walk forward. It was soon apparent that a convoy was moving out. They went at a brisk walk, not a trot. The swaying, rocking movement rekindled her disorientation. Her head swung with the horse's motion, making it seem that the entire world was oscillating, wavering, sweeping along the path of a pendulum. From time to time, she heard a woman's wordless cry, quickly cut off.

Nausea swept over her in wave after wave. The points of glowing light reappeared behind her eyes. Her body seemed to elongate and stretch thin—thin—thinner, fraying into gossamer strands.

It wasn't real, she knew that. It wasn't real and it was dangerous to be caught up in the hallucinations. She searched for a defense, a shield.

Neave, can you hear me?

The lights intensified their movements, like the buzzing of angry insects. Her head throbbed and the hard pommel dug into her ribs. Her shoulder joints went from being on fire to going numb. She could no longer feel her hands.

Despite the cramping in her muscles, she drifted in and out of consciousness. She was too exhausted to stay awake. From time to time, the horse halted, and she heard the men's voices and sometimes that of the *kyorebni* woman. She hoped someone would offer her water, but no one did.

Coolness gave way to heat. Her throat went from cottony to sickeningly dry. Her stomach clenched, compressed by the weight of her body and the swaying motion of the horse.

Breathe ...

If she vomited, the foul stuff would remain within the hood. She would feel worse than ever if it did not choke her.

Breathe ...

They went on, occasionally halting, or climbing and descending, scrambling over rougher terrain. Leora's thoughts returned to her companions, praying to whatever god would listen that Duna had gotten safely away. And Neave—she'd heard her sister's voice when she first awoke in the tent. She *had* to believe that Neave was alive and nearby. She could not bear it if they were truly separated. No, she would, she *must* find a way to communicate.

Leora had sufficient mental clarity for only one thing at a time, one single point of focus. *Let Neave be well. Let her still have her starstone. Evanda, if you ever heard my prayers, grant this blessing ...*

On and on the hours stretched until finally, the horse came to a halt. She heard men speaking and an occasional feminine whimper. She wriggled around on the saddle, trying to ease the pressure on her ribs.

"Stop that!" came a man's voice, heavily accented.

She almost wept when she felt the rope joining her wrists and feet loosen. Hands pulled her from the saddle. Her feet touched the ground, but her knees folded and she crumpled to the ground. The next moment, the hood was jerked off her head. She lay on her side, sobbing with pain and relief. Wetness streamed across her cheeks to drip onto the ground.

At least I can feel something.

In front of her face was gravelly soil and ground-hugging plants. She inhaled, smelling spicebush, dusty and faint.

"Water," she called out, lacking the strength to sit up. "Please."

"Save your breath," said the woman to Leora's left. The voice sounded as dry and rough as Leora's own. "They want us ... weak. Begging ... makes it worse."

The woman looked quite young, barely into her teens, small and neatly built, wearing a lady's riding dress. Red-tinted blonde hair hung loosely around the shoulders, and a dark bruise swelled one cheekbone. The gray eyes looked unfocused, weary.

"I'm Leora Hastur. Who are you?"

"Glynnis Ridenow."

♦♦♦

Someone was poking her, poking at her mind with her name. Poking at her back with something small and hard. And annoying. And persistent. She didn't want to wake up. Didn't want to *feel*.

Her eyelids felt scratchy, encrusted with sand. Her vision blurred with a rush of tears. There wasn't much to see other than near-darkness. But her hearing was sound enough as she caught the word, *water*. A raspy voice saying—no, *asking*.

"*Water?*"

She thrashed around, struggling to sit upright, and finally managed it. The sun had gone down, leaving a silvery sweep of emerging stars. The horizon suggested a broken landscape with little vegetation. It offered few clues as to where she was.

Beside her sat Glynnis Ridenow. Other women sprawled in groups of two or three, although she couldn't tell how many or what they looked like in the failing light.

Please all the gods that Neave is among them!

She made out a tent and men moving about, ghostly gray, and a picket line of riding animals. Near the tent, orange light flared, a cooking fire.

A figure in flowing, sand-white robes approached, pausing at the nearest pair of women, carrying what looked like a leather water bag. It took all her self-control not to crawl on her belly toward it. At her side, Glynnis Ridenow whimpered.

Please.

The figure was taking their time or perhaps taunting the women. And then it came to her in a moment of unexpected clarity that the thirst and the withholding of water, the delay, and the blows and *"Quiet!"* and the blinding hood and the ropes that enforced helplessness were designed to humiliate. To subjugate. To turn desperation into abject submission.

Then I will give them what they want.

As hard as it was to wait, she forced herself to do it. She let her head fall forward, concentrating on her breathing—slow, slower. In that self-compelled stillness, she caught a glimmer of emotion from the figure— satisfaction, almost gloating.

How could she know that? She had no starstone. She felt its absence in every pulsation of her heart, and yet.

And yet.

Step, step, pause. Step. Pause.

Finally, the figure stood before her. "Water? You want?" There was no mistaking *Kyorebni*-voice.

"Yes." She kept her head bowed. Let the old woman think her defeated.

A splash answered her, along with a clashing of metal links. She raised her eyes. A wooden dipper lifted from a leather bucket, then swung toward her. She was half afraid that *Kyorebni*-voice would snatch it away or grant her only a sip before spilling the rest on the ground. But the old woman held the dipper steady while she drank.

Relief coursed through Leora's body. Nothing had ever tasted so ambrosial as that stale, leather-imbued water. When she paused to catch her breath, *Kyorebni*-voice turned to Glynnis Ridenow and allowed her to drink, alternating between the two. Was this kindness? Or the same care that a shepherd would take of the flock he intended to slaughter?

As the old woman moved back and forth, Leora noticed her bracelets, which were linked by a chain running through a loop set into a wide, ornamental belt. The chain was long enough for her to use her hands, although if she reached out with one, the other was drawn tight against her waist.

What kind of monster chains a person like this?

Kyorebni-voice moved on.

The water was cool, and in the falling air temperature, it leached the heat from Leora's body. She curled in on herself as best she could as shivers racked her. After trial and error, she and Glynnis managed to huddle together, forming a spoon shape to share body heat. After a time, one of the men covered them with a tattered blanket. The blanket stank of old animal sweat, but it kept off the worst of the chill.

She drifted in and out of sleep, for how long she could not tell. She dreamed, half-memories too close to nightmares and too formless to recall. During one of her wakings, she saw or rather sensed that Glynnis was also conscious.

Keeping her voice to a whisper, Leora said, "I think we can speak without being overheard as long as we are very quiet."

Glynnis nodded.

"How did you come to be captured?" Leora asked.

"My cousin and I were on our way to Serrais. I don't know what happened to her after we were waylaid. The men of our escort were wounded. One, I think, was killed." Glynnis sounded so sorrowful, Leora wondered if the slain man was someone she cared for.

Connor, be safe.

"I am sorry," Leora said.

"And you," Glynnis said in a small voice, "what is your story?"

"My sister and I were on the road with a single female servant."

"You had no protectors?" Glynnis sounded aghast.

"We did, but they were separated from us by weather in rough terrain. We'd hoped to join up further along." A sigh lifted Leora's chest. "We were wrong."

"So they do not know what has befallen you. They cannot come to your aid. Ai, me!" Glynnis was silent for a moment. "Your kinswoman and the servant—do you know what happened to them? Did they escape … and might they summon a rescue party?"

Leora shook her head, wishing she had better news. Glynnis sounded so tentative and yet so hopeful. "I do not know what happened to Duna. I hope she got away—I think she did. But I heard my sister's voice in the tent where I awoke."

"With Evanda's blessing, she is well."

"I pray the same for your cousin."

"I wish—" Glynnis sniffled, "—I wish I could give you a hug, *breda*." Glynnis used the inflected term meaning, *chosen sister*. She sounded very young.

Leora pressed against the other woman's back.

After a few moments, Glynnis said, "I heard the men talking about a woman who died. They said she was a witch and they took her amulet from her, and that killed her. I think she was one of those with *laran* and it was her starstone they took. I hope it was not your sister."

Leora's heart beat too fast and too loud. "I don't know," she murmured. "My starstone was taken from me, but it must still be insulated. Did that happen to you, too?"

"Oh, *that*." Glynnis forced a laugh. "No. I have *laran*, of course, but my family did not think it worthwhile to give me a starstone. I was very sick for a time when it first awoke, but my mother said I should ignore the visions and they would go away."

Leora recoiled at the idea of a child with *laran* being dismissed in this way. Did no one think to send her to a Tower? Or, more aptly, was there a Tower where she could have been sent?

"I'm sorry about your starstone," Glynnis said. "Did it hurt very much when they took it?"

"I was unconscious." Then: "What do you know about these men?"

"The *kiharim*, they call themselves. They appeared out of nowhere when my grandfather was a child. They didn't even speak our language—neither *casta* nor *cahuenga*!" The more she talked, the more she reminded Leora of Sharina. "They seemed content to wander the sand lands until about five years ago, when they began raiding our lands for livestock, wood, and harvested grain. That's when they carried off our women and any women travelers they could lay their hands on."

"What do they want with us?"

"I've heard that we are to be slaves, but others say they want us for wives." Glynnis made a rude sound. "As if *this* were any way to woo a bride! Did you see the chains on Karwa?"

Karwa must be Kyorebni-*voice.* Leora nodded.

"I overheard one of the men tell Karwa that now we will all go deeper into the Dry Lands, where even if we escaped, we would perish before we reached help," Glynnis said.

I will find a way.

Glyniss's chattiness was beginning to wear. Making no effort to suppress a yawn, Leora said, "I am sorry, but I am very tired."

"Oh! No need to apologize! I rattle on, I know—my cousin is always complaining about it—and it's been *such* a relief to have someone to talk to. I feel as if we were sisters, yes? But you are right, we must rest for whatever comes tomorrow."

◆ ◆ ◆

The next day began with a blast of night-chilled air as the blanket was yanked away. Leora sat up so quickly that her vision went gray for a moment. Around her, the camp was waking, men saddling the animals and *Kyorebni*-voice uncovering the captives. A woman sobbed, wordless sounds of despair.

Another day, Leora thought. *Duna, I hope you made it and are free.*

Then Glynnis said, "I'm glad you are with me, *breda*," and Leora knew for a certainty that she must find a way to free not only herself and Neave but also this girl who had called her *sister*.

"Up!" *Kyorebni*-voice—Karwa—strode up and down, striking some captives and hauling others to their knees by their bound hands. "Up!"

Leora clambered to her feet and helped Glynnis to rise. Although her muscles were tight from immobility and cold, she strained to get a better look. The men herded the captives, who had been in pairs, into a single group. Most had mouse-brown or blonde hair, not strawberry gold like Glynnis. Nowhere was a woman with Neave's flame-bright hair and gray eyes.

She must focus her mind. To call out silently, to make telepathic contact as she had so many times since her *laran* had awakened.

Neave! Sister, can you hear me?

Nothing, only a leaden silence. Yet she had reached Neave's mind in the onslaught of her threshold sickness. She had not yet been given a starstone then, so might it be possible now?

Neave!

Pain shot through her temples. Her gut clenched. Sour saliva filled her mouth. She would not give up, she would *not!* Not if there were the slightest chance of pushing through this Zandru-cursed deadness in her head. Of being *heard*. Of reforging the mental bond she and Neave had shared since that first contact … She poured all her will, all her power, all her desperate longing into one last scream.

NEAVE!

Please, please, please let her hear me!

As if in answer to her desperate call, the group of women parted and there—

NEAVE!—

—*there—red hair, red like fire!* Red like her own.

Neave was standing beside a woman so like Glynnis, they might be sisters. Or cousins. She turned to meet Leora's gaze. A purpling bruise darkened one cheekbone.

Leora choked back a sob. Her heart soared. She trembled with relief and exhaustion. It was all she could do to not rush to her sister. They might both be at risk if their relationship were known. These men would not hesitate to threaten one to force the obedience of the other.

Eyes bright, Neave nodded—*I understand*—before Karwa hustled Leora and Glynnis away.

After a ration of water and a rotation at the latrine area, the men divided the prisoners into two groups, one of which was mounted. Leora and Glynnis were tied by their bound wrists behind a horse. They were to walk today, instead of riding. She concentrated on keeping an even stride and taking deep, regular breaths. Glynnis stumbled a few times before Leora said, "Watch me, and move as I do."

The caravan filed along a spit of gritty sand. To either side rose mounds covered by thorn-trees and gray, feathery spicebush. Here and there, outcroppings of black rock thrust upwards like the charred bones of giants.

Gradually, Leora's disorientation eased. The worst effects of losing her starstone seemed to be fading. Whether from the exercise or the knowledge that Neave was alive, her mind felt clearer, stronger. Now she could think … and plan.

When the sun hung directly above them in a cloudless sky, sweltering heat poured down. The wind left Leora's eyes burning. Thirst returned, greater than ever. She was stumbling by the time they halted at a dell, sheltered in a cleft in the hills. Here a spring fed into a pool. The horses were watered first, then the men. The women would come last.

While trying to ignore the maddening scent of the water, Leora spotted Neave again. Their gazes met and locked. Although Neave looked weary, her eyes were clear. *Was it possible—could she still have her starstone? How?*

One of the men brought them in pairs to the pool opposite the muddy mess left by the horses. The water was turbid but cool. Leora sank to her knees and scooped up handfuls, gulping and rinsing her sweat-crusted face. Her guard made no move to stop her. She drank and washed and drank some more. Along the edge of the pool, other captives were doing the same.

When everyone had had their fill, they were allowed to sit under the trees. Leora contrived to be next to Neave. With a pointed glance, Neave indicated Karwa, on guard and alert. Leora scooted closer so that one hand made contact with Neave's bare forearm. Physical touch and proximity catalyzed telepathic rapport. Images and emotions flooded into Leora from her sister's mind, bits of memory of their capture—a blow that sent Neave reeling with dizziness and nausea—Neave half-conscious as Karwa searched her—hands pawing through her clothing—skimming over but missing the small gem folded into her waistband—a flash of terror as the old woman seized Leora's stone in its insulating pouch—a rush of love and gratitude.

Sweetling, you are alive and lucid, Neave said. *How is this possible?*

She has not touched my starstone, or else I would be dead or insane, Leora replied

I feared she had given it to one of the men as a treasure.

Hope flared in Leora. *Does she still have it? Where is it kept?*

I think one of the men has them—yours and two others.

Leora sensed the effort it took for Neave to converse telepathically without holding her stone in her bare hand. Taking it from its hiding place would surely result in its discovery.

One woman—died when hers was taken, Neave went on, pausing more frequently. *Another is now mind-dead—I overheard. I am—so glad—you survived.*

Why was your starstone not seized, too? How did you conceal it?

After a long moment and a sigh, Neave answered, *At Aillard—I had gotten into the habit—of carrying it in a fold at my waistband. Not—pouch or locket—or sash.*

Leora shuddered. If only she had not kept hers in a pouch on a thong around her neck, so easy to find … but all the smiths in Zandru's forge could not make time run backward. She must look forward, and that meant finding a way to get free.

In response, Neave formed a mental image of the two of them, unbound and mounted, racing for home. It was hardly realistic, given their present condition, lack of knowledge of the terrain, and how closely they were watched. Yet Leora sent back her own hope, not just the two of them but the entire group of women arriving, dusty and footsore, at Lindar Castle. The castle people rushing to meet them, the exclamations of gladness, the tears of relief.

We cannot free everyone, Neave objected.

I will not leave even one of us behind.

◆ ◆ ◆

The caravan got underway, with the women who had walked switching places with those who had ridden. They went on, trudging through gaps between the mounds. The pace was moderate but unrelenting. Hunger gnawed at Leora, worse than before. Finally, as the light seeped out of the eastern sky and one of the moons appeared, they stopped at another wooded area. Leora was so tired, she wanted to throw herself down on the dry, curling grasses. The other captives were in a similar condition or worse.

The next day unfolded much in the same manner, and the day after that. The women rode for half each day and walked the other half. Each midday, they stopped where there was water and shade. The low, rolling terrain flattened into sand dotted by clusters of rabbitbrush.

At last, they crested a sandy ridge to look over a plain of shimmering white, like the bed of an ancient ocean. Below, greenery flanked a cluster of oddly shaped buildings. Beyond the town rose cliffs the color of blood-washed chalk.

As they descended, the men burst into song. The words sounded harsh and ancient. Leora knew enough of their dialect by now to gather the sense of it:

"We are the men of the sun, of the sand!
Red is the dawn, and red the river!
Our strength is a knife honed by drought and storm!
Like the god of the well, we will rise again!"

Entering the town was like stepping into another world. Branches with wide, spreading leaves met overhead in a cool green tunnel. The air smelled fresh and moist, laden with spices. Leora wanted to pause and take it all in, to inhale the soothing herbal scents. It was all she could do to stay on her feet.

The shadowed avenue opened into a plaza bordered on two sides by walls of sunbaked mud bricks that shimmered like ice where the sun lit them. In the center of the plaza, women in pastel veils dipped jugs into an open well. Their chains rang softly, almost musically, with their movements. Beyond, men and women clustered around booths heaped with green and orange vegetables, bright fabrics, and small metal objects. Beside the well, a fountain shot jets of water into the air. Leora thought she must be dreaming—so much water in this arid land, and in so public a place! A symbol of hope that the desert might bloom? Or an ostentatious show of the reigning lord's wealth?

The party approached the largest building on the far side. By its size and ornamentation, it resembled a palace. The surrounding wall was higher and more heavily decorated than the others. Two men in garish tunics stood guard at the entrance, holding bared sabers. They stepped aside as the women approached, swinging open the gate of bleached wood inlaid with thin strips of copper—a fortune's worth! Passing through, the women were jostled into single file, and then into a spacious courtyard.

Karwa ushered Leora and several other women, including the young cousin of Glynnis Ridenow, to the principal building. Although Leora glanced around for Neave, she could not see her or sense her. Neave must be in the second group, beyond the limited reach of Leora's unaided *laran*. The separation left Leora uneasy. Anything could happen in a place like this.

Once inside, darkness enfolded Leora, temporarily blinding her. The air was dank chill.

"Move!" Karwa half-dragged her forward, and when Leora moved too slowly, one of the guards shoved her from behind. She found herself in a windowless, low-ceilinged passageway, along with the other women in her group.

The passage turned, and turned again. Suddenly, they emerged into a blaze of daylight, a courtyard of some sort. Leora's eyes watered from the brightness. They cut across it, along a colonnaded walkway, and into a door at the opposite end. The palace seemed to be a square or rectangular structure with gardens in its hollow center. That might make an escape more complicated but offered more places in which to hide.

Leora's group arrived at a bathing chamber, with sunken tubs of tiles glazed in blues and greens. Benches and chests of woven reeds lined the sides of the room. They were met by a trio of young women wearing loose trousers, knee-length sleeveless vests, and belts of linked metal discs. Chains joined their bracelets through a loop in the front of the belts. Fillets of matching metal held back their hair—black and brown and blonde. None had the red that distinguished *laran*-Gifted families.

The black-haired woman addressed them in *cahuenga*, "Be welcome to the house of Lord Narram. We are to prepare you to become proper wives."

Wives *might mean greater freedom*, Leora thought, *and more chances to escape*. She hoped.

The other captives cringed, pulling away from the approaching attendants, but Leora faced the black-haired woman. "Wives, you said. What does that mean?"

With an anxious glance at Karwa, the black-haired woman replied, "To be a wife is to serve your husband in all things and to wear his chains with the same pride with which he bestows them upon you."

The Ridenow girl sobbed, "Chained? Like an animal? No, I can't! I won't!" She whirled back toward the door. Lightning-quick, the guard caught her by the hair and yanked hard. With a shriek, she landed flat on her back. Her skull thumped on the stone floor. The sound was hollow, sickening. For a heartbeat she lay there, unbreathing. Then her chest heaved with a gulping inhalation and she curled on her side, hugging herself and sobbing weakly.

"So! This the way!" Karwa proclaimed, emphasizing her words with a metallic clanging of her chains. "Be warn! Next time—" She pointed to the saber-bearing guard and made a gesture of slitting a throat.

None of the women moved. The only sound was the choked weeping of the woman on the floor.

Do not rebel openly, Leora cautioned herself. *Wait for an opening.*

Wait for Neave.

She turned back to Black Hair with gaze downcast and a self-effacing smile, one that said, *I am no danger to you.* This girl might be an ally … or an informer, a lackey. "Hello. What is your name? How did you come to be in the service of Lord—Narram, you said he is called? Were you born here or taken prisoner like us?"

Black Hair flushed, a swath of red across her cheeks. "It is not my place to tell such things. Please, my lady—" with a nervous glance at Karwa, "do not ask."

Leora drew back, stung by the terror in the girl's mind. "I'm so sorry," she murmured, inclining her head. "I have no wish to cause you difficulties."

The Ridenow girl was weeping again, pushing away the attendant's hands. She would fail, Leora thought, and likely lose whatever freedom a feigned submission might buy her.

Black Hair began removing Leora's bonds and then her travel-stained garb. At first, Leora submitted without protest, it seemed such a benign thing, to be tended to—and there was the bath, tempting—

Then a thought shook her, *Neave carries her starstone in the waistband of her skirt! If they take away her clothing—*

They might find it! And even if they do not—what will it do to her? Can she survive losing it?

What if one of them thinks it's a pretty bauble—and touches it?

In a whirl of panic, Leora snatched up her skirt and tunic. She held them against her chest. "No, please! This is all I have left of home! Please let me keep it—and my sister, the same! For comfort, please!"

Black Hair gave her a suspicious look. "What do you want those old things for? They're so torn and filthy! Lord Narram would never allow a woman in his household, either his wife or a woman he gives to one of his nobles—to wear such disgraceful rags." She took a firm hold of the garments with another worried glance at Karwa. At *Kyorebni*-voice.

"Please, lady, do not make a fuss. If she sees you are disobedient, you will be punished." Lowering her voice even more, "We will *both* be punished. You said—you said you would not make trouble for me. Please, just get into the bath. It's very pleasant, you will see."

Leora allowed the girl to take away her clothing. She would gain nothing by resisting. No help would come to Neave that way.

Wait. Wait and watch. But the words rang hollow in her mind. Against so many, what chance had she, even with her starstone?

What chance does Neave have?

If I do nothing, if I give up … she will have none.

She was Neave's chance, her only chance, and for Neave's sake, she wrestled with her rising despair. Fought it and shoved it down where she could not hear its treacherous words.

I do not know the way out of here, but I swear by all the gods I will find it!

◆ ◆ ◆

The first pool was shallow enough to sit in, the water warmed by an underground hot spring. Heat seeped into her aching muscles. Black Hair was right, it was pleasant. *Good, let her think I have given in.* Karwa left them to usher in the next group. Leora remained alert, watching the guard and studying the exits.

The attendants brought out brushes and cakes of soap. Leora had never been bathed by another person, not since she was a child. It was a peculiar thing to have her back scrubbed and her hair washed. Drying came next, and then a massage with unguents that smelled of roses and citrus. Finally, Black Hair escorted Leora and the others to a dressing chamber, leaving the other attendants behind to deal with the next group. The clothing was pastel-hued, thin, and flowing, the sort of garment that would mean her death by freezing at Neskaya. It would be impossible to run in the flimsy sandals. She'd go faster barefoot.

Next came a belt of linked metal rings with a loop through which a chain might pass. When an attendant approached, carrying matching bracelets, trailing those fetters, Leora recoiled instinctively.

No!

Her silent cry reverberated … echoed. The sobbing Ridenow girl cringed visibly, then lifted her head and stared at Leora with a bewildered expression.

She should not have been able to hear me.

Only a moment had gone by. The attendant was still speaking rapidly in a dialect Leora could not follow. By signs, the woman conveyed that the bracelets would not be put on at this time, only checked for size.

She reached out to Neave's mind. *Be ready.*

And felt a ghostly ripple of an answer.

Be ready, she repeated to herself. She schooled her expression to meek obedience. And waited. And watched.

When the primping and painting were done, the captives were ushered into another room—the palace was a maze! —with a table bearing a pitcher and cups. An older woman who could have been Karwa's twin stood guard over the captives as an attendant poured water from the pitcher.

Leora took her turn and gulped down the water, flat but refreshing. She finished it and held out the cup. To her relief, she was given more. Afterward, she waited with the others along the far wall. Despite the harsh stares of their guards, they managed to exchange a few words. Leora opened her mind as best she could, intent on gleaning even the smallest detail—

Leora, help me! Neave's mental signature carried the raw edge of panic. *Help—*

—No, no!—desperately fighting—*Keep off!— Don't—*

HELP!

Images flashed through Leora. She saw the world through Neave's eyes, heard with Neave's ears, felt the same sensations—

—hands holding her, tearing at her clothing—

—the ripping sound as seams parted and worn fabric shredded—

—the outer layers in a heap on the floor—

—a tug and a wrench at the waistband—

Fingers like raptor claws grasping the tiny gem that glowed with shimmering light, the mirror of Neave's *laran*—

—reeling, the world warping into chaos—

—the blue-white light fracturing—

—screams echoing through her mind—

—echoing … echoing …

Leora almost lost her balance and fell against the wall. The last thing she wanted was to attract attention by fainting. *Breathe! Calm down …*

Neave? Are you there?

There was no answer.

Neave? Sister, sweetling, answer if you can!

And then Leora sensed—not an answer, but not an absence, either. An illusion arising from how desperately she wanted to hear from Neave? A dying echo, a remnant of the bond they had long shared, but nothing more?

Leora … came from deep in Neave's mind, her personality, her talent.

How could that be? Neave's starstone had been wrested from her while their minds were open to one another. She had been awake and aware, fighting desperately … but Leora had been unconscious when her own was taken.

I have to find it … get it back for her … But how?

Neave, hold on. Evanda, if ever you blessed us, watch over her!

◆ ◆ ◆

Leora approached the old woman at the water table. "Excuse me, madam," she said, enunciating the *cahuenga* with care. "I have a humble question, but I do not wish to offend."

Gimlet eyes regarded her. "Hmph."

"What happened to the clothing we were wearing? I know it's unfit for his lordship's sight, but might it be possible to obtain an item or two? Keepsakes?" She had to guess the correct term. "For comfort?"

"Must ask husband," the water woman replied with a dismissive gesture. "Holds everything. Gives everything." She meant *Once you wear his chains.*

Leora felt sick. And then furious. And then resolute.

"Do I have any say in who this husband is to be?"

Quick as a whip, the old woman slapped Leora. The chain drew her other hand tight against her belt, but she'd had ample experience with exactly how far she could reach. The blow was hard enough to make Leora's ears ring but not enough to tear her beautiful—*bridal*—clothing.

Eyes watering, Leora struggled upright. "When … when will I meet my husband? So I can ask him?"

"Lord Narram decides. If lucky, you go to his." The water woman added with a shrug, "Please husband, give him many sons, he generous. Old rags—bah! No need."

"There was an—" Leora paused, hesitating to say, *amulet* for fear of evoking superstitious dread, "a pendant among my belongings. A silken bag on a cord. How might I ask for it as a wedding gift?"

The water woman looked as if she would like to spit in Leora's face. "Husband will decide."

If Lord Narram were accustomed to dealing with captives who were overwhelmed and confused, she could use that to her advantage.

A horn sounded from beyond the door, and a quartet of armed guards entered. The attendants arranged the captives into a double line. They filed through yet another garden, then into a large, high-ceilinged chamber. Columns covered with brilliant mosaics ran alongside a carpeted, central aisle. A half-dozen men in striped robes, wide belts, and ornate headdresses turned to gawk at the captives.

At the far end stood a backless chair of crimson-streaked wood. Its arms and sides were carved like vines, and it looked sturdy enough to hold three men. The man who occupied it was of substantial girth beneath brocade robes and bands of metallic embroidery. His sandy gray hair was plaited in a dozen braids, and his beard had been waxed and sculpted. He regarded the captives, his eyes slits of unreadable darkness.

More painted and bejeweled captives entered the chamber. Their despair washed over Leora. She recognized Glynnis Ridenow, proud and ashen, as if hope as well as tears had drained out of her. Neave was the last, near to fainting and barely able to stay on her feet, half-carried between two attendants. In the back of Leora's mind, she was screaming silently, over and over. Leora dared not close her *laran* barriers or she'd lose what little communication they had, so she endured it as best she could. Even so, when the attendants dragged Neave into the center of the room and threw her down on the carpet before Lord Narram, the sight came as an almost physical blow.

Neave's face was a bloodless mask. Livid purple surrounded her eyes. Crimson stained her lips. With an obvious effort, she clambered to her feet and faced Narram, legs braced, hands clenched at her sides. With an act of equal will, Leora held herself still. Her training as a Keeper had fortified her self-control. The only thing that might have betrayed her, had anyone the skill to notice, was the slight tensing of her jaw muscles.

Memories surged in her mind, a hundred moments of Neave's kindness—Neave nursing her through threshold sickness—Neave patiently teaching her to use her starstone—Neave's warmth and ready laughter as a balm to her youthful angst—

—Neave tending to her wounds, physical and psychic, after the fire—

I would not have survived without her.

—Neave's joyful greeting at Aillard Castle—

If she dies, if she suffers any lasting harm from this ordeal, I will show them what a daughter of Hastur is capable of! I will exact vengeance in every drop of Narram's blood.

One of the guards who had accompanied Neave's group bowed before approaching the Dry Land lord, then approached the throne. The guard murmured briefly, words Leora could not make out, then gestured at Neave.

Narram's expression hardened, his brows drawing together. He straightened in his chair. His invisible shadow lengthened over the room. Nobody moved, yet everyone shrank in stature.

Except for Leora. Her only movement was to open her fists. She did not want her fury to dissipate into muscular tension, but to gather. To build. She'd been taught that it was impossible to use unaided *laran* for more than close, low-energy tasks, or to speak mind-to-mind except with physical contact.

Yet she had done it. She had done it as a terrified child and as a trained *leronis*. And as a Keeper.

Narram did not notice her defiant posture. His attention was now focused on his audience—his nobles and the women who cowered before him. His chest swelled as he pulled his shoulders back. When he spoke, his voice filled the chamber.

"*We are the men of the sun, of the sand!*" he chanted, and with each syllable, the guards pounded the butts of their halberds against the ground.

"*Red is the dawn,*" Narram called, and the other lords responded, "*And red the river!*"

"*Our strength is a knife …*"

The answer, rising in intensity, "*Honed by drought and storm!*

"*Like the god of the well …*"

The final phrase reverberated through air and wall and sky. "*We will rise again!*"

The echoes of the final syllables died away.

Leora's heart hammered against the cage of her ribs, but her thoughts were clear. Power flowed along her *laran* channels. It came from within her and through her. From the minds of the other women, even those with not enough talent to be worth training? From the heart of Darkover itself?

"We are the men of the sun, of the sand," Narram repeated, this time not in the ringing timbre of earlier but low-pitched, intense. "We are the *kiharim*, and our honor is pure. It shines like the sun. It opens for us the gates of heaven. It makes fertile our loins that we engender many sons."

Now his tone shifted, along with his attention. "For our *kihar* to remain strong, we shun those who would sully us. The deformed. The perverted." He paused, his gaze now resting on Neave. "The unrighteous."

Agreement rumbled through the chamber.

"Those who renounce the paths of foulness can be rendered acceptable. We have already freed some of their fetishes, according to the wisdom of our fathers. But others—" and here he glared at Neave again, "—others have resorted to stealth. But the eyes of the *kiharim* pierce all deception."

Narram paused as a man in a striped gray and white robe and elaborate headdress—a counselor or perhaps a physician—carried in a pile of clothing. Leora recognized the garments as Neave's.

On top of them sat a glowing blue-white gem. "Behold, great lord!" the counselor proclaimed. "Behold the vile talisman of the witch! She attempted to hide it in her garments. Thus shall we unmask all wickedness!"

Narram seized the skirt, bunching it around Neave's starstone, and held it aloft. "Now the world will witness the consequences. Woe to any who defy the law of the *kiharim!*"

"No … please, no," Neave whimpered. She fell back to the floor. Agony shrieked through Leora's mind. For a man of such malevolent intent, a man without a shred of *laran* sensitivity, to handle her sister's starstone, even buffered—

A chill ran through Leora. Perhaps he did not know what that would do to Neave: searing agony in mind and body, a moment of madness, and then death.

He does *know. It's exactly what he intends. To make her an object lesson for us all.*

I will not allow it! I will stand for Neave, and Glynnis, and every other leronis *he would destroy!*

Words rippled through her mind. *I stand for the memory of Callista, who had too much* laran *but not the training to use it wisely, and my sweet Sharina, who had none and was destroyed, nonetheless.*

She stood at a crossroads between the ravening fires loosed by Callista, the desolation of war, between darkness and grief and her own nightmares, and a tower of incandescent blue set in a field of golden grasses. A place of peace as well as beauty. A school, a haven. A sanctuary for those with precious Gifts against the cruelty and avarice of the world …

Arilinn whispered through her mind.

Energy surged up in Leora. Her *laran* channels ignited with blue-white power.

Narram shook out the folds of the skirt. The gem fell to the floor, the sound muted by carpet and silken wrapping. It rolled a short distance before coming to a halt. As Narram bent over to retrieve it, a cry went out from the assembly, astonishment and grief, and anticipation. *Hunger.*

Neave's hair had fallen across her face like a veil. A shroud. She lifted her head, her eyes locking on Leora's, as the last person she would ever look upon in life.

I will not allow *it!* stormed through Leora's mind.

She was no longer a woman of flesh. She was a vessel of faceted crystal, a reservoir of the storm arising in her. It battered against her barriers, demanding release.

Crouching, Narram reached for the starstone—his fingers brushed its facets—

—Neave cried out in terror—her eyes white and wild—

Leora opened herself to the tempest within her. She reached into the maelstrom to draw upon its power. Using all her Keeper's authority, she hurled it—

"*STOP!*"

The Dry Land lord froze in place. Air hissed through his clenched teeth. Blood suffused his face. Sweat shone on his face. He fought to move, to lift just one hand, just one finger, all to no avail.

Throughout the chamber, silence hung in the air, throttling speech.

"Uhnnn," Narram groaned. His chest heaved with the effort of even that small sound.

Leora hushed him with a glance.

"You will return the stone to its owner," she said. "You will restore mine, as well as any others you have stolen. Then you will release all your captives and provide us with the means to return home. Or you will suffer the consequences."

Rage swelled within her. It was getting increasingly difficult to control, dividing her attention from the scene before her. The days of privation had taken their toll. She knew what would happen if she let loose. If she fed it with her unchecked will.

A tumult of wildfires, dwarfing Callista's fiercest flames ... minds burning up like torches ...

... a city leveled ... mountains cracking, rivers boiling ...

... A god clad in living light striding through the world of men, crushing everything in his path ...

The confrontation must end quickly. Leora didn't have much reserve left.

Turning back to Narram, she restored his will.

"You?" Narram's voice, once assured, now sounded thin and shrill. "Who—who are *you* to tell your master what he must do? You are nothing, you are nobody! You are a witch without a talisman. It was taken from you!"

"I am Leora Hastur, *leronis* and Keeper." Unearthly calm rang in her words.

"I care not who you claim to be! Your boastfulness means nothing here. We of the *kiharim* know how to deal with insolent women—*thus!*"

He bunched a length of fabric around Neave's starstone. With one hand he grasped a corner and shook it out, so that the starstone would drop into his bare, cupped hand—

As the starstone tumbled free, the last dregs of Leora's restraint fell away. Unbridled *laran* exploded through her. Brilliance flooded her mind. Her channels ignited into blue-white flames.

She was no longer flesh and bone and blood, but a blazing crystalline form—a living matrix.

The power that she drew upon came from Darkover itself. It streamed forth, across sands and hills, no longer confined to a chamber in the Dry Land palace. It surged over mountains and lakes, blasting its way through rock and wall and tower. From the starry sweep of skies to the deepest cavern below, from the storm-tossed seas to the glaciated Wall Around the World, her power reached everywhere.

Aidan Hastur scrambled to his feet, his pen skittering across the paper, ink splattering. In a nursery at Carcosse Castle, twin girl babies wailed, their senses jarred open. On the fields of Alton and Aillard, men reined in their horses, frozen in alarm. A Ridenow lord crumpled on the training yard, screaming as he pressed his hands over his temples. Across the Hellers, *leroni* whose minds she'd touched responded like lightning flares—Luis-Jorje at Tramontana, and at Neskaya, Padraik answering in gladness and astonishment, and Rosmerta-Anne and Ilona and Juana, her old circle, her friend and Keeper, Mikhail Toman—and further still, more and more—until it seemed every person with a scrap of *laran* reacted to her mental blast.

Within the blue-white radiance, an incarnation took shape—a man bathed in shimmering light. His right arm lifted, revealing the ethereal form of a sword … from some other time, a time yet to be … wielded by a far-future kinsman …

If I summoned him, Aldones Himself would come. I am Hastur, and this is my Gift.

—a woman crowned in springtime joined the Lord of Singing Light, then a king of frozen hells and a woman dark as moonsless night. They bent toward her, immense.

Daughter of Hastur … whispered through her mind. *This realm is not meant for you. Your human body cannot sustain it. Return now to your place, and live …*

Remember who you are … Remember what you have done.

What have I done?

Carried aloft, Leora looked down on the Dry Land oasis. Everywhere, buildings lay in ruin, stones shattered down to their atoms and smoking pits where there had once been gardens. The earth itself had cracked, fractured into dust. Here and there, a straggling tree remained. Women and children cowered terrified in the rubble. In the central plaza, only the well and part of the palace—the part that sheltered Leora and the captive women—remained standing. Around the shattered wreckage, a lifeless desert stretched in every direction.

I leveled a settlement. I slaughtered gods know how many Dry Landers. And I did it with my unaided laran.

She'd been taught it was impossible. A starstone was the only method known to amplify a person's natural *laran*, except for telepathy between minds in close proximity.

And yet, as a child in the throes of threshold sickness, she had reached her sister's mind. And yet, the fires of the Carcosse attack still burned in her memory.

And yet.

Was it possible that she—her mind, her flesh, her spirit—had become a *living* starstone?

What I have done … What I have become …

As slow and certain as the movement of mountains, as swift as the flight of a sparrow, Leora came back to herself. Her eyes focused on the throne before her and a flame in the shape of a man.

The chamber came into focus. Color leached back into the world. Soot now streaked the mud-brick walls. The flaming man was no more than flickering embers. A touch, a breath would crumble him into ash. Around the room lay others, their bodies crisped black. Except for the murmuring of the captives huddled together, all was silent.

Neave was on her knees, cradling her starstone between her hands. She looked up at Leora through tear-flooded eyes.

Neave had set up a place to tend the wounded, a flat space beside a tumble of stones that was once a building. She was helped by Glynnis and her cousin, Silvia, along with a handful of freed captives with herbal-woman skills. The few remaining trees, likely from a courtyard garden, provided mottled shade, the best that could be found.

Straightening up, Neave ran the back of one hand across her forehead, smearing the sweat-caked dust. Leora thought her sister had never looked so weary, or so determined. She remembered a passing comment in a letter Neave had written during the years at Neskaya, a guarded reference to ghosts from the Carcosse war.

What of my *ghosts? Of the people of this town? Did they all deserve such a death?*

Did I have a choice? And what must I do now?

Leora walked up to Neave and held out a cup of water diluted with wine. Black Hair, whose real name was Ysabet and who hailed from a small village in Aillard, had discovered several barrels of the stuff and used it to make the water safe. "Drink this."

Accepting the cup, Neave sniffed and made a face, for the mildly alcoholic liquid had a sour taste, but gulped it down.

"Come, sit down," Leora said. "You've been on your feet for hours. You'll make yourself ill if you keep going."

"You should rest, too." *I will if you will.*

Leora glanced at the women crouching beside the wounded. *I think they're still afraid of me.*

Neave handed back the cup. *I'm not.*

"You're my bossy big sister," Leora pointed out.

Neave shrugged, meaning that such a comment did not deserve a reply. *I'm fine. I don't need to sit down.*

You do.

Neave faced her, hands on hips. *Now who's being bossy? Gods above, Leora, every telepath on the planet must have felt you! I've never heard of such power and range. You brought down Narram's palace and the remaining half of the town isn't safe. Is it any wonder that women who've been through—*she stumbled, *—through what we went through are wary of you?*

"Besides," Neave added aloud. "It isn't everybody. There's me and Glynnis and Ysabet, and others. Even the rest understand they owe you their freedom. Give them time. They'll all come around."

Leora collapsed on the broken stone, her ragged skirts bunching around her legs, and blinked back tears. Instinctively, she reached for the starstone that had been discovered in Narram's treasure chest. The stone warmed to her touch even as its crystalline pattern warmed her mind. The resonance had changed from its familiar pattern, as if her mind remembered being a living starstone and longed for it. She struggled to filter out the barrage of sensations, although that could have been in part because she was bone-tired.

She could not afford to be weak, not now. Not when there was so much yet to be done. Wounded who needed *laran* healing as well as ordinary medicine. Supplies to be dug out from the wreckage and sorted. They were days and days of travel from anywhere, no help was coming because nobody knew where they *were*, who knew how long the food and water would hold out, and *where was Duna?*

She wiped her eyes, swore silently, and laid her head down on arms folded over bent knees. *Don't cry don't cry don't cry.*

Neave hunkered down beside her and brushed fingertips across Leora's bare wrist. *Sweetling ...*

Shade fell over both of them, dimming the harsh afternoon.

What now? Leora straightened up.

"Pardon, *vai leroni.* I didn't like to disturb your rest, but I didn't know who else to tell." The voice was light and clear, one of the younger girls. Dayna, yes, that was her name. She was one of the lucky ones who seemed to be doing well. Not like Glynnis, who awoke screaming every night.

That was me once. I must find a way to help her.

"What is it, *chiya?*" Leora asked.

"For one thing, that old—" the girl was about to use an expletive for a malicious woman, but left it at "—*person.* Karwa. She died a little while ago. Nobody wanted to go near her or we would have realized earlier."

Kyorebni-*voice*. A sigh wafted through Leora. Had Karwa a family who would mourn her? Who loved her once? Finding out was yet another task that would be hers because no one else had the will or strength to do it.

"Put her body with the others," Leora said resignedly. "We'll cover them with stones. Was there something else?"

"Oh, yes! Ailis, the one who's always climbing trees, she went up and says there's dust off to the west. Maybe northwest? Riders, she thinks."

Leora scrambled to her feet. *More of these awful* kiharim? Or, hoping against hope, her own people?

◆ ◆ ◆

Starstone clenched in her fist, Leora strode to the edge of the encampment. Many of the survivors were already there, some holding on to one another in anxious silence, others chattering. She heard the words *rescue* and *strangers*. And *kiharim*.

"Go hide as best you can," she ordered, shooing them off. "We don't know who these people are. They could be Narram's kin." One of the women squeaked in fright.

"Come with me." Dayna took the hands of the two nearest and hurried them toward the section of town wall that was least damaged. A few tarried, glancing at the approaching dust clouds. "Come *on!*" she repeated, and sent them scurrying after the others.

"I'd like to wait with you." Glynnis approached Leora, her step hesitant. Since the fall of Narram, she'd worked tirelessly with the survivors, often stinting herself on food and sleep. "If that's all right."

Leora gave her a searching look. Her friend's face was paler than usual. "I can protect you better if you're with the others."

"I will have to face my fears eventually," Glynnis replied with a small, proud lift of her chin. "It might as well be now."

"All right, Get behind me, and don't distract me."

"I'll look after her." Neave put her arm around the Ridenow girl's shoulders.

Leora peered into the distance as the sand-colored clouds approached. They could only have been kicked up by horses, approaching fast. The sound of hooves grew louder. Now she could see banners whipping in the wind above the billows. Gold and green—she didn't recognize whose colors.

Closing her eyes, she focused on her starstone. Men … and horses … the men's minds radiating anxiety and hope. And fear. Anger and grief—

they had dealt with Narram's kind before. Had followed the *women-stealers* to find empty sands and desiccated corpses. From one came a flash of memory … dry bones, scraps of cloth, and a wedding bracelet. A *catenas* wedding bracelet.

She did not know if these men had come as saviors or as executioners. *They do not know what to expect, but they are afraid of me.*

Men who are frightened can do dreadful things.

The first riders slowed to a walk, their horses picking through the debris. Leora felt the tension in their hands as they tightened on the reins, the restiveness of the horses, sensed the emotion behind their murmured epithets. Even though they knew from Leora's psychic blast that something terrible had occurred, the actual sight of the wreckage shook them.

"Papa!" With a cry, Glynnis sprinted toward the foremost rider, who looked to be their leader, with a tabard of green and metallic gold. He leaped from the saddle and caught her in his arms. Her sobs rang through the air, but they were sounds of joy.

Leora murmured to Neave, "Get her cousin. She should know that her kinsmen have come."

Neave nodded, grinning. "She will be right glad of it."

A few minutes and a hundred sobs later, the Ridenow lord lifted his daughter's arms from around his neck. His gaze fastened on Leora. His brows were fair, almost blond, as was his hair caught back with a copper clasp.

Leora felt the touch of his mind on hers, his *laran* untaught but unmistakable. She sensed the presence of his starstone; likely, he'd been given one but not tutored in its use. Given what Glynnis had said, it was no wonder he had not received proper training. Perhaps a time would come when everyone with *laran* would spend at least a season at a Tower, learning the basics.

With one hand, he placed Glynnis behind him. The fingers of his other hand closed on the hilt of his sword. His eyes narrowed as he asked, "Are you the one responsible for what happened here?" *Are you the one who shook the world with your mind?*

The moment rested on a sword's edge. A mistake, an arrogant tone, a defensive phrase could shatter it. Ridenow was not her enemy, not yet, but more was at stake here than Leora's personal position. The balance of alliances on Darkover might collapse if this discussion went wrong.

"I am Leora Hastur, *leronis* and Keeper. You know my father, *Dom*

Aidan Hastur. And my sister's kin, the Aillards. Surely, that must speak for my character. I ask you to keep an open mind until you have heard the entire story."

Ridenow's gaze tracked from her filthy hair and sun-reddened cheeks to her bare, muddy feet. Leora heard his thought as if he had spoken it aloud. *Why should I believe anything you say?*

Glynnis grabbed her father's arm with surprising force and turned him to face her. "Papa, Leora is my *breda* in misfortune! We comforted one another when Silvia and I were first seized. I—I do not think I would have survived without her care. And then—" her eyes grew round, "—then, when we were about to be married off to the cronies of that disgusting *toad*, Narram, she set him *on fire!* and brought down the palace and everything, just as you see—with her *laran!*"

It warmed Leora's heart to see Glynnis bubbling over with such enthusiasm. So might Sharina have spoken, had she been in the same place.

"Oh!" Glynnis cried. "I am forgetting my manners. Please forgive me. Leora, this is my father, *Dom* Ewen Ridenow. Oh, and here is Silvia!"

Neave had come back, holding the hand of Silvia, the younger Ridenow cousin. Bursting into tears and cries of, "Uncle, you have come!" the girl ran to him. Their reunion made Glynnis cry again. The sound brought Dayna and the other women out to investigate. Exclamations of "We are rescued! Help is here!" swept through the survivors.

Neave slipped her hand through Leora's elbow. "Come on, sweetling. Let's let them celebrate. Our turn will come." She bit her lip as they walked toward the area where the wounded lay, and Leora knew she was thinking of Connor. Whether he would come after them. Whether he had heard of their plight. Whether he might not be able to find them. Whether he had become another victim of the Blackstones.

She wished she could offer reassurance but not false hope. Connor had no detectable *laran,* so he would not have sensed the use of her Gift. Could she reach his mind? Curling her fingers around her starstone, which now rested in a pouch Ysabet had sewn from a scrap of Dryland silk, she sent out a mental call.

Connor!

And felt a fleeting glimmer. Not a link, not any sort of contact bearing the stamp of his personality. Perhaps he was thinking of her, of Neave.

◆ ◆ ◆

Shadows lengthened across the ancient sea bed. Only the brightest stars shone, but more emerged with each passing hour. Lord Ridenow had directed his men to establish an encampment outside the remains of the Dry Land town, with shelter for the wounded, and a hot meal and soul-warming fires for everyone else.

The freed captives sat around the fires, talking and laughing. Their eyes shone with more than tears. Leora, sitting between Ysabet and Glynnis, sensed their relief. Now it was safe for them to hold their heads high, to weep and to sing, to say their names and where they were from without fear of punishment.

Ewen Ridenow and his captain watched from the edge of the circle. Leora sensed his gaze upon her. He was keeping his distance to allow the women to enjoy their liberation; some of them remained wary of strange men. She excused herself, untangled her arm from the hold Glynnis had on her, and went to stand beside him. Silvia was telling a story with many gestures and a great deal of uproarious laughter.

"They know they will go home," she said. "Thanks in no small part to you."

"I was the closest. Others will come." He meant, but did not say aloud, that he was sorry for having misjudged her.

Clearing his throat, he went on, "I will escort my daughter and niece home as soon as they can travel. After what they have endured—the little my Glynnis has been able to speak of, and the others—who have been too long without a father's protection," with a gesture toward the fire circle. "It is my duty to stand in stead of a father to restore them to their families."

Leora forbore to point out that these women had survived brutal conditions without the aid of male relatives. She had not needed a man to gain her freedom, she had done it herself. Yet, Lord Ridenow wished to act honorably. His words were not meant to sound arrogant but rather, kind. He wanted his kinswomen to return to their former lives, for this whole terrible episode to be over.

For some of us, it will never be over. Even if Darkover and all its great lords forgot, she could never return to the life she'd led before need and desperation awoke her Gift.

Ewen was looking at her, expecting her to say something. "That is not only honorable but generous," she said.

"You and your sister will come with us to Serrais, where you will be our honored guests. From there, I will send word to your kinsmen."

Glynnis emerged from the firelight. "Papa, you said just now that you want to bring us all home. I cannot speak for Silvia or the others, but I—I do not *want* to go home. I want to go wherever Leora goes, whether that is to Hastur Castle or the Wall Around the World or the far side of Mormallor, I don't care."

Ewen placed his hands on his daughter's shoulders. "*Preciosa*, you have been through a terrible ordeal. Naturally, you feel unsettled. I cannot blame you for clinging to the friend who shared your captivity. But as your father, I must choose what is best for you. You belong at home with your family."

Glynnis clenched her fists at her sides. "I know you speak from love, Papa, and that is why I am not *furious* with you for saying such a thing. You have no *idea* what I have been through and what I need now."

Leora stared at Glynnis, struck by the change in her young friend. Glynnis had gone from being a prisoner to a nightmare-ridden survivor to this, a young woman standing her ground.

Ewen's shock was like a physical blow. Facing him, Glynnis radiated defiance. Leora's heart ached for them both.

Leora turned to Glynnis. "I will not forsake you, *breda*, that much I promise. But the world goes as it wills and not how you or I would wish it. Your father is right." She gave Ewen a sharp look, and he stilled his next words. "You and I have obligations to our families, and they to us. I must go home, to Hastur Castle. I have matters to settle, and I must reassure my family that I am alive and well."

"Glynnis, you belong with those who cherish you," Ewen said in a voice resonant with feeling.

Leora imagined the same scene playing out for every other captive. Some would welcome the embrace of their families, the security of what they had known. Yet some would see it as another form of confinement, being locked in with memories of horror with no escape.

"And then?" Glynnis had not looked away from Leora.

"I will send for you once I have established a place for us," Leora said. "A Tower where your mind and spirit can be restored. Ordinary healing may not be enough. It wasn't for me after the Carcosse war. I had to master my *laran* to make peace with my past. That may be true for you, or you may find that with time and the care of your family, you find contentment in your life."

Ewen's hostility softened, although he had the sense to keep quiet.

"I don't *want* to wait." Glynnis sounded very young.

"Yet wait we must. Will you not allow your father to console you? Does he not have your love, as you have his?"

Eyes bright, Glynnis allowed her father to gather her into his arms. She whispered, "Papa."

Leora left them murmuring comfort to one another. As for herself, there was much to sort through, everything from her reunion with her father to the betrothal she could no longer honor to the reactions of the great lords to her planet-spanning *laran* to how she was going to get the financial and material support for her Tower. For now, it was enough.

Dawn glimmered over tents and cookfires, and piles of baggage ready to be loaded up. Leora looked over the encampment, standing beside Ewen Ridenow. "We must leave in the next day or two," he remarked. "There is no reason for delay, since your healer—" he meant Dayna, "—tells me the last of the wounded are now well enough to travel."

"I agree. There is no purpose in remaining here any longer." And many reasons not to tarry: the well was drying up and what little food they'd been able to salvage from the town was almost gone. As it was, they would have to ration meals for the journey to Serrais. The proximity of Ewen's men was proving difficult for a few of the freed captives, even with the men camping outside the town and the women free to find sleeping space behind the crumbled walls. Conditions might be even more cramped on the road. The sooner they got started, the sooner they would reach their destinations.

Yet she could not help wishing for another arrival—her father, the Aillards, even Kennard Lindar—*and Connor, where was he?*—so that she need not go to Serrais. Ewen had shifted from suspicion to respect, although she did not entirely trust him once he was back in his stronghold.

They discussed the remainder of the preparations, which women could walk and which must ride, and how to accommodate the survivors who could not tolerate the closeness of riding pillion with a man.

"Glynnis must go with me," Ewen said, even though she had previously insisted she was strong enough to walk.

Leora sought out her young friend and urged her to reconsider. It was clear that he wasn't going to offer a ride to anyone else. "Grant your father this small kindness. He has not gotten over his fear of losing you."

"Put that way, I will," Glynnis said. She meant, *Since you ask it of me.*

The following morning, the tents were taken down and what little packing remained was completed. Leora noticed a slender boy not out of his teens hunkered down at the edge of the camp. She wondered what his story was. Shy and silent, he gave off an aura of half-remembered torment. She'd asked Ewen about him when she first noticed him. According to Ewen, the boy had crept into a Ridenow outpost in the dead of winter and been taken to Serrais. Terrified of being cast out, the boy had been eager to earn his keep. When Ewen determined to rescue his daughter and niece, the boy had indicated, through signs and drawings, his knowledge of the route. Besides scouts ahead and behind, rotated among several of Ewen's men, they now had a guide.

They set off, Leora at the front of the column alongside Ewen and Glynnis. Their speed was limited to that of the slowest walker and decreased even further as they scaled the inner slope of the ancient sea bed. Past the wall's shelter, winds stirred up gritty sand. They halted at the crest to give those on foot a breather. Ewen distributed scarves to the freed captives to protect their faces.

With the town behind them, stretches of dusty grit gave way to low rises marked by feathery spicebush. The party increased their speed over the relatively flat ground. After several days, the guide indicated an area of green ahead. Here they found plentiful water and shelter from the sun.

The hour being only a little past midday, Ewen called for an extended rest. Horses and humans drank their fill, and water supplies were replenished. Ewen ordered his men to the far side of the picket lines so that the women had privacy to wash. Dayna, along with Silvia and a younger woman started a splashing game until Neave pointed out how much mud they were churning up.

"Mark me, you'll be eating mud with your dinner."

The girls waded out of the pool and lay, wet and giggling, on the bank.

"How young they are." Neave lowered herself beside Leora on a rock a little way from the water's edge. "Were we ever that carefree?"

"I never knew you as a child," Leora pointed out. "But I was much, much worse. Sharina and I used to get into the worst scrapes, and Father—" Her words trailed off. How long had it been since she'd spoken of Sharina in anything but grief? And guilt?

Let it go, she told herself. *Remember that Sharina would have forgiven you long since.* Her sister's memory shifted from pain to nostalgia and remembered affection. *She would want you to live a happy life.*

Now that the women had finished bathing, some of Ewen's men moved about the picket line, tending the horses. Others stood about, joking, as they washed out socks and dust-coated scarves. Beyond them, on a slight rise above the bank, the Dry Land boy sat by himself.

Leora brushed bits of moss from her skirt and ambled over. Through her *laran* senses, she picked up the boy's aching loneliness and, beneath it, a red-black cloud of memories. He looked up, eyes white-rimmed, as she approached.

"I didn't mean to startle you," she said quietly. "May I sit?"

He nodded, a sharp dip of his chin.

She folded her legs, sitting close enough to get a clearer image of his energon channels yet not so near as to spark his alarm. He watched her out of the corner of his eyes as she began talking, using tone and cadence to soothe. His tension eased a little. He no longer had the quality of a trapped animal.

"I think something terrible happened to you," she said, deliberately not looking at him, "and that is the reason you do not talk." She felt, rather than saw, the subtle jerk of his head, the clench of his jaw. "Something terrible happened to me, too. Oh—" with a glance toward the other women, "—when I was a child. My home was attacked and many people lost their lives. My sister was one of them, and I almost died, too."

She went on, letting the story unfold. He leaned toward her, his rising interest plain. Through her heightened sensitivity, she felt the heat and churn of his emotions. When, finishing, she met his gaze, he did not flinch.

"I would like to help you if I may," she said. "If you wish it."

One hand fluttered to his throat. He cried in rage and denial and terror so brutally suppressed as to be cut off entirely from his voice.

She nodded, "Yes," and held out her hand. He rested his fingers on her palm, the skin rough with callus, the nails bitten to the quick. The touch sharpened her reading of him. Like most people, he appeared on the surface to have only low-grade *laran*. She thought of Glynnis, who had a great deal more but had never been allowed to develop it. This boy—*yes, there*—as deeply buried as his voice, scabbed over by lashings of clotted red and char—*a spark*.

Cradling her starstone, she reached for the crystalline pattern that enhanced her *laran*. At her psychic touch, tendrils of the boy's remembered abuse softened. Lifted. Fell away. Not all, for that would require painstaking healing work in a protected environment. But enough so that when she returned to herself, the boy was smiling, his cheeks streaked with wetness.

"Ciarran." The name came like rusty hinges swinging open. He jabbed one thumb at himself. "Ci-*ar*-ran."

"Ciarran," she repeated, to his enthusiastic nod. "I am Leora."

To say more might strain the boy's newly discovered voice. After promising to work with him further and find a place where he could receive more comprehensive care, Leora left him.

Leora woke from a near-doze in the afternoon warmth when Neave returned with a hunk of dried meat pounded with fat and bits of dried sour cherries. "I raided Lord Ridenow's private larder," Neave said. "Or rather, I asked Glynnis and she dug it out for me. There isn't anything that girl would not do for you. She has a serious bout of hero-worship."

"Mmmm." Leora nodded in between mouthfuls. Renewed strength poured through her. "As for Glynnis, I am the first *leronis* who has taken her seriously. And I am not kin, which is sometimes an advantage."

"I suppose." Neave's gaze drifted to where the Dry Land boy—*Ciarran*— was bent over a bridle, stitching repairs. He was humming. "You did well with him."

"A beginning only. Like Glynnis, he needs more care than I can give under these conditions."

"You helped both of them," Neave pointed out.

Leora faced her sister. "Which I cannot do as Lady Lindar … or Lady Anything-Else." She added silently, *I am a Keeper. A leronis. A healer.*

A teacher, Neave said.

My place is in a Tower, not a castle.

Neave's eyes shone with understanding. She brushed her fingertips across the back of Leora's wrist, a telepath's butterfly touch. *You mean to withdraw from the betrothal to Kennard.*

I do not see that I have a choice. Yet I do not know how to handle such worldly politics. If it were a Tower matter, I would have no difficulty. But Father made such a big point of the consequences should that treaty fail … Her thoughts came out in a rush. *Will Kennard accept my decision, do you think? And Father! What am I to tell him?*

"Of those the easiest to deal with is Kennard," Neave said with a smile. "You have not seen him and Valentina together, as I have. If the treaty can be arranged any other way, I doubt Kennard will object. In fact, I suspect he will release you with a glad heart."

Valentina? … yes, that makes sense. The color in her cheeks as she confessed she liked Kennard very much. *"Leora, I do not think your family could find you a better husband."*

"Could it be so simple?" Leora wondered aloud.

"And yet," Neave replied with candor, "you forged a way for Connor and me when it seemed impossible. I cannot begin to repay you, but as a beginning, I will stand by your side."

Leora grimaced. "I shall need it. But Father—and the treaty he worked so hard to put together! How am I to manage that?"

"My dear," Neave said with a laugh, "one problem at a time! Leave Father for tomorrow. I cannot speak for him, for he and I have had only sporadic contact since I went to Aillard, but circumstances have changed. Not just the treaty, but Father's rise to pre-eminence among the powerful lords—*Comyn*, they call themselves, 'Equals'—not to mention that every telepath in the realms now knows how immensely strong you are."

I simply wish to build my Tower for people like Glynnis and Ciarran and all the others who so desperately need a place where they can master their laran—*and live there in peace.*

In answer, Neave squeezed Leora's hand. *Given how determined you have always been and how worthy your goal, I believe you will achieve it. Look at how many obstacles you have already overcome.*

"Hmm." Leora rested her head on Neave's shoulder, thinking how comforting it was to be understood. "What of you, sister mine?"

"Ah, me? I cannot return to Aillard," Neave murmured. "I will have to go home. That is where Father is, so where Connor must be." She sighed. "And where I shall be."

"And I, for a time."

"I am glad of that."

The nights grew colder as the days shortened. Midsummer Festival seemed an eon in the past. At night, Leora and Neave wrapped themselves in a single blanket for warmth. They whispered like the close sisters they had never been before. Sometimes, Neave would become quiet, and Leora knew she was thinking of Connor.

The land sloped downward, leaving behind the windswept rocky ground. The landscape grew tamer and the going was easier. Birds were more numerous, as were antelope and rabbit-horns. A thread of a trail emerged, then broadened, intersected another, and became a road.

They passed a familiar-looking crossroads framed by scrubby trees and a crumbling rock wall. The hair on Leora's neck prickled.

This is the place. This is where it happened. Already fatigued from trudging so far on foot, she swayed on her feet.

"My lady?" Ciarran, at the head of the party, turned back just as she caught her balance.

The sound of his voice, now a low tenor with usage, broke the moment's vertigo. "Do not fret for me. I'm well enough—" with a glance at Neave, who had caught her reaction and gone a shade paler. "'Tis memory, that's all."

Seeing the place as it was, not as how memory painted it, steadied her. They had come from *that* direction, leading back toward the Blackstone Hills. And *here* was where the Dry Land bandits had lain in wait …

"Yonder lies our road." Ewen pointed to the branch leading due west. "We'll be at Serrais within the tenday."

If Connor comes looking for us, he will not know where we've gone, said Neave.

Ewen promised he would send messages to Hastur, and Lindar and Aillard, as well.

A longer wait. Neave sighed.

Their conversation was broken by the sound of hooves from the direction of the Blackstone Hills. Drawing his sword, Ewen shouted a warning. His men did the same, forming a defensive circle around the women.

Ciarran nudged his pony closer. *I will defend you!* The telepathic thought rang through her mind.

"There! That's where we were set upon!" A woman's voice—

Duna! Leora bolted in the direction of her friend's voice. Past the crumbling rock wall, around a brush-sheltered bend—the road angled up—

"What the—" Ewen shouted. "Come back!"

And there was Duna, mounted on a fine-boned riding chervine, and behind her, a knot of men in the colors of Aillard, Lindar—and her own Hastur!

The foremost Hastur rider cried out, "They're here!"

Leora had known that voice since she was a child. "Neave!"—with a glance over her shoulder—"Neave, it's Connor!"

Connor burst into the crossroads and was on his feet before his horse had slid to a halt. A rush, a touch on her shoulder, no more. Eyes searching behind her. Neave ran up to him, laughing and crying and throwing herself into his arms. He held her so close, they might have been a single person.

Their joy almost brought Leora to her knees. Tears blurred her vision. She could not speak. She heard, half-aloud, half-telepathic, Connor saying, *"I will never let you go, never again, not while life is in me."*

"Nor I, you," Neave replied.

The two parties came together in a jumble of horses and men, men mounted and on foot, women on foot and riding double, Duna sliding off her chervine and hugging first Leora and then Neave. Above the clamor and milling came the forlorn cry of a chervine. Their old pack animal trotted up, panting and bleating until it reached Duna and leaned into her.

"Godsforsaken creature follows me everywhere," Duna muttered. Then, to the sisters, "You're safe, the both of you!"

"Duna, *you're* safe," Neave said. "How—?" She broke off as Ewen guided his horse forward.

"My lord, I am Connor Darriell, paxman to Lord Aidan Hastur." Connor went on to introduce an Aillard captain, head of the guard of the wedding emissary, and Rannirl Cornwell from Lindar. "I had nearly arrived at Lindar when Duna, the friend and attendant of the *vai leroni* Leora and Neave Hastur, found me. She told me that they'd been kidnapped by Dry Land ruffians and she had just barely managed to remain free."

Leora met Duna's eyes, recognizing her friend's resolute spirit. *I bet it was more than "just barely." Doranna chose well in sending her with me.*

Connor had gathered a rescue party from Lindar, including the captain from Aillard, an experienced fighter, and several of his men. With Duna as their guide, they had retraced her route to the crossroads, intending to follow the only remaining road in the direction of the Dry Land. At each point of his story, the freed captives murmured in wonder. Ewen made no response, sitting silent and tight-faced on his horse.

Ewen thought the value of the captives arose from their family connections. The daughters of the most powerful man on Darkover would make formidable bargaining tools … He intended to pressure Connor to accompany him to Serrais. He saw Connor as weak, emotional, apt to concede rather than risk the women. If it came to a fight, he was sure he would prevail.

Anger flared in Leora. She had not escaped storm and slavery, only to be exploited for political influence. She pitched her voice to be heard throughout the crossroads.

"Thank you for all your efforts on our behalf, Lord Ridenow," she said. "May there be goodwill and amity between us from this day forward."

Approval and not a little surprise at her forwardness rippled through the gathering.

"What does this mean?" Ysabet asked. "Where are we to go?"

"Dinna worry," Duna said with a friendly smile.

"I will answer that question presently," Leora said. Then, back to Ewen, "Now that my father's paxman is here, my sister and I no longer require your *protection*"—with a slight emphasis on the word. "You are free to escort your kinswomen back to Serrais with a clear conscience that now *all of us* will be looked after. As for you, my sisters—" turning to the former captives, "—you may choose. Serrais with the Ridenow family, or Hastur with me, or Aillard or Lindar—and then anywhere else you wish to go."

A moment of stunned silence answered her. These women had endured having all choices wrested from them. A few looked near paralyzed and unable to absorb this news. Others buzzed with hope.

"I know you mean well," Ewen said, fixing his gaze on Leora. "But given what the Dry Land slaves have endured, proper thought must be given to their care. We have a plan, one that you agreed to. It would be rash to set aside all preparations on a whim." As he spoke, his hand crept to the hilt of his sword. He did not grasp it, but the threat was unmistakable.

Connor drew Neave behind him. He shifted his stance, weight balanced, body angled, hand ready to unsheathe his blade. Leora motioned to him to hold. He nodded, although he did not relax.

One hand resting lightly around the pouch containing her starstone, Leora took a step closer to Ewen. "Lord Ridenow, I speak for my father when I say neither of us wishes to imperil the friendship between our two realms. At the same time, he will not look kindly upon any action that delays our return home. Are you willing to disregard my father's influence and power? Then let me remind you of what *I* am capable of."

Ewen drew back, his hold on the reins so tight that his horse threw up its head in protest, tail lashing.

Neave, standing at Connor's shoulder, gasped audibly. *Leora! Is such a provocation wise?*

To allow his challenge to pass would be the greater folly, Leora responded. *I am not afraid of him.*

Neave was right in counseling against a needless confrontation. Leora knew that she must keep her focus on her goal. Had she not promised Glynnis a place of healing and study? And Ciarran?

She lowered her hand. "Lord Ridenow, I repeat my desire to continue the friendship so well begun. Consider, if you please, that my determination to be speedily reunited with my family in no way diminishes my gratitude for all the help you have given us. We will part ways here, giving due thought to the others in your care. Will you meet me again in a happier time?"

"Yes, Papa," came the clear, light voice of Glynnis, riding pillion behind him. "Think if our situation were reversed. Would you not want me to hurry home to you?"

Ewen's shoulders rose and fell. In surrender, Leora thought. She had seized the advantage in calling for cordial relations between Serrais and her influential father. But against the logic of his daughter, the Ridenow lord had no defense.

"Put that way, I must agree," he said. "There, there—" to Glynnis's entreaty, "—you will see your friend again before long."

Ewen surprised Leora by suggesting a division of his supplies so that Connor's party had enough for the women who would go with him. Ewen and his quartermaster, and Connor and the Aillard captain negotiated the logistics, with Duna keeping a watchful eye, making suggestions, and muttering that soldiers had no idea of what women needed. Neave joined Leora in speaking to each of the freed captives about where they wished to go.

When everything had been divided and the two parties ready to be on their way, Glynnis came up to Leora. Trailing her were her cousin and Dayna, who had decided to go to Serrais.

"I will never forget you!" Glynnis threw her arms around Leora.

"Nor I, you, little sister." After a long moment, Leora pulled back to look the younger woman in the eyes. "Remember what I promised? That there would be a place for you to train and heal, should you need it? And even if not, this may be the beginning of harmonious relations between our families."

Sniffing, Glynnis nodded, then joined her father and slightly more than half the women headed toward Serrais. In the end, Leora, Neave, Duna, Ysabet, and the rest would accompany Connor to Lindar. The fastest rider was sent to bring news of the rescue to Hastur Castle.

◆ ◆ ◆

Lindar's seat was not a stronghold but a sprawling manor house of rust-hued stone and mullioned windows surrounded by gardens. It sat atop a pleasant hill, flanked by a trading town, garden plots, and orchards. Rolling plains stretched into the distance. The travelers arrived near dusk, and when the huge red sun dipped toward the west, its rays limned the waving grasses with gold. In the hazy distance, Leora made out two peaks. She could not remember seeing them in her visions, yet a thrill ran through her at the sight.

A welcome party waited on the steps of the manor house. Among them were Kennard and an older man and woman, all dressed simply in finely woven wool.

Kennard came forward. "*Leronis* Leora, I cannot express how relieved we were to learn of your safe return. When your party did not arrive in the expected time, we feared the worst."

"Many things have changed since you and I last met," Leora replied. "On behalf of my companions as well as myself, I thank you for your hospitality."

Kennard presented Leora, Neave, and Connor to his father, *Dom* Octavien Lindar, and his maternal aunt, *Domna* Kendria Vallonde, who served as the Lindar chatelaine.

Leora thought the Lindars looked careworn rather than aged by years. She noticed, also, their modest garb. *I must take care that they do not suffer from the loss of my dowry. They may live comfortably, but compared to the Aillards, they are at a disadvantage.*

Domna Kendria took charge of the guests. In short order, she arranged rooms, baths, clean clothes, and hot meals. Everyone, family and guests alike, crowded around a long table to eat, drink *shallan* and hot spiced wine, and listen to Kennard's young sister and her music tutor playing on reed flute and *rryl*.

As tired as Leora was when she tumbled into bed, she lay awake for what seemed like a long time, listening to her sister's even breaths. Her thoughts jumbled together—whether *Dom* Octavien would accept her offer—*Kennard* would, she was sure—how the Aillards would react—what could go wrong—and Father!—Connor was so confident of his approval. And the looming, unanswered question about repercussions from her destruction of the Dry Town—members of every great family would have felt her *laran*—

I will worry myself into a frazzle at this rate!

In her mind's eye, she saw the golden field and two peaks in the hazy distance. It called to her, whispers that were longing but not yet words.

This, this *is my goal. My dream.*

With the vision shimmering in her imagination, she fell asleep.

The next morning, she dressed in her borrowed clothes and found her way to the dining area from last night. Kennard and his father were just finishing their breakfast.

"*Dom* Octavien, *Dom* Kennard," she began. "I would like a word with you both at your earliest convenience. In private, if you please, except for my sister and my father's paxman."

An hour later, the two Lindars, Leora, Neave, and Connor gathered in *Dom* Octavien's library, a snug, firelit room that reminded Leora of her father's study. It was smaller and fewer books lined the shelves, but it had the same sense of slightly shabby comfort. Leora opened by thanking the Lindars for meeting with her.

"After your ordeal, I quite understand if you wish to postpone your nuptials," Octavien said gravely.

Leora caught a flare of emotions from Kennard, so tangled she could not tell them apart, hope and sorrow being the foremost. And resignation. Hurriedly, she strengthened her *laran* barriers. She had picked up his feelings without conscious intent. During her captivity, her sensitivity, even without the aid of her starstone, had been an advantage. Now it amounted to an intrusion, a rudeness.

"Given the circumstances, I consider the betrothal annulled," Leora replied. "Kennard will have no difficulty finding another, more suitable wife. As for myself, my fervent desire is to withdraw to a Tower where my talents can be put to constructive use."

A swift rush of color suffused Kennard's cheeks. Octavien said, in a voice that quavered a little, "That cannot be, *vai dami—vai leronis*. The fates of two realms rely upon this marriage treaty. I am sorry to insist if this is no longer your wish, but the marriage must go forth."

"That cannot take place without my consent, and I have already stated my intentions." Leora gentled her tone. "But your concerns are valid. The best solution is one that benefits all parties. Therefore, I have asked *Mestre* Connor, as my father's voice in these matters, to put forth a plan to ensure peace and mutual prosperity for you and our Aillard cousins."

Oh, well done! came from Neave.

I have had time to think this through. Leora cast her sister a sidewise smile. *If I am to gain my freedom here at home as I did in the Dry Land, I must act properly political. I once thought worldly affairs were very different from those of the Tower, but now I understand the similarities.*

Connor sat straight in his chair, unconsciously mimicking Aidan's posture. "When Lord Hastur was brought into this matter, it seemed that the best, perhaps the only solution to the generational tension between you and your neighbors was a union by marriage. That is no longer necessarily the case. For one thing, *Tenerésteis* Leora has withdrawn her consent. One might also argue that her captivity in the hands of ruthless brigands renders her no longer suitable."

"I didn't mean—" Kennard realized his error and broke off speaking.

"Hrrumph." His father scowled, then turned his attention back to Connor. "We withhold our opinion on this point, leaving open the option of returning to it. Meanwhile, what do you mean by *no longer necessarily the case*? Is there an alternative?"

"Hear me out." Connor leaned forward, his expression intent. "Our world has changed, and we must change with it. The Comyn are moving toward diplomacy instead of conquest to resolve our differences. With Lord Hastur acting as mediator and sponsor, you can forge an alliance based upon mutually binding agreements, verification of trust, and common benefit."

"Say more," Octavien said in a dazed voice.

Connor went on to describe the particular provisions, including designating borders and trade, and procedures for resolving disputes. "At a future time, once trust has been established, the agreement might include making restitution for past injuries."

Leora was greatly impressed by Connor's thoughtfulness and clear articulation of his points. This was not the paxman of her childhood but a mature adult who shared her father's values, his dream of peace, and even his oratorial style. By the time he summed up, Octavien was nodding and smiling, and Kennard was not even attempting to hide his relief. Neave beamed with pride.

"Since we are agreed in principle, the next step is to obtain a commitment from Lord and Lady Aillard," Leora said, rising. "To that end, we must depart as soon as may be. May I impose on you to care for the women we freed from the Dry Town ruffians, assisting those who have homes to return to and providing for the rest?"

"Of course, of course!" Octavien exclaimed. "And I will provide additional mounts and an escort for your safety. I shall dispatch a message to Aillard Castle without delay, and to your father, as well."

"I will accompany you," said Kennard, rising also. "It is appropriate that a member of this family be present and *Mestre* Rannirl is still recovering from his travels."

Leora was not in the least surprised by either announcement. And from the expression on Kennard's face as she expressed her thanks, she had made not one ally, but a generation of allies.

"I have one more thing to ask," she said, walking beside Kennard. "On our way here, I spied a stretch of plains with the view of the two peaks. Who owns it?"

"I know the place," Kennard said. "I thought of it when you asked me about the color of the grass. It was at the ball in Hastur Castle, do you remember? It doesn't belong to either us or Aillard. We've grazed cattle there from time to time over the years, but the grass is poor quality." He grinned wryly. "It's probably the only thing we haven't fought over."

"If I wanted to found a Tower there, would you help?"

His answering grin said he would dig the foundations himself.

◆◆◆

Aillard Castle
To Aidan, Lord Hastur
Dear Father,

I take the opportunity to tuck a letter in with the documents Connor is sending to you, detailing the agreement he has worked out between Aillard and Lindar in place of a marriage alliance. The storm that descended on our arrival has abated, although our hosts assure us this is a temporary lull and travel remains unsafe. However, a messenger on a fast horse may get through before the snows close us in. I trust that you received the news that Neave and I were released from captivity of a Dry Town chief named Narram. He is no longer a threat to anyone. I have formed the basis of a mutual alliance with Dom Ewen Ridenow, whose daughter and niece I befriended during our captivity. This may be to our advantage.

I assure you again that I am well, as is Neave. She is very happy. Please convey our love to Mother and the rest of the family.

Adelandeyo,
Leora, Keeper

◆ ◆ ◆

Midwinter
To Damisela *Leora Hastur*
My dear,

The news that you had not arrived at Lindar Castle sent me into such a frenzy of worry. I feared so many things, each worse than the other, so that I almost made myself ill. Jessamy, sweet girl, offered to take care of me, although she is now indisposed with her fourth child. I sent her a note forthwith that she was to stay at home, and then took my nerves in hand.

Your father tells me we are not to expect you—well, I am not sure when. You must not imperil your health by unseasonal travel. Once the snow melts, I hope to see you. There is to be a convocation or council of sorts of all the important nobles in Thendara after Midsummer. I hope to see you here afterwards, if it can be arranged.

Do not fear, I will not pressure you to remain. It is clear to me from your last visit that you no longer consider this your home, although of course, you will always *be welcome. After your recent, dreadful experience, it's understandable if you wish to withdraw to a Tower. A second betrothal offer is not to be expected, nor do I believe you would wish it. I know how little I understood your life since you first left us. I pray to the Blessed Evanda that whatever your heart desires, you may find it.*

Your loving
Mother

◆ ◆ ◆

Past Midwinter
To Leora Hastur, Keeper
Dear Leora,

Events are moving more quickly than I expected. The idea of a council of Comyn peers has caught on and I must go to Thendara early to make arrangements. The Elhalyn have a large house that can host the meeting temporarily. If this becomes a recurrent event, we will need a larger place.

Nevertheless, the subject most eagerly anticipated is one you know. Despite the support from Aillard and Ridenow, as well as Lindar and some of the smaller houses, the question of a hitherto unknown form of laran, *an extremely powerful one at that, must be answered. It is essential that you present yourself to the council.*

I have attached the address and directions to the house I have engaged for our use. I expect to see you no later than a tenday before the opening of the council, date below. I have sent word to Connor that I require his assistance as soon as he can make arrangements for you and your sister.

In closing, I remind you of my grandfather's watchword, which has become the motto of our house: Permanedó. *"We shall remain."*

Aidan, Lord Hastur

◆ ◆ ◆

Early spring
To Leora Hastur, Keeper
Aillard Castle
Breda,

I wish I could capture Father's surprise when Connor and I showed up on the doorstep of his rented Thendara house! He was gracious about it, naturally, but also mystified that I—or you!—would do as we wish and not as he commands.

Connor and I will be married here shortly after the formal session. Domna Graciela will be livid, but as she is not my mother, I feel no obligation to indulge her feelings. The only people whose presence matters to us are you, my dear sister, and Father—once he gets used to the idea.

While Connor is sequestered away with Father, I've been exploring. Thendara is a bit like a calf grown so fast it doesn't know what to do with itself, but also a bit like a scorpion-ant nest. This council of Father's has brought about a parade of balls, street fairs, musical performances, and general merrymaking. I have met a number of Gifted youngsters with no training in how to use their laran *beyond surviving threshold sickness and keying into their starstones. All, or should I say almost all, are enthusiastic about a season or two at a Tower. One young woman with the strongest telekinesis I have yet seen said it's been like going through life knowing you can see colors when the world has only shades of black. Or trying to sort pollen grains wearing gloves. I will tell you more when I see you, which cannot be too soon.*

Your loving
Neave

The long Darkovan winter had broken, warming to a spring of blossoming fruit trees that filled the air with fragrance and layered the ground with petals. Even here in Thendara, where Aidan had made his way as fast as a sturdy horse could negotiate the roads, a sense of cheerfulness prevailed. Now the fruit of those same trees was ripening. So, too, were his own affairs.

He and Connor stood before the brass-bound gates leading to the Elhalyn house, endowed with heavy stone walls, stabling for a dozen horses, two wings of residence, and an enormous great hall. He had thought it ample for the Comyn convocation when Gabriel-Alar Elhalyn had offered it. Now that word had spread beyond his initial outreach, more attended every session. Today's meeting, the last before the final ball, was sure to be crowded.

Leora and Neave, resplendent in new-made cloaks of velvet trimmed with *marl* fur, came into view along the broad street. They were accompanied by Captain Derry and the woman Leora had brought from Aillard, originally from Neskaya. *Duna*, that was her name. Competent and fearless, she bullied even her chervines, notoriously difficult beasts, into adoration.

"Sorry we're late." Neave gave Aidan a quick kiss on the cheek, a familiarity that never failed to delight him, before standing beside Connor.

Leora stood apart, holding herself with the aloof poise of a Keeper. At the same time, she remained his sweet Leora, fierce and loyal, inquisitive and stubborn, and most of all, loving. Since their reunion in Thendara, he had come to respect how much more she had become. When she met his gaze, her smile was warm. "Father."

He closed the distance between them so that his voice would not carry. "Are you ready?"

"Father, we have been over the arguments a dozen times. I said then and I say now that if storms, fires, and Dry Town brigands cannot deter me, then a civilized discussion stands no chance." She lowered her voice. "Will you trust me now, as I have trusted you?"

He could not control how she behaved in the council or what she said and did. Perhaps he had never had that power. He would stand beside her, even so, and use his hard-won prestige in her cause.

Her eyes widened—she had caught his thought. She mouthed the words, *Thank you, Papa.*

"Let's go in," Connor said.

Past the doors, they continued through a wide, stone-walled foyer, where Derry and Duna remained with the other servants, and into the great hall. Banners in the colors of each realm hung from the balconies. Lord Elhalyn had gone to great lengths to prepare for the session, with cushioned chairs for the head of each house and benches for other family members. Aidan had insisted on two chairs of equal size. Connor and Neave would have places of lesser importance, but he meant for Leora to be accorded the same privilege that he enjoyed.

About half the audience had already taken their places. The other half, noticing Aidan's arrival, went to their seats. The Ridenow lord inclined his head to Leora as she passed. Lady Aillard smiled and nodded. Kennard Lindar sat beside Bettina in token of their alliance.

After everyone had settled, Gabriel-Alar Elhalyn stepped into the central space in front of his own chair. He must have been seventy or eighty years of age but did not show it, tall and whipcord-thin, with a mane of colorless hair. He raised his six-fingered hands and began speaking in a rich, musical voice.

"Kinsmen, nobles, and fellow Comyn—" He had used the same phrase to open each of the previous sessions, emphasizing that here, in this place of truce, they were all equals. "On this historic occasion, I bid you welcome for what I hope will not be the last time. We have discussed many matters during our time together, some of which we have resolved. Others will require deeper thought, study, and negotiation. At least, the shortage of nuts is not yet upon us, for we have all heard the saying about eating them without breaking their shells."

At this, a ripple of muted laughter passed through the assembly. It was a nice touch, Aidan thought, considering the serious topics they had grappled with. Yet, despite initial wariness, they had reached a consensus on the value of such a council, a place to meet under truce, a forum for resolving frictions. Perhaps eventually, a venue for making mutually beneficial laws and adjudicating inheritance disputes. Many pledged to contribute funds for the construction of a citadel that would belong to all, so that no one family would wield undue influence over the others. The Comyn Castle would take generations to build, but they had begun.

"Next year," Lord Elhalyn went on, "if the gods are willing, we shall meet again to carry our plans further. Tonight, we shall celebrate the season in fellowship. But there remains one final issue to consider. I refer to the demonstration of a new form of *laran* as exhibited by *Damisela*—excuse me, *Tenerésteis* Leora Hastur."

Leora stood, her cloak falling across the back of her chair to reveal a loosely belted robe of crimson. A sharp inhale passed through the council. The color was bold, audacious. Aidan thought, *One day all Keepers will wear red to demand recognition.*

Throughout the great hall came scattered mutterings of disapproval … and fear. Since the opening of the council session, some had made it clear that they saw Leora as a troublesome woman with a Gift notable only for its destructive potential. The folk of Alton, Di Asturien, and minor clans like Castamir, Montray and Lennart—they did not know what had really happened. All they knew was what they had *felt*, those of them with *laran*, and the reports of the ruins. The aftermath, not what had gone before. The truth went beyond their common understanding. If only it were possible for her to speak to the entire assembly telepathically, when deception was impossible, as she had spoken to him. Convinced him. Or a way—a *laran* technique—to guarantee the truth of her words. He'd heard rumors of a spell of truth being explored at Tramontana. But that would not help Leora now.

They would trust *his* words without hesitation, simply because he was a man and a Hastur. Was a Keeper's word not just as binding? Outraged on Leora's behalf, Aidan got to his feet to stand beside her.

"Lord Hastur, we have called your daughter to account, not you." *Dom* Gabriel-Alar's tone lost its prior warmth.

Aidan pitched his voice to ring out. "I stand with her not only because she is blood of my blood. I am here to ensure her words are not lightly dismissed, and because her Gift affects us all."

"That is why we require answers about her role in the destruction of a Dry Land oasis and the concomitant loss of life by means of a *laran* weapon previously unknown to us. *Tenerésteis*—" to Leora, "—will you answer?"

"You want to know what happened?" Leora held herself proudly, her voice as clear as a silver bell. "As you know, I was one of many women abducted by Dry Land bandits. What you may not have heard is that it is their practice to seize the starstones from any Gifted women they captured."

At this, a ripple of emotion passed through the assembly. Possibly, they had *not* heard, although Aidan thought it likely they had dismissed it as rumor.

Leora was speaking again. "They did this atrocious thing to control us, their captives, out of superstitious fear. They have no *laran* and regard it as sorcery. Sometimes, they would deliberately lay hands upon the stolen stones, sending the women into shock and death." She paused to let the impact of her statement sink in. "They were preparing to auction us off as chattel, as slaves forever chained—for that is how they treat their wives."

In the moment of shocked silence, Ewen Ridenow stood up. "I attest this to be true, for my Glynnis was one of the captives. The story she told was harrowing. Beaten, deprived of water, of food, even of sight. And always under the threat of rape, torture, and death. She still has nightmares of that time."

Many in the audience cried out in sympathy. *What if that had been* my *daughter?*

Ewen went on, "Without the actions taken by Leora Hastur, my daughter and niece would now be lost. I tell you, we are in debt to the *tenerésteis* for putting an end to this menace, for protecting our loved ones as we should have done. We ought to be praising her, not accusing her. Not condemning her. To put it bluntly, that is what we are doing, isn't it?"

Lord Elhalyn's expression did not change except for the swift unclenching of his jaw. Clearly, he had not expected Ridenow's challenge or the solidarity it evoked.

With this beginning, the Comyn Council looks to have an … interesting future, Aidan thought.

"Kinsmen and nobles, fellow Comyn," he said, echoing the opening address. "This assembly has no authority over the Keeper, Leora Hastur. She has not offended any of you, yet you are perilously close to offending *her*. Therefore, I move to close this discussion. It is petty-minded, rooted in fear instead of honor, and is beneath us."

All eyes went to Lord Elhalyn as presider. His complexion was naturally so pale that it was difficult to discern if more blood left his cheeks. "We are not—" he cleared his throat, "—not exactly—bringing charges against the *vai leronis.* We seek only to understand what happened. If you have no further objection, Lord Hastur, may we proceed?"

"Whether or not I have an objection depends upon what the next question is." Aidan switched his gaze to Leora. She gave him a brief nod, *Let's finish this.*

"Very well, then," said the Elhalyn lord. "*Tenerésteis,* how is it that you were able to prevail against these bandits when you no longer had your starstone in your possession? You are a trained Keeper, but still … We know that unamplified *laran* is limited in scope and reach, and is capable of only small acts. Is this not the case?"

Aidan sensed a flare of triumph from Leora and knew that this was the opening she had been waiting for.

She fixed the men in each section with an iron stare. "The Dry Town lord believed I could do nothing. *I* believed I could do nothing. But what if there is a Gift none of us dared imagine—the Gift of being able to harness one's full *laran* capacity a thousand times over, without a crystal? Of being, as it were, a *living matrix*?" She paused again to let her words and their implications achieve their full effect.

"I have that Gift," she said, pitching her voice to hold their attention.

The Hastur Gift, Aidan thought. Perhaps she ought to have phrased it that she *was* that Gift, but the semantic difference did not matter.

"We are still beginning to fully understand what *laran* can do," she went on. "For every Gift we recognize, there might be a dozen, a hundred yet to be discovered. We use our talents for healing and building and other peaceful purposes, but we have also upon occasion employed them as instruments of war. Like children playing with sharpened swords, we give no heed of where all this will lead."

Aidan felt a blow to his heart. *Callista's fire … Melanie dying in the attack … men paralyzed with horror, their minds burned out … and how much more?* Guilt gnawed at him. He did not believe he'd had a choice at the time. He could not envision an end to the escalation of such terrible weaponry and the ages of chaos they would bring about … but Leora could.

"Which brings us to the question of what to do about a Gift such as mine." She raked the assembly with her gaze, with every bit of her authority as a Keeper and a Hastur. Some had the grace to look embarrassed.

"I know what you're thinking." Her voice rose, more adamant with each phrase. "As my father pointed out, you have been pondering what to do with me. You think I'm a woman whose mind has broken under pressure.

You think—Zandru alone knows what I might do if I'm crossed or a whim takes me. You're afraid I might turn the power of my Gift against *you*."

She paused, took a breath. Lowered the pitch of her voice. Every breath hushed, as everyone strained to catch her next words.

"My lords, do you really think you can control someone with *laran* like mine? Would you dare treat a male *laranzu* with such contempt?"

Murmurs swept the assembly. Some considered her questions, debating the most prudent response. Others, quick to take offense, muttered their disapproval.

We must stop her—

But she had them now, as surely as if she held them in the palm of her hand. The air shimmered with her power. She seemed to be limned in blue fire.

"I will put it to you another way," she said. "How can such power be nurtured? How can it be trained to be useful instead of destructive? What ethical principles must guide those of us who possess these Gifts?"

She speaks of a path to peace.

He had never been more proud of this daughter of his. In this hour, in this moment, she had surpassed him.

The Elhalyn lord cleared his throat, as if he had been waiting to interrupt her. She silenced him with a look.

"Those who possess Gifts must be sent to a Tower for training. Where else can they be safely taught and, if necessary, contained?"

"A Tower, yes …" came from Ardais.

"Listen to her!" Lady Aillard was on her feet. "She speaks the truth!"

"Excellent idea—but in which realm?" Lord Alton demanded. "Who will control such a Tower?"

"Hush! Let us hear what she had to say."

"The only responsible—*honorable*—way to deal with *laran*, whether a Gift such as mine, a talent that drives a young person to the brink of death, or even one thought to be so slight as to be unworthy of a starstone—is in a Tower. We already lack sufficient places and teachers for all those who need them. Therefore, I propose the founding of a new Tower—and yes, I do intend that I should be its first Keeper.

"There is but one thing for you to decide, my lords. This new Tower will come into being with your support or without it. If you believe as I do that an untrained telepath is a danger to everyone, including themselves, and if you can imagine a world transformed by what our minds can accomplish, then will you join me in this enterprise? What say you? Are you with me?"

Aidan sensed the hesitation in the chamber. None of these men wanted to be the first to rally around a woman, even if she was a Hastur. Their emotions mixed fear and doubt with grudging respect. If they could find a credible way to dismiss her, they would seize upon it.

And yet, her words had had an impact. He could see it in their faces and sense it in the air.

"I will!" he announced. "Leora's Tower will have the full support and resources of Hastur. Now, who will join me?"

"What Ridenow can do, we shall. You have my word!" from Ewen.

"And Aillard's," said *Domna* Bettina.

Kennard was on his feet now, his voice rising above the others. "We have already agreed to donate land for this Tower, as well as what we can contribute towards its construction. It's probably the only thing Lindar and Aillard have agreed upon in the last century."

As the laughter died down, Lord Elhalyn recovered his voice. "You make a persuasive argument for the establishment of a new Tower, *vai leronis*. Is it the will of this council that such a Tower be established with our consent and endorsement?"

A chorus of *Ayes* answered him. The support was not unanimous, but it was enough.

The last business being concluded, the assembly broke up. Lord Elhalyn stood beside the door, speaking with each departing noble. "That's over with," someone said, and then another said something about celebrating at the ball tonight.

Connor came up, grinning. "You did it, you really did it!" Neave threw her arms around Leora. Aidan could have sworn he saw tears in the eyes of both sisters.

Aidan remained until the hall had almost emptied. He glanced down at Leora, noting how composed her expression was. *A Keeper's calm.* When she met his gaze, a thought rose in his mind.

Permanedó, the Hastur motto. "We shall remain."

Whatever was done and said here will remain, as well.

"So you shall have your Tower," he said. "Not that I ever doubted it. What will you call it?"

"I have known its name since I first dreamed of it as a child." She slipped her hand through the crook in his arm as they followed Connor and Neave to the door.

"And what is that?"

"Arilinn."

EPILOGUE

Five Years Later

To Leora Hastur, Keeper
Arilinn Tower
Preciosa,
Yes, of course I will come. Mikhail has granted leave to any of us who wish to join your new Tower at Arilinn.
My heart is ever yours,
Padraik
Neskaya Tower

◆ ◆ ◆

To *Dom* Ewen Ridenow
Serrais
Dear Father,
Thank you for the baskets of Midsummer flowers. They smell like home. What a lovely way to celebrate the festival.
I no longer have nightmares or episodes of unreasoning panic. You were right to trust Leora. She and the other healers here are exceptionally skilled in treating injuries of the mind. I hope to be of similar service to others. Learning to use my Gift has strengthened me in many ways.
I send my love to you and Mother, and much happiness to Silvia on her betrothal to Beysel Aillard.
Adelandeyo,
Glynnis Ridenow, monitor
Arilinn Tower

◆ ◆ ◆

To Leora Hastur, Keeper
Arilinn Tower
My dearest sister,
Our daughter is born, healthy and perfect. We have named her Melanie. Connor insists I rest now, but it's really so he can have her to himself before Graciela wants her chance. We are all enchanted with her, even Father. Especially Father.
Visit when you can.
My love always,
Neave Hastur-Darriell
Hastur Castle

"Arilinn was not the oldest of the Towers, but it was the proudest … claiming that the first Keeper had been a daughter of Hastur's self."

—The Forbidden Tower